"GONNA TIE ME TO THE BED?"

she asked, and sat up against the pillows, watching him as he approached.

He did not answer her.

He came to the bed and sat on its edge, the red silk tie in his right hand.

"What'd you find?" he asked.

"What?" she said.

"You were searching the house. What'd you find?"

"Searching the *house*? Don't be ridiculous."

Blue eyes wide. Frightened.

"Did you find the ID cards?" he said.

His voice was very low. He was holding the tie with both hands now, the tie dangling loose between his hands.

"What ID cards?" she said.

Her voice was quavering.

"You're lying." he said.

The tie whipped out, looping over her head, forming a sling behind her neck, yanking her off the pillows. . . . She felt herself being pulled off the bed, sliding off the bed, put out a hand to stop her fall, and then felt herself being yanked up sharply by the tie. "No, please," she said, gasping for air . . .

SCIMITAR

A NOVEL BY

John Abbott

Island
BOOKS

ISLAND BOOKS
Published by
Dell Publishing
a division of
Bantam Doubleday Dell Publishing Group, Inc.
1540 Broadway
New York, New York 10036

Photo on page 76 reproduced with permission of Camera Press/Globe Photos, Inc.

Photo on page 78 reproduced with permission of UPI/Bettmann

ISBN: 0-440-21550-1

Reprinted by arrangement with Crown Publishers, Inc.

Printed in the United States of America

Published simultaneously in Canada

June 1993

10 9 8 7 6 5 4 3 2 1

This is for my brother
PETER ABBOTT

1

Tomás was talking about a head floating in a toilet bowl. This had been years ago in Houston, in the building where he'd lived. They'd heard yelling upstairs and he'd gone up with his sister and his brother-in-law, this shabby little walkup where they were living at the time, climbed the stairs with the smell of rancid oil and stale cooking in the hallway, a whiff of marijuana drifting from one of the apartments, knocked on the door to 3C, and a woman opened the door and told them in Spanish that her husband had just suffered a heart attack. But there was a bloody cleaver in her hand.

"He's in the bathroom," she'd told them in Spanish.

In the bathroom, the man's decapitated body was lying alongside the tub, and his head was floating in the toilet bowl.

"Gross," BJ said.

Pudgy and short, with blue eyes and straight brown hair styled at a barber's college, BJ looked like a Georgia redneck farmer. Actually, he was a preppy WASP,

1

born and bred in Connecticut, a product of Choate and then Yale where—to hear him tell it—he'd learned not to pee on his hands, although graduates of Harvard also claimed that singular distinction. He peppered his speech with teenage colloquialisms, sometimes sounding more like a Valley Girl than a man with a medical degree. He was now rolling his baby blues in bug-eyed horror at the very thought of a severed head in a toilet bowl.

Tomás relished his revulsion.

Like a dedicated sadist, he described in meticulous detail the woman in the blood-stained slip, her hands dripping blood, strings of blood in her hair, flecks of blood on her face—

"Barphsville!" BJ shouted.

—and then went on to describe the appearance of the bathroom, which to Tomás resembled the chicken market back home in Houston, Texas, where birds with their throats slit and their feathers drenched with blood hung upside down on hooks and flapped out the last minutes of their lives against white-tiled, blood-spattered walls. The *pièce de résistance* of his gory tale was the severed head itself, wedged into the toilet bowl, the bald scalp intersticed with chop wounds, the throat ending in a jagged tatter of torn and lacerated flesh where it had been severed from the body.

Sonny was enjoying both Tomás's story and BJ's discomfort.

The singles bar was in downtown Los Angeles, not too distant from the hospital, but far enough away to make it seem safe. Safe from what, he didn't quite know. Safe to get drunk, he imagined. Safe to indulge profligately, without any of the teaching staff accidentally wandering in to cluck collective tongues over the unseemly behavior of doctors in residence.

The Doctors Three, they called themselves.

Sonny himself, BJ, and Tomás, whom they sometimes called Tomasito because of his diminutive stature. Small-boned and thin, with straight black hair and eyes as black as midnight, Tomás moved with the grace of a butterfly, his slender fingers floating on the air now as he described in more intimate detail the anatomy of the long-ago woman in the pink slip, who kept insisting that the two-piece corpse in the bathroom had achieved its present bipartite condition via a heart attack.

"That was when I knew I wanted to be a doctor," he said.

The Doctors Three.

All of them in their second year of residency at what was known in the trade as "a busy hospital," or "a hands-on hospital," meaning a hospital with more than its fair share of broken heads and bullet wounds. Come next June, they would each and separately venture out into the wide, wide world of internal medicine. They had met at the hospital as strangers with Doctor of Medicine degrees. They were now fast friends, albeit somewhat drunken ones, BJ already half in the bag, Little Thomas not far behind him, and Sonny trying to stay sober long enough to determine whether the leggy blonde at the bar was in actuality tossing her lilting laughter exclusively in his direction.

Tomorrow would be Saturday, the twentieth day of June. Tomorrow night, the beast that was Los Angeles would bellow and roar once again, and the citizenry of this fair city on the Pacific would begin flooding into the Emergency Room, complaining of a wide variety of fractures, contusions, and wounds. Normally, the Doctors Three were on rotating duty in various and separate parts of the hospital, the better to see you, my dear. But on the weekend, all three of them were needed downstairs to breach the tide and stanch the flow of blood. This Friday-night respite was a necessary part of the process, Sonny guessed, a time to regroup and recharge, a time of merriment in anticipation of a good night's sleep before the—

The blonde's lilting laughter floated his way again.

He turned to face the bar.

Their eyes met.

No question about it. I'd Like To Know You Better, her eyes said. His said the same thing. Hers were blue, his the color of tarnished brass, an admixture of his father's brown and his mother's blue, the genes tangled over centuries of invaders in two different lands. His complexion was the color of California sand.

"See you guys later," he said, and pushed back his chair.

BJ whispered something to Tomás. Tomás laughed.

As he crossed the floor toward the crowded bar where the blonde was still in apparently delighted conversation with a girl at her left elbow, Sonny was aware of his own good looks and the stir, the *buzz*—or so he imagined—that accompanied his very passage through a room. His looks were what most women considered exotic, this mingling of East and West, the dusty complexion and green-grey eyes, the brown hair with its lustrous shine, the aquiline nose and sensuous mouth he'd inherited from his father, the tall muscular body that was a legacy from his mother's side of the family. The blonde turned on her stool as he approached, swiveling away from the girl on her left, welcoming Sonny by crossing outrageously long legs sheathed in an extremely brief blue-leather mini. Blue stockings. He loved blue stockings. Pantyhose, actually, he guessed. Blue high-heeled patent-leather pumps. Her eyes flashed. A paler blue than the pantyhose. She was wearing a white silk blouse with little pearl buttons down the front. Long blond hair hanging loose around the perfect oval of her face. Red, red lipstick, you expected a more orangey color on a blonde. Blue eyeliner. A dazzling smile that could have kleig-lighted a Hollywood premiere.

"Hi," he said, "I'm Sonny," and extended his hand.

"I'm Corrie," she said.

"Okay to join you?"

"Sure," she said.

He took the stool beside hers. She swiveled to face him. She smelled of spring flowers in bloom, he wondered what perfume she was wearing. The bartender waddled over. He was a big fat man wearing green suspenders. He looked jolly and eager to please.

"Sir?" he asked.

"Beefeater's on the rocks, please," Sonny said.

"Lady still okay?"

"Corrie?"

"Please," she said, extending her glass. "It's . . ."

"Corona and lime, right," the bartender said, and smiled, and waddled off again.

"So," she said.

"So," he said.

"Is Sonny your real name?"

"Are you ready?" he said.

"That bad, huh?"

"Try Krishnan Hemkar."

"Say *what*?" she said.

"Krish . . ."

"Yeah . . ."

"Nan . . ."

"Okay . . ."

"Hem . . ."

"Uh-huh . . ."

"Kar. Krishnan Hemkar. It's easier when you break it up."

"That's what *you* think," she said, and laughed. "What is it, anyway? Russian?"

"Indian," he said.

"Which tribe?" she asked.

"Not *American* Indian," he said. "*Indian* Indian. Calcutta, New Delhi, Bombay, like that. My father was Indian."

This was the lie.

The eternal lie.

"He met my mother in Rajistan. She's British."

Embroidering the lie. By rote.

"I thought maybe you were Hispanic," she said. "From a distance, you and your friend looked Hispanic."

"My friend, yes," he said. "Me, no."

"Why Sonny?" she asked.

"Lots of Indians are called Sonny. I really don't know why."

"Lots of Italians are called Sonny, too," she said. "Didn't you see *The Godfather*?"

"No, I'm sorry, I didn't."

"Well, Sonny Corleone. He was Italian, you know. Not James Caan, but the character he plays. In the movie. In the book, too. Sonny."

"Yes," Sonny said.

"I loved *Jewel in the Crown,* too," she said. "Did you see that one?"

"No, I'm sorry."

"On television? You didn't see it?"

"No."

"It was all *about* India!" she said, her eyes widening, her face registering surprise and perhaps outrage that someone of Indian descent had not watched a show that was all *about* India.

"I don't watch much television," he said. "Or see many movies, either. When I'm not at the hospital, I'm home studying."

"Oh?" she said. Interest flashing in the blue eyes. Was

it possible that the handsome Indian was also a *med* student? Or perhaps even a *doctor*? Half the interns in the United States of America were Indian. Press your bedside buzzer at two in the morning, you got a guy in a turban and baggy pants, wearing a little black plastic nameplate with white letters that read Dr. Vishwambhar Prakash. When you were sick, the whole world was Indian.

"I'm a doctor," he said, ending the intensely suspenseful moment.

"No kidding?"

"No kidding. Dr. Krishnan Hemkar. Sonny Hemkar."

"Well. I'm pleased to meet you," she said, and extended her hand. He took it. They shook hands. They held hands briefly. She withdrew her hand. She smiled at him.

"Beefeater's on the rocks," the bartender said, "Corona and lime. Pour it?" he asked Corrie.

"Please," she said. "With a head, please."

He poured the beer over the squeezed lime.

"Keep the tab running, sir?" he asked.

"Yes, please," Sonny said.

The bartender went off again. Sonny raised his glass.

"Cheers," he said.

"Cheers," she said.

Their eyes met again.

"What's the Corrie for?" he asked.

"Guess," she said, and pulled a face. "Corinne. Isn't that *awful*?"

"Actually, I like it," he said.

Another lie. Minor league, but a lie nonetheless; Co-rinne was possibly his *least* favorite name in the entire world.

"It's a diminutive of Cora," she said. "Which in Greek means 'maiden.' Which in itself is a laugh," she said, and smiled. Meaning she was *not* a maiden. As if any woman in her mid-twenties, which is what he guessed she was, could in this day and age be mistaken for a maiden. Nonetheless, she'd informed him. Which was encouraging. He would have to remind her, later, that she'd been the first to bring up sex, however re-motely. "So were you *born* in India?" she asked.

"Yes, but we moved to England when I was very young."

The lie, the lie.

"How young?" she asked.

"I was eight months old."

"Then you were just a baby."

"Yes."

"Then, actually, you were *raised* in England."

"Yes."

"So really you *could* call yourself English if you wanted to, couldn't you? I mean, your mother's English, isn't that what you said . . . ?"

"Yes."

". . . and you lived in England from when you—how old were you when you came to America?"

"Eighteen."

"How old are you now?"

"Twenty-nine."

"To go to college, or what?"

"Yes, college."

"Where?"

"Princeton."

"I went to U-Mich," she said. "I wanted to be a writer."

"Do you still write?"

"Yeah, insurance," she said, and laughed.

"Would you like to sleep with me tonight?" he asked. She looked at him.

"That was fast," she said.

"Yes," he said, smiling, nodding, ducking his head in the Little Boy manner that had worked for him on far too many previous occasions. He had never had trouble bedding any girl or woman he'd wanted. Never. At the same time, he often felt that he was at their mercy, felt that each time a seduction succeeded for him it was contradictorily he himself who'd succumbed to a force beyond his control.

"So?" he said, and smiled boyishly. "What do you say?"

"Why not?" she said.

So much for safe sex, he thought.

Shower at six in the morning, leave the apartment, dash home to douche or whatever it was they did afterward to ward off evil demons and venereal disease. In all fairness, she *had* asked him for a brief sexual history —he'd made it as brief as possible—and then insisted that he use a rubber, which he'd always felt was tantamount to skiing on grass. The night had been only moderately exciting, and he was not surprised to find her long gone when the alarm went off. He looked at the clock again. He had hit the snooze button at eight; it was now twenty minutes to nine. The sheets smelled of stale sex. He stretched his arms over his head, yawned, and then threw back the covers and got out of bed.

The apartment was insufferably hot.

Something wrong with the air conditioner, he'd been begging his landlady to fix it ever since the heat wave began at the beginning of the month. He went into the bathroom, performed what BJ called The Morning Rites of Passage, and then washed his hands as if he were scrubbing up for brain surgery. There was something wrong with the hot water, too, this damn apartment. He yanked a big white bath towel from the rack and, drying his hands, looked at himself in the mirror over the sink; he did not feel even vaguely positive that he could cope successfully with the day ahead. Wearing only the big towel—white against his dusty skin, the hard flat belly and dancing pecs courtesy of Nautilus three times a week—he came out into the kitchen, put up the coffee, and poured himself a glass of orange juice. The time was 9:06 A.M. by the digital clock on the countertop microwave; it felt like the middle of the night. A note was propped up against the toaster. He picked it up. In a hasty scrawl, she'd written: *Adored it, I'll call you.*

Don't bother, he thought.

The telephone rang.

11

So soon?

He lifted the receiver from the wall mount.

"Hello?" he said.

"Scott?"

A British accent detectable even in that single word. But . . .

"Who's this, please?" he asked.

"Mrs. Jennings," she said.

Nothing valid yet.

"And the first name?"

"Priscilla."

"Go ahead, Mother," he said. "This is Scott."

There was a slight pause. Then she said, "Are you awake, Scott?"

His heart lurched.

"I'm an early riser," he said.

The proper response.

"I have good news," she said.

"Tell me."

"I think I've found an apartment for you."

"Where?"

The proper words, the proper sequence.

"Here in New York."

"How did you find it?"

"In *The New York Times*."

Essential information.

"How much are they asking?"

"Twenty-five."

More vital information.

"That sounds reasonable."

"And will you let me know when you get here?"

"You can be sure," he said.

The proper sign off.

He put the phone back on the wall hook.

His heart was pounding.

At ten minutes past noon that Saturday morning, it was still raining in New York City, a relentless summer rain that drilled the pavement surrounding the sidewalk telephone. In New York nowadays, you couldn't even go into a proper phone booth to escape a downpour. There were only these ridiculous little *shells*—not even those, really. Just these stingy little—Gillian was at a loss for a word to describe them. Listening posts? Narrow and constructed two abreast, with a plastic divider falsely promising privacy between them. The phone *position*— as good a word as any—alongside hers was still vacant. She fished in her handbag for another quarter, dialed a number, and listened to the insistent ringing on the other end.

"SeaCoast," a male voice said.

"Mr. Scopes?" she said.

"Who's this, please?"

"Priscilla."

"Go ahead, Mother. This is Arthur."

"Arthur, I'm calling about the shipment we were expecting."

"Which shipment?"

"From Los Angeles."

"Yes, go ahead."

13

"It will be here on the twenty-fifth."

"Very good. And will you keep me informed?"

"You can be sure," she said, and hung up.

She put the receiver back on its hook, felt automatically for her quarter in the coin return chute, and then stepped out boldly into the rain. Her umbrella was one of those flimsy little folding jobs the size of a rolled tabloid newspaper when it was closed. Open, it seemed incapable of braving the unseasonably fierce wind. As she turned left at the corner, into the full onslaught of the wind roaring eastward through the narrow canyon from the Hudson, she felt certain the umbrella would either flip inside out or else be torn from her hands. The umbrella was red. She held it like a small shield, pushing it into the wind and the rain, muttering to herself about the dreadful weather. She was drenched to the skin by the time she reached her apartment building on West End Avenue.

Sighing audibly, she stood in the small entrance hallway for a moment, catching her breath, marveling that she had neither drowned nor been blown to bits and pieces. She shook out the umbrella, pulled it into its miniaturized state, fastened its Velcro strap, and then reached into her handbag for her keys. They were lying on the bottom of the bag, alongside the muzzle of a Walther 9-mm Parabellum pistol. Casually, her hand moved the gun aside to get at the keys. She unlocked the glass-paneled inner door, and climbed the steps to the second floor of the building. There were two keys to the locks on her apartment door. She was home at last.

She put her bag and the umbrella on the hall table, took off her soaking wet raincoat, hung it on the brass coat-rack near the mirror, and then stepped out of her low-heeled walking shoes. Barefooted, she padded into the bedroom and began getting out of her wet clothes.

The apartment was what they called a two-bedroom in this city, but which was in reality a one-bedroom with a small dining room that converted into either a second bedroom or what she used as a sitting room. The living room faced south and was quite sunny on good days, and the kitchen had been entirely redone only two years ago. There was only one bathroom, this off what was laughingly called the master bedroom, which—given its size—might better have been called the maid's room. She unbuttoned her blouse, unzipped her skirt, yanked down her pantyhose, unclasped her bra, stepped out of her panties, and dumped the whole lot unceremoniously on the floor in a sodden little pile. Naked now, she looked at herself appraisingly in the full-length mirror fastened to the closet door, dismayed as always to recognize yet another time that the good full breasts were beginning to sag ever so slightly, the once flat tummy was developing a most unattractive bulge. She supposed this was forty-nine. If so, she wondered what dread calamities *fifty* would bring. Eyes still a clear and penetrating blue, however, hair at least reminiscent of the blond it had been in her youth, silver threads beginning to show among the gold, but legs still long and lithe and shapely, a woman's legs never changed. She went into the bathroom and turned on the shower.

She was drying herself some fifteen minutes later when she heard the front door opening.

She remembered all at once that she'd left her handbag on the table in the hall.

Near the front door.

Her pistol was in the handbag.

"Yes?" she called.

Silence.

Perhaps she was mistaken.

"Is someone there?" she called.

More silence.

And then a board creaking under someone's footfall.

She dropped the towel at once, stepped swiftly out of the bathroom, and was moving toward the bedroom where she kept a second pistol in the nightstand beside the—

He loomed suddenly in the narrow hallway.

A giant of a man wearing a black trenchcoat and a black rainhat pulled low on his forehead, black gloves, a black pistol in his right hand, it looked like a Colt, it suddenly exploded.

The first bullet was low, he'd been going for her throat, the muzzle of the gun had been tilted up toward her head. It shattered her clavicle instead, sent her reeling back from the impact, colliding with the wall, bouncing off the wall in a frantic half-turn toward the bedroom, the gun, the spare gun in the—

The second bullet took her in the back, high up between the shoulder blades. It knocked her stumbling forward through the entrance door of the bedroom, sent her falling to the floor beside the small pile of damp clothing she had removed not twenty minutes ago. On her knees, she scrabbled toward the bed, threw herself headlong across the bed, and was stretching to reach the nightstand on the far side when the third bullet took her at the back of her head. She did not feel this one. It blew out her forehead and spattered tissue and bone and brain matter onto the wall and onto the top surface of the nightstand where the Browning automatic rested on a pile of pink panties in the top drawer.

The man leaned over her and fired again, unnecessarily, into what was left of her head. Then he hurriedly left the apartment and walked out into what was now a cold, slow, steady drizzle.

2

The next holiday would be the Fourth of July.

Independence Day.

It said so on the mimeographed sheet tacked to the bulletin board on the wall opposite Geoffrey's desk. This was one of the easier ones. Like Christmas or Good Friday. Some of the others—like Martin Luther King, Jr., Day or Memorial Day—were a bit more difficult for an Englishman to remember, no less comprehend.

The mimeographed notice had been sent round at the beginning of the year, two copies to each registry, intended to be seen by all staff in the Hong Kong Office, the Embassy in Washington, the North America Department FCO, the UN Department FCO, the Resident Clerk FCO, and all Consular Posts in the USA. It was flanked on Geoffrey's bulletin board by another mimeographed sheet listing the addresses and telephone numbers of all British Consulate General offices in the

United States and yet another sheet listing all the police precinct telephone numbers here in New York City.

Actually, Geoffrey was not at the moment the least bit interested in *any* of the mimeographed information fliers. He was, instead, consulting a properly *printed* sheet that had been produced by the Cartographic and Map Section and distributed early last year to every British Consulate in the world, including the one here in New York. Its headline, boldly marching across the top of the page the way the redcoats must have done at Lexington or Concord, read:

**STANDARD TIME ZONE EQUIVALENTS AT FCO
OVERSEAS POSTS
WHEN 12 NOON (GMT) IN LONDON**

The letters GMT stood for Greenwich Mean Time.
The letters FCO stood for Foreign Consular Office.
The FCO for which Geoffrey worked here in New York was called the British Consulate-General, and it was located on the ninth floor of an office building on Third Avenue, between Fifty-first and Fifty-second streets. From Geoffrey's corner office, he could look south for quite a ways downtown, and he could also look west across Third Avenue to the front of the Seventeenth Precinct across the street. He was, in fact, looking *east* this morning, if spiritually rather than actually; he was consulting the printed Overseas Posts chart to ascertain what time it was in Kathmandu.

It was now 9:00 A.M. on a bright Monday morning, the

twenty-second of June. Adjusting for Daylight Savings Time, which had last month sprung the clocks ahead both here and in London, Greenwich Mean Time was now 2:00 P.M., which made it 6:40 P.M. in Kathmandu, which did not adjust its clocks to suit the seasonal fashions, and which was rumored to be the second worst foreign post to which a person could ever be assigned.

At 5:00 P.M. Kathmandu time, Alison would have taken her leave of Snuffy, as Her Majesty's Consul-General there was familiarly called (although his proper name was Sherwood Spencer Hughes), and would by now be showering and dressing before leaving for dinner at either the Del Annapurna or the Soaltee Oberoi, both five-star hotels. He would give her a bit more time to put on the finishing touches, and then he would call her at 10:00 A.M. sharp here in New York, which would catch her at 7:40 P.M. before she left her apartment. There in the shadow of the Himalayas, they dined late.

The *worst* foreign post, of course . . .

Well, actually, there seemed to be several.

Saudi Arabia. Oh, dear Lord, the stories he had heard about *that* place! Or the Ivory Coast. And long-time foreign servants had told him it was a toss-up between Ceylon and Ulan Bator as to which was the most utterly boring. But they all agreed that Dakar had to be the absolute worst in the world, perhaps the entire uni—

The telephone rang.

For a brief delirious moment, he imagined it might be Alison calling *him*!

He turned from the bulletin board and the benign gaze of Queen Elizabeth staring at him from a poster above it, snatched the receiver from its cradle, and said somewhat breathlessly, "British Consulate, Turner speaking."

"Yes, hello," a man's voice said. Nasal and veddy veddy British. A Colonel Blimp adrift in Manhattan, the first Distressed British National of the week.

"Yes, sir, how may I help you?" Geoffrey asked.

Three minutes past nine on a Monday morning, and already a DBN on the line.

"Yes, hello, can you hold a moment, please?" the man said.

"Certainly," Geoffrey said, and waited.

And waited.

And waited.

He was about to hang up when the man came back on the line.

"Yes, sorry," he said, "my wife was bending my ear. What I need to know, young man . . ."

Geoffrey wondered how the man knew he was young.

". . . is how a person would go about establishing residency in the U.K., do y'follow me?"

"Are you a British national, sir?" Geoffrey asked.

"I am indeed. Born and bred in Manchester."

"Then, sir, why would you need . . . ?"

"No, no, this is for a *friend* of mine," the man said. "A Yank. Plans to move to Kent, lovely spot, d'you know it? Hawkhurst? Quite lovely."

"Yes, sir, quite lovely indeed."

21

"My friend's sixty-seven years old, been retired for some time now. Can you tell me what the requirements would be?"

"To apply for entry clearance as a person of independent means?"

"Well, yes, I should imagine that's what he'd be. Is that what you call it? A person of independent means?"

"Yes, sir. If, in fact, that's what he is. In which case, he would need to prove that he has under his control, *and* disposable in the U.K., a sum of not less than a hundred and fifty thousand pounds . . ."

"That much, eh?"

"Yes, sir, or income of not less than fifteen thousand pounds a year."

"I should imagine he gets at least that much in retirement pensions, shouldn't you think? Fifteen thousand pounds?"

"I have no idea, sir."

"Well, I shall have to ask him then, shan't I?"

"Yes, sir, that would seem a good idea. And then, if he wishes to apply, he can write to this office for the proper forms."

"Thank you so very much, young man. You've been most helpful."

"Happy to've been of service, sir," Geoffrey said, and put the receiver back on its cradle, still wondering how the man had known he was *young*. Something in his voice? His telephone manner? Surely, if the DBN had been standing here before him, looking at him across the desk, he'd have seen nothing about Geoffrey to indicate he was but twenty-four. For this was no callow-faced pimply youth growing a sparse mustache in a vain bid for maturity. Rather, here were the lean good looks of someone whose forebears were part Welsh and part Scottish, the smoldering dark eyes, the high cheekbones and thrusting jaw, the thick black hair, somewhat tousled now at a quarter past nine in the—

The telephone again.

He picked up the receiver.

"British Consulate," he said, trying to make his voice deeper. "Turner here."

Another DBN, a woman this time, reporting that her handbag had been stolen, along with all her money, her credit cards, and her passport. Not an unusual distress call. Geoffrey took at least one of these every day of the month, more of them in June, which was the busiest month. He asked the woman where she was staying, gave her the telephone number of the police precinct closest to her, and advised her to report the crime there and then to come directly here to file an application for a new passport.

He hung up wondering whether the stolen passport activity was heavier in a city like Chicago or Houston. Detroit. That was probably the worst of the lot, but there wasn't a British Consulate there. New York was a choice post, he still marveled at the good fortune that had landed him such a plum as his second assignment. First crack out of the box had been Dublin, but one didn't join the foreign service to be sent directly around the corner.

He had entered the service as a vice consul at the age of twenty-two, with a good university degree—a first in History, actually—and coming in as a Grade-9, which paid a starting salary of twelve-thousand quid a year. This had been more than enough in Dublin, one could live there like a king on that amount of money. Here in New York, though, where he was living "on-Manhattan" as opposed to somewhere in the boonies, everything was much more expensive, and he could barely make ends meet at thirteen-five, his new Grade-8 salary.

And he had to admit that the glamour of the city sometimes paled beside the incessant tiresomeness of the daily routine here in the Passport and Visa Section. Process some thirty-thousand visas annually, and another thirteen-thousand passports, and one could with justification call the repetition deadly dull. And when it got to be June, as somehow it always did, one might say the routine became numbing. He sometimes felt that if he never saw another Pakistani, Bangladeshi, Ghanaian, Indian, or Afghan applying for a visa to—

And yet, there were times when New York . . .

Well, not now. Certainly not now. The temperature had been insufferably hot since the beginning of the month, and now that the expected humidity was here— the Yank forecasters quaintly called it the Three H's, for Hazy, Hot & Humid—there was no relief except out at the Hamptons, which seashore required hours of motoring to reach and tons of money to enjoy. He wondered abruptly if there was a chance in hell that Alison would join him on her holiday. He would ask her again tonight, when he—

But why on earth wait? It was now a quarter to ten, and with a nine-hour-and-forty-minute—damn it, even *Dakar* didn't have such a peculiar time-zone difference. Forty less fifteen came to . . . yes, it was seven twenty-five in Kathmandu, where Alison was undoubtedly all lipsticked and lovely. He would wait another five minutes and call her at seven-thirty on the Dorothy.

The call went through without a hitch, miracle of miracles.

Her voice sounded as clear and as sharp as if she were in a phone booth on Madison Avenue, rather than in a room thousands of miles away.

"Are you coming to New York?" he asked.

"I don't know yet," she said.

"Allie, please, you'll *love* it here."

"It's just that I miss London so terribly much," she said.

"Don't you miss *me*?"

"Of course, I do, Geoffrey, but . . . can't you possibly time your holiday to coincide with mine? So that we can *both* go to London?"

"I've been to London," Geoffrey said. "I joined the foreign service to get *away* from bloody London."

"I just don't know," Alison said.

"New York is a *won*derful city," he said. "It's enchanted, Allie, you'll love it. Especially during the summer. Even *with* the Three H's. And . . ."

"The three *what*?"

25

"The Three H's. Happiness, Humor and . . . uh . . . Halvah. Besides, don't you want to help Mrs. Thatcher celebrate?"

"Who? What on earth are you talking about?"

"Mrs. *Thatcher*! She'll be here on a personal visit, Allie . . ."

"Well, who cares about *that*? I've seen her thousands of times on the telly. Even here in Nepal."

"Ah, yes, but have you ever danced in the same room with her?"

"Done *what*?"

"Danced, my dear. The light fantastic. There'll be a big ball on the first, and we're both invited."

"We are?"

"Indeed. I've been handling a great many of the arrangements, you see . . ."

"You have?"

"Mmm, yes."

"And you say we've been invited to . . ."

"Yes, she extended the invitation personally."

"Geoffrey, are you pulling my leg?"

"Have I ever lied to you, darling? Our beloved former Prime Minister will be arriving at the end of the month, just before the Americans start their yearly celebration in honor of our eviction. Attila the Nun, the Iron Maiden, the Redoubtable Maggie, will be here in lieu of Mr. Major a day or two before *you* get here! So what do you say *now*, luv? Care to join us?"

There was a long pause on the line.

He waited for what seemed a lifetime.

26

Then a voice said, "Excuse me, sir, you asked me to interrupt at . . ."

"Yes," he said, "just a moment, operator. Allie?"

"Yes, Geoff."

"Anyway, sir, it's three minutes."

"Thank you. Allie?"

"Yes, Geoff."

He hesitated.

"Please say yes."

There was another long pause.

He thought he would die.

He waited.

"I don't know, Geoffrey," she said, at last. "It's just that I really had my heart set on London, truly. I just miss London so terribly much."

"Well . . . think about it, would you?" he said. "I'll call you tomorrow, will that be all right?"

"Snuff's having a party for staff tomorrow."

"I'll call you *after* the party, all right?"

"Well, try me, but I may be late. Goodbye, Geoff, I have to run now."

"Allie? Allie, wait a . . ."

There was a click on the line.

"Damn," he said, and jiggled the rest bar. When the operator came on, he asked her for time and charges, and then leaned back in his chair and wondered why on earth he'd lied to Alison.

His expertise, such as it was, lay in passports and visas, in which section he worked with a consul and three other vice consuls, all of them women, all of them

British, all of them ugly. Normally, such a lowly serf would have had nothing whatever to do with the impending visit of someone so lofty as the Nun. But because this was a rare occasion for the consulate—her visits normally took her to California, to see her old buddy Ronnie—every available man and woman had been pressed into service to smooth the arrival and ease the passage of the former Lady from Number Ten. Even so, the extent of his involvement had been minimal at best. He had hardly, as he'd claimed to Alison, handled "a great many of the arrangements." In fact, all he'd done . . .

Well, last week he'd telephoned the Canadian Consulate-General—who'd invited Mrs. Thatcher to attend the gala on Canada Day, the first of July—in an attempt to determine whether the tables would be rectangular or horseshoe-shaped, the better to collaborate on a seating arrangement that would offend neither Mrs. T. nor the Canadian Prime Minister. The young woman to whom he'd addressed this pressing problem was a dimwit with an accent that sounded American, but which—she assured him at once—was Canadian. He had only by the end of the week learned that the main table would, in fact, be horseshoe-shaped, and that among the visiting dignitaries would be the President of Mexico, here to honor Canada on this its special day, and incidentally to remind America that Mexico, too, shared a border, albeit to the south.

It seemed to Geoffrey that an equitable seating arrangement would place Mrs. Thatcher between North and South, so to speak, but he'd been informed by the head of Admin Section that the rules of diplomatic form and procedure as they applied to receptions were to be strictly followed. He was later informed by Chancery that the Canada Day gala was to be considered an "official" reception in that the guests had been invited exclusively by reason of their position, and the dinner was being offered in honor of a head of state, in this instance *two* heads of state and one former head, which was what made the situation so partic—

The telephone rang again.

He glanced at the clock.

Five minutes to ten in the morning.

He lifted the receiver.

"British Consulate, Turner here," he said.

"Detective Delaney, Twentieth Precinct," the voice on the other end said.

"Yes, sir, how may I help you?" Geoffrey said.

"We've got a homicide victim," Delaney said.

"Oh, dear," Geoffrey said.

"Yeah, woman shot with a Colt .45, which I guess you know is a big mother. Looks like she caught four, maybe five slugs, it's hard to tell 'cause the head was totaled."

"I see," Geoffrey said.

He abhorred many of the words the Yanks used. Totaled. To indicate utterly demolished. With a gun that was a big mother. To indicate exceptionally large. The words seemed particularly inappropriate in describing what had been done to a woman's *head* during the commission of a violent crime.

"Yes?" he said.

"Cleaning woman found her when she came in this morning, sprawled on the bed, blood all over everything, her brains on the wall."

Geoffrey winced.

"This is on West End Avenue, just off Seventy-Third," Delaney said.

"Yes?" Geoffrey said.

"Her name's Gillian Holmes, like in Sherlock."

"Yes?"

"She had a British passport in her handbag."

The Eagle had left Los Angeles last night at ten minutes past eleven, Pacific Time. It was now ten minutes past 8:00 A.M., Mountain Time, and the train was scheduled to stop in Phoenix in twenty minutes. Sonny had been awake and dressed since dawn.

The sleeper he'd booked was a deluxe bedroom with a sink, a vanity, and its own private toilet facilities and shower. Both the upper and the lower berths had been made up for sleeping when he'd boarded the train last night at Union Station. He'd slept in the extra-wide lower berth, which he'd been informed would become a sofa during the day. There was also an armchair in the room, and a wide picture window past which the Arizona countryside flashed in early Monday morning splendor. The windows on the corridor side of the compartment were curtained.

He had rung for the porter as soon as he was dressed and had been told the dining car would not be opened until they left Phoenix. But he offered to bring Sonny a cup of coffee and some sweet rolls if he wanted those now. Sonny asked him to please change the bed back into a sofa before he brought the coffee and rolls. The porter flashed a wide grin and said he'd be happy to, sir.

Sitting now with his coffee and warm rolls, Sonny faced the direction in which the train was speeding, and watched the magnificent landscape outside. By this time tomorrow morning, they'd be in San Antonio, Texas. On Wednesday morning, they'd be pulling into St. Louis, Missouri, and by mid-afternoon they'd be in Chicago. He'd connect there later that evening with the Lake Shore Limited to New York. If all went as scheduled, he would arrive there at 1:40 P.M. on Thursday, the twenty-fifth.

How much are they asking?

Twenty-five.

Giving him the absolute deadline for arriving in New York. Twenty-five. The twenty-fifth of June. Knowing he could not possibly take an airplane because airport security devices had a nasty way of detecting weapons packed in one's luggage.

He sipped at his coffee.

He had been told several months ago that one day soon his years and years of waiting would be over. He suspected what the assignment would be; one did not forgive easily in his part of the world, and it had been too long a time now. But even without knowing the complete details—the actual target, though he felt he had already guessed correctly, the date, the location, the

31

number of people, if any, who in addition to himself would be involved—he could feel a rising sense of excitement. After all those years and years of training, all those years and years of waiting in a foreign land among people he despised, his patience would finally be rewarded by success. At last they would permit him to serve his country with honor and with pride. He awaited only his final instructions. The rest was already in his hands and in his head.

He looked at his watch.

Seven minutes past seven.

In ten minutes, they'd be in Phoenix.

And shortly after that, he would enjoy a hearty breakfast in the dining car.

He felt very good about everything.

She had seen him last night when they were boarding the train, but she pretended not to notice him this morning as he came into the dining car. He was possibly the handsomest man she'd ever seen in her life. She had to admit that her knowledge was somewhat limited; she was only nineteen years old. But she was not altogether inexperienced, and to her discerning eye he seemed not only extraordinarily good-looking, but extremely self-assured as well.

She could not tell what color his eyes were from where she sat midway up the car, either blue, or green, scanning the tables, meeting her own eyes briefly before moving on, and then flashing with sudden light as the train emerged from a tunnel and sunlight splashed into the car, causing him to squint. She even liked the way he squinted. Eyes scrunching up, and then the face relaxing again, a faint smile touching the mouth. Humor at his own expense, a grown man ambushed by sunlight. She wondered how old he was. She'd once dated a thirty-year-old. Thirty was too old, but she didn't think he was that old, God he was handsome! She went on pretending not to notice him, busying herself with the menu again, and was genuinely surprised when he appeared at her table.

"Excuse me, is anyone sitting here?" he asked.

She was too startled to speak.

"Hello?" he said, and smiled again.

"Hello, hi," she said. "Sorry, I . . ."

"I didn't mean to . . ."

"No, no, I was just . . ."

"*Is* anyone sitting here?"

"No. No, please sit down. Please."

"Thank you."

He pulled out the chair.

Green. They were green. Or actually a greenish-grey. She guessed. She forced herself to take her eyes from his face. She busied herself with the menu again. He was watching her. She felt suddenly flustered. She wondered if she was blushing.

"Anything good?" he asked.

"What?"

"On the menu."

"Oh. I . . . uh . . . haven't decided yet. I mean

. . . there are *lots* of good things, but I don't know what I want yet. Would you like to look at it?"

"I'll get one from the waiter," he said.

"You can have this one if you like. Really."

"No, that's all right."

"Really. I think I know what I'm having, anyway."

"I thought you didn't know."

"I always have eggs," she said, and shrugged.

"And are you having eggs this morning?"

Faint smile on his mouth. Was he laughing at her? Or did she delight him? Full, sensuous mouth . . .

"Yes, I think I will be having the eggs this morning," she said.

"As usual," he said.

"Yes," she said, and smiled.

"In which case, I'll accept the menu," he said.

She handed him the menu.

"Thank you," he said. He was still smiling, studying her face. "I'm Sonny Hemkar," he said.

And realized his error at once.

"How do you do?" she said.

Damn it. Force of habit. Too late now. He held out his hand. Awkwardly, she reached across the table for it.

"I'm Elita Randall," she said.

"That's a very unusual name," he said.

"It means 'special person,'" she said. "In Latin."

"Randall?"

"No, Elita. The word 'elite' comes—oh, you're putting me on, right?"

"And *are* you a special person?" he asked.

Still holding her hand. The waiter was watching them. Sonny holding her hand that way. Sonny. He couldn't be thirty. Nobody named Sonny could be thirty. He had such a beautiful mouth. She suddenly felt like kissing him. Just as suddenly, she took her hand from his. Gently.

"*Are* you?" he asked.

"Am I what?"

"A special person."

"Yep, that's me. Gorgeous, intelligent . . ."

"You forgot modest," he said.

"Right, modest, too," she said.

"You are," he said. "Gorgeous."

"Thanks," she said, "but I know I'm not. I wouldn't have said it if I really thought I was."

"How old are you?" he asked.

"How old do you think I am?" she said.

"Fourteen," he answered.

"Oh, sure."

Did he mean it?

"Or fifteen, maybe," he said.

He wasn't smiling. Maybe he meant it. Did she really look like a teeny-bopper? She was wearing faded jeans and a floppy sweater, maybe they *did* make her look younger than she actually was. But fourteen? Even fifteen?

"Right," she said, "I'm the youngest soph at UCLA."

But suppose he *really* thought she was fifteen?

"Is that where you go to school?" he said.

"Yes."

"Good school."

"Yes."

"What's your major?"

"I want to be a social worker."

"Hard work," he said.

"Yes, but it's what I want to do."

"Good," he said, but it sounded like a dismissal. Perhaps because he picked up the menu at the same time.

"What do *you* do?" she asked.

"I'm a doctor," he said from behind the menu.

Stuck with it now. Go with the truth. Or at least the partial truth.

"Really?" she said. "Do you practice in L.A.?"

"I'm in residence there."

True enough. But . . .

"I'm going back East to see my mother. She isn't feeling well."

"Oh, I'm sorry."

"I'm sure it's nothing serious," he said, and lowered the menu. "I think I'll have the eggs, too," he said. "Is your home in New York?"

"Yes. Well, my mother's. I'll be staying with her for the summer." She paused and then said, "They're divorced. My dad's with the Army in Germany. He's a colonel."

Sonny raised his brows appreciatively.

"I hardly ever see him anymore," Elita said, somewhat wistfully.

"You must have done a lot of traveling around," he said.

36

"Oh, yes. Well, an Army brat, you know. By the way, I'm not really fifteen."

"You're not?" he said, feigning surprise. "I thought you were. Your name's Lolita, so I thought . . ."

"No, it's *Eli*ta. E-L-I-T . . . you're putting me on again, right?"

"How old are you *really,* Elita?"

"Nineteen. How old are you really?"

Please don't say thirty, she thought.

"Twenty-nine," he said.

She felt enormously relieved. Twenty-nine wasn't quite thirty. But try to sell that to her mother. Mom? Hi, I just met this gorgeous guy on the train, I think I'm in love with him, he's twenty-nine years old. Mom? Take your head out of the oven, Mom.

"What's funny?" he asked, and she realized she was smiling.

"My mother," she said.

"What about her?"

"Are you Mexican?" she asked.

"Why? Is your mother Mexican?"

"No, but are you?"

"Do I look Mexican?"

"Sort of."

"My complexion?"

"I don't know what. This . . . sort of exotic look you have."

"Oh my," he said, "exotic," and waggled his eyebrows like Groucho Marx.

"Are you?"

37

"No, I'm part Indian and part British," he said.

She wondered if that was better. Hello, Mom? He isn't Mexican, you can climb down off the windowsill. He's British, Mom. Well, part Indian, I guess.

"*Indian* Indian, right?" she said.

"Yes," he said.

Which is really a whole lot better than Comanche or Chippewa, Mom. Wait'll you see him, he looks like a young Dr. Zhivago, whatever that actor's name was. Only better looking.

"What part of India are you from?" she asked.

Careful, he thought.

"A little town called Jaisalmer," he said.

"Where's that?"

"Close to the Pakistan border. Have you ever been to India?"

"No. But my dad was stationed near there when I was twelve."

"Oh? Where?"

"Burma," she said.

He signaled to the waiter. Everything he did, his every motion, seemed smooth and accomplished. He made something as simple as signaling to the waiter seem like a liquid hand gesture in a ballet. Careful, she told herself, this can get complicated.

"Who's Lolita?" she asked.

"A little girl who fell in with a dirty old man," he said.

"Oh my," she said, and rolled her eyes.

"Yes," he said.

"And did she come to a sorry end?"

38

"Yes, sir," the waiter said, "are you ready to place your order?"

"Elita?"

"I'll have the eggs, over medium, please, with bacon."

"Orange juice? Coffee?"

"A small orange juice. Do you have decaf?"

"Fresh brewed."

"I'll have a cup, please."

"Sir?"

"Same as the lady," Sonny said. "All the way down the line."

"Yes, sir, thank you, sir," the waiter said, and walked off grinning.

"Tell me more about Lolita," she said.

The call from London came just as The Eagle was approaching Texas. The train had by then come through Arizona and almost all of New Mexico, and was on the outskirts of El Paso. On the train, it was still three-thirty in the afternoon, Mountain Time. In New York City, it was five-thirty on a hot summer evening.

When the telephone rang, Geoffrey was just about to hit the four-number combination that would unlock the inner door to what the consulate personnel called "the airlock." The security measure had been installed in 1984, several weeks after Libyan terrorists killed a policewoman in London. The airlock consisted of a pair of steel doors flanking an empty cubicle. One door led to the inner offices. The other door led to the waiting room. Each door had a different combination lock on it.

You opened one door, locked it behind you, and then opened the second door. The airlock had been designed to dissuade entry by anyone intending mischief. Geoffrey had already pressed the first number of the combination when Peggy Armstrong, one of the vice consuls in Passports and Visas, called in her high, shrill voice, "Geoff, for you! It's the Mainland!"

He wondered whether hitting the first number of the combination and then leaving it at that would cause alarms to go off and security people to descend upon him in hordes. Nothing on the alarm panel indicated what one should do in order to abort. He waited, fully expecting total disaster. Nothing happened.

"Geoff!"

Peggy's voice again.

"The *Main*land!"

Why she insisted on calling Britain "the Mainland" was totally beyond him. He sometimes suspected that Peggy had descended from another planet and was only now coming to grips with living on earth. She did somewhat resemble an alien being, what with frizzed red hair sticking out all over her head, and enormous brown eyes magnified by equally enormous goggles. A totally bug-eyed, flat-chested wonder, standing beside his desk now in tweeds better suited to the moors than to the Three H's of a summer in New York, telephone receiver in her hand, thoroughly exasperated look on her homely face.

"Thank you," he said coolly, taking the phone and hoping his tone of voice conveyed the annoyance he'd felt at being yelled down like a fishmonger.

"Turner speaking," he said as Peggy marched off in a huff, presumably to her waiting spaceship.

"Geoffrey, ho, it's Miles Heatherton here."

Heatherton worked in the Consular Department of London's Foreign Office, in a street near St. James's Park called Petty France. Geoffrey had telephoned him earlier today, immediately after the Twentieth Precinct biked over the passport they'd found in the murdered woman's handbag. He'd given Heatherton the number on the passport, the woman's full name—Gillian Holmes, as in Sherlock—and the date and place of issue, in this instance June of last year in London. All routine. As required, the woman had listed in her passport the names, addresses, and telephone numbers of two persons to be notified in the event of an emergency. One was a brother named Reginald Holmes, who lived in London. The other was a friend named Jocelyn Bradshaw, who lived thirty-six miles west of London, in Henley-on-Thames.

"Sorry to be getting back to you so late on this," Heatherton said, "but we ran into a bit of a problem."

"What do you mean?" Geoffrey asked.

He could not imagine anything so urgent that it could not have waited till morning. This was a routine notification of next of kin, and it was now past ten-thirty in London.

"Well," Heatherton said, "we tried the numbers you gave us for these people—the one in London, and the other in Henley—and we got two *other* people entirely."

"I'm sorry," Geoffrey said, "I'm not following you."

41

"There's no Reginald Holmes at the London number, and no Jocelyn Bradshaw at the Henley number."

"Moved, have they?"

"Well . . . no, it doesn't appear so. The people who answered the telephones said they've lived at those addresses for the past ten—well, ten years in the case of the London man, seven for the one in Henley."

"Uh-huh," Geoffrey said. He hadn't the foggiest notion where Miles was leading.

"Which I thought decidedly peculiar in that these are the identical addresses listed in the passport," Heatherton said.

"Are you saying the addresses and phone numbers in Miss Holmes's passport do, in fact, exist, but the people she's listed as brother and friend do not *live* at those addresses?"

"That's exactly the case," Heatherton said.

"Then where *do* they live?"

"There are thirteen Holmeses in the London directory, and two of them are Reginalds. Neither of them had ever heard of a woman named Gillian Holmes."

"How about Henley?"

"Not a single Jocelyn Bradshaw there."

"Mmm," Geoffrey said.

"Or in London, either, for that matter. We checked on the offchance."

"Mmmm."

"Yes. Exactly what *we* wondered."

"How do you mean?"

"Why the false names?" Heatherton said.

"Yes."

"Yes," Heatherton said.

"And what did you conclude?"

"Well, that's what's taken me so long to get back."

"Miles, I seem to be having enormous difficulty following you tonight. Perhaps you ought to ring me sometime tomorrow morning, when we've both had . . ."

"The passport could have been issued anywhere in the U.K., you see, even though you'd told me it was written in London."

"Yes. Last June."

"The woman was how old?"

"She listed her date of birth as 1943."

"That would have made her forty-nine."

"Yes."

"And she'd never had need of a passport till last year? Woman living so close to the Continent? Never traveled abroad in all her forty-nine years?"

"Well, perhaps she was a homebody," Geoffrey said. "Or this may have been a simple renewal."

"No, it wasn't a renewal. Nor quite that simple, either."

"How do you know?"

"We've run her through, Geoff."

"Run her . . ."

"Through the computer, yes. That's what's taken all this time. I must admit I didn't like the smell of it from the start. Otherwise, I'd have let it go till morning. But . . ."

"Perhaps you should have done," Geoffrey said. "I really hate to see you working so late on my be . . ."

"In retrospect, I'm glad I didn't. She's not in the computer, Geoff."

"How do you mean?"

"I mean the British government has issued scores of passports to women named Gillian Holmes over the years, but none of them was born on February 9, 1943, in Colchester, England."

"Then . . ."

"Moreover," Heatherton said, "the number on the passport, although valid, was the number issued to a Scottish passport holder named Hamish Innes McIntosh, who was born in Glasgow on the third of November, 1854, and who most certainly should be dead by now."

There was a long silence on the line.

"Then you're saying the passport is counterfeit," Geoffrey said.

"Yes, dear boy," Heatherton said. "That's precisely what I'm saying."

She had looked for him at lunchtime and again at dinner, but he had not come to the dining car, and she was beginning to wonder if he'd taken ill. Well, he was a doctor, he should know how to take care of himself, and yet she was concerned. The man sitting across from her at dinner was an elderly tractor salesman from Burbank, who was on his way to Chicago to meet with a son from whom he'd been estranged for the past seven years. His eyes welled with tears when he talked about the young man, who sounded like a Grade-A shit to Elita.

The man explained to her that they had crossed over from Mountain Time to Central Time when they'd left El Paso at six P.M., at which time she should have set her watch ahead an hour, although she wouldn't have to touch it again because it would remain Central Time all the way to Chicago. But, of course, if she was traveling on to New York . . .

"Yes, I am," she'd said.

. . . then she'd have to set it ahead yet another hour when they crossed over from Valparaiso, Indiana, to Warsaw, Indiana. He warned her to be very careful in New York, as it was a very dangerous city. She had the good grace not to tell him she'd been born and raised there.

On her watch now—which, as instructed, she'd set ahead at the dinner table—it was already twelve minutes to midnight, *wherever* they were. They had left the station in Little Rock at eleven-thirty or thereabouts, so she guessed they were still in Arkansas, although it all looked the same out there in the dark. She wondered again if Sonny was sick. She thought of going back to the dining car to ask the porter who'd served them breakfast if *he* knew what had happened to the Indian gentleman. Half *British,* Mom, don't forget. Was it possible he'd got off the train earlier than she'd expected? But he'd told her he was traveling to New York.

She left her seat in the coach section, and walked forward to what they called the Sightseer Lounge, which was a two-story car with a café on the lower level and these huge wraparound picture windows upstairs. She looked briefly into the café. A waiter was leaning against the serving counter. Otherwise, the place was empty. She debated going back to her seat, and then went upstairs instead.

He was sitting in one of the lounge chairs at the far end of the car.

Looking out at the star-drenched night.

Thoroughly absorbed in his own thoughts.

So very beautiful.

"Hi," she said.

He turned, looked up, smiled.

"Hi," he said.

"Mind if I join you?"

"Please," he said.

She took the chair alongside his.

"Are you okay?" she asked.

"Sure." A puzzled look crossed his face. "What do you mean?"

"I haven't seen you around," she said.

"I looked for you at lunch," he said.

"Oh? When was that?"

"Around two."

"I went in at noon."

"Must've missed you then," he said.

"Too bad," she said.

Silence.

The stars wheeling overhead. The night flashing by.

"Did you have dinner?" she asked.

"No, I wasn't very hungry."

"Well, sure, if you eat lunch so late."

Silence again.

The rattle of the wheels over the tracks, the evenly spaced clickety-clacks. Outside, the telephone wires swooped and dipped from pole to pole, and clouds scudded across the sky.

"Which car are you in?" she asked.

"I've got a sleeper," he said.

"Doctors must make a lot of money."

"Not *this* doctor. My mother paid for it."

"Ah."

"Ah," he repeated.

Another silence, longer this time.

"Listen, would you like to be a good Samaritan?" she asked.

"Sure."

"I mean, if it isn't any trouble."

"No trouble at all."

"I ordered a scotch at dinner and they carded me, would you believe it? I mean, on a goddamn *train*— where you have to change your watch every five minutes and you never know *where* the hell you are—they refuse to serve me 'cause I'm not twenty-one. Could you do me an enormous favor and ask the waiter downstairs for a scotch and soda, please, before I die of thirst?"

"I'd be happy to," he said, and got up at once.

"Wait, let me . . ."

But he was already on his way.

He came back with two drinks in actual glasses, never

mind cardboard containers. His estimation in her eyes went up at least two-thousand percent; she hated to drink whiskey in anything but a glass.

"How much do I owe you?" she asked.

"Don't be ridiculous."

"Is your mother paying for these, too?"

"Cheers," he said in dismissal, and clinked his glass against hers.

"I owe you one," she said. "Cheers."

They both drank.

"You have *no* idea how good this tastes," she said. "What are *you* drinking?"

"Gin."

"I've never developed a taste for gin," she said.

"I feel the same way about scotch."

They sat sipping their drinks.

Alone with him in the car, alone with him and the stars and the night and the dark silence of the entire universe, she felt as if she'd known him a long, long time.

"Why'd you decide to become a doctor?" she asked.

Her voice softer now, almost a whisper.

"I wanted to help people," he said.

"That's totally amazing," she said. "Because that's just why *I* want to be a social worker. So I can help people."

"I can't think of anything nobler," he said.

"I totally agree."

"I just hope I never change my mind about it. I see so many doctors . . . well, I'm sure you know. They forget why they went into it in the first place. They forget the purity . . . the innocence . . . the dedication. They become nothing more than businessmen of another sort. I hope I never get that way."

"That's very beautiful," she said.

"I mean it sincerely," he said.

"You're a very beautiful person," she said.

"Well . . . thank you," he said. "That's very kind of you. Thank you."

"Do you feel you've known me a long time?" she asked.

"Yes. Since at least this morning," he said.

"Oh, stop it," she said, and playfully tapped his hand. "I'm being serious."

"Yes, I feel I've known you a *very* long time."

"Honestly?"

"Honestly."

"Because *I* do. I feel I can tell you anything I'm thinking . . . or feeling . . . or hoping . . . and you won't laugh at me. I think that's very rare. And very beautiful," she said.

"I think *you're* very beautiful," he said.

"Oh, sure."

"Gorgeous and intelligent and the youngest fifteen-year-old at UCLA."

"You know, I really *believed* you?" she said, turning to him and putting her hand on his arm. "That you thought I was fifteen?"

"You didn't."

"I did, I swear to God. I kept wondering, does he

really think I'm only fifteen? Do I seem *that* immature to him?"

"On the contrary. You seem very mature."

"People are always telling me I seem older than nineteen."

"Well, you do. There's a very . . . serious and sensitive side to you, isn't there?"

"Yes," she said softly.

"Which is in such marvelous contrast to your playfulness."

"I *love* having fun, don't you? Don't you just *love* doing fun things?"

"I do."

"Unexpected things."

"Yes."

"Things that . . . oh, you know!"

She took her hand from his arm, raised it suddenly, tossed it in a What-the-hell gesture, and then put it immediately on his arm again. He covered her hand with his own. She turned to look into his eyes.

"Elita?" he said.

"Yes, Sonny?"

"Would you like to sleep with me tonight?"

"Yes, Sonny," she said, "I really would."

She would always remember this night—or at least while it was happening she thought she would remember it always—as the night she stopped being a girl and became a woman. Because no matter what she and the other college girls her age told themselves about being women and wanting to be called women, she knew in her deepest heart that nineteen was still a girl, nineteen was still a teenager, and a teenage girl was simply not a woman, any more than a teenage boy was a man.

Sonny Hemkar was no teenager.

He's no teenager, Mom. I thought you'd be delighted to learn that. Mom? Please, Mom, come in off that fire escape, okay?

Until now—until this night in his sleeping compartment, the countryside flashing by outside, the train speeding through the darkness—until these deliriously empty hours of the night when she was full of him and full of herself, Elita had known only three men intimately, all of whom she now realized were merely boys, although one of them had been twenty-four years old. Until now—

There was something frightening about the intensity of his passion.

She found herself wanting to say No, don't kiss me, even as his lips found hers and even though she wanted desperately for him to kiss her. She found herself wanting to protest his hands on her breasts, heard herself actually saying, "No, please don't touch my breasts," longing for him to touch her.

He unbuttoned her blouse . . .

"Please don't," she said.

. . . spread the blouse in a wide V over her bra, his hands cupping her breasts, urging them out of the bra . . .

Please don't, she thought.

51

. . . her breasts overflowing the bra, "Oh, please no," she said, her nipples stiffening to his touch.

She had already told him how much she really did want to sleep with him tonight, but now she kept repeating over and over again in her mind and aloud, please don't, please don't, breathless in his fierce embrace, terrified by her own response to his ardor.

Never in her life . . .

His hands were everywhere, her blouse and skirt falling away, dropping to the floor of the compartment in a clinging whisper of cotton and silk. There were suddenly lights outside, flashing past in a blur, some sort of village or town, traffic lights and street lights, window lights, bright circles and rectangles in an otherwise pitch black landscape. The lights flickered momentarily on her breasts and her belly. She was virtually naked now, standing before him in high heels and panties, her bra still fastened but pulled below her breasts. He did not remove the bra. He could easily have unclasped it to allow her breasts complete freedom, but he chose instead to keep them in partial bondage, lifted by the restraining nylon cups, their sloping tops and nipples elevated to his hands.

The lights of the town fell behind.

A new and deeper darkness enclosed them.

In the darkness his lips found her mouth again. His hands consumed her breasts. Her own hands hung limply at her sides. She could feel the nylon of her panties brushing the insides of her arms, just below the elbows. Her panties were wet, she was afraid he would touch her down there and discover that she was soaking wet, but she wanted him to touch her, find her, and she willed him with all her might to let his hand drop between her legs and into her panties where he would find her achingly wet for him, but he would not release her breasts.

She leaned into him, her hands still hanging loose at her sides, leaned into him with her nipples and her breasts, offering them to his passion as if in sacrifice, her entire body seeming to rush upward into her nipples, hard and burning and yielding to his hands where they worked her relentlessly. She was beginning to feel dizzy. She thrust her tongue into his mouth and jutted her hips toward him, searching for him, finding him hard against the nylon panties, don't take off all my clothes, she thought, please don't . . .

Reading her mind . . . seeming to read her mind . . . he did not, would not release her from the bra, choosing instead to keep her partially restrained, nipples bursting . . . did not, would not remove the bikini panties . . .

But yes, oh Jesus . . .

Yes.

. . . rolling them down now, over her hips, down to . . .

Yes, that's it, she thought.

. . . just where the tangle of her pubic hair began . . .

Find me, she thought.

53

. . . the waistband pressing against the upper side of the blond triangle that defined her . . .

Please don't, she thought.

She could not later remember how long he kept her poised between girlhood and womanhood. She could not later remember how long she stood there partially clothed, leaning into his questing hands, trembling as he probed her, discovering her wetness, exploiting her wetness, quivering beneath the onslaught of his incessant touch. When at last he lifted her onto the bed and spread her legs to the darkness and to the night and to his brilliant hardness and murderous passion she thought No, don't fuck me, but he was already fucking her, oh *yes* how he was fucking her, and she knew she would never in her lifetime be the same again.

3

Never in his life had Geoffrey Turner been inside a morgue. Even this early in the morning, there were people working in blood-stained smocks. Bloated bodies on stainless steel tables. Blood dripping into stainless steel basins. Everywhere Geoffrey looked, he saw the obscenely exposed *insides* of human beings. But the greatest obscenity was the stench. It was the stench of putrefaction, a sickly sweet odor that made him want to wash out his nostrils with salt water. The detective with him seemed not to mind any of it at all.

The detective's name was Al Santorini.

He was not the same detective who'd called the Consulate on Monday to report the murder of a British subject. *This* one was a detective from Homicide. He explained that in this city, at this particular point in time, Thursday morning, the twenty-fifth day of June . . .

"It changes practically every day," he said, "but this is what it happens to be at this particular point in time . . ."

—the precinct detective catching the original squeal, even if it was a murder, was usually the one who followed the investigation through to its conclusion.

"If there *is* a conclusion," Santorini said. "Lots of them end up in the open file."

But in this particular case, where the victim was someone believed to be a foreign national, and where now there seemed to be some question about whether the person really *was* British . . .

"It's merely that we believe the passport is a forgery, you see," Geoffrey said.

"Yeah, I understand that," Santorini said.

He was somewhat taller and broader than Geoffrey, with a shock of very black hair hanging on his forehead, and dense black hair curling over the collar of his shirt. Forty-two, forty-three years old, Geoffrey guessed. A rough-hewn streetwise look about him. Brown eyes that matched the color of his sports jacket. Rumpled brown slacks and unpolished brown loafers. Smoking a cigarette, even though one of the doctors sawing open a skull looked up every now and then and frowned at him. Detective/First Grade Allan Santorini, Homicide Division.

"The point is, that's why I took over the case," he said. "Well, me and my partner. Jimmy Halloran, you ever hear of the Grey Ghost?"

"No," Geoffrey said.

"He used to play ball for L.I.U.," Santorini said. "He holds the record for most bases stolen in college baseball."

"I'm not too familiar with the sport," Geoffrey said.

"Yeah, well," Santorini said dryly. "Anyway, he's famous. *Used* to be famous before he became a cop. The Department frowns on famous cops."

"I would imagine," Geoffrey said. He was thinking it was rather like the foreign service. They didn't want anyone to shine. Brilliance was a definite handicap. "But you see," he said, "the fact that she was carrying a forged British passport doesn't necessarily mean she was British to begin with, don't you see?"

"Oh, sure, but her landlady seems to think she *was.*"

"Well, how would she have known?"

"From the funny way she *talked.*"

"I see," Geoffrey said, and cleared his throat.

"The landlady says she sounded English. Not British, she didn't use the word British. She said English."

"I see."

"So that's all we're going on so far. So far, what we're going on is an English lady with a phony British passport, or so you tell us, who gets shot four times and immediately cashes in. Also, we found two weapons in the apartment, a nine-millimeter Walther in the lady's handbag, and a Browning automatic in the night table alongside her bed. So this doesn't seem like your usual English lady taking a stroll in Piccadilly, does it?"

"*If* she's English at all," Geoffrey said.

The smell in this place, and the fact that Santorini kept insisting the dead woman was *English* when for all anyone knew she could be Czech or Lithuanian or *Mongolian* for that matter, was beginning to irritate

Geoffrey. He didn't know why he was here in the first place. On the phone, Santorini had said something about positive identification, but how was he supposed to positively identify a woman he'd never seen in his life who, into the bargain, had been carrying a forged British passport? The doctor looked up from the open skull he was examining and again frowned at Santorini, who took a last puff of his cigarette and then ground it out in a small stainless steel cup that may have contained a pint of blood not half an hour ago.

"What I'd like you to do," he said, "is take a look at the corpse."

Oh, great, Geoffrey thought.

"You realize," he said, "that I've never laid sight on this woman, don't you? So my taking a look at her now, especially in her present unfortunate condition . . ."

"Yeah, her head all blown away," Santorini said, and shook his own head sadly.

"Yes, exactly," Geoffrey said, "could *hardly* serve any purpose now, could it?"

"Well, looking at her *head* wasn't exactly what I had in mind," Santorini said.

"You told me you wanted a positive identi . . ."

"No, what I told you was I thought what we found might help *you* guys get a positive ID."

Geoffrey looked at him.

"So come take a look at her," Santorini said, and walked over to where a man in a white uniform was sitting behind a desk reading a magazine. "We're here for the Jane Doe," Santorini said, and showed the man

58

his shield. The man stood up without saying a word,
leaned over the desk while he finished the paragraph
he'd been reading, closed the magazine—which Geoffrey now saw was one of the American girlie books—
and then walked to a stainless steel door set in a stainless steel frame. He opened the door. A chill rushed
into the room.

It was not the chill of death—although at first Geoffrey thought it might be, given the circumstances—but
was instead the chill of a refrigerated compartment. He
followed the attendant and Santorini into a vast cool
room, listened to them haggling over *which* unidentified
female Santorini wanted to see—apparently there were
three such stiffs, as the attendant called them, in residence at the moment—and was relieved, he guessed,
when they finally settled on the woman who'd been
brought in this past Monday.

The attendant opened a small door and rolled out a
tray.

The woman on the tray was naked and blond.

Part of her face and most of her skull were entirely
gone.

Geoffrey wanted to throw up.

"Take a look at the left tit," Santorini said.

Geoffrey looked.

Tattooed just below the nipple was what appeared to
be the silhouette of a sword:

A tiny green sword.

He was just coming out of the shower that Thursday morning when Elita noticed the tattoo.

At 6:25 last night they'd boarded the Lake Shore Limited in Chicago, and were already eating dinner when the train passed South Bend, Indiana. She drank a single scotch before dinner—no one asked her for identification—and two glasses of white wine during dinner, and then they went back to his bedroom again. And while the rest of Indiana, and then all of Michigan and Ohio, flashed by outside in the darkness of the night, she gave herself to him as she had the night before and the night before that, again and again and again, mindlessly and completely. By dawn, when the train entered New York State, she was utterly exhausted.

It was now a little past nine in the morning.

They planned to eat a late breakfast before the train pulled into the Albany-Rensselaer station. They were scheduled to arrive in Penn Station at twenty minutes to two that afternoon, and she was hoping he would take her to lunch in New York, although he'd made no mention of it thus far.

She was lying naked on the wide lower berth where all last night they'd made love, a faint, pleased smile on her face, her long blond hair fanned out over the pillow, her head turned toward the closed bathroom door. The train was still heading eastward, it would not begin its true southern descent until they left Albany. The compartment's picture window was facing north, it splashed a cold clear light into the room, broken occasionally by the dappling of infrequent trees along the track. The bathroom door opened.

He came out into the sharpness of sunlight streaming through the window, materialized like some dusty pagan god wearing only a white towel around his waist, his brown hair wet and plastered to his head, his grey-green eyes reflecting the light, his face breaking into a grin when he realized she was observing him solemnly and silently and—well, reverentially, she supposed, and felt suddenly embarrassed.

There was another glint of green, echoing the green of his eyes, darker in hue, curling like a misplaced eyebrow on his left pectoral, just below the nipple. She realized all at once that it was a tattoo, and further realized that it was a sword . . . well, some sort of sword . . . one of those swords you saw in the waistbands of guys wearing turbans and baggy pants . . . *that* kind of sword.

"Is that what I think it is?" she asked.

"Is *what* what you think it is?" he said, drying himself now, the towel in his hands and no longer around his waist, his cock—he had taught her to call it a cock, and not a dick or a prick—his *cock* faintly tumescent even in repose. Her first boyfriend . . . well, the first boyfriend she'd known *intimately*—had called it a dick. That was when she was sixteen. The other two had called it a prick. That was when she was respectively seventeen and just nineteen. Last night, when she stopped being a teenager altogether, Sonny had informed her that a prick was what you called a son of a bitch. A *cock* was what he was about to put in her mouth.

"It *is* a tattoo, isn't it?"

"Oh," he said. "This."

And looked down at his chest as if discovering it for the first time.

"A samovar, right?" she said.

He burst out laughing.

"No," he said. "Not a samovar."

"Well, what do you *call* that kind of sword?"

"A scimitar," he said.

"Yes, that's what I meant," she said, and felt suddenly childish, suddenly the teenage girl again and not the woman she'd become, the woman he'd miraculously caused her to become. Still drying himself. The towel behind his back, an end in either hand, working the towel. His cock hanging there. Moving slightly with the movement of the towel. Like a pendulum. Hanging there. Moving. Waiting to be touched. By the woman, not the girl, not the child. She had a sudden desire to take him in her mouth again.

"Where'd you get it? The tattoo, I mean."

Her eyes on his cock.

"In San Francisco," he said.

"When?"

"I was still very young. Just out of medical school."

"Why a sword? A scimitar."

"Why not? The other new residents were getting mermaids and hearts and such. I figured a scimitar would be more original."

62

"Why green? To match your eyes?"

"No, it was St. Patrick's Day. We'd gone up there for the weekend. I thought green would be appropriate."

"Bring it closer," she said.

He walked to the bed. She reached out to touch the tattoo.

"Cute," she said.

"Thank you."

"This, too," she said.

Geoffrey placed the call to Nepal at 1:00 P.M. sharp, New York time. He had eaten a hamburger and french fries at his desk, washing his lunch down with a Diet Coke, waiting for the appropriate time to call. By his calculation, it was now 10:40 P.M. in Kathmandu. Alison should be in her apartment and in bed at this hour, with nowhere to rush off to and plenty of time to talk. The phone rang once, twice, three times . . .

"Hello?"

A man's voice. A brusque tone even in that single word. Had they put him through to the wrong number? Halfway across the bloody world?

"Yes, hello," he said, "excuse me, I'm trying to reach . . ."

"Who's calling, please?"

Same brusque tone, more impatient now.

And then, somewhere in the background, "Who is it, Spence?"

Alison's voice. But who . . . ?

"Is Miss Haywood there, please?" he said.

63

"Who *is* this?"

The voice thoroughly impatient now, virtually rude.

"Geoffrey Turner. May I please speak to Miss Haywood?"

"Moment."

And off the line.

Muted voices in the background.

Spence who?

"Hello?"

Alison again. On the phone this time.

"Who was that?" he asked at once.

"Spence," she said.

"Who's Spence?"

"You know very well who Spence is."

"No, I'm afraid I don't. Who in bloody . . . ?"

"Sherwood Spencer Hughes," she said.

Sounding every bit as impatient as *Spence* himself had a moment earlier. Sherwood Spencer Hughes, Her Majesty's Consul-General, familiarly known as Snuffy, except apparently to a certain female Grade-9 who called him Spence and in whose rooms he happened to be at—what the hell time was it?

"What's Snuffy . . . ?"

"People *do* call him Spence, you know."

"I'm sure," Geoffrey said. "But what's he doing at your place at this hour of the night?"

"Late meeting," she said.

A shrug in her voice.

"Alison?" he said.

"Yes, Geoffrey?"

64

Cool. Precise.

"Alison . . . what's going on, would you mind telling me?"

"I assure you nothing's going on."

"Then what . . . I call your place at whatever the hell time it is there, and Snuffy answers the . . ."

"Geoffrey, I'm truly sorry, but this is an inconvenient time for me. As I told you . . ."

"Inconvenient? I'm calling all the way from . . ."

"Yes, but we're in the midst of a meeting here."

"Well, I'm *awfully* damn sorry about your meeting, but . . ."

"I'll have to ring off now," she said.

"Not before we . . ."

The phone went dead.

"Hello?" he said. "Alison?"

And looked at the receiver in his hand.

Snuffy? he thought.

He's sixty-two years *old*!

One moment he was there, and the next he was not. He was carrying only a single suitcase, whereas she was carrying trunks and trunks full of clothes, which she probably should have shipped by UPS as her mother had suggested. But until these past several nights of ecstatic instruction, she'd been merely a rebellious teenager who'd objected automatically to *any* suggestion her mother made, and so the tons of trunks—well, actually *one* camp trunk and two oversized suitcases.

Plus a duffle full of dirty clothes.

And a traveling case with her cosmetics and perfumes in it.

And her tote, which contained—in addition to her wallet and Kleenex tissues and chewing gum and hairbrush and whatnot—a pair of jogging shoes which she would have put on if she'd been alone and not with Sonny. Sonny preferred heels. So she stood now with her luggage, wearing moderately high heels and a trim blue suit, no hose because of the suffocating heat, long blond hair pulled back in a cool, elegant, and she hoped womanly bun, the tote slung over her shoulder, waiting for him to come back with a porter.

Penn Station looked worse each time she saw it.

When she'd been home for the spring break, she thought it couldn't possibly get any worse, there was just no way on earth it could look more like New Delhi, she had to ask Sonny if he'd ever been to New Delhi and did Penn Station look worse? Although he'd already told her he'd been born in London and had spent most of his childhood and young manhood here in the United States, which didn't come as much of a surprise since he didn't sound British at all, despite his mother.

The big wall clock across the terminal read five to two.

It would probably take him a while to find a porter. She tried to remember the last time she'd seen a porter in Penn Station. Most of the people who came through the station day and night were commuters who didn't need porters. In any case, there seemed to be a dearth of them here on the upper level where there was not a similar scarcity of homeless people. She hoped none of them came over to beg from her; she found them frightening. Then again, there were a lot of things that frightened her; she did not think of herself as a particularly strong or self-sufficient person. The fact that she hadn't even been able to buy herself a drink on the train, the fact that she'd had to ask a strange man—well, he *had* been a stranger at the time—to intercede on her behalf . . .

At two o'clock, she wondered what was keeping him.

At two-thirty she realized he simply wasn't coming back.

The Hilton on Sixth Avenue was the sort of hotel in which a person could lose himself entirely. Host to conventioneers from everywhere in the United States, popular as well with tourists from all over the world, the hotel was normally booked to capacity, a condition Sonny found entirely suited to his current needs.

He had kept a dozen credit cards active and in readiness for the past ten years, preparing for just the contingency that had brought him to New York today. The reservation here at the Hilton had been made under the name to which one of those alternate credit cards was issued. His original name, the name given to him at birth, was buried so deep in GID files he'd almost forgotten it himself. Here in America, he'd been Sonny Hemkar for what seemed forever. But his train reservations had been charged to an American Express card made out to one Albert Gomez. As he checked into the hotel now, he offered Albert Gomez's Visa card. Gomez was leaving a clear trail that led to a post office box in Los Angeles. Dr. Krishnan Hemkar—Sonny Hemkar to his friends and associates—had disappeared from that city on the twenty-first of June. When and where he could safely surface again was anyone's—

"Enjoy your stay, Mr. Gomez."

"Thank you."

The desk clerk tapped a bell. A uniformed bellhop appeared at Sonny's side, took the proffered key and registration slip, and said, "Good afternoon, sir, is there just the one bag?"

"Just the one," Sonny said.

"If you'll follow me, please, sir," the bellhop said, and lifted the bag and began walking through the crowded lobby toward the elevators, Sonny following him like a quarterback behind a blocker. In the elevator, the bellhop said, "Will you be with us long, sir?"

"Not very."

"You've hit some nice weather. A little hot, but much better than the rain we had last week, don't you think?"

Sonny nodded.

He hated idle elevator talk. It was like elevator music. Vapid and dull. Worse in New York than anywhere else in the United States. He supposed that all the service people here were instructed to bend over backward in an effort to dispel the city's reputation for surly rudeness. Chattered on aimlessly where no conversation was necessary at all. A total waste of time in that the city's reputation was well earned and no amount of empty servility could disguise it.

Sonny had known that when the call finally came it would most probably summon him to one of two places: New York or Washington. As a result, he had learned both those cities intimately, acquiring a working knowledge as well of Los Angeles and San Francisco, the two *next* likely candidates. But—

—I think I've found an apartment for you.

Where?

Here in New York.

Telling him where.

All things considered, he guessed he was glad they'd chosen New York. There were a great many ways to get *out* of New York. Washington was far easier to blockade. And once this was over—

"Here we are, sir, 2312."

The bellhop unlocked the door, allowed Sonny to precede him into the room, and then came in to do his stand-up routine about the air-conditioning and the television set and the wake-up calls and the restaurants available here at the hotel, seamlessly performing his little tip-seeking dog-and-pony act, which Sonny rewarded with two dollars and a friendly smile he hoped was masking his impatience.

The bellhop left.

Sonny went immediately to the telephone.

He dialed the number from memory.

The phone rang once, twice, three times . . .

"Hello?"

A man's voice.

Sonny hung up at once.

The ringing telephone scared hell out of Santorini.

Alone here in the apartment where the English lady had been killed, early afternoon sunshine streaming through the windows and slanting onto the bed where her blood had soaked into the covers and mattress, alone here with the evidence of sudden violent—

And the goddamn *phone* rings!

He yanked the receiver from the cradle.

"Hello?"

A sharp intake of breath on the other end.

And then silence.

And a click indicating the caller had hung up.

Santorini wondered why.

He knew he could not go to the apartment.

And will you let me know when you get here?

Her words on the telephone.

He had just tried to let her know he was here, but a man had answered the phone, and he knew that no one but Mother would *ever* have answered the private line in her apartment, no one but she herself was *permitted* to answer that phone, this was the simple hardfast rule.

But a man had indeed answered it.

If Mother had answered Sonny would have used her code name at once. Priscilla. The name premised on the s-c sequence, Priscilla Jennings, the s-c buried in her given name. He had no idea what her everyday cover

70

name might be; he knew that whatever name she'd been given at birth was as deeply buried in the archives as was his own. But she'd been expecting a trade call today, and she'd have asked for his code name . . .

Who's this, please?

Scott Hamilton.

. . . and only then would she have proceeded with, "Go ahead, Scott. This is Mother."

He could not go to the apartment. If she'd been discovered, then going there might put the entire operation in jeopardy.

How did you find it?

In The New York Times.

His fallback position.

He picked up the phone again, dialed the bell captain's extension, and asked him to send up a copy of today's *Times*. The paper came up some ten minutes later. It was already a quarter to four. He opened the newspaper to the Classified ads, and began searching through the Help Wanted columns. The heading fairly leaped off the page.

LANDSCAPE GARDENER WANTED
SAN FRANCISCO AREA EXPERIENCE
ESSENTIAL.
NO OTHERS NEED APPLY. TOP SALA . . .

His eye skipped to the number at the bottom of the ad. He dialed it, and a woman answered the phone.

"Hello?"

71

"I'm calling about your ad in the *Times*," Sonny said.

"Which ad is that, please?"

"For a landscape gardener."

The s-c sequence.

"Have you had experience in the San Francisco area?"

Repeating the sequence.

"Yes, I have."

"Do you have references?"

"I worked for Priscilla Jennings."

"Can you tell me your name, please?"

"Scott Hamilton," he said.

"I'm Annette Fleischer," the woman said. "Go ahead, Scott."

Repeating the name immediately after confirmation of it. The essential double-check. Had she not said the name again, he would have ended the conversation at once.

"I tried to call Mother," he said, "but . . ."

"Mother is dead."

A silence on the line.

Sonny waited.

"Where are you now?" she asked.

"The Hilton. Room 2312."

"When are you available?"

"I'm available now."

"Can you come here?"

"Where are you?"

She gave him an address on the upper east side.

"Give me half an hour," he said.

72

"I'll be expecting you," she said.

He waited.

There was a silence on the line. She was waiting for his prompt.

"And will you be there?" he asked, supplying it.

He would not go to meet her unless she responded correctly.

"You can be sure," she said.

He had never seen the woman he'd known on the telephone as Priscilla Jennings. His control. Mother. The woman who, he'd been told, would one day awaken him from sleep. The woman who had, in fact, awakened him last Saturday morning.

Now he wondered what she'd looked like.

His new control—if such she turned out to be—was a woman in her mid-fifties, he supposed. Dark brown eyes, a vaguely Mediterranean look about her except for the reddish-blond hair, clipped close to her skull like a medieval archer's helmet. She was wearing a grey cotton cardigan buttoned up the front over ample breasts. Her dark skirt was festooned with cat hairs. There were cats everywhere Sonny looked. At least ten or twelve cats in the apartment, one of them sleeping on the windowsill, another perched on the upright piano, yet more flopped on cushions or silently stalking the small apartment. Everywhere, there was the faint aroma of cat piss. Mrs. Fleischer poured tea. Sonny listened to the sounds of summer filtering up from the street and through the open window where the cat snoozed. He was thinking

73

that never in a million years would anyone guess this woman was one of them.

"So," she said. "When did you arrive?"

"This afternoon," he said.

Not a trace of accent in her speech. She could have been Greek or Turkish, even Israeli, but nothing in her speech revealed a country of origin. Her hand pouring the tea was steady.

"Where's Priscilla Jennings?" he asked.

"Pardon?" she said, and raised her eyebrows. Faint polite inquisitive look on her face.

"Priscilla," he said. "Jennings."

"I don't believe I know her," Mrs. Fleischer said. "Milk? Lemon?"

"Lemon, please."

She caught a wedge of lemon between the jaws of a small pair of silver tongs. She dropped it on his saucer. She passed the saucer to him. He was wondering why she was now denying the existence of his previous control. She had acknowledged her name on the phone—but no, she may only have been confirming the s-c sequence. It was quite possible she knew nothing at all about her. Yet she had informed him that Mother was dead. What . . . ?

"Did you get a chance to sleep on the train?" she asked.

"Yes," he said, and thought suddenly of Elita. And just as quickly put her out of his mind.

"Are you well rested then?" Mrs. Fleischer asked.

"Completely."

"Completely awake?" she asked.

"I'm an early riser," he said.

Their eyes met.

She smiled.

"I have your instructions," she said.

Voice low and steady.

He had been waiting for these instructions from the time he was eighteen. He had come to America eleven years ago, trained and prepared, and had been anticipating these instructions ever since. He leaned forward now.

She opened her handbag. She removed from it a glossy black-and-white photograph, some three inches wide by four inches long. Handing it to him, she said, "She'll be here for the Canada Day celebration on the first of July. Security will be tight, access difficult."

He looked at the photograph.

And felt mild disappointment.

Had they awakened him for this? Merely this?

"The celebration will take place at the Plaza Hotel on Fifth Avenue and Central Park South, are you familiar with it?"

"Yes," he said.

"The Prime Minister of Canada will be there, of course, as well as the President of Mexico. But Mrs. Thatcher is only your secondary target. Your *primary* target . . ."

"Yes, who will that be?"

". . . may or may not be present at the dinner that night, we haven't been able to ascertain that as yet. In any event, you must not do anything to jeopardize your main objective. There's a possibility you can kill two birds with one stone, so to speak . . ."

A faint smile.

". . . but only if your primary target . . ."

"Who?" he asked.

". . . is present at the dinner and ball. Otherwise, you'll have to wait till the Fourth of July," she said, and grimaced. "Their big holiday, Inde*pen*dence Day. There'll be a ceremony at the Statue of Liberty which he is scheduled to . . ." She hesitated, studied his face. "They told me you were familiar with New York."

"I am."

"You seemed puzzled when I mentioned the Statue of . . ."

"No, I was only wondering *who*."

"I want to make certain, first, that you understand you can't be diverted from . . ."

"Yes, I do understand."

"The whore is relatively minor."

"Yes."

"If you can accomplish *both* objectives, all to the good. But you mustn't sacrifice *purpose* to expediency. Forget *her* if you must . . ." A nod toward the photograph in his hand. "But get *him*."

"Yes, who?" he asked again.

She handed him another small photograph.

"Him," she said.
Sonny looked at the picture.

And then, truly puzzled now, he looked up at Mrs. Fleischer.

"The whore because . . ."

"Yes, I realize, but . . ."

". . . without her, the bombing would have been impossible."

"Yes, but . . ."

"He has not forgotten," she said. Hatred burning in her eyes now.

"*None* of us has forgotten." The hatred leaping into his own eyes, enflaming them. "But . . ."

"Nor has *God* forgotten. Or forgiven."

"Allah be praised," Sonny said.

"Praise God, for there is no God but He."

There was a silence. They sat staring at each other, memories flaring. One of the cats mewed softly. The silence lengthened. At last, Sonny asked, "But why have we chosen . . . ?"

"This will make it clear to you," she said, and handed him an envelope. "The letter will explain. When you've read it . . ."

He was already reaching into the envelope.

"Not now," she said. "There's a telephone number in the envelope. Call it after you've read the letter. Ask for Arthur Scopes. You are not to contact me again. I have never entered your life, I no longer exist. Do you understand?"

"I understand," he said.

"May God go with you," she said, and snapped her handbag shut.

The click sounded utterly final.

4

Carolyn Fremont was in the midst of packing for the move to Westhampton Beach, carrying clothing from her bedroom dresser to the open suitcase on her bed. Elita was slumped listlessly in an armchair near the window in her mother's bedroom, early morning sunlight streaming through the partially cracked blinds, touching her blond hair with fire. Carolyn knew the signs well; Elita was in love again. Or, worse, Elita was in love again and had once again been abandoned.

"How anyone as bright and as beautiful as you are," she said, "can manage to get herself *abandoned* as often as . . ."

"I wasn't *abandoned*, Mom," Elita said. "There was just some mixup at Penn Station."

"Who is this boy, anyway?" Carolyn asked.

The two were in the Park Avenue apartment Carolyn had received as part of the divorce settlement from her former husband, Ralph Talbot Randall, known to her forevermore as The Late Colonel. The $1,939 alimony check she received each and every month was made out to her maiden name, which she'd begun using again even before the divorce was final. This sum was exactly forty percent of The Late Colonel's salary. She had also received in settlement the house in Westhampton Beach, a brand-new (at the time) green Jaguar convertible, and child support and college tuition for Elita. Which served the bastard right for starting up with his gorgeous sergeant, a twenty-seven-year-old (at the time) redhead with spectacular tits but no brains at all.

"He's not a boy, Mom, he's a man," Elita said.

"I'm sure," Carolyn said, and rolled her eyes.

Her eyes were as blue as her daughter's—well, perhaps Elita's were bluer in that The Late Colonel's eyes were blue as well, and their offspring had been twice blessed genetically. Carolyn's hair had been as light as her daughter's when she was her age, but over the years she and an assortment of beauticians had patiently guided it to its present shade, the tawny color of a lion's mane. At thirty-nine, Carolyn was leggier than her daughter, fuller of breast, infinitely more attractive in a womanly way, and certainly not a person anyone would ever *abandon*.

"His name is Sonny," Elita said.

"I thought he wasn't a boy," Carolyn said.

"He's twenty-nine years old."

"And he still calls himself *Sonny*?"

"His real name is Krishnan."

"Is *what*?"

"Krishnan Hemkar."

81

"I see," Carolyn said, and went to the dresser for another stack of slips. Carrying them to the open suitcase on the bed, she wondered whether twenty-nine was too old for Elita, remembered that there was a fourteen-year age difference between her and her former philandering husband, decided ten wasn't too terribly bad, after all, and then realized she was already marrying off the child to someone named . . .

"*What'd* you say it was?"

"What was?"

"His name."

"Krishnan Hemkar."

"You sound like you're clearing your throat."

"That's his name, Mom. He's half-Indian, half-British. And when you meet him, I hope . . ."

"Oh, am I going to meet him?"

"*If* you meet him, I hope you won't make fun of his name."

"I have a friend named Isadore Lipschitz, and I've never made fun of *his* name, so why should I make fun of Christie *Hemmar's* name?" Carolyn said, and shrugged and went back to the dresser. "How many sweaters should I take?" she asked aloud.

"Krishnan Hemkar," Elita said.

"Whoever. I'm sure he's delightful, stranding you in Penn Station."

"I wasn't stranded, Mom. I managed to get my bags outside *all* by myself, and get a taxi *all* by myself . . ."

"Mama's big girl," Carolyn said, carrying sweaters to the bed. "Are you coming out with me tomorrow?"

"I thought I'd stay in the city for a few days."

Carolyn turned from the suitcase, a white pearl-buttoned cardigan in her hands. She looked at her daughter. "Why?" she asked.

"I just got home," Elita said. "I want to spend a few days in New York before running out to the beach."

"The city's going to be an oven all week long."

"So what? I like hot weather."

"Since when?"

"Sometimes it gets very hot in L.A."

Carolyn kept looking at her.

"It does," Elita said.

"There'll be a message on the machine, you know."

"What do you mean?"

"Giving the Westhampton number. If anyone calls."

"That's not why . . ."

"If this Sonny person calls."

"I just want to spend some time in New York, that's all. And he's not this Sonny *person*."

There was a long, strained silence. Carolyn kept looking at her daughter.

"Elita?" she said at last.

"Carolyn?" Eyebrows raised, faint mocking tone.

"I *hate* when you do that," Carolyn said.

"Do what?"

"Mimic me."

"Sorry."

"And call me by my first name."

"Gee, sorry."

"You *know* I hate that. I'm not Carolyn, I'm your goddamn mother."

"Yes, Mother."

"You're staying here because you're hoping he'll call, aren't you?"

"I told you why I'm staying here."

"Because you hope Sonny *Lipschitz . . .*"

"*Goddamn it, Mom!*"

"*. . . will call. You're going to mope around here in the apartment for the next . . .*"

"*I am not!*"

". . . three, four days . . ."

"I told you I . . ."

". . . waiting for some goddamn *Indian* you met on a train . . ."

"He's half Br . . ."

". . . to call you! Instead of . . ."

"I'll come out sometime next week, okay?"

". . . instead of for *once* in your life exhibiting the tiniest bit of pride and self-*respect*!"

"Mom." A pause. As lethal as her sudden glare. "I don't *want* to go to Westhampton tomorrow, okay?"

"Okay, fuck it."

"Nice talk," Elita said.

Carolyn turned away from her and hurled the pearl-buttoned sweater into the suitcase.

The two detectives who'd caught the squeal were pounding up the steps ahead of Santorini. One of them was called Hawk for Hawkins because his first name was

Percival and anyone who called him Percival or even
Percy would have risked a mouthful of knuckles. He did
not look like a hawk at all. He looked, in fact, more like
a bear. Two hundred and fifty pounds if he weighed a
dime. Wearing a blue polyester suit he'd bought at some
discount joint. White shirt and red tie. Beer barrel belly
hanging over his belt. Sweating bullets as he climbed the
steps.

His partner was black. The strong silent type. Wearing his hair in what they called a hi-top fade, looked like
some kind of upside down flower pot sitting on top of
his head. Plaid sports jacket, looked like wool, the guy'd
never heard of tropical weight fabrics. Tall and slender,
maybe a bit over six feet, a hundred sixty-five pounds
stepping out of the shower onto a scale. Big knuckled
hands of a street fighter. Eyes as black as midnight. Skin
the color of a coconut shell. Santorini figured him for
the sharper of the two. And the more lethal. Down
here, this was the One-Nine. If he ever worked anything
down here again, he had to remember to ask for Lyall
Gibson, which was the black guy's name.

Hawkins was doing all the talking. Puffing up the
stairs, throwing the words over his shoulder. Santorini
was doing a little puffing himself; the victim was in an
apartment on the fifth floor of the walkup. There were
the usual cooking smells you found in any building in
this city, even some of the expensive condominiums.
Made you want to puke sometimes, the smells in the
hallways. They kept climbing. Hawk kept talking.

". . . saw the inter-departmental alert you guys put

out, figured this one would *really* interest you. You'da got it anyway, sooner or later . . ."

"Not necessarily," Santorini said.

He was not eager to take on another case. The stiff rightfully belonged to Gibson and Hawkins, they were the fucking cops who'd caught the squeal. So why were they busting Homicide's balls?

". . . the coincidence and all," Hawkins was saying.

"It's no coincidence, Hawk," Gibson said.

He pronounced it *co*incidence, the way people from the South pronounced *um*brella or *po*lice. Santorini figured he hadn't been up North too long. Either that or he'd picked up his speech patterns from a mother who'd been born in Mississippi or Georgia.

"I hate these buildings got no elevators," Hawkins said.

"No doorman, either," Gibson said.

"No doorman, she gets a coupl'a bullets in the head," Hawkins said.

Santorini wished he had a nickel for all the homicide victims he'd seen who had doormen *and* a couple of bullets in the head. They were on the fourth floor now. One more to go. They turned and walked across the landing to the next flight of stairs. As they began climbing again, he could see a pair of blue uniformed trouser legs at the top of the stairwell. Puffing, he followed the two detectives onto the landing. The uniformed cop was standing outside the door to apartment 5A. The A, some kind of metallic shit that wasn't real brass, hung crookedly from one screw.

"How you doing?" Hawkins said to the cop outside the door.

"Okay," he answered.

"Everybody still here?"

"Yes, sir. Except the M.E., he just left."

"They didn't take away the stiff, did they?"

"No, sir. Lieutenant gave strict orders Homicide had to see it first."

"Well, this here's Detective Santorini from Homicide, we're gonna go in now, show him the body."

"Yes, sir."

Santorini wondered what all the fuckin' fuss was about. Dragging him all the way down here to look at some dame got shot in the head 'cause she didn't have a doorman? Why couldn't he have viewed the corpse at the morgue? A stiff was a stiff no matter where or how you looked at it. They went into the apartment. At least it *smelled* better than the morgue. Big burly guy in a grey tropical suit and wearing a greyish straw fedora came over with his hand extended.

"Lieutenant Costanza," he said, "we got something good for you."

"I wonder what it could be," Santorini said, thinking he was making a joke about calling Homicide in to see yet another dead body. But everybody here was looking so serious and solemn, like they just found the latest victim of Buffalo Bill; the trouble with too many cops nowadays was they saw too many fuckin' movies.

"Over here," the lieutenant said.

The dead woman was surrounded by what had to be a

dozen cats, all of them looking confused. One of them, a white cat with yellow eyes, was sitting closest to the woman and meowing incessantly.

"Goddamn cats," the lieutenant said.

The woman herself was half-seated, half-lying on a sofa with floral-patterned slip covers. There were two overlapping bullet holes between her eyes. The slugs had torn out the back of her skull and splashed the wall behind her with blood the color of the slipcover flowers. Her hair was clipped short, a sort of reddish color, but not as bright as the blood. She was wearing a grey sweater. The M.E. must've unbuttoned it a bit to slip his stethoscope onto her chest; she had good firm breasts. Santorini figured she was fifty, fifty-five years old, a woman who might have been good-looking when she was younger. There were cat hairs all over the grey sweater.

"Her name's Angela Cartwright," Hawkins said. "We found a passport with her name and picture in it."

"A British subject," Gibson said.

So *that's* the coincidence, Santorini thought. Two fuckin' Brits get killed in the same week, right away they run to Homicide.

"You know . . ." he started to say.

"M.E. noticed this while he was examining her," Costanza said, and unbuttoned the dead woman's sweater to reveal her white brassiere. Gently, almost tenderly, he eased her left breast out of its restraining cup. Just beneath the nipple, Santorini saw:

"We figured it tied in with the one in your alert," Costanza said. "Two Brits, both of them with swords tattooed on their chests."

"Guy kills 'em and tattoos 'em," Hawkins said, and shrugged at the simplicity of it all.

Santorini knew this wasn't the case; the coroner's report had indicated that the tattoo on the last victim had not been a fresh one at all.

"Anyway," Costanza said, "we figured we'd turn it over to you right away."

Terrific, Santorini thought. Now I'll get to talk to that dumb fuck at the Consulate again.

Arthur Scopes had chosen the venue himself; his private office at SeaCoast Limited had been swept for listening devices and further equipped with a babbler to confound long-distance ears. On the telephone, he told Sonny that he knew the place was completely sanitary. The words *private office* conjured for Sonny a wood-paneled area offering both space and solitude, with windows overlooking on one side Seventy-second Street and on the other Columbus Avenue. But as the ancient elevator in the soot-stained building creaked and whined its way up to the third floor, he began to realize that his expectations may have been a trifle ambitious.

SeaCoast was at the end of a narrow hallway that contained two other offices, one an accountant's, the other a firm that repaired electric shavers. The door to the shaver-repair firm was standing wide open. An electric fan swept back and forth over a counter opposite the entrance, wafting cool air into the hallway as Sonny walked past. At eight-thirty this morning, just before he'd left the hotel, a television forecaster was predicting temperatures in the high nineties.

The words SeaCoast Limited were lettered in black on the upper, frosted-glass panel of the company's entrance door. Sonny grasped the brass doorknob, turned it, opened the door, and found himself in a smallish room where two people—one an Asian girl, the other a white male—sat at desks with telephone receivers to their ears.

A pair of windows at the far end of the room admitted midmorning sunlight. The room was noisily air-conditioned by a single window unit in the window on the left, a virtual babbler in itself. The Asian girl was speaking in what Sonny assumed to be Chinese. The white male was saying ". . . three-ninety-nine a pound for the chicken lobsters, six and a quarter for the jumbos. May I take your order, sir?"

An organizational cover beyond reproach. A legitimate business that could withstand even close scrutiny. Sonny was impressed. The Chinese girl—she was in her twenties, Sonny guessed—finished her conversation, turned from the phone, and asked, "May I help you, sir?" Her speech was entirely accent-free. She was wearing a white blouse and a blue mini-skirt that rode high on her upper thighs. Sandals with white leather thongs.

Good Chinese-girl legs. Long black hair fastened with a blue plastic barrette. Sonny had recently read that Chinese women were undergoing cosmetic surgery to remove the folds in their eyelids and make their eyes look rounder. He figured the women in China were going crazy.

"I have an appointment with Martin Hackett," he said.

His everyday cover name.

"And your name, sir?"

"Scott Hamilton."

"One moment, please."

She rose in a single fluid motion, smiled briefly, and went to a closed door Sonny assumed was Hackett's private office. She knocked . . .

"Yes, come in."

. . . opened the door, entered, and closed it behind her. Sonny waited. The white male on the phone was still giving prices to whoever was on the other end of the line. He did not so much as glance at Sonny. The Asian girl came out, said, "Mr. Hackett will see you now," and stood aside for him to enter.

The door eased shut behind him.

He was looking at a large man wearing a white cotton jacket of the sort people wore in supermarkets. Embroidered in red over the breast on the left-hand side of the jacket were the words SeaCoast Limited. The man's looks were clearly Arabian. Black hair and dark brooding eyes, an aquiline nose. A strapping man of the desert stuffed into a cheap white jacket that was too tight across his shoulders. But this was no camel herder.

"I'm Arthur," he said, and smiled, and rose, extending his hand.

Arthur Scopes. The *Martin Hackett* was for civilians, but Arthur was the code name he'd be using for the business at hand.

"Nice to meet you," Sonny said.

"Sit down, hmm?" Arthur said, and indicated a straight-backed wooden chair in front of his very dark, virtually black, indeterminately wooden desk. The windows here in the front office faced the Columbus Avenue side of the building. On the street below, Sonny could hear cab drivers impatiently honking their horns. The walls were painted a grim shade of grey. There were two pictures hanging on the wall behind the desk, one of what appeared to be a French landscape, the other of a laughing peasant girl with golden curls. Sonny took the chair. It was uncomfortable.

"So," Arthur said. "You've been briefed, hmm?"

"I've been briefed, yes."

"Have you read the letter?"

"I've read it."

"Does it explain everything?"

"Everything," Sonny said.

He had read the letter at least a dozen times. Remembering the events it had triggered, he became enraged all over again, the anger igniting his eyes—but only for an instant. He was a professional; there was work to be done here.

"What happened to Mother?" he asked.

"Mm, Mother," Arthur said, and tented his fingers. Huge hands. Blunt fingertips. Manicured nails. "She was murdered," he said.

Sonny's eyebrows went up.

"We don't know who or why. We're watching it closely. This may be a countermeasure of some sort."

"How was she killed?" Sonny asked.

"Gunshot wounds. All we really know so far is what we've read in the newspapers. The police are still investigating. I'll keep you informed."

"I hope you will. If my back needs covering . . ."

"Oh, no question, we'll let you know at once." He hesitated a moment, and then said, "Were you told this is a No-Fail operation?"

"No."

"That's what it is. Does that trouble you?"

"Not particularly. I've been trained for any eventuality."

"You understand, don't you, that a pistol is out of the question?"

"Yes. That's what No-Fail . . ."

"Because pistols aren't infallible, are they?" Arthur said. "We don't want him surviving, the way Reagan did. And we don't want him left a vegetable, either. He's to be *eliminated,* hmm? Cleanly. Completely. And anonymously."

Sonny looked at him.

"We'll claim no credit afterward, we want no later retaliation. Just kill him, Sonny. And vanish."

Or die if I must, Sonny thought.

"Do you understand?"

"I understand."

"Good. What will you need?"

"A drop."

"Use SeaCoast."

"Can I have deliveries made here?"

"Of course."

"Are we still using the same cobbler?"

"McDermott, yes."

"Is he at the same address?"

"Yes. East Seventieth Street."

"I'll also need some basic information."

"What sort?"

"Precinct numbers, the addresses of police supply . . ."

A buzzer sounded on Arthur's desk console. He hit a
button.

"Yes?"

"A Mrs. Fremont on four," the Chinese girl said.

"I told you not to disturb us."

"She said it's urgent."

Sighing heavily, Arthur hit another button on the console and picked up the receiver. "Hello?" he said, and
listened for a moment. "No, don't be silly," he said,
rolling his eyes heavenward, "always plenty of time for
you." He listened again, nodded, said, "Mmm, I see.
Yes, a *very* good idea, and I quite agree it's of para-
mount importance to make certain the fish is fresh. But,
you know . . . SeaCoast is a wholesaler, hmm? Yes. To

restaurants and fish markets and the like. Uh-huh. Uh-huh. Yes, I see. Well, what I *could* do . . . hmm? The seventeenth, did you say? Well, that's . . . well, let me see," he said, and glanced at his desk calendar. "That's still three weeks off, I'm sure I could . . ." He rolled his eyes again, impatiently this time, and listened for what seemed an interminably long time. "What I was going to *suggest*," he said, "was that I put you in touch with a retailer on the island . . . yes, I'll be happy to do that. I'll find a good one and get back to you. I'm sure I have your number, but let me have it again, hmm? Uh-huh," he said, writing, "uh-huh, good. I'll call you as soon as I . . . what? Oh. Thank you. The seventeenth, yes, I'll put it on my calendar. Good talking to you," he said, and hung up and expelled his breath in exaggerated exasperation. "A neighbor," he explained. "She's having a *fish* party, God help me."

Sonny smiled.

"You were saying?" Arthur said.

"Police supply houses, police precincts . . ."

"You're planning elementary substitution, hmm?"

The "hmm?" was an annoying verbal tic that threaded his conversation like a shiny metallic wire.

"I'm not sure," Sonny said. "But I'll need to know which precinct the Plaza is in . . ."

"Of course. But you realize, don't you, that we're still not sure he'll *be* at the Canadian affair?"

"I'll be there, anyway."

"Ready to improvise, hmm? Play it by ear, so to speak."

"No, I'll have a plan by then."

"It's not that far off, you know."

"I'll have a plan, don't worry."

"You'll want to check out the Baroque Room . . ."

"Is that where the . . . ?"

"Yes, sorry. I got that today."

"Still at the Plaza?"

"Yes. The Baroque Room at the Plaza Hotel. It'd be convenient if he *did* decide to come, wouldn't it? Get him and the bitch at the same time, hmm? But I haven't yet heard if that's likely. The Statue of Liberty'll be harder. It's on an island, you know . . ."

"I know."

". . . and security will be very tight, I imagine. So . . ."

"I'll need the number of *that* precinct, too."

"I'll get it for you. But . . . I was about to say . . . if you're planning to go in as a cop, it might be extremely difficult. The space is too confined, and getting close to him . . ."

"That's what I'll have to figure out."

"Be much easier at the Plaza. Big ballroom, lots of space to roam around in, lots of exits and entrances. Even so, it won't be easy. I don't know what kind of security the British will provide for Thatcher, if any at all, now that she's out of office, but I'm sure the Canadians and Mexicans'll have agents all over the place. And if Bush *does* show up . . ." Arthur rolled his eyes. "Be literally thick with them, hmm?"

Sonny nodded. He was thinking that either way—the

ballroom or the island—he might have to do a lay-in job. He didn't want to discuss that quite yet, not until he knew for sure what his weapon would be and how he would . . .

"What weapon did you plan to use?" Arthur asked.

Mind reader, Sonny thought.

"I don't know yet. I didn't know this was a No-Fail till just . . ."

"Of course. The point is, will you need help?"

"Maybe."

"You'll let me know, of course."

"Of course."

"You know," Arthur said, and hesitated. "The Canadian affair is on the first. That's only five days away."

"I realize that. But I got here as soon as I could. My outside deadline . . ."

"Of course, I'm merely saying. The point is . . . if you have to go for the second option, that's only three days later. So if you'll need any weaponry assistance from us . . . will you be considering explosives, for example?"

"I'm not considering anything yet."

"Because we have a man who can rig whatever kind of . . ."

"So can I."

"Of course. Forgive me. I'm merely saying we can help you with whatever . . ."

"Yes, I understand."

"Good. Phone me if you . . ."

"The Chinese girl and the other one, are they . . . ?"

"Not Scimitar, but yes, with us, of course. She's not Chinese, by the way. She's from Bali."

"Oh."

"In any case, you don't have to go through the Sea-Coast line. The number you have is my private line and completely secure. As I told you."

"How soon can you get me the information I need?"

"I'll put someone on it . . ."

"Because the sooner the . . ."

"I was *about* to say I'll put someone on it *immediately,* hmm?"

All at once, it was clear to Sonny that Arthur did not enjoy having his authority questioned. Fuck him, Sonny thought. Time was of the essence here, and he preferred directness to convolution. His plans had to be formulated as soon as possible, the one for the ballroom, the contingency plan for the island. If Arthur couldn't get the information he needed quickly, then he would go elsewhere for it.

"I'll need some cash, too," he said.

"How much?" Arthur said at once.

"A few thousand for now. Perhaps more when I know what my plans will be."

"Fine," Arthur said, and opened the bottom drawer of his desk. He took from it a small grey metal cash box, unlocked it, and removed from it a sheaf of banded hundred-dollar bills. Breaking the paper band around the bills, he began counting them out.

"You know how important this is to us, don't you?" he asked, counting, his head bent.

"I do," Sonny said.

"You won't fail us, hmm?" he said, and looked up sharply, his eyes meeting Sonny's.

"I won't," Sonny said.

"I hope not," Arthur said, and smiled, and handed the bills across the desk to him. They felt new and crisp. "Anything else?" he asked.

"Is there a safe house? If I should need one?"

"Of course."

"Where is it?"

"In Westhampton," Arthur said.

The call from Miles Heatherton came at twelve-ten that Friday afternoon, just as Geoffrey was leaving the office for lunch. A glance at his watch told him that his stomach was understandably growling and that, incidentally, it was already a bit past closing time in London.

The first words Heatherton said were, "Are you having us on, Geoff?"

"How do you mean?" Geoffrey asked.

"This *second* passport notification request."

Geoffrey had rung London at eleven this morning, shortly after Santorini had left the consulate office. The detective had seemed almost gleeful that yet another British subject had turned up dead in this insufferably hot and murderous city. With an identical scimitar tattoo on her breast, no less. Which report Heatherton had received silently and non-committally, promising to call on Monday. It was not yet Monday. It was merely lunchtime today—and thank God it's Friday, as the natives were fond of saying. Geoffrey waited now for whatever dire information Heatherton was about to transmit.

"Having you on how?" he prompted.

"The two persons she listed in the passport?"

"Yes."

Get *on* with it, he thought.

"Non-existent," Heatherton said.

"I see."

"And it's the same passport."

"How do you mean?" Geoffrey asked.

"As the first one. The name on it is different, of course, Angela Cartwright on this new one, as opposed to Gillian Holmes on the first one . . ."

Oh dear, Geoffrey thought.

"And the dates and places of birth are different as well. Colchester in 1943 for the Holmes woman, London in 1937 for the Cartwright woman."

Oh dear dear, Geoffrey thought.

"Which are almost certainly false names," Heatherton said, "since, you see, the passport numbers are identical."

Geoffrey glanced at the number he'd copied from Angela Cartwright's passport before making his call to London this morning.

"Which number," Heatherton said, "is the number of a passport issued to the same Hamish Innes McIntosh."

Born in Glasgow, Geoffrey remembered.

"Born in Glasgow," Heatherton said.

In 1854, Geoffrey remembered.

"In 1854," Heatherton said. "So what we have here is a case of two women claiming to be British subjects, for reason or reasons as yet unknown, seemingly unrelated save for the identical passport number and the rather curious tattoo adorning their, ah, respective bosoms."

Geoffrey sighed audibly.

"I've turned this over to MI6," Heatherton said flatly. "I rather imagine someone in New York will be contacting you."

Geoffrey looked at the calendar.

"When?" he asked.

"Depends how urgent they feel it is, wouldn't you say?" Heatherton said. "There are two corpses already, you know . . ."

But *not* British subjects, Geoffrey thought. So why . . . ?

"So perhaps they'd like to move on this before there are any *more* of them, eh?" Heatherton said. "How's the weather there in New York?"

"Beastly," Geoffrey said.

"Quite the same here," Heatherton said, "but in a different way, I'm sure. I wouldn't plan on dashing off to the mountains, by the way . . ."

Shit, Geoffrey thought.

". . . or the seashore," Heatherton said, "until the man from MI6 has made contact. Shouldn't want him to think you rude, eh?"

Geoffrey looked at the calendar again.

Friday, the twenty-sixth day of June. He had, in fact,

planned to go to the seashore tomorrow. A friend in New Jersey . . .

"What do *you* think those bloody scimitars represent?" Heatherton asked.

"I haven't the foggiest," Geoffrey said. "When do you think this chap will be contacting me? To be quite frank, I'd made arrangements for the weekend, and the thought of hanging about in New York, waiting for a telephone call . . ."

"I shouldn't think it would be before Monday," Heatherton said. "But, Geoff . . ." His voice lowered. "I really wouldn't leave the city, were I you. Truly."

Shit, he thought again.

"Toodle-oo," Heatherton said, and hung up.

5

It was still only a little past one on Friday afternoon, but Santorini felt like he'd been sitting here in front of the computer for a month and a half. The computer was called Fat Nellie, for the letters FATN stamped into a metal plate screwed onto its back. Santorini didn't know what the letters actually stood for, and he didn't give a damn. He had trouble enough *working* the damn thing, without having to concern himself with technicalities.

The fucking computer was driving him crazy.

First of all, because he wasn't sure how you spelled *scimitar.*

It took him close to half an hour to realize that just possibly the word was spelled with an *s-c* like in *scissors* instead of just a plain *s* like in *simple,* or a *p-s* like in *psycho,* this was *some* fuckin' language, English.

What he was trying to do was come up with a scimitar tattoo, preferably, if there was any such thing in the files. But in addition to scimitar tattoos, he asked the computer to locate any *sword*-shaped tattoo because he was willing to settle for anything that even *looked* like a scimitar. And then, for good measure, he threw in sword-shaped scars or birthmarks as well, which he hoped might possibly give him something that related to the two dead broads with scimitar tattoos on their tits, stranger things had happened.

He had started his search by limiting it to New York City and by further restricting it to felony arrests over the past five years. Those arrests would of course include murders, since homicide was a felony as every schoolboy and schoolgirl in this city knew from watching television and movies and—in some instances—from having *committed* one or two themselves, murders. The same way that every kid in this city, from the third grade on up, knew that a kilo was the equivalent of two point two pounds. Never mind any *other* mathematical formulas; they could be failing algebra and geometry or even elementary-school arithmetic, but they all knew for sure that a kilo of cocaine or heroin was two point two pounds of the shit.

Which is why Santorini suspected he should try spelling *scimitar* with an *s-c*, stranger things were possible.

Bingo! Right off the bat, he came up with more *scimitars* than he could shake a sword at.

There were two street gangs in Brooklyn named Scimitar. One of them was the Scimitar S.A.C., which letters stood for Social and Athletic Club, like fun. The other was just plain Scimitar, but the computer indicated the gang was now defunct; Santorini wondered if the Scimitar S.A.C. had taken over the name of the gang that had preceded it in time and exceeded it in reputation. Both gangs, past and present, tattooed these funny little swords on their right hands, on the ball of flesh where thumb joined index finger.

There was also a street gang in the Bronx that called itself Scimitar Psychos, but they preferred tattooing the Persian sword on the forearm—except for the gang's female members. The debs called themselves Scimitar Psycho Bytches, and they preferred to tattoo the little curved sword—well, well, well—on the upper slope of the breast, where the tattoo would be visible in a bikini, a halter top, or even a low-cut blouse. But the computer indicated that the oldest of the Bytches was only nineteen, scratch Gillian Holmes and Angela Cartwright, or whatever their square handles were.

Santorini kept scrolling.

A guy named Curtis Langdon had slain three nurses in the Bedford-Stuyvesant area of Brooklyn four years ago and had carved onto their cheeks a mark that faintly resembled a curved sword. The newspaper had taken to calling him the Scimitar Killer. According to the computer, though, Langdon was languishing upstate at Attica, where he was doing life plus ninety-nine.

A woman named Alice Hermann had drowned her six-day-old infant in the bathtub of her apartment in a Queens housing project a year and a half ago. Among the physical characteristics identifying her was a tattoo on her left arm showing a heart pierced by a curving sword. Well, who the hell knew? Except that she, too, was doing time in the Women's Division of the Bedford Hills Correctional Facility.

There were several other men and women with similar sword-in-heart tattoos . . . that was the trouble with such a wide search . . . and a man with a scar that resembled a curved sword or scimitar . . . and a remarkable number of men and women alike who had birthmarks shaped like curved swords or scimitars . . . and . . .

Santorini leaned closer to the screen.

In Manhattan, three years ago, a terrorist group named *Simsir* had claimed credit for planting an explosive device that detonated in the Iraqi airlines terminal at John F. Kennedy airport. One of the group had eventually been arrested, convicted of arson and reckless endangerment, and sentenced to twenty years in prison. He had escaped last fall and had not surfaced again. His name was Mustapha Hayiz and he was listed as an Iranian national.

In Persian, the word *simsir* meant scimitar.

Sonny walked past Bergdorf Goodman on the corner of Fifty-eighth Street and Fifth Avenue and paused to look in the corner window, where a plastic blond mannequin, dressed in crisp white and black, looked coolly indifferent to the sweltering heat beyond the plate glass. He himself was wearing a tan tropical suit, matching shirt and tie, and brown loafers. Under his arm, he carried a brown leather Mark Cross portfolio with a gold-plated clasp. He looked at his watch: 1:23. He had made his appointment for 1:30.

He turned the corner onto Fifty-eighth, walked partway up the street, almost to the Fine Arts theater, and then crossed Fifty-eighth and walked past the fountain and small park outside the Plaza. Huge flags, only one of them American, hung limply over the entrance doors to the hotel. A dozen or more limousines were parked outside, their windows down, their chauffeurs looking pained by the heat. A doorman, uniformed in white trimmed with gold braid, hailed a taxi for a woman who waited at the top of the steps under the merciful shade of the hotel marquee.

Sonny glanced at her as he walked by and pushed his way through the revolving doors. Following the directions he'd received on the telephone, he walked past the Palm Court and to the left, and then went straight ahead and up a flight of carpeted steps to the mezzanine level, following the signs to the Terrace Room. His appointment was with a woman named Karin Lubenthal in the Catering Department. He had told her on the phone that he wished to make reception and banquet arrangements for his sister's wedding next June.

The wooden sign was painted white, edged with gold, trimmed with a double scallop at all four corners, and fastened to the wall with a pair of brass fleurettes. It read:

CATERING * SALES
CONFERENCE SERVICES
OFFICES

The receptionist just beyond the door was a woman in her late twenties, wearing a wispy red summer dress, her dark hair cut in bangs on her forehead. A laminated identification tag was clipped prominently to the sash of the dress.

"I'm Mr. Morris," he said. "I have a one-thirty appointment with Miss Lubenthal."

"Yes, sir, please have a seat," the woman said. "I'll let her know you're here."

He sat in an upholstered straight-backed chair on the wall perpendicular to the desk. There were several brochures on the table beside the chair. One of them was titled *Wedding, Plaza Style*. It showed on its all-pink cover a bride all in white. The other was larger—some six by twelve inches, he reckoned—and was simply titled *The Plaza*, in elegant gold script lettering against a background that looked like marble. He was opening the first brochure when the receptionist said, "She'll be with you in a moment, sir."

"Thank you," he said, and then, conversationally, "Do you all wear those tags?"

"Pardon?" she said.

"The ID tag. It *is* an ID tag, isn't it?"

"Oh. Yes, sir. All hotel employees are required to wear them."

"Why's that?" he said, studying the tag more closely now.

"Well, for security," she said. "We don't want unauthorized people wandering around the halls."

"I would guess not."

108

"For security, that's all," she said, and shrugged.

A redheaded woman who appeared to be in her mid-thirties came down the corridor, stopped several feet from where Sonny was sitting, smiled, and said, "Mr. Morris?"

He stood up at once and extended his hand.

"Yes," he said. "How do you do?"

"Karin Lubenthal," she said, and took his hand.

"Where's *your* tag?" he asked.

"What?" she said, puzzled.

"Your ID tag."

"Oh. In my desk drawer," she said, still puzzled.

"Only checking," he said, and smiled.

"I just finished telling him we all have to wear them," the receptionist said.

"Well, don't report me," Karin said, and winked at her. "Won't you come with me?" she asked Sonny, and then led him down a carpeted corridor to the office's inner recesses. She was wearing a pleated white skirt and a navy blue blazer. She looked altogether nautical, and quite patriotic if you counted her red hair.

"So your sister's getting married," she said.

"Yes. You may think it unusual . . ."

"Not at all."

". . . for me to be handling the arrangements . . ."

"No, we get different members of the family all the time."

"Both my parents are dead, you see."

"I'm so sorry."

They were passing conference spaces, or consultation

spaces, he didn't know quite what to call them, they certainly weren't *offices* per se. Merely spaces partitioned one from the other . . .

"They died a long time ago," he said. "I virtually raised my sister, which is why I'm here today."

"Not at all unusual, won't you come in, please?" she said, and smiled, and indicated one of the partitioned spaces, in which there was a desk and several chairs. She sat in the chair behind the desk. He took one of the chairs in front of it.

"First," she said, "let me give you my card. People sometimes have trouble spelling the last name."

"Thank you," he said, and accepted the card, and glanced at it. Looking up again, he said, "Just the way it sounds," and then took out his wallet and tucked the card into it.

She waited till he'd put the wallet back in his pocket, and then she asked, "Has your sister chosen an exact date yet?"

"No. It'll be next June sometime, but . . . oh my," he said. "Are we already too late?"

"No, no," she said. "We sometimes get people who book two years in advance, but there's still time, please don't worry."

"Phew," he said, and smiled.

"How large a party will this be?" she asked.

"The exact figure isn't set yet," he said. "I expect somewhere between a hundred and a hundred fifty people."

"I see you have both our brochures," she said.

"Yes, but I haven't had a chance to . . ."

"If you'll open the back cover of the larger one . . . yes . . . and just flip back the flap there . . . that's it . . . you'll see a page with some floor plans on it . . ."

"Yes," he said, nodding.

". . . and below them, a chart."

"Yes."

"If you'll look at the floor plan . . ."

Sonny looked at it.

". . . in the upper right-hand corner there," Karin said, "just above the Grand Ballroom—I don't think you'd want the Grand Ballroom, would you? It's much too large for something like this."

"I quite agree."

"But the Baroque Room is very popular for wedding receptions. Do you see it on the plan there?"

"Yes, I do," he said.

"I'll show you the room itself later on, of course," she said. "That, and also the Terrace Room. You passed through the Terrace Foyer on the way in . . ."

"Yes . . ."

". . . which is right here on the mezzanine floor, and also very popular for wedding receptions. Do you see the floor plan there? Just under the plans for all the other rooms? It's separated from the others because they're all on the first floor."

"Yes, I see that."

"Now if you take a look at the chart . . ."

"Yes."

"Right there below the floor plans . . ."

"Yes," Sonny said, and looked at the chart.

"You'll see that the Baroque Room is almost twice the size of the Terrace Room—a bit more than forty-four hundred square feet as opposed to *twenty*-four hundred."

"Yes. Sixty-three by seventy . . ."

"As opposed to sixty by forty."

"Yes."

"I personally find the Terrace Room more intimate . . ."

"It looks small."

"No, the floor plan is deceptive."

"I think my sister might prefer the larger room."

"The Baroque, yes, a lovely room. I'll show you both, of course, and I'm sure she'll want to look at them personally before she makes a final decision. Where will the wedding take place?"

"That hasn't been decided yet."

"Because we do weddings here, too, you know."

"No, I didn't know that."

"Yes, we do. In which case, should you decide to have the wedding here, we would set up the room itself—whether it's the Terrace or the Baroque . . ."

"I think the Baroque might please her more."

"Let's say the Baroque then . . . we'd set that up for the wedding, and then retire to the foyer for the before-dinner cocktail reception, while the main room is being set up for dinner. The before-dinner reception . . ."

And now, as Karin told him all about the open bar

and the deluxe brands, and the medium-priced French wine . . .

". . . although we've recently begun serving a very good American wine as well . . ."

. . . and the passed hors d'oeuvres, and the buffet with four or five hot selections . . .

. . . Sonny listened for opportunities to ask the questions that had brought him here in the first place.

She was talking now about the dinner itself, explaining that the menu consisted of an appetizer, a salad, an entrée with vegetables and potatoes, medium-priced red and white wines, a champagne toast, and dessert, which included a wedding cake.

"All of this is open to change or addition, of course. For example . . ."

. . . if the bride wanted them to serve a whole smoked salmon during the before-dinner cocktail reception, it would cost an additional eight dollars per person. Or if she requested a more expensive champagne for the toast . . .

"We normally use a Louis Roederer, which is very good," Karin said.

"Yes, very," Sonny agreed.

. . . but if she wanted a more expensive champagne, the basic price would be adjusted accordingly.

"We're very flexible," Karin said.

"What *is* the basic price?" Sonny asked.

"Two hundred dollars per person, whichever room you choose. Plus a gratuity of nineteen percent for the waiters, the two captains, and the maître d'."

"Where do you get your waiters?" he asked.

"How do you mean?" she said, puzzled.

"Well . . . do you hire waiters especially for the occasion, or are they . . . ?"

"No, they're all Plaza Hotel waiters. We have our own staff."

"Do they wear little ID tags like the one in your desk drawer?" he asked, smiling, making a little joke.

"Well, they wear *name* tags, actually," she said, and returned his smile.

"How many will there be?" he asked. "Waiters."

"One for every ten persons. And the same waiter will handle the same table all night long. That's important."

"Do they all know each other?"

"What a strange question," she said.

Careful, he thought.

"What I mean is, have they *worked* together before? Do they work well as a team? I wouldn't want . . ."

"Oh, I see. Yes, they're all familiar with each other."

"What sort of uniforms would they wear?"

"For a summer wedding, black trousers and white jackets. Black bow ties, of course."

"What if one of them gets sick?"

"Sick?" she said.

"Yes. Or three of them. Or five? Would this cause utter confusion? Or would . . . ?"

"Oh, I see. No, there wouldn't be a problem. These are all union waiters who work on a rotation basis. We have fifty or so on order, and if one gets sick, we fill in with another one. Don't worry, you'll have a full complement, one for every ten people, no matter *what* happens."

"Who'll be in charge?"

"I'm sorry, I don't . . ."

"Well, for example, if a waiter *should* get sick, who'd be the one to call in a substitute wait . . . ?"

"Oh, I see. Our Banquet Executive Director. He'd be there on the night of the reception, making certain everything went smoothly."

"I'm sorry I'm asking so many questions."

"Not at all."

"I don't mean to be so picky."

"I'm happy to help you."

"I just want to make sure everything is perfect for her."

"Naturally."

"What does the two hundred dollars include?"

"Well, let me tell you what it *doesn't* include."

"Please," he said.

He would get back to his questions later. He had almost come too close there a minute ago, and he didn't want to raise her suspicions. For now, he listened to all the bullshit. Flowers were not included in the basic price, but the hotel recommended a florist named Ernest, with whom they'd had excellent results. Music was also not included, but she could highly recommend the Jerry Carlyle Orchestra—"No relation to the competitive hotel," she said, and smiled. And the photographer they recommended was a man named Allan Curtis, who . . .

"I think my sister has her own photographer in mind," Sonny said. "But can you tell me a little about security? I know she'll be concerned about crashers . . ."

"We provide a Plaza security guard."

"Uniformed?"

"No, wearing a plain dark suit."

"No ID tag?" he said, and again smiled.

"Yes, an ID tag," she said, and returned the smile. "*And* a little name plate. White lettering on black plastic, totally discreet."

"And just that one guard is enough?"

"We usually find one sufficient. He's equipped with a radio, of course, and is in constant touch with our security office. He'll make certain no uninvited guests, or curiosity seekers . . ."

"How do you mean?"

"Well . . . people who hear music, and become curious, and try to poke their heads in, see what's going on . . . he'll make sure nothing like that happens."

"And just the one guard can take care of that?"

"Oh, yes."

"Because . . . well . . . I didn't want to disclose this . . . but . . ." He lowered his voice. "My sister is marrying a rather well-known performer . . ."

"Oh, I see."

"And I wouldn't want any uninvited photographers or . . ."

"I quite understand. We can provide beefed-up security, if you like . . . or, you know, you can hire your *own* security people, if that's what you'd prefer. We're flexible, either way."

"I'm not comparing this to any sort of political function, mind you," Sonny said, "he's not *that* important. But what sort of security would you provide for a . . . ?" He searched for an example, and then rolled his eyes and said, "A Democratic fund-raiser, say, where there'd be senators and governors . . . maybe a movie star or two . . . something like that."

"We can supply whatever kind of security you'd like," she said.

"But for something like that . . ."

"We handle all sorts of events," she said. "You have no idea how many heads of state stay here at the hotel in total anonymity. When you feel free to let me know who the groom is, we can recommend the proper precautions, and see to it that your sister's every wish is fulfilled."

"I'd appreciate that," he said.

"Would you like to take a look at the rooms now?"

"Just the Baroque, I think," he said.

At twenty minutes past two that Friday afternoon, Geoffrey Turner was talking to the American girl when Lucy Phipps, the secretary shared by him and two other vice consuls, buzzed him from outside. He glanced up at the clock, an annoyed little frown furrowing his brow.

"Yes?" he said into the microphone on the phone console. He hadn't yet quite caught the hang of the newly installed "communications system," so he said the word again, not certain she'd heard him the first time. "Yes?"

"There's a gentleman from Her Majesty's Government here to see you," Lucy said.

"Which branch?" he asked.

"Customs and Excise," Lucy said. She always sounded as if she were shrieking. Her shrill irritating voice sounded like a cross between an air raid siren and a banshee. Come to think of it, she sounded a great deal like Peggy Armstrong, one of his co-vice-consuls. Two singularly unattractive women. Here in Passports and Visas, Geoffrey was sure there was a conspiracy afoot to surround him with the plainest women in all the whole crumbling empire.

"I'm sorry," he said, "he'll just have to wait. I've someone with me at the moment."

"I know," Lucy said, "but he said it was urgent."

"Just ask him to wait, won't you?" Geoffrey said as pleasantly as he could manage, and smiled forbearingly at the girl sitting on the other side of his desk. "I shan't be much longer."

"He looks *terribly* impatient," Lucy whispered.

"I'm sorry," Geoffrey said, and clicked her off. "Now then," he said, "as I understand this, Miss Randolph . . ."

"Randall. Elita Randall."

"Sorry, I thought I'd . . ." He glanced at his note pad. "Randall it is, terribly sorry."

"That's all right," Elita said.

"As I understand it," Geoffrey said, and was momentarily distracted by her legs. Frightfully good-looking woman, this one. *Girl,* he supposed. Couldn't be a day over seventeen, could she? "This . . . ah . . . friend of yours," he said.

"Acquaintance, actually," Elita said, aware of his wandering eyes, lifting herself slightly off the seat of the chair, and tugging at her mini. "I met him on a train, actually."

"Ah, yes," Geoffrey said, aware that he'd made her uncomfortable, cursing himself for it, and looking away in contrition, busying himself with the pad on his desk and the pencil in his hand. "And you say he's British?"

"Well, his mother is."

"Would you know her name?"

"I'm sorry."

"How about his father? Is he British as well?"

"He's Indian."

"And his name?"

"I don't know that, either."

"I see. Well, what's this *fellow's* name? The one you met on the train."

"Krishnan Hemkar," she said.

"Ah, Indian indeed," he said. "How old is he?"

"Twenty-nine."

"May I ask your age, Miss Randall?"

"Why do you need to know that?"

"Well, I don't, actually. I was merely curious."

"I'll be twenty in February," she said, somewhat defiantly.

Which meant she was scarcely four months past her

nineteenth birthday. But whereas seventeen would have put her completely out of range, nineteen wasn't totally unacceptable. On the other hand, he had dated nineteen-year-old American girls who wanted to discuss nothing but movie stars.

"Krishnan Hemkar," he said, looking at the name he'd written on his pad. "And, of course, you don't have his address or his tele . . ."

"No, I don't."

"Of course not, or you wouldn't be here, would you?" he said, and smiled.

"No," she said. "I wouldn't."

"Would you know what sort of passport he might be holding?"

"Well, I know he was born in India . . . someplace near the Pakistan border. He told me the name of the town, but I can't remember it."

"Mmm," Geoffrey said. "Would you know if he's a British subject?"

"Well, he said his mother's Brit . . ."

"Yes, I know, but . . ."

"And he told me he was raised in England. He came here when he was eighteen."

"Would you know if he's now an *American* citizen?"

"No, I'm sorry. He's a doctor."

"I see."

He looked across the desk at her. Wide blue eyes beseechingly returning his gaze. Please help me find my lost Indian friend. But how?

"You see," he said, "without knowing . . ."

"I just . . . it's important that I locate him."

"I'm sure, or you wouldn't be going through all this trouble, would you?"

"No, I wouldn't," she said.

"Well," he said, "let me run his name through the computer . . ."

"Oh, thank . . ."

". . . when I get a free moment."

Her face fell.

"If you'll let me have a number where I can reach you . . ."

"When can you do that?"

"I beg your pardon?"

"Run his name through the computer."

"Well, I have someone waiting just now . . ."

"Yes, I know," she said. "I heard."

"But my diary looks relatively clear afterwards, perhaps I can get to it sometime later this afternoon."

"That would be very nice of you," she said.

"Could I have the telephone number, please?" he said.

She gave him her mother's number, watching as he wrote it onto his pad, making dead cert he was writing it down correctly, this Indian chap was obviously of some importance to her. She thanked him again, rose, smoothed the short wrinkled skirt over her thighs and her behind, told him she'd be home all afternoon if he found the information she needed, and he promised again to try to get to it this afternoon. He offered his hand in farewell. They shook hands briefly and she went out, the door whispering shut behind her. His heart was pounding. He went to the intercom on his desk, buzzed Lucy Phipps, and said, "What's the gentleman's name?"

"Sir?" Lucy said, sounding like a startled siren.

"The gentleman from H.M. Customs."

"Joseph Worthy, sir."

"Show the worthy gentleman in," Geoffrey said, rather pleased with his own little joke, which of course Lucy Strident did not catch at all.

6

Sonny did not place the first of his three calls until three o'clock that Friday afternoon.

By that time, he knew exactly how he would kill the President.

Sitting on the bed in his room at the Hilton, he dialed the 800 number and listened while it rang on the other end. A recorded female voice told him he had reached Gem Inorganics in Lewiston, Maine, and then advised him which button to push for product pricing, product availability, or sales. He pressed the number-one button on his phone. A live woman said, "Gem Inorganics, how may I help you?"

"Can you tell me in what quantities you sell dimethyl-sulfoxide difluoride?" Sonny said.

"Do you have the catalogue number on that?" the woman said.

"I'm sorry, no."

"Just a moment," she said.

He waited.

"Dimethylsulfoxide dichloride?" she asked.

"Di*fluoride*," he said.

"Oh, yes, here it is," she said. "That's 37468 in the catalogue. The two-gram size is ninety-five dollars, and we've got it in stock. The ten-gram size is three hundred and fifty-two dollars . . ."

"Do you have that in stock?"

"Let me check that, sir."

There was a pause. Scrolling her computer screen, he guessed.

"Yes, sir, we do."

"Is there any limit on how many I can order?"

"However many you need, sir. On a ten-by-ten, we could probably do a special pricing for you."

"I won't need as many as that," he said. "Can I order two of the ten-gram size?"

"Yes, sir, certainly. If you'll have your purchasing department call us with a purchase-order number, we'll invoice your accounting department."

"Thank you," he said, and hung up.

He called again ten minutes later. Pressed the number one again. Got a different woman who said, "Gem Inorganics, how may I help you?"

"I'd like to place an order, please," he said.

"May I have your account number?" she said.

"We don't have one yet. This is the first time we've placed an order with you."

"All right," she said cheerfully, "I'll have to get some references from you later on. Meanwhile, do you have the catalogue number on the item you want?"

"Yes, it's 37468. In the ten-gram size."

"One moment, please," she said.

He waited.

"37468," she said, "dimethylsulfoxide difluoride, the ten-gram size, and it's in stock. May I have your name please, sir?"

"Hamilton Pierce," he said.

"And the name of your corporation?"

"SeaCoast Limited," he said.

"The address and zip, please?"

He gave her SeaCoast's address on Seventy-second and Columbus.

"And your phone number?"

He gave her the phone number.

"The purchase order number on this?"

"127 dash 024," he said.

"127 dash 024, yes, sir. That'll come to seven hundred and four dollars plus tax."

"Can you FedEx the order to me?"

"Yes, sir, but it'll be expensive."

"How expensive?"

"Well, it'll be a hazard shipment, so that's ten dollars right on top. Did you want this a one or a two?"

"A one or a . . . ?"

"Delivery, sir. One day or two?"

"One-day, please."

"I'd say the delivery charge'll come to something like forty dollars, more or less."

"Fine. When can you send it?"

"It'll go out today."

125

"Before you get our references?"

"I'll trust you on those till you send them. Do you have a fax?"

"I do."

"Just send me three business references and one bank reference. You can address those personally to me, my name is Anne Burroughs."

"I'll get that out right away," he said. "Thank you."

"Thank *you*, Mr. Pierce."

He hung up, dialed Arthur at SeaCoast, filled him in on the conversation he'd just had, and asked him to fax the requested information to Miss Burroughs. Arthur said he would have it taken care of at once.

"While I have you," he said, "the Statue of Liberty is in the First Precinct and the Plaza is in the Eighteenth."

"Thank you," Sonny said.

"What's dimethylsulfoxide difluoride?"

"An insecticide," Sonny said, and hung up.

He'd used a wire garrote the first time he'd killed anyone.

By the time he was seventeen, he had killed three men. By the time he was twenty—and an undergraduate at Princeton—he had killed yet another person, a girl this time. Since then, he'd been asleep. Waiting. And now, at last, the opportunity. There would be no personal glory here, none except the secret glory in his heart. Complete anonymity, Arthur had told him. Retribution without recognition. No credit claimed this time. Do the job and disappear. Take satisfaction in the knowledge that the debt had been paid, the score settled.

And although he was willing to give his life to achieve the goal entrusted to him, the No-Fail designation did not make such a sacrifice mandatory. Do the job and do it well, covering all tracks before and after, leave the victim or victims unmistakably dead, and then move on. He had been trained to kill and to escape intact. He would do both exceptionally well when the time came.

The first man he'd killed was an Egyptian spy posing as a rug merchant in Tripoli. In an operation of small consequence except as a training exercise, Sonny had gained entry as a seller of figs, snapping the wire loop out of his basket and around the Egyptian's neck in a cobra-like strike that left him dead within seconds. His escape route was through the Old City, white walls and minarets, the smell of eucalyptus leaves, past the Mosque of the She-Camel, and down Jama ad-Duruj, and past the Osman Pasha Mosque, losing himself in dark and narrow alleys twisting downward to the sea, until at last the sparkling blue of the Mediterranean surprised him.

That had been the first time. There were two other men after that—one in Egypt, the other in Chad—and then the girl. Here in America. The only one he'd ever regretted. Sixteen years old. A sophomore at McCorristin High in Trenton, some fifteen miles from Princeton, where he'd been studying at the time. Francine Dumar, whose father was Alex Dumar, a GID agent whose cover was working as an insurance claims adjustor for the Prudential. Francine had been observed in conversation with a man from Langley, and it was assumed that Washington was taking a serious run at her in an attempt to nail her father as a spy. That she'd been receptive seemed undeniable. GID figured it would merely be a matter of time before they turned her completely.

The assignment was top priority in that one of their own was in imminent danger and remedial action was imperative. This may not have been a true mayday situation, where exposure and arrest—or even termination—of an agent was imminent; the job fell just short of an emergency Code Red designation. But it was serious enough, and Sonny's orders were unmistakable. In the trade, "measles" was the international nomenclature for any killing engineered so that death would seem to have occurred either accidentally or through natural causes. Francine Dumar had to be eliminated, but discreetly. Francine Dumar had to contract a deadly case of measles.

He arranged her suicide. Overdose of the sleeping pill Seconal—which he'd forced down her throat one cold November night while her parents were attending a concert at the War Memorial on West Lafayette. Suicide note in her own handwriting—duplicated by their cobbler in New York. Sonny's initial research had indicated that she was very popular at school, and also sexually promiscuous. The note explained in adolescent prose, which he himself had composed, that her period was three weeks overdue and she thought she was pregnant. Entirely plausible, given her reputation. He still considered it a brilliant touch, considering how inexperienced he'd been at the time.

Francine Dumar. A beautiful girl with long dark hair and brown eyes. He remembered that she'd been wearing nothing but a nightgown when he came into the small development house through a back door he'd picked with a nail file, the way he'd been taught at Kufra. She'd pleaded for her life. He'd pulled her head back by the long dark hair, forced the pills into her mouth, clamped his hand over her nose and mouth until she was compelled to swallow. Thirty-five of them, ten more than the lethal dose. She was comatose on the bedroom floor before he left the house. He knew she would be dead before her parents got home from the concert.

Saddest assignment he'd ever had.

Her father later defected, possibly suspecting that his only daughter had been murdered by his own people. His name appeared regularly on GID hit lists, but Langley had given him a new identity and so far he hadn't surfaced anywhere.

Sonny looked at his watch.

He planned to revisit the Plaza early tomorrow morning, this time without the informative Miss Lubenthal as a mentor and guide. With her eager assistance today, he had learned the location of the pantry servicing the Baroque Room . . .

"May I take a peek into the kitchen, please?"

"Well . . . why would you . . . ?"

"I just want to make sure it's clean."

JOHN ABBOTT

"Clean? Well, I can assure you it meets the highest sanitary standards. In any event, that isn't the kitchen. It's the pantry. The kitchen is downstairs."

"Oh. Well, how does the food get up here?"

"On the elevator."

"And is the pantry where they prepare it for serving?"

"Yes."

"Well, may I take a look at the pantry then?"

"I'd be happy to show it to you, but there's an Orthodox Jewish wedding tonight, and the caterer might not like . . ."

"The caterer?"

"Are you familiar with the word *trayf*?"

"I'm sorry, no."

"Well, I just don't think he'd like us in the pantry while he's setting out his kosher dishes and things."

. . . and had also been able to locate and mark in memory all the exits leading from the room. Tomorrow morning, he would wander the back stairs without Miss Lubenthal in tow, searching for both an escape route and a possible lay-in location, should his final plan call for one. Earlier this afternoon, under guise of asking about a dais for his sister and her bridal party . . .

"Do they ever do that? Sit at a separate long table?"

"Oh, yes, to avoid seating conflicts between the two families. That way, the bride and groom, together with the bridal party, sit at a table on a raised dais, and there are no problems. Here in the Baroque Room, we normally . . ."

. . . and had gone on to show him where the dais was

usually placed, there on the left, with the huge arched windows facing the park at right angles to it.

That's where Thatcher'll be sitting, he'd thought.

And maybe Bush as well.

With an exit door close by, leading to the pantry on the left. And directly ahead, a visible flight of steps climbing upward.

He would reconnoiter those steps tomorrow morning. Meanwhile . . .

He picked up the receiver again, and dialed the 800 number for Epsilon Chemical Supplies in Meriden, Connecticut.

The liaison officer seemed not at all bothered by the fact that counterfeit British passports were in circulation. Apparently, this was a common occurrence and not something to get one's feathers—

"In any case," Geoffrey said, "it was only *one* passport. That is, they were one and the *same* passport, with different names in them, you see. The dead Scotsman's passport, that is."

The liaison officer glared at him.

His name was Joseph Worthy, or so he'd said, who knew what it might really be? He explained to Geoffrey at once that he was not with Her Majesty's Customs and Excise Office, as he'd told the noisy Miss Phipps, but served instead as liaison between M16 and the Foreign and Commonwealth Office, of which the British Consulate here in New York was an integral part. It was the Secret Intelligence Agency, in fact . . .

"SIS, M16, call it what you will," Worthy said.

. . . who'd contacted him early this afternoon to report the alarming fact that two women with identical green scimitar tattoos had been found dead in Manhattan, both of them carrying false British passports. The passports, he was now saying, were of no interest whatever to him. Sixpence a dozen, buy them in any local pharm . . .

"Well, surely not," Geoffrey said.

"Figure of speech," Worthy said.

"I should hope so."

"The scimitar tattoo, on the other hand, *is* something of concern, especially since a former prime minister will be here in the city a fortnight from now."

"Nine days from now, actually," Geoffrey said.

"Worse yet," Worthy said. "Who's the police officer investigating these homicides?"

"A man named Allan Santorini. He's with Homicide North. In the Twenty-fifth Precinct uptown."

"Seem any good?"

"A typical New York detective," Geoffrey said, and shrugged. Unwashed, unshaven, and uncouth, he thought.

"Does he have any idea what those green scimitars might mean?"

"No. And neither do I."

"Does the name *Sayf Quasīr* mean anything to you?"

"No, what is it?"

"It's an elite Libyan intelligence group."

* * *

"It's an Iranian terrorist group," Santorini said.

"Simsir," the other man said, and nodded. "I'm familiar with it."

They were sitting in the twelfth-floor offices of the Federal Bureau of Investigation at 26 Federal Plaza downtown. Santorini had called here the moment he'd made his computer discovery. The special agent with him now was named Michael Grant. He was fifty-three years old and balding, and he told Santorini that his biggest recent assignment had been rounding up a gang of rustlers—here in the East, would you believe it, rustlers!—who'd been dumb enough to move cattle interstate from New York to Pennsylvania, thereby invoking the wrath of the federal agency. Through the windows behind him, the Statue of Liberty and the Jersey shore were clearly visible.

"Do these people tattoo themselves?" Santorini asked.

"Not to my knowledge," Grant said.

"Little sword on their breasts?"

"I'm not *that* familiar with them."

"Little scimitar? Because it means scimitar in Persian, you know. *Simsir.*"

"I didn't know that," Grant said. "In any case, they're out of business. They were very active during the Iran-Iraq War, claimed responsibility for the assassination of several top-level Iraqi diplomats. But I haven't heard anything about them since that bombing at JFK, back in . . ."

"That's what I wanted to ask you about."

"We caught a punk named Mustapha Hayiz—there're no state or federal statutes against terrorism, you know, the Bureau got called in 'cause the bombing took place at an airport . . . interstate, international, all that jazz. We found him living like a camel-driver in a room in Philadelphia, big terrorist hero, the whole place stinking of human excrement. He wouldn't tell us who his accomplices were—for all we know, he was operating solo on the airport bombing. Anyway, we sent him up for a long, long time—but he broke out last October, don't know where the hell he is now. Probably back in Teheran, clenching his fists for the television cameras."

"How many others were there in the group?"

"Originally? Five or six. All these terrorist groups with the high-sounding names—the Holy This and the Holy That, the Masked Ones, the Islamic Legion, the Flaming Sword, the Volcano, the People's Bureau for Solidarity and Horseshit—these're sometimes two, three guys who know how to put together a bomb, and another dumb bastard who's willing to sacrifice his life delivering it."

"Any women in these groups?"

"Sometimes. Why?"

"We found two dead women tattooed with green scimitars."

"Well, green, now you're talking Libya," Grant said.

"Which is what concerns us," Worthy said. "Do you remember the Yvonne Fletcher incident?"

"Of course I do," Geoffrey said.

"April 17, 1984," Worthy said, and nodded solemnly. "St. James's Square, London. Outside the Libyan embassy . . . well, they called it the People's Office. There were demonstrators outside . . ."

Geoffrey could still remember that day.

He was sixteen years old at the time, home from Eton, visiting his parents. A quiet Tuesday in London, five days before Easter. St. James's Square tree-shaded and still save for the chanting of the demonstrators. The BBC news cameras were covering the event dutifully but routinely; in a democracy, one became used to demonstrations for or against everything on earth. The police were there as a matter of course; they were always on hand to make certain a crowd didn't go entirely berserk. But no one, least of all Geoffrey, was prepared for what happened next.

He was watching the screen only casually, glancing up every now and then from the thriller he was reading, an addiction he'd picked up from his mother. He had reached the part in the book where the female detective was out in a rainstorm, tracking a rapist, when all at once he thought he actually *heard* thunder, and then realized in an instant that the sound had come from the television set—but it wasn't raining in London that day. And then he recognized with a start that what he'd heard was gunfire. Actual gunfire. Not the kind you read about. *Real* gunfire. He looked up sharply. On the television screen, people were shouting, and policemen were rushing to where a young woman in uniform was lying on the pavement—dead, as it later turned out.

Someone inside the embassy had fired an automatic rifle from the first-floor window, killing her instantly.

"We had that bloody embassy under siege for ten days," Worthy said now. "Then somebody decided to allow the bastards clear passage home. Diplomatic immunity. For murderers." He grimaced sourly, shook his head. "We still haven't resumed relations with Libya . . . well, of course you know that."

"Yes," Geoffrey said.

He was still thinking about that dead policewoman lying on the pavement.

"So now we have two of Quaddafi's elite intelligence people abroad in New York a week before . . ."

"Five days, actually," Geoffrey corrected. "And they're not quite abroad anymore, you know. They're both dead."

"Five bloody days before she gets here," Worthy said. "Which seems quite a coincidence to us."

Geoffrey didn't see any connection whatever. He said nothing.

"I understand the Consulate here has been handling the banquet arrangements," Worthy said.

"No, sir, not the banquet itself. The *Canadian* Consulate is looking after that. All I did was consult with them on the *seating* arrangements for the main table. So that Mrs. Thatcher might not be inadvertently offended. That was the extent of my participation."

"Where have they seated her?"

"Well, let me show you the diagram," Geoffrey said, and opened a desk drawer and took from it a copy of the sketch the Canadian Consulate had sent him. Worthy studied it:

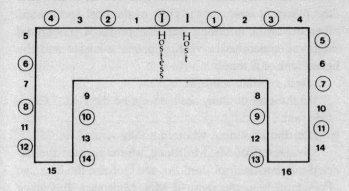

"In keeping with protocol," Geoffrey said, "the visiting prime minister is considered to be at home when he attends an embassy affair. The Canadians have quite properly granted him the presidency of the table, here at the center, with his wife on his right, both of them facing the entrance doors."

Worthy looked puzzled.

"Do you see where the places are marked with the Roman numeral one?" Geoffrey said. "That's where Mr. and Mrs. Mulroney will be sitting. The Canadian P.M. and his wife."

"What do all those little circles mean?"

"The circles indicate ladies. The usual seating arrangement for these affairs is boy-girl-boy-girl, as you see it here."

"And where will *our* girl be sitting?"

137

"Well, I had something of a row about that with an idiot at the Canadian Consulate, who mistakenly assumed that the Consul-General and his wife should take the places of honor to the right of the host and hostess respectively. I informed her that protocol was crystal clear as concerned a visiting prime minister and the president of a repub . . ."

"*Former* prime minister."

"In the eyes of many she'll *always* be the P.M.," Geoffrey said.

"Be that as it may, where *are* they seating her?"

"To the left of Mr. Mulroney, where you see the circled number-one position. Mr. De Gortari, the Mexican President, is to the right of Mrs. Mulroney. But all of this may go up in smoke, if what I hear is true."

"What is it you hear?"

"That someone very high up may be dropping in. A surprise guest. In which case, there'll be something of a brouhaha regarding the seating arrangements. I'll stick to my guns regarding Mrs. Thatcher's place of honor, of course, but . . ."

"How do you mean someone very high up?"

"Here," Geoffrey said, and tapped his forefinger on the desk.

"Here in the consulate?"

"No, no. Here in the *States*."

"*How* high up?"

"If they'd told me, it wouldn't be a surprise anymore, would it?"

"When *will* they tell you?"

"If it becomes necessary to move Mrs. Thatcher, I'd imagine."

"And when will that be?"

"I haven't the faintest."

"May I have a copy of this?" Worthy asked.

"I'll have one run off," Geoffrey said, and took the seating arrangement from him, and pressed a button on his phone console.

"I'll want to know immediately if her position at the table is changed."

"I'll call the moment I hear anything."

"Because we'll be planning very tight security," Worthy said, and winced as Lucy Phipps's voice blared out of the speaker.

The third call Sonny made was to a firm called J.D. Bowles Laboratory Sales, Inc., in St. Paul, Minnesota. He spoke to someone in sales, telling her he wished to order some isopropyl alcohol. She looked up the item in the company catalogue, told him it came in 480-milliliter bottles and sold for $9.75 plus tax, how many bottles did he want? He told her he would need only one, and said he wanted one-day FedEx delivery. She said it would go out in the morning. When she asked him his name and company affiliation, he told her he was Hamilton Pierce of SeaCoast Limited and gave her the firm's address and telephone number. She asked him what sort of company it was.

"We do research," he said.

"Can you be a bit more specific?" she asked.

"We do a wide variety of experiments for private physicians," he said.

"Can you tell me how you plan to use this product?" she asked.

This surprised him. Isopropyl alcohol was common rubbing alcohol, harmless even in the hundred-percent concentration stocked by a chemical supply house.

"We're running toxicity tests on rats," he said.

"Toxicity tests on rats," she said, obviously writing. "Very well, sir. Someone will call you regarding billing. Meanwhile, this will go out tomorrow."

"Thank you very much," he said.

Nodding, he put the receiver back on its cradle.

The photography shop was located on the second floor of a brownstone on East Seventieth Street, between First and Second avenues. There was a tailor shop on the ground floor and a palm reader on the first floor, and then the photography shop at the rear of the second-floor landing. Sonny did not get there until a little past five that Friday afternoon.

A man named Angus McDermott ran the shop. Four years ago, he had prepared Francine Dumar's suicide note from a sample of her handwriting. Sonny told him he was looking great, which wasn't quite true. McDermott had lost a lot of weight in the past four years, and his normally ruddy complexion was now somewhat sallow, his reddish hair thinning. McDermott was gay; Sonny wondered now if he'd contracted AIDS since last he'd seen him.

"How can I help you this time?" he asked.

There was the faintest burr in his voice. He had once lived in Glasgow, Sonny knew, but he was certain the man's heritage wasn't Scottish; the cover name was as false as his own Krishnan Hemkar. The night he showed Sonny the perfect suicide note, handwritten on Francine's own stationery, they got drunk together in a Third Avenue bar. In the empty hours of the night, McDermott confessed his abiding hatred for the United States, but never once mentioned what had provoked such murderous rage. Sonny got the feeling a woman was somehow responsible, but he knew better than to ask McDermott.

The studio in which McDermott worked was fronted by a huge picture window that flooded the room with natural light. Pale blue backing paper hung behind a raised platform on one wall. A half-dozen power packs were on the floor near the platform, their cables snaking to strobe lights on stands topped with grey umbrella-shaped reflectors. A Polaroid was mounted on one tripod, a Nikon on another. A green door on another wall was marked with a red hand-lettered sign that warned the room beyond was a darkroom.

They were sitting now at a long table strewn with snippets of film, grease pencils, magnifying glasses, developer, metal clips, capped lenses, order forms, and a half-empty bottle of Heineken beer. Sonny took from his jacket pocket an envelope containing the card Karin Lubenthal had given him. Careful to handle it only by its edges, he placed it on the table before McDermott, who picked up one of the magnifying glasses, leaned over the card, and studied it:

KARIN LUBENTHAL
CATERING MANAGER
(212) 759 3000 FAX (212) 759 3167
FIFTH AVENUE AT CENTRAL PARK SOUTH NEW YORK, N.Y. 10019

"What do you need?" he asked, still peering through the glass.

"An ID card."

"What on it?"

"The hotel seal, my name, my . . ."

"Do you want the seal in gold, as it is here?"

"Yes. Exactly as you see it."

"What else?"

"My name, my picture . . ."

"Do you have a photograph?"

"I thought you might take one today."

"Sure. What else on the card?"

"Across the bottom, in bold letters, the word *security*."

"Do you have a sample of the type?"

"No. A good block lettering will do."

"What color?"

"Black."

"How about the photograph? Color, or black and white?"

"Color."

"Do you want the card laminated?"

"Yes. With one of those little fastener clips on it, so I can pin it to my jacket."

"Plastic strap and fastener," McDermott said, nodding.

"Yes."

"How big should it be?"

"Two and a half by four, approximately."

"Seal at the top . . ."

"Yes."

". . . in gold, photo where?"

"On the right-hand side of the card."

"Name on the left then?"

"On the left, yes."

"What name?"

"Gerald Ramsey."

"And the word *security* across the bottom, block lettering, in black."

"Yes."

"All caps or just initial cap?"

"All caps."

"Do you need this card back?" he asked.

"I have no further use for it."

"How does Monday sound?"

"Tomorrow would be better."

"Tomorrow's a bit early."

"Sunday then."

"I suppose."

"Early Sunday morning."

"Well . . ."

"Time's short."

"All right, Sunday before noon. Need anything else? A birth certificate? A . . . ?"

"No."

"Driver's license?"

"Yes."

"What name?"

"Same as the Plaza card."

"How about ID cards?"

"Have you got NYPD stock?"

"Yes."

"I'll need one for the First and one for the Eighteenth. Both of them detective ID's."

"What grade?"

"Second."

"Any particular name?"

"James Lombardo."

"You've got it."

"Can you make up an FBI card?"

"Yes, I've got blanks in stock."

"Put the name Frank Mercer on it."

"You plan to be all these people?"

"I don't know yet. How about Secret Service?"

"Don't know what it looks like, never had a call for one. Sorry."

144

"No problem," Sonny said, but he was clearly disappointed. "Can we take the pictures now?"

"Whenever you're ready."

From a phone booth outside The Food Emporium on the northwest corner of Second Avenue, Sonny dialed the number she had given him on the train.

"Elita?" he said. "Hi, this is Sonny."

"Oh, God," she said.

"Ever been to the Statue of Liberty?"

"Oh, God," she said, "it's you!"

7

It had been a long hot Friday, but Saturday was even hotter.

At ten minutes to two that afternoon, the temperature in Washington, D.C., soared to ninety-nine degrees Fahrenheit, shattering the ninety-eight-degree record set for this day on June 27, 1980.

Agent Samuel Harris Dobbs was sweltering in the lightest-weight seersucker suit he owned. His immediate superior, Daryll Phillips, had taken off his jacket, and pulled down his tie, and was sitting in his shirtsleeves behind his big uncluttered desk, the Treasury Department seal on the wall behind it. But this was the boss's office here, and Dobbs didn't feel he could risk the liberty of making himself quite so much at home. Not with Phillips seeming to have a hair across his ass this hot summer day.

"I don't like surprises," he told Dobbs.

"Nossir," Dobbs said.

146

"I don't care it's a president or some sheek fum an Arab nation, it don't make no never-mind to me."

"Nossir."

"I don't like this last-minute sputterfuss, I got to send a team to New York, beef up the security there."

Dobbs was thinking he didn't much like it himself. He had promised Sally they'd take a trip to Pennsylvania next weekend, have a sort of second honeymoon in Bucks County. Booked the room and everything, his wife had been looking forward to it since early May. Now Phillips was telling him he'd have to leave for New York this afternoon, take five other agents with him, be there all weekend and through the first of July. And for what? To make sure security at the goddamn Plaza Hotel would be tight enough to suit the goddamn Republicans, and then to give the New York field office a hand at the goddamn *Canada* Day banquet, whatever the hell *that* was.

Dobbs hated Republican presidents.

He'd learned to hate Reagan and his witchy wife when he was working for them as part of the White House detail, hated all the things the President and his fine *lady* had stood for. Alone in bed with Sally, Dobbs would rage at how Nixon had only tried to *steal* the goddamn country whereas Reagan was now trying to *murder* it. Sally would tell him to hush, Sam, he'd lose his job or something.

He told Sally the only way he'd get out of this rotten job was to throw himself across that son of a bitch when another crazy bastard like Hinckley tried to kill him.

That was more than eleven years ago, before he got transferred to the Omaha field office, where he learned how much better it was to be in Washington, even working for Republican presidents. He never stopped believing it was Nancy who'd had him transferred because one day he was thirty seconds late opening a goddamn *door* for her!

Hating them both, he'd loved all the Reagan jokes they began telling . . .

There's this banquet at the White House, okay?

And Reagan is sitting next to Nancy, and one of the White House waiters appears by her side to take her order, explaining that they're serving either roast beef or filet of sole, which would she prefer?

And Nancy says, "I'll have the roast beef, please."

"Yes, ma'am," the waiter says. "And the vegetable?"

"He'll have the same," Nancy says.

. . . rejoiced when the son of a bitch got caught with his hand in the Iran-Contra cookie jar, but knew he'd wiggle out of it somehow—gosh, I'm terribly sorry, I just don't remember.

God, how Dobbs had hated him, *still* hated him.

But if Reagan had merely *killed* the nation, it was Bush who was now attempting to *bury* it, and Dobbs hated him even more than he had his predecessor. In fact, it was a good thing he was no longer part of the White House Secret Service detail; he might have killed *this* president himself.

Got a domestic crisis?

Just bomb a foreign country.

Follow in the footsteps of the Great Communicator, who'd used military force against Lebanon in 1982, and Grenada in 1983, and Libya in 1986 and finally in Honduras in 1988. The Great Communicator. Who'd once sent a *Bible* as a gift to the Ayatollah Khomeini, the leader of a *Moslem* nation. Bombs and bibles, how stupid could a person get?

So along comes Haji Bush, hero to millions, conqueror of Iraq, a fearsome nation with the gross national product of Kentucky, still bloated with his Commander-in-Chief importance, still managing to ignore the minor problems like dope, crime, collapsing cities, and civil rights so long as the Big Parade went on and on and on. The Washington newspapers were full of scathing editorials about him running off to New York where, golly, he could stand before that lady in the harbor on the Fourth of July, and, gee, wrap himself in the flag yet another time, and, wow, take advantage of all those big patriotic sound bites in an election year.

Reagan and Bush.

Two presidents too many.

Dobbs hated them both.

"Here're your plane tickets," Phillips said. "Enjoy the trip."

They each had different agendas.

Sonny was here to observe and to record.

Elita was here on an outing.

In the distance, they could both see the Statue of Liberty sitting far out on the water, the sky clear behind it. But Sonny was registering a sign advising that Battery Park closed at 1:00 A.M., and Elita was noticing a pair of lovers strolling hand in hand, one white, the other Asian. On her right, Elita saw a man selling green foam-rubber Statue-of-Liberty crowns, and wondered if she would appear childish buying one. On his left, Sonny saw a low, greyish-brick building with the metallic letters UNITED STATES COAST GUARD across its facade—and wondered if there would be Coast Guard cruisers circling the island when the President made his Independence Day speech.

They bought tickets for the ferry in a round, red brick building that reminded Elita of a sun-washed cloister, and Sonny of a roofless fortress. The tickets cost six dollars each. Sonny had a camera around his neck. He posed her in front of a large posterlike sign headlined PLANNING YOUR VISIT TO LIBERTY ISLAND.

They boarded the ferry at two-fifteen.

Elita was wearing running shorts, a white T-shirt, and sandals. Sonny noticed that she wasn't wearing a bra. He was wearing chinos, a striped polo shirt, and jogging shoes. She thought he looked exceedingly handsome, dressed so casually. She did not know that he had dressed to blend in with what he'd suspected would be a tourist crowd.

There was a babble of foreign tongues everywhere around them. Elita found the mix of nationalities exciting; Sonny found them boring. He understood many of the languages, but did not reveal this fact to Elita. A French girl reading aloud from a guidebook to New

York City was informing her friends that the island they were heading toward was once called Bedloe's Island and was the site of the old Fort Hood, the outlines of which now formed the starlike base of the statue. Sonny found her voice monotonous. A German girl approached a man whom she'd heard speaking in her own language, and asked if she could have a single cigarette —*eine einzige Zigarette, bitte*—because there was no place to buy any on the boat. Sonny found her bold. The man gave her the cigarette she'd begged, and then, in English, asked, "Do you have fire?"

"Danke ja, ich habe," she said, and went back to where she'd been sitting on the port side of the ferry.

The ferry was called Miss Liberty. It was moving out from Battery Park now in a southwesterly direction, approaching toward the distant copper statue from her right, where she clutched a tablet in the crook of her arm . . .

". . . *sur laquelle est écrite la date du quatre juillet, dix-sept cent soixante-seize* . . ."

"How thrilling it must have been," Elita said over the sound of the French girl's voice. "Approaching her as they came into the harbor."

"Yes," Sonny said.

"The immigrants, I mean."

"Yes."

He was wondering how he would get back to the mainland once he'd accomplished his mission.

The soaring downtown towers of the financial district were behind them now; the island and Liberty were

151

coming closer and closer. A Japanese girl sat beside him and began changing the film in her camera. She was wearing a T-shirt that read DISNEYLAND, TOKYO. Her friend said something to her in Japanese, which Sonny could not understand. A Hassidic Jew in a black suit, flat black hat, and snowy white beard stood at the railing, staring beyond Liberty to where Ellis Island sat on the horizon. The French girl kept babbling from the guide book . . .

"*. . . fond de la base jusqu'à la torche est quarante-six virgule cinq mètres. Pour avoir accès à la couronne, il faut monter trois cent cinquante-quatre . . .*"

The pilot of the ferry headed her straight for marker thirty-one, then brought her around so that she slowly revealed the statue first in profile, then in a three-quarter view, and then dead-on, the folds of her garments cascading to the pedestal in a flow of green copper, the left arm cradling the tablet, the sleeve of the raised right arm falling back, the golden torch in her right hand capturing the rays of the early afternoon sun, the sky behind her a vibrant blue. Viewing the statue as the boat circled her, revealing her as if in separate frames of motion picture film, Elita felt a fierce patriotic pride mixed with a sense of place and history. Sonny felt nothing.

The boat circled the island and came into the dock. In the distance, Elita could see the American flag flying from a tall flagpole. This, too, thrilled her. Sonny was busy looking down at a sign on the dock:

At the
Statue of Liberty
All Packs,
Packages,
Briefcases, etc.
are Subject to
Search

They came down the gangway and onto the dock. A high shed-like structure opened onto a wooden walkway that led to a huge brick-paved circle at the center of which stood the flagpole Elita had seen from the deck of the ferry. A tree-flanked esplanade—similarly paved with brick and ornamented with rectangles outlined in blue tile—led to the rear of the statue, standing tall on her pediment, a seeming halo of light around her crown.

"What happened to you at the train station?" Elita asked. She'd been dying to ask this from the moment he'd called, but had only now found the courage to do so.

"First, I couldn't find a porter," he said. "Next, I ran into a guy I went to Princeton with, and he dragged me off to . . ."

"But I was standing there waiting for . . ."

"Well, I had your number. I figured you knew I'd call."

"Then why didn't you?"

"But I did."

"It's been three days."

"I lost the slip of paper."

153

"What slip of paper?"

"The one I wrote the number on."

"Then why didn't you look it up in the phone book?"

"I didn't know your mother's first name. There are *dozens* of Randalls in the Manhattan . . ."

"She uses her maiden name now. It's . . ."

"Besides, I finally found the slip of paper."

"Well, in case you lose it again, her name's . . ."

"I've already written it in my book."

A National Park Service ranger wearing olive drab trousers, a tannish-green shirt, and a Smokey the Bear hat was waving tourists onto one or another line on either side of the center doors leading into the base. He was a tall, burly man with blue eyes and a reddish-brown mustache, and he kept chanting, "Admission is to the right or left. No admission through the center doors. Admission is to the right or left, depending where you want to go."

"Excuse me," Sonny said.

"Yeah?" the ranger said, and then immediately to the approaching crowd, "Admission is to the right or left, depending where you want to go. No admission through the center doors. Yeah?" he said again.

"How do we know which line to get on?" Sonny asked.

There was a National Park Service patch sewn to the ranger's shirt over his left pectoral. A little brass National Park Service shield was pinned over the pectoral on the right. Below the shield was a narrow brass rectangle with the ranger's name stamped onto it: ALVIN RHODES.

"Where do you want to go?" he asked.

"Well, until we know which line goes *where*," Sonny said, "how can we . . . ?"

"The line on the left is for people who don't know where they're going," the ranger snapped, and then began chanting again, "Admission is to the right or left, depending where you want to go. No admission through the . . ."

As it turned out, the line on the left wasn't for people who didn't know where they were going, but was instead for people who wanted to climb the stairs going up to the crown. A girl tending the rope at the head of the line told Sonny they were looking at a twenty-two-story climb . . .

"That's three hundred and fifty-four steps," she said.

. . . and maybe a wait of two to three hours. If they wanted her advice, they'd get on the other line and take the elevator up to the pedestal.

"Get a good view of the harbor all around that way, save yourself a lot of sweat and strain. Here's a plan, shows you where the pedestal is," she said, and handed him a printed drawing of the "Planning Your Visit" sign he'd photographed on the mainland:

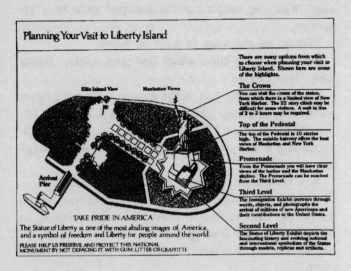

Planning Your Visit to Liberty Island

There are many options from which to choose when planning your visit to Liberty Island. Shown here are some of the highlights.

The Crown
You can visit the crown of the statue, from which there is a limited view of New York Harbor. The 22 story climb may be difficult for some visitors. A wait in line of 2 to 3 hours may be required.

Top of the Pedestal
The top of the Pedestal is 10 stories high. The outside balcony offers the best views of Manhattan and New York Harbor.

Promenade
From the Promenade you will have clear views of the harbor and the Manhattan skyline. The Promenade can be reached from the Third Level.

Third Level
The Immigration Exhibit portrays through words, objects, and photographs the arrival of millions of new Americans and their contributions to the United States.

Second Level
The Statue of Liberty Exhibit depicts the fascinating history and evolving national and international symbolism of the Statue through models, replicas and artifacts.

Ellis Island View   Manhattan Views

Arrival Pier

TAKE PRIDE IN AMERICA

The Statue of Liberty is one of the most abiding images of America, and a symbol of freedom and Liberty for people around the world.

PLEASE HELP US PRESERVE AND PROTECT THIS NATIONAL MONUMENT BY NOT DEFACING IT WITH GUM, LITTER OR GRAFFITTI

"What do you think?" he asked Elita.

"Sounds good to me," she said.

"I'll let you through," the girl said. "Just cross over to the other line."

"Thank you," Sonny said.

He was thinking he would remember Alvin Rhodes. He was thinking, *I hope you're here on the Fourth, Alvin.*

They were in the open space where Liberty's original torch was now displayed, a large rectangle surrounded by an upper level, which he guessed was the Second Level indicated on the Planning Your Visit sketch. As they walked toward the people waiting on line for the elevator, Sonny looked up and saw signs indicating there were restrooms upstairs. He spotted a staircase, took Elita's elbow, said, "There are restrooms up there," and led her toward the steps. She wondered if he had read her mind.

The men's room was on one side of the open rectangle, the ladies' room on the other. Again, their agendas were different. Elita simply had to pee. Sonny was looking for a likely lay-in spot, should the plan call for one. An open wooden door led into an angled alcove that shielded the men's room from the corridor outside. He ran his palm over the door, seemingly studying the paint job, while actually checking out the lock. A man passing by looked at him curiously, and Sonny said, as if commenting admiringly, "They painted it to look like bronze," which in fact they had. The man nodded in vague agreement and hurried into one of the stalls. The lock on the door was a spring latch, fitted with a keyway on the outside. A wooden wedge held the door open. Sonny glanced behind the door and saw a push bar on the inside. Mickey Mouse time.

There was another door in the little alcove, painted grey and right-angled to the entrance door. Someone had left it either accidentally or deliberately ajar, open perhaps some eight to ten inches. As Sonny passed it, he glanced into the darkened room beyond and saw a pail with a mop in it. The room was a utility closet. The outside of the door was fitted with a circular keyway. He walked past at once, hurrying through into the main section of the restroom. There were the requisite number of urinals, stalls and sinks. You could lay in overnight in a stall, but if a cleaning man came in to mop up—

The man who'd agreed with him about the imitation bronze door was coming out of the closest stall. He washed his hands at one of the sinks, glanced sourly at the blowers attached to the wall, dried his hands on his handkerchief instead, and left the room. Sonny took a position at the end of the row of urinals. A man at the other end was taking forever to pee. Sonny waited for him to finish, waited for him to leave the room—without washing his hands—and then zipped up his fly. He went to the sinks, quickly washed his hands, dried them inadequately on one of the wall blowers, and moved immediately to the grey utility closet door. He yanked the door all the way open, checked its inside surface in an instant. A thumb latch. Nothing else. No knob on the door, no push bar. Just the latch, designed to spring the lock in case someone accidentally trapped himself inside. He feigned elaborate surprise at having entered a closet. But there was no one in sight as he backed out into the alcove again; his little act hadn't been necessary at all.

Elita was waiting for him in the corridor. He glanced over the railing, said, "That elevator line looks long," and suggested that they walk up to the pedestal.

It turned out there was no way they could walk all the way up. But the steps at the far end of the corridor went up to a landing and then another flight of stairs, ten steps in each flight, and then to a level with some kind of telephone exhibit that was out of order at the moment . . .

Out of order, he thought. Yes. Good.

. . . and then two shorter flights of steps leading up to three pairs of exit doors fashioned of thick plate glass framed in bronze—*real* bronze this time. Deadbolts on all of them, inside and out. He pushed open one of the doors in the middle set, and allowed Elita to precede him outside, where he took a picture of her standing beside a stanchioned sign that read STAIRS TO GROUND LEVEL, with an arrow pointing toward the doors they'd just come through.

They walked all around the star-shaped level; this was where the old fort had stood. Actually the shape was less a star than a square with a series of angular bastions protruding from it, two on each side except for the one facing the harbor channel, where a larger bastion jutted out. Standing at the point of this larger abutment, looking up directly into the statue's face some hundred or more feet above, it was easy to see why the sculptor had oriented the front of his statue in this direction, at the mouth of the Hudson, and visible to any vessel passing through the Narrows.

It was also easy to determine that *here* was where the President would give his Independence Day speech. Here where the television cameras could pan up and away from Bush's solemn, sincere candidate's face to the great impassive face of the lady in the bay. Whether they set up the speaker's stand and microphones on this level . . . or the level above . . . or the one above that . . .

"Let's see if there are any more stairs going up," Sonny suggested.

"This is fun, isn't it?" Elita said, and squeezed his hand.

She stood virtually naked in her mother's bedroom, the room cool and dim now that sunshine had abandoned the Park Avenue side of the building, Sonny standing behind her, his hands on her breasts as they faced the vanity mirror. She could feel him stiff against her, erect between her cheeks, watching herself in the mirror, watching them both in her mother's mirror.

She was wearing a white garter belt she'd taken from her mother's lingerie drawer, sheer white nylon stockings, red patent-leather, ankle-strapped, outrageously high-heeled pumps, also her mother's. She looked like a recklessly disheveled nurse wearing chorus-girl shoes designed by the devil. The shoes lifted her buttocks, raised them to his probing cock. She hoped he wouldn't try to . . .

"Bend over," he said.

"Listen, I don't want you to . . ."

"Hands flat against the mirror."

She leaned into the mirror, obeying him, palms flat against it, face turned, cheek against the reflecting glass. She was truly frightened now, there was something about him that was sometimes terrifying.

"Lift it to me," he said.

"Please don't," she said.

And felt him probing her nether lips, felt him sliding familiarly into her wetness below, and lifted herself to him in gratitude and relief. Standing taller in her mother's heels, she accepted him deeper inside her, and began throbbing almost at once, wave after wave of uncontrollable spasm seizing her as she strained against him, gasping, accepting him completely, melting against him, dizzy with pleasure, flush and faint and "Fuck me," she said, "fuck me, oh fuck me . . ."

She lay beside him on her mother's bed. His eyes were closed. He looked utterly peaceful and relaxed. She wondered if he'd learned to do all those things in medical school. The things he did to her. Did they teach you that in medical school?

"How many girls have you done this to?" she asked.

"Done what to?"

"What we just did."

"Thousands," he said.

"I'm serious," she said. "How many?"

"Nine hundred and ninety-nine," he said.

He was kidding, of course.

Wasn't he?

"No, seriously," she said.

"Why do you want to know?"

His eyes were still closed. With her forefinger, she began tracing the green scimitar tattoo on the underside of his left pectoral.

"I want to be special," she said.

161

"You are special."

"How am I special?"

"You're passionate, and . . ."

"Well, anyone can be passion . . ."

"And responsive, and inventive, and . . ."

"How am I inventive?"

"You have a lively, inquisitive . . ."

"Mind? Give me a break."

"Cunt, I was about to say."

She fell silent. Finger still idly tracing the tattoo, wondering if she could dare . . .

She decided to risk it.

"I don't like that word," she said.

"Oh?" he said, and seemed to go suddenly tense beside her.

Immediately she said, "I didn't mean . . ."

"That's okay," he said, and sat up. He turned to her, smiled in polite dismissal, swung his legs over the side of the bed, and began walking toward where he'd draped his clothes over her mother's chaise lounge.

"Sonny?" she said.

"Yes?"

"What'd I say?"

"Nothing," he said, and pulled on his Jockey shorts.

"Where . . . where are you going?"

"Home," he said.

She was off the bed in an instant, rushing naked to him. He was reaching for his trousers. "No, don't go," she said, and hurled herself against him, wrapping her arms around his waist.

"Let go," he said.

"Sonny, please, I didn't mean to . . ."

"I said let go."

"Please, I'm sorry, please don't . . ."

The telephone rang.

"Answer your phone," he said.

"Sonny, I don't want you to . . ."

"Answer it," he said.

She went back to her mother's bed, lifted the receiver on the bedside phone, said "Hello" dully, and watched him as he pulled on his trousers and reached for his shirt.

"Miss Randall?"

"Yes, who . . . ?"

And recognized his voice. The jerk from the British consulate.

"This is Geoffrey Turner," he said. "I hope I'm not disturbing you."

"As a matter of fact . . ."

"I've run your friend's name through the computer," he said. "I'm happy to say . . ."

"I've already found him," she said. "Thanks, anyway."

"Well, good," he said. "If I can be of any . . ."

She covered the mouthpiece.

"Sonny, wait," she said.

". . . further assistance . . ."

"Thank you," she said, "I appreciate . . ."

And covered the mouthpiece again.

"Sonny, please!"

"Miss Randall . . ."

"Please, I'm very busy just . . ."

"I was wondering if you might be free for . . ."

"Thank you," she said again, and hastily put the receiver back onto its cradle and hurried across the room to where Sonny was sitting on her mother's plush velvet ottoman now, putting on his loafers. She forced herself onto his lap, threw her arms around his neck, lifted her lips to his face, tried to kiss him on the mouth, but he twisted away from her. She kissed his cheeks instead, his nose, his forehead, showered his face with kisses, murmuring "Please, Sonny, I love you, please, oh please . . ."

His voice low and steady, the words measured, he said, "Don't ever tell me what you don't like."

"I won't," she said.

"Ever," he said.

"I won't, I promise."

"Now get over there," he said.

She looked bewildered for a moment. Where did he want her? In front of the mirror again? Or was he . . . ?

"The bed."

Fearful she would anger him again, terrified she would lose him completely, she moved swiftly to the bed and sat on its edge.

"Lie down," he said.

She nodded obediently. Swung her legs onto the bed. Raised herself on her elbows to look toward where he was still standing motionless near the ottoman. Her heart was pounding, she could scarcely breathe.

She now knew that she would do whatever he asked her to do.

Whenever.

Forever.

The story was on page eight of that afternoon's *New York Post*. Santorini easily could have missed it, especially since he was eating a meatball grinder while reading the paper and was concentrating on not getting tomato sauce all over himself.

The story said that Margaret Thatcher would be here on the first of July, to attend a Canada Day celebration at the Plaza Hotel.

Santorini looked at his calendar.

The first was a Wednesday.

Four days from now.

Only yesterday, the FBI nemesis of Eastern cattle rustlers had briefed him on the counter-intelligence panic that had followed the 1986 bombing of Tripoli. At the time, the CIA, the FBI, and Britain's counter-intelligence people were all convinced that the Libyan leader had dispatched hit teams to kill Ronald Reagan for having ordered the raid, and Margaret Thatcher for having allowed the American bombers to overfly her country. Only after months had gone by without any actual assassination attempts were the concerned agencies able to relax their vigilance.

"But green is Libya's color," Grant had told him.

"Green, huh?" Santorini said.

"Green. Their flag used to be red, white, and black with a little gold eagle on it . . ."

"Little gold eagle, huh?"

"Yes, but Quaddafi changed it to solid green. The whole thing's green. Just this big solid green flag."

"Solid green, huh?"

"Green, right. Now your scimitar, come to think of it, is on the Saudi Arabian flag, with some squiggly Arab writing above it, probably means Allah be praised or some such shit. And *that's* a green flag, too, though not solid green like the Libyan one."

"So maybe this is something Saudi Arabian, huh?" Santorini said.

"Well, it could be *anything,* who knows with those troublemakers over there? If the *Israeli* flag was green, I wouldn't put it past *those* lunatics, either. The whole Middle East is full of maniacs, you ask me. But theirs is blue and white with a Star of David on it."

"Blue and white, uh-huh. The Israeli flag."

"Yes. But Libya has a thing about green, you see."

"A thing about green, huh?"

"Yeah. Well, you know, Quaddafi's got this vision about a state based on the masses—pretty original, huh?—which he tells all about in these three little booklets he calls the Green Book."

"Three of them, huh?"

"Yeah, but he calls all three of them the Green Book. Singular."

"Why singular?"

"Go ask him."

166

"Or green?"

"Who knows with these lunatics? The point, man, is your swords are green, am I right? The tattoos? So maybe this *is* something Libyan, who the hell knows?"

Especially since Margaret Thatcher's coming to town, Santorini thought, and we've already got two dead British ladies on our hands.

8

Elita was just approaching the Third Avenue building when the man from the British consulate came out onto the sidewalk.

"Mr. Turner!" she shouted.

He stopped dead in his tracks, turned, looked at her, seemed puzzled for the merest instant, and then said, somewhat curtly, "Miss Randall."

"I was just coming upstairs," she said.

"I'm dreadfully sorry," he said, "but I'm on my way somewhere. If you can come back in a few hours . . ."

"I just wanted to ask . . . when you called me Saturday . . ."

"I *am* in a frightful hurry," he said.

He did indeed seem as if he were anticipating a starting gun, his very stance giving the impression of a man already in motion. He was wearing the same grey suit he'd had on the last time she'd seen him, a striped gold and blue tie on his white shirt. His dark eyes were darting now, signaling his eagerness to move.

"Can I walk with you?" she asked.

"If you like," he said, and turned and started off. She caught up with him, fell into step beside him.

"I'm sorry about Saturday," she said.

"Mmm, yes," he said, "but this is Monday, you know, and I'm very busy."

"I know I was abrupt."

"Well, I wouldn't say you were abrupt," he said. "I'd say you hung up on me."

"Yes, I suppose I did."

"Mmm," he said.

He was walking as though his shoes were on fire, long strides scorching the pavement. She was having trouble keeping up with him.

"But I *was* in the middle of something," she said.

"Mmm."

"I'm sorry. I really am."

"That's quite all right," he said, sounding not the least bit mollified. "Why were you coming to see me today?"

"Well . . . I've lost him again."

"I see. Your young man."

"I thought I'd found him, but then he . . . well, he went off without telling me where I could reach him and . . ." She shrugged. "He's disappeared again."

"Something of a magician, eh?"

"Well . . ."

"Does his little disappearing act at irregularly spaced intervals."

"I guess he's shy," she said defensively.

169

"I guess he must be."

They were walking through heat that seemed three-dimensional. Everywhere around them, people moved along the sidewalks as if in slow motion. The homeless lay in torpor against the walls of the buildings, dressed for the summer heat in shorts and tank-top shirts. They passed one man who was picking at scabs on his legs, passed a woman with rat's-nest hair piled high on her head, wearing a voluminous skirt, a dirty white long-sleeved blouse, and black high-topped sneakers; she was sitting on a flattened cardboard carton, reading *The New York Times*. Elita saw the look of disgust on Geoffrey's face, and suddenly wondered how this city must appear to foreigners.

"But on the phone Saturday," she said, "you told me . . ."

"I scarcely had an opportunity to tell you *anything*," he said.

"I *said* I was sorry," she reminded him.

"Mmm," he said.

"I am."

"Mmm."

"You told me . . . you were *starting* to tell me . . . well, I had the impression you'd located him."

"Your impression was wrong."

They were approaching Alexander's now. She had never particularly liked the sleazy stretch of pavement that ran past Alexander's and Bloomingdale's on the next corner, but now—in the presence of this somewhat stuffy representative of the Crown—it looked particularly sordid. Geoffrey seemed to be the only man on Third Avenue who was wearing a suit. The others were wearing shirts, long-sleeved or short, collared or T. She was suddenly glad she'd worn a dress. Cotton, to be sure. With sandals. But nonetheless a proper dress, rather than the shorts and halters on many of the women moving sluggishly along the avenue. Geoffrey moved along the sidewalk like a royal frigate steaming past tugboats in a crowded harbor. He was beginning to annoy her. The way he moved so goddamn fast, the slightly superior and supercilious look on his handsome face, as if he were smelling something particularly noisome and was merely too polite to hold his nose.

"You said something about being happy to . . ."

"Yes, I had some information about the fellow," Geoffrey said. "But I did not indicate in any way whatever . . ."

"What information?" she asked.

They were on the corner of Fifty-ninth and Third now, waiting for the light to change. The moment it did, he sprinted for the opposite curb. She almost tripped trying to keep up with him. A cab driver blasted his horn at them even though the light was nowhere near turning against them.

"Will you for Christ's sake slow *down*!" she shouted.

"I'm late," he said, and glanced at his watch without really noting the time and without breaking stride.

"Where are you going?" she asked. "The coronation?"

"Close but no cigar," he said.

"What information do you have about him?" she asked.

"Krishnan Hemkar," he said. "Doctor of Medicine."

"Yes," she said. She had already told him this. It was nothing new.

"There was nothing on him in our computer, British mother or not," Geoffrey said. "But you said you'd met on a train coming from Los Angeles, so I . . ."

"Yes."

". . . called our consulate there and asked them to conduct a routine paper chase . . ."

"Oh good," she said.

He broke his pace for only an instant, giving her the look an exasperated older brother might have given a dumb kid sister who'd floated his stamp collection in the kitchen sink. Their eyes locked, blue on brown. He began walking again, even more swiftly, it seemed.

"There is, in fact, a Dr. Hemkar in residence at a hospital in Los Angeles. A call there netted a home address and a telephone number. I can let you have those," he said, "in case you'd like to make further inquiries yourself."

"That was very kind of you," she said.

"What was?"

"Calling the hospital."

"My colleague in Los Angeles made the call, not me."

"Either way, it was very kind."

They were waiting for the light to change on the corner of Fifty-ninth and Park.

"You have to go the moment it turns green," he said.

"If you expect to get past the median and all the way to the other side."

"I know," she said.

"I despise Park Avenue," he said.

"I *live* on Park Avenue," she said.

"Then you should make it narrower," he said, and then, "There it goes," and bolted off the sidewalk. She ran after him, past the median divider, onto the opposite curb.

"If you'll let me have the number," she said, "I won't bother you further."

She sounded very British. She guessed it was contagious.

"It's back at the office," he said.

"Couldn't someone . . . ?"

"I was ready to give it to you on Saturday, but you hung up on me."

Still sulking, she thought. The stupid ass.

"Well, isn't there anyone who . . . ?"

"Lucy would never find it." He saw her puzzled look. "My so-called secretary."

"I really would like to get started on this."

"Yes, I realize. But I *do* have this other business to attend to, you see."

"Maybe if you told *me* where it was . . ."

"Quite out of the question. Besides, I don't know *where* I put it, exactly. I'd have to look for it. You're fortunate I didn't just toss it in the wastebasket when you hung up on . . ."

"Look, are you going to carry that to the grave?"

"I beg your pardon."

"I mean, get *off* it, okay? I've apologized six times already, do you want me to slit my throat?"

"We're here," he said.

They were standing in front of the Plaza Hotel.

The ASPCA had taken away all the cats, but the place still stunk of their piss. Santorini opened all the windows the minute he got in the apartment, leaving the door open—CRIME SCENE sign still tacked to it—so's he could get a crosscurrent of air. But it was so fuckin' hot today you prolly couldn't even find a breeze at the beach, which is where he wished he was instead of sniffing around a dead lady's whatnots. He'd had to go up the One-Nine to get the fuckin' key to the padlock on the door, and a fat lot of good that done him. He'd been here for almost an hour now, going through every closet and drawer in the place, but so far he'd come up with nothing. Truth was, he didn't know what the fuck he was looking for.

If this really *was* some kind of spy shit here, where was the shortwave radio and the little book of codes? Where was the list of safe houses? Where were the dozen passports in different names? Where was the little vial of poison you had to swallow if you got captured by the enemy? So far, all he'd found were dresses and skirts and sweaters and socks and bras and panties and overcoats and shoes and checkbooks with the lady's name, Angela Cartwright, printed on them, and some letters from somebody with the same last name in Liverpool, England, probably a relative, Jesus, it stunk in here.

He decided to go through the lady's garbage.

Going through the garbage was something most cops hated doing, which is why he was guessing nobody from the One-Nine had yet gone through it. You could tell by just a casual glance at anybody's garbage whether or not it had been sifted. This garbage did not look as if it had been touched by human hands since the time it was placed here in the pail under the sink, whenever the fuck *that* had been. The lady was already dead since Thursday, and here it was Saturday already, who knew *how* long the oldest of the garbage had been sitting here? *Cop* hands, neither, for that matter. Just one look at this shit under the sink and Santorini knew it was pristine, so to speak. Between the stink of the garbage and the stink of the cat piss, he wished he had a gas mask.

He got down to work.

Top layer first, because usually the top layer was the closest in time to the victim's hour of departure from this earth, may she rest in peace, he thought. Peeling off all the shit layer by layer, studying it, placing it on the newspapers he'd spread on the kitchen floor, this was some terrific job here. If the pay wasn't so good—gimmee a break, willya?—he'da left the job in a minute, become a spy himself, go to bed all over the world with exotic girls trying to pry secrets from him. All over the world. Istanbul, wherever that was. Lots of spies came from Istanbul.

Going through the shit bit by bit, wanting to pinch his nose together, but his hands were all dirty already. Then going through it all over again, wondering how much money spies made, thinking if this limey lady here in this apartment was a spy, sword on her tit or not, he would *eat* all this garbage. Spies were supposed to be glamorous. The stuff in this lady's closet and drawers reminded him of what his Aunt Christina used to wear. And the leftovers in this lady's garbage pail were the kind somebody with no imagination at all would eat, weren't spies supposed to be inventive? Creative even?

Was plain yoghurt creative? Empty container of it, coffee grinds clinging to the inside of it, Jesus. Half a squeezed grapefruit, covered with mildew. A rancid stick of butter. Or margarine. Or whatever the hell it was. When was the last time anybody emptied this garbage pail? At least a dozen empty cans of cat food. Seafood Delight, and Beef and Cheese Mix, and Liver and Eggs, the cans stinking worse than all the other garbage and the cat piss combined. Crumpled restaurant menus, undoubtedly slid under her door and never making it past the kitchen. Unopened junk mail, did she used to take her mail into the kitchen and open it at the counter here? Empty bottle of cheap white wine. Was the lady a wino? Spies drank absinthe, didn't they? And smoked cigarettes in long black holders. Crumpled piece of pink paper torn from the phone pad on the counter, under the wall phone there. He smoothed out the sheet of paper.

A telephone number was written on it in pencil:

586 – 7000

And under that:

2312

Well, well, he thought.

The Baroque Room was gorgeous.

While Geoffrey talked to a tall gangly man from the Canadian Consulate, Elita wandered the room aimlessly, luxuriating in its grandeur. Geoffrey—who sometimes sounded as if he had a wad of marbles in his mouth—had introduced the man as Sully or Solly or Selly Colbert. She learned his full name only when he handed her his card: Selwyn Colbert, Jr. Selly sounded totally American. He was wearing a dark suit, shirt and tie.

The floor was covered wall-to-wall with a thick carpet that featured an oval floral design in its center, surrounded by a royal blue field studded with a smaller flower pattern. The carpet's border was ivory highlighted with blue and scattered with the same floral motif. At the far side of the room, windows hung with darker blue drapes admitted sunshine and showed glimpses of summer green in the park across the street. Ceiling chandeliers echoed themselves in wall mirrors, casting a glow as golden as the sun's. A huge painting of

177

a landscape hung on the wall right-angled to the windows. Even now—when uncovered tables showed only bare wood in sharp contrast to the chairs around them, upholstered and tufted in white—the room had an ambiance of serenity and dignity. She visualized herself in a long shimmering gown, dancing to the music of an orchestra with a violin section.

They were going over some sort of seating plan.

She overheard Selly saying he could see no problem about seating *him*—whoever that might be—to the left of Mrs. Thatcher; they were good friends. Besides, protocol definitely dictated that Mr. De Gortari should have the seat to the right of Mrs. Mulroney, and he was certain the U.S. people would have no objection to that. So, for all intents and purposes—and Geoffrey could report this to *his* people—Mrs. Thatcher would be seated exactly as had been originally planned, to the left of Mr. Mulroney, with her pal sitting right beside her— with his hand on her knee under the table, no doubt. Selly smiled to indicate he was making a little joke. Geoffrey did not return the smile. Selly sighed, rolled up the seating plan he'd been showing to Geoffrey, and then shook hands with him. Passing Elita on his way out, he told her how nice it was to have met her, and then loped out of the room.

Geoffrey took an inordinately long time studying the landscape painting on the wall, seemingly lost in thought. At last, he walked to where Elita was impatiently waiting for him.

"Care for some lunch?" he asked.

"I was hoping we could go back to your office for the . . ."

"The price one must pay," he said, and grinned like a shark.

When the telephone rang at a quarter past one that Monday afternoon, the Balinese girl picked up the receiver and said, "SeaCoast Limited, good afternoon."

"Good afternoon," a man's voice said, "this is Michael Rubin at Epsilon Chemical Supplies?"

"Yes, sir?"

"In Meriden, Connecticut?"

She had been prepped for a possible call.

"Yes, Mr. Rubin," she said, "how may I help you?"

"May I speak to Mr. Pierce, please? Hamilton Pierce."

"Out of the office just now," she said. "May I be of assistance, sir?"

"I wanted someone in your Order Department," Rubin said.

"This is the Order Department," she said.

"Well . . . last Friday afternoon, a Mr. Pierce placed an order for five hundred milliliters of isopropylamine . . . with one of our salespersons, Mrs. Carpenter."

"Yes, sir?"

"Can you tell me what sort of firm SeaCoast is?"

"We do research, sir."

"What sort of research?"

"I'm not really certain, sir, this is the Order Department."

"Does Mr. Pierce work in the Order Department?"

"Yes, sir, he's *head* of the department. Was there someone else you'd like to speak to?"

"Do you have a Safety Director?"

"No, sir, we're just a small firm. But perhaps you'd like to speak to Mr. Hackett, sir. He's our executive vice president in charge of research and development."

"Yes, put him on, please."

"Just one moment, sir."

She put him on hold, buzzed Arthur's inner office, and said, "It's Epsilon Chemicals on five. A Mr. Rubin. Wants to know what sort of research we do."

"I'll take it," Arthur said, and pressed the five button on the base of his phone. "Martin Hackett here," he said. "How may I help you?"

"Mr. Hackett, good afternoon, this is Michael Rubin. We had an order last Friday from your Mr. Pierce . . ."

"Yes, sir, Hamilton Pierce."

"Yes. For five hundred milliliters of isopropylamine. As you know, this is a highly flammable substance . . ."

"Oh yes."

"And it's our policy to . . ."

"Of course."

". . . check with the ordering entity to learn how the substance will be used."

"SeaCoast is at present conducting experiments in toxicity."

Exactly what Sonny had advised him to say.

"Of isopropylamine?" Rubin asked, sounding surprised.

"Of a great *many* reagents," Arthur said. "Isopropy-lamine is only one of them."

"What are some of the others?"

"Aliphatic and aromatic amines, for the most part . . ."

Listing the classes of compounds Sonny had supplied.

". . . and also some pyridines," Arthur said. "That is, a wide variety of tests on nitrogen-containing organic compounds."

"I see," Rubin said. "Well, thank you, sir, I appreciate your time. I notice there's a one-day FedEx request on this . . ."

"You mean it hasn't gone out yet?" Arthur said.

"Well, normally, sir . . ."

"When *will* it go out?"

"You'll have it tomorrow morning before eleven."

"I hope so," Arthur said, and hung up.

He was flirting, and she was fidgeting.

They were lunching in the Palm Court, downstairs in the Plaza's lobby. Violinists were playing. Geoffrey was telling her how exciting he found his work in the foreign service. Every time he said the word *foreign,* she realized that to him America was a foreign country. He told her that only recently he'd been visited by a homicide detective looking into the murders of two supposed British subjects, and that . . .

"That *is* exciting," she said.

She was thinking, Let's finish this goddamn lunch and go get Sonny's phone number.

". . . both of them were tattooed," Geoffrey said, and rolled his eyes.

"My," Elita said.

"Under their breasts," Geoffrey said, and wondered if he was being too bold, raising the subject of tattooed breasts over turkey and tomato sandwiches on toast. With iced tea. He decided to abandon this possibly offensive conversational line and switched the topic instead to the impending visit of Mrs. Thatcher, which was another exciting aspect of work in the foreign service.

"That's why I came here today, in fact," he explained. "To check on the seating arrangements. There's a certain protocol that must be followed to the letter with heads of state."

"I'm sure," she said.

"To the letter," he repeated.

She was wondering if whoever answered the phone in Los Angeles would know where Sonny might be in New York.

The violinists played on interminably. She hoped they would not come to their table; there was nothing she found more embarrassing. Geoffrey was explaining how important his role had been in making certain the prime minister was properly seated. It all had something to do with Canada Day, a gala dinner and ball, prime ministers and presidents among the invited guests . . .

"Would you care to join me?" he asked.

"Sorry?" she said.

"That night. Would you care to come with me?"

"Well, I . . ."

182

"I'd be honored," he said.

She looked at him. He was, in his stuffy British way, quite handsome. Very dark eyes, which he lowered now under her scrutiny. High cheekbones and good jaw, a faint cleft in it. Thick black hair combed casually to give him an exceptionally youthful appearance. She wondered suddenly how old he was. At their first meeting, he had asked her how old she was, and she had tried to make herself seem twenty. Her guess was that he couldn't be much older than that himself—twenty-two or -three, perhaps. A mere boy in comparison to Sonny.

He raised his eyes again, looked at her hopefully, almost entreatingly.

"I don't think so," she said.

If the dais was set where the cooperative Miss Lubenthal indicated it was normally set, and if Thatcher and Bush were sitting side by side at the table, as Sonny expected they would be, then he could eliminate both targets in the wink of an eye. His escape route was clear. Directly up the stairs to the left of the room, then around and down again to the Central Park South lobby. Out the door into the street and then down into the subway. New York's subway system was a safe house in itself.

But if the President *didn't* show . . .

Well, his orders were clear.

There's a possibility you can kill two birds with one stone, so to speak, but only if your primary target is present at the dinner and ball. Otherwise, you'll have to wait till the Fourth of July.

On his visit to Liberty Island last Saturday, he had learned that it would be closed on the Fourth until noon, at which time regular ferry service would resume. This meant that the President would be making his speech sometime that morning. The exact time had not yet been announced in the newspapers, but he knew that it would be. His tentative plan was to lay in the night before. He knew he could carry a gun onto the ferry and onto the island—no one had searched anyone yesterday, and he doubted that anyone would bother him on the third of July. The last boat left the island at six-thirty. He would not be on it.

But security on the Fourth would doubtless be exceptionally tight: the Secret Service for sure, with park rangers as backups, and possibly cops from the First Precinct as well. He had seen only one ranger wearing a gun last Saturday: a good-looking woman with a .357 Magnum on her hip. The others were carrying walkie-talkies in their holsters. He was positive they would *all* be armed on the Fourth. So whereas he'd be carrying a gun that day, he would not use it except in self-defense. As Arthur had pointed out, guns were not infallible, and this was a No-Fail operation.

Bush would undoubtedly be arriving by helicopter. Good photo op, the chopper with the presidential seal on its side, coming out of the sun to land on the wide brick circle with the American flag flapping on a tall flagpole at its center. Walk him to the statue itself, cameras following, the President tossing quips and waving his hand—Hello, folks, here's the once and future President of the United States. Into the base of the monument, up the same stairs they'd taken on Saturday and out onto the star-shaped Fort Hood level. Sonny felt almost positive that this was where the speech would be delivered. More room here for maneuvering cameras, more opportunities for utilizing Liberty herself. The levels above were narrower, more restrictive to creative camera work.

The way Sonny looked at it, this entire appearance was one giant political photo op and the President's men would be bending over backward to give the networks whatever assistance they needed. The Fort Hood level was the spot Sonny would have chosen if he were running CBS or ABC. The President standing against the high whitish stone wall behind him, the lady herself soaring above him into the sky. Place one of your cameras at the point of the star for your full shots of the statue, another midway toward the podium for your medium shots of the President with flags flying all around him no doubt, yet another camera for those sincere close shots. Yes, that's where it would take place. Sonny would be ready for any other contingency, but he knew in his deepest heart that the President would die where Fort Hood once had stood.

He did not think there would be security on the level directly above the President, if only because the television pictures would then show men in blue suits lined up like vigilant tin soldiers, a bad image to project. Position your men instead at the stairs leading to the level above, out of view of the cameras. Keep your security on the Fort Hood level out of camera range as well, creating the impression of a fearless leader of the people, standing bold and unafraid before the worldwide symbol of freedom.

So unless he got to him first at the Canada Day celebration, what he planned to do . . .

The telephone rang.

Sonny picked up.

"Hello?" he said.

"Mr. Gomez?" Santorini asked.

He was standing in the lobby downstairs, using one of the house phones. His earlier call from the precinct had informed him that the guest in room 2312 was registered as Mr. Albert Gomez. Now he was here to find out just who Albert Gomez was, and why the number of his hotel room was scribbled on a scrap of paper in a dead lady's garbage.

There was a silence on the line.

"Mr. Gomez?" he said again.

"Yes?" a voice said at last.

"This is Detective Allan Santorini, Homicide North?"

"Yes?"

"I wonder if I could have a few minutes of your time."

"Well . . . sure," Sonny said. "Homicide, did you say?"

"Homicide North, yeah."

"I don't understand."

186

"We're investigating a case, I'd like to ask you some questions."

"A murder case?"

"Well, yeah, that's what we do. Investigate murder cases."

"What's a . . . *murder* case got to do with me?"

"Well, nothing, actually," Santorini said. "There're just some routine questions I'd like to ask you."

Routine questions, Sonny thought.

"Whose murder are you investigating?" he asked.

"I'll tell you when I see you," Santorini said. "If you'd like to meet me in the lobby bar, I promise I won't take more than ten minutes of your time."

There was a long pause on the line.

"Mr. Gomez?" he said.

"Why don't you just come up here?" Sonny suggested.

9

There was no answer at the number Geoffrey had given her for Sonny's apartment. She let the phone ring twenty times, and then dialed the number again in case she'd made a mistake the first time, and let it ring another twenty times before hanging up. The second number he'd given her was for the hospital where Sonny worked. She dialed that next, slowly and carefully. It was a quarter to two in New York, ten forty-five in Los Angeles.

She told the woman who answered the phone that she wanted to talk to someone in Personnel, please. The nurse, or whoever the twit was, asked Elita what this was in reference to—she *hated* when underlings in doctors' offices or hospitals did that. She said, "It's a private matter, thank you." Like a vaginal *itch,* she thought, as if it's any of your goddamn business.

"Personnel," a woman's voice said.

"Yes, this is Elita Randall," she said. "I'm calling from New York City."

"Yes?"

"I'm trying to get an address here for Dr. Krishnan Hemkar, I wonder . . ."

"I'm sorry, we don't give out personal information on staff."

"This is regarding his mother," Elita said. "She's very ill."

Which was sort of what Sonny had told her on the train.

"It's important that I get in touch with him," she said.

"I'm sorry, Miss, but . . ."

"Before she dies," Elita said.

There was a long sigh on the line.

"How do you spell the last name, please?" the woman asked.

"Hemkar. H-E-M-K-A-R."

"Just a moment, I'll connect you with the page operator."

"No, I don't want to *page* him," Elita said. "He isn't in Los . . ."

The line went dead.

She's cut me off! Elita thought. The stupid . . .

"Page Operator," another female voice said.

"Yes, this is Elita Randall," Elita said, "I'm calling from New York City."

"Yes, Miss, whom did you wish paged?"

"I'm trying to get some information on Dr. Hemkar," she said. "I don't want him paged, he isn't . . ."

The line went dead.

Elita visualized a page going out all over the hospital,

speakers blaring, "Dr. Hemkar, please call the operator, Dr. Hemkar, please pick up," or whatever the hell it was they announced in hospitals.

"Hello?" a voice said.

A male this time. Somewhat preppy sounding.

"Hello," she said, "this is Elita Randall, I'm calling from New York. I'm trying to locate Dr. Krishnan Hemkar, but the page oper . . ."

"You and everybody else," the man said.

"What?" she said.

"Who'd you say this was?" he asked.

"Elita Randall. Who's this?"

"Dr. Welles," he said. "Benjamin J. Welles. Did you say New York?"

"Yes, I'm calling from New York. I've lost track of Sonny . . ."

"Is he in New York?"

"Yes. Well, yes."

"You don't know how happy this makes me. We've been worried stiff out here."

"What do you mean?"

"Well, he disappears from sight without a word, we thought he'd been kidnapped or something. That's why I answered the page. I thought it might be someone who . . ."

"Well, no. Actually I'm trying to locate him, too. Would you know his mother's phone number here in New York?"

"I thought she lived in Paris."

"No, he came here to see her. New York. She's here in New York."

"That's funny, his father works in Paris, I'm pretty sure that's where they live."

"No, she was sick, and he . . ."

"Are you sure we're talking about the same person?"

"Well, Sonny Hemkar," she said, "how many Sonny Hemkars can there be? I mean, that isn't exactly a common . . ."

"From Los Angeles, right?"

"That's where he . . . excuse me, but how well do you know him?"

"We're very close friends."

"And he . . . never mentioned he was going to see his mother in New York?"

"Never mentioned he was going to New York at *all*. I've got to tell you, his job is at risk out here. If you see him, tell him BJ said he'd better . . ."

"When did *you* see him last?"

"I had brunch with him a week ago Sunday. Called him a little after eleven that night, got no answer."

Because he was already on the train by then, Elita thought.

"And you don't know where he is now?" she asked.

"No, I don't. I wish I did."

So do I, she thought.

"If you see him, tell him he'd better have a damn good story for Hokie."

"Who?"

"Dr. Hokinson. He'll know."

"I'll tell him."

If I find him, she thought, and hung up.

He lowered the windows on the rental car the moment he realized he was getting close to the ocean. Salt air wafted in over the marsh grass. He took a deep breath and turned the car onto a narrow, packed sand road that was undoubtedly impassable in any kind of heavy rain. Today, though, the sky was a magnificent robin's egg blue, wisps of clouds brushed across it by a mild and languid breeze. He heard now the hollow rasping sound of surf rolling in against the shore. And smiled.

The house loomed suddenly ahead.

He looked at his watch.

Three twenty-seven.

It had taken him an hour and forty minutes to drive here from the city.

He parked the car, got out, stretched, and looked up at the house. The smile was still on his face. There was nothing quite like this in Southern California, where he had spent the past six years of his life. The beach houses out there—even those that were unabashed reproductions of Cape Cod cottages—had none of the authentic look that this one so effortlessly achieved. Here, the outside walls were covered with sun-bleached shingles the color of seagulls. The roof was shingled with cedar shakes streaked brown and black, eroded by time and weather, twisted and gnarled. Sand-drifted pieces of flagstone led to a front door painted a blue faded paler than the sky.

Everywhere around the house, tufted sea oats and plumed pampas grass leaned in the mild ocean breeze, gently rustling. Something spidery and green sent long tendrils across the sand, trailing off in every direction. Sonny climbed a dozen or more rickety wooden steps to the top of the high dune and looked out over a beach more magnificent than any he'd seen in California. The Atlantic Ocean stretched endlessly before him, the roiling water a bluish-grey reflecting sunlight in tiny sparkling glints, waves rushing in against the sand, tumbling and receding again, whispering. He took a deep breath, all at peace with himself and the world. This was exactly what he wanted.

All he'd said to Arthur was, "I need that safe house."

Walking back to the car, he unlocked the trunk and took from it the single large bag he had carried from Los Angeles. Fishing in his pocket for the key Arthur had messengered to the hotel, he walked up the sand-strewn flagstone path to the pale blue door at the front of the house. There was an absolutely appropriate tarnished brass knocker and doorknob. He inserted the key into the keyway, twisted it, and gently shoved the door inward.

Sunlight splashed through the French doors at the far end of the room, beyond which he could see a spacious deck overlooking the beach and the ocean. There was an immediate aroma that brought back to him memories of every summer seaside house he'd ever known, a combination of mustiness and damp, mildew and salt air. The room itself was furnished casually, almost sloppily, with slip-covered sofas and easy chairs that looked as if they'd come from a thrift shop on La Cienega. A rolltop desk stood against one of the unpainted cedar walls. There was a standing floor lamp with its shade hanging crooked, and a footstool with an upholstered needlepoint top. Rows and rows of books on rickety plank shelves hung on the cedar wall opposite the desk, where a partially opened door revealed a simple kitchen with more windows facing the sea. It was altogether charming, exactly what a beach house—not to mention a *safe* house—should be.

He carried his suitcase up a steep, narrow staircase to the floor above, where a door at the top of the landing opened onto one of the bedrooms, again facing the sea and streaming late afternoon sunlight. A canopied bed with a paisley-patterned quilt on it was just to the left of the entrance door. The sliding glass door opposite the entrance door opened onto a deck narrower than the one below. He slid open the door and went to stand outside.

The sea moved restlessly below.

There was a house close by on the left, architecturally similar to this one, but with a weathered wooden fence on all sides save the one facing the ocean. Some fifty yards to the right, there was yet another house, storied and gabled with a wide deck running along its ocean-front side. On the northern side of the house, the side facing Sonny, there was a hidden second-story deck some twelve feet square, catching only scant sunlight now, a wooden fence guaranteeing complete privacy—except for a narrow sunwashed section of deck against the wall of the house, visible from where Sonny stood.

A woman was lying in that narrow space now.

Lying on her back in the space near the wall, soaking up the last slanting rays of the sun on the one section of deck vulnerable to observation from above.

The woman was naked.

Long blond hair fanning onto the striped inflated mat beneath her. Echoing blond hair tufting brazenly at the joining of her legs. Black sunglasses covering her eyes. Firm breasts flattening gently in repose, lolling toward her arms where they rested one off, one on the mat, the palms of her hands turned upward as if in supplication. Brown sandals rested on the deck beside the striped mat. An open book with a red jacket was lying face downward alongside her; Sonny could not read the title from this distance.

Unaware of his presence, she lay all golden in the sunshine. Time seemed to stop. He was vaguely aware of the ocean nudging the shore, the sound of a record player up the beach, music floating, muted laughter drifting. Silently, he stood watching her.

And suddenly she sat up, and rose, almost in one motion, stretching her arms over her head, shaking out her hair, bending like a dancer to retrieve her sandals and her book, closing the book, the sandals dangling from one hand, totally oblivious of him until . . . she must have sensed something. An unseen observer. A presence. She glanced upward all at once, and saw him where he stood transfixed on the upper deck.

She stood tall and motionless, the book in one hand, the sandals in the other, her head tilted toward the deck above, black sunglasses reflecting sunlight and sky and shielding her eyes from him. She stood that way for several breathless moments, looking up at him in seeming defiance, still and silent in the sunshine. And then, in brief dismissal, she turned her back to him, tight tanned buttocks swiveling as she walked to a sliding glass door at the side of the house, and opened it, and entered the house without a backward glance.

The truck from Advance Laundry Service was covered with scrawled graffiti. The company was located in the South Bronx and the trucks were parked overnight in an area enclosed by a cyclone fence, hardly a deterrent to determined graffiti writers. The white side and rear panels of the truck were simply too tempting to ignore. So it rode through town looking like an inner-city wall, hardly an image to project, especially when Advance listed among its customers some of the better hotels in New York.

At four o'clock that afternoon, Sammy Leone backed the truck into the Hilton's loading dock on West Fifty-third Street, climbed down from behind the wheel, walked directly to the steps leading up to the platform, and rang the bell set in the metal jamb that framed the service doors. A uniformed security guard opened one of the doors, recognized Sammy, said, "Hot enough for you?" and beckoned him in.

It was cooler inside, but not much. The service doors were in constant use, and each time one of them was opened, a blast of hot air rushed in to dilute the effects of the air-conditioning. Most of the hotel's soiled linens had already been separated into rolling canvas bins provided by Advance, separately brimming with towels and washcloths, sheets and pillow cases, tablecloths and napkins. The laundry from the Hilton alone would fill the entire back of Sammy's truck; it was straight back to the Bronx when he finished here. He wheeled the first of the bins out onto the loading platform, opened the truck doors, and rolled the bin deep into the truck. This is pneumonia weather, he was thinking. You go from air-conditioning to heat and then back to air-conditioning again. He was starting to wheel the second of the bins out to the truck when he noticed a Hilton laundry cart sitting near the elevator doors.

"What's that?" he asked the security guard.

"Just came down," the guard said.

"Anybody separated it yet?"

"Don't look that way."

"Shit," Leone said, and tried to remember what he'd just wheeled outside. Towels? Sheets? "This stuff's supposed to be separated before I get here," he said.

"They usually do that over by the chutes," the security guard said, and gestured vaguely toward some inner recess of the service level.

Leone wheeled the cart over to where the company

bins were standing. Wearily, he began separating the laundry, sheets here, towels there, muttering about people not doing the goddamn jobs they were *supposed* to do, napkins in this one, washcloths over there, sheets here, reaching blindly into the cart behind him, identifying whatever he pulled out, and tossing it into its appropriate bin. He reached into the cart again, touched something sticky, and yanked his hand back.

It was covered with blood.

He looked into the cart.

A man was lying on top of the remaining laundry.

An icepick was sticking out of his left eye.

From the bedroom window of the beach house she'd received in settlement from The Late Colonel, Carolyn Fremont looked down at the rear of the house next door. The man she'd seen on the deck not an hour ago was out back there, examining the potting table under the deck. Late afternoon sunlight struck his dark hair, glanced off the high cheekbones and smooth planes of his face. How on earth could any of Martin Hackett's friends be quite so attractive?

Hackett himself was a crashing uneducated bore, a man who'd made his fortune selling live Maine lobsters to restaurants and fish markets. Whenever he discussed lobsters, and he did so with the fervor of a true believer, he reminded you that the lobsters were *live,* as if anyone would want to buy a *dead* Maine lobster. The people he invited as house guests were either restaurateurs or somehow connected otherwise to fish and other types of seafood. A total lot of bores.

The dark stranger turned away from the potting table, his brow furrowed. Was he going to pot some growing things? Did he have a green thumb, the little darling? She was suddenly glad her daughter hadn't joined her here in Westhampton. Being alone here would be a definite advantage should Martin's guest decide to stay awhile. Crony of the Lobster King, here are the keys, pal, enjoy yourself. But where was Martin when a person needed him? Carolyn, I'd like you to meet a friend of mine, he's . . .

Yes, what? Another restaurant owner, another big fisherman?

He'll be here for . . .

How long? A week, ten days, the entire summer, oh God, wouldn't *that* be wonderful!

His name is . . .

What? Who?

The way he'd stared at her. Eyes devouring her. She'd stared right back at him, daring him. You want to look at me? Fine, go right ahead. How do you like it? Want some of it? Fat chance. Eat your heart out.

She looked at the clock.

Almost four-thirty.

The cocktail party at the Cabots was supposed to begin at six. Nobody in the Hamptons was ever on time, especially to a cocktail party, but she hadn't even showered yet.

She took one last look at him . . .

He was heading back into the house now . . .

. . . and wondered what his favorite color was.

Ozzie Carruthers was supposed to be relieved at five o'clock, and he did not particularly welcome a visit from the Secret Service at fifteen minutes before quitting time. The two men resembled lean bookends. Both of them wearing blue suits that looked entirely too heavy for this weather. White shirts. Dark ties. As somber a pair as he'd ever met. One of them introduced himself as Agent Dobbs, the other as Agent Dawson. The men shook hands all around, and then Carruthers asked how he could help them. He could not resist looking up at the wall clock, a covert glance that was not wasted on Dobbs, who had been trained to detect the slightest suspicious movement in a crowd.

"Miss Lubenthal in the Catering Department told us you'd be in charge of hotel security on the night of the party," Dobbs said.

"The Canada Day affair," Dawson said.

"That's right," Carruthers said.

He was a former Marine who kept himself in shape with thrice-weekly visits to Nautilus, where he worked out on the machines and with free weights as well. Carruthers gauged a man's worth by his muscles, and these guys looked entirely too flimsy for the job; these guys could press twenty pounds between them, he'd be surprised.

"The Canadian Consulate has provided us with a

seating arrangement," Dobbs said, reaching into the inside pocket of his jacket. "What we'd like to . . ."

"They sent me one, too," Carruthers said, and unrolled a larger plan than the reduced Xerox copy Dobbs took from his pocket.

"What we'd like to do," Dobbs said, unintimidated, "is check the room the function'll be in, see where we can put our people for the best possible security."

"Happy to show it to you," Carruthers said.

He was thinking this was a case of overload, pure and simple. Security for the Canadian Prime Minister, security for the Mexican President and the former British P.M., and now Secret Service protection for . . .

"Our regular people here in New York'll be carrying the brunt of it," Dobbs said, as if reading his mind. "We're just a team of six, lend them a hand."

"Big affair like this one," Dawson said, "lots of people, lots of opportunity for mischief."

"Well, we don't get too much mischief here at the Plaza," Carruthers said, sounding miffed.

"'Specially when there'll be such big guns here," Dawson said, totally oblivious.

"Come on, I'll show you the room," Carruthers said.

She was writing him a long letter when the telephone rang. She was telling him that if he didn't appreciate her as a person, if he thought all he could do was walk out whenever he felt like it, disappear into thin air like a ghost or something, then she wanted nothing further to do with him. Her concentration was intense; when the phone rang, she almost jumped out of her skin. She went from her desk to the bedside table, and picked up the receiver. On the wall alongside her desk, there was a poster of Boy George, a holdover from her teeny-bopper days. Sonny made her feel like a damn teeny-bopper all over again.

"Hello?" she said.

"I know it's been a long time since we've seen each other . . ."

Geoffrey Turner.

". . . and I must apologize for not having called sooner . . ."

Little touch of humor there; she'd left him at the consulate not four hours ago.

". . . but what are you doing tonight?" he asked.

"Why?"

"I'd like to see you," he said.

"You just saw me," she said.

"I know."

A long silence.

"Elita . . ."

The first time he'd said her name.

It sounded very British on his tongue.

Elita.

"*May* I see you tonight?"

But suppose Sonny calls? she thought.

"Elita?"

"What time?" she asked.

* * *

The first thing Dobbs noticed were the steps in the alcove off the far corner of the room.

"Where do they go?" he asked.

"Upstairs," Carruthers said.

"What's up there?"

"Business offices."

"Any access to other parts of the hotel?"

"Sure."

"What kind?"

"An elevator. And fire stairs down the hall."

"Let's take a look," Dobbs said.

Sonny had spread the various ID cards on the dining room table, where they could catch the late afternoon sun streaming through the windows. *Live at Five* had just come on. A black woman named Sue Simmons seemed to be running the show, never mind the blond guy with her. Telling all about the detective who'd been found in a laundry basket at the Hilton Hotel this afternoon. Sonny kept studying the fake ID cards.

The one for the Plaza was particularly good. So were the two Detective Division cards. He'd never seen an FBI card, but the seal looked legit and McDermott undoubtedly had copied it from a real one.

A young woman named Perri Peltz was now doing a remote outside the loading platform at the Hilton. She was here with Lieutenant Hogan, she was saying, of Homicide North. Hogan was a short man with a face reddened by the heat. His shirt collar looked too tight. He was wearing a hat, Sonny couldn't believe it. He was telling Perri Peltz that Allan Santorini had been with Homicide North for twelve years. Good detective, good man.

"Any idea what he was doing here at the Hilton?" Perri Peltz asked.

"None at all."

"Was he conducting an investigation that might have brought him here?"

"I have no idea. The manager tells me Santorini spoke to him earlier today, but . . ."

Uh-oh, Sonny thought.

"What about?"

"He wanted to know who was in room 2312."

"Have you learned anything about that?"

"The room was registered to a man named Albert Gomez."

Goodbye, Albert, Sonny thought.

"Hispanic?" Perri Peltz asked.

"Possibly. The bellhop who carried his bag up described a man some five feet ten inches tall . . ."

Eleven, Sonny thought.

". . . weighing about a hundred and seventy pounds . . ."

Sixty-five.

". . . with light eyes and dark hair."

"Was Detective Santorini armed?" Perri Peltz asked.

"He was."

"But as I understand it, when his body was found, the gun was still holstered, isn't that right?"

"Yes, it was," Hogan said, and shook his head.

"Santorini was an experienced detective. How anyone could have taken him so completely by surprise . . ." He shook his head again.

Sonny grinned.

He had stabbed him in the eye the moment he'd entered the room.

"Is it your opinion that the murder took place where the body was found?" Perri Peltz asked.

"I would rather not comment on that," Hogan said.

"Thank you, sir," Perri Peltz said, and turned away from him to look directly into the camera. "This is Perri Peltz, News Four, New York," she said, "reporting from outside the Hilton Hotel on Fifty-third Street and Sixth Avenue. Back to you, Chuck."

Chuck was the blond guy—Chuck Scarborough, a good code name for a Scimitar agent. He began talking about New York City's deficit. Sonny watched Sue Simmons trying to look solemn about it all, but managing only to look cute as hell. He reached over to snap off the set, gathered up the cards, and returned them to the leather Mark Cross portfolio. He was carrying it toward the steps leading upstairs to the bedroom when a knock sounded at the front door.

"Who is it?" he called.

"Carolyn," a woman answered.

"Just a moment, please," Sonny said. He dropped the portfolio on the lowermost step, where he'd remember it later, went to the door, unlocked it, and opened it wide.

The woman he'd seen naked on the deck earlier today was standing there.

Wearing a white dress.

High-heeled ankle-strapped white sandals.

Blond and tanned and blue-eyed.

"Hi," she said, sounding surprised. "Is Martin home?"

"I'm sorry, no, he isn't," Sonny said.

She was trying to peer into the house, past his shoulder. Blue eyes looking faintly suspicious. Was it possible she didn't recognize him as the same man who'd . . . ?

"I'm Scott Hamilton," he said. "Martin's house guest."

"Carolyn Fremont," she said.

"How do you do?" he said, and extended his hand. She took it. Their eyes met. Locked.

"I live right next door," she said. "I was on my way to a party . . ."

He was still holding her hand. Eyes sweeping her body. Lingering on the swell of her breasts in the low-cut white dress.

". . . at the Cabots', and I thought Martin might have been invited, too. He knows them . . ."

Still holding her hand.

"I thought we could walk over . . ."

His hand warm around hers.

". . . together."

Her sentence trailed.

She shrugged like a little girl.

Retrieved her hand.

Shrugged again.

"Well," she said.

"Won't I do?" he said.

They had come back down to the Baroque Room again.

"We'll want to put one of our men at the bottom of those steps and another one at the top," Dobbs told Carruthers.

"Block access in and out of the room that way," Dawson said.

Carruthers was thinking they'd only be doing what ten thousand security people had done before them.

"You might want to think about putting somebody at that door coming from the pantry, too," he suggested.

This had also been done ten thousand times before.

"Good idea," Dawson said.

"Way I've got it," Carruthers said, "cocktails'll be served at seven, dinner at eight, dancing afterwards. What time do you expect . . . ?"

"Around six-thirty," Dobbs said. "Check out the room and anything leading into it."

"I was asking about *him*. What time do you think *he'll* be getting here?"

"Our New York people'll have that information. I'll let you know sometime tomorrow."

"I want to make sure he gets a nice welcome," Carruthers said, and smiled. "Lots of people are mighty fond of that man."

"I'll bet," Dobbs said.

* * *

Sunset was expected at seven thirty-three.

In the Hamptons, a cocktail party invitation for six
P.M. was usually honored at seven. People drifted in and
out in a variety of costumes. Those who planned to go
home after the drinks and finger food generally arrived
in casual beachwear ranging from jeans to shorts to—on
one memorable occasion in Easthampton—a woman
wearing only high heels, a bikini bottom, and a gold
chainlink top she'd purchased in the city of Rome.
Those who planned to go on to dinner at one of the
local eateries came dressed in what some of the host-
esses called Casual Elegant. For the men, this usually
meant blue blazer, pale slacks, and white shirt open at
the throat, with or without a colorful ascot. Some
women actually managed to look both casual and elegant. Others, loaded for bear the way Carolyn was tonight, arrived in more blatantly seductive outfits; the
white dress was recklessly low-cut, tight across the behind, and high on the leg. Sonny was wearing white
slacks and a purple crew-necked Ralph Lauren shirt.

On the deck of the Cabot house tonight—while the
assembled guests, some fifty in all, waited to "ooh" and
"ahh" yet another magnificent sunset, ho-hum—the talk
was mostly about the murder that had taken place at the
Hilton Hotel.

A woman who introduced herself as Dr. Sylvia Hirsch
—who Sonny later learned from Carolyn was a noted
psychiatrist—was holding forth on the theory that the
murder had been homosexually motivated, an icepick

being the weapon of choice in such murders, although she was surprised the victim's hands hadn't been tied behind his back with a wire hanger.

"Mr. Gomez?" he'd said.

"Yes, come in, won't you, please?" Sonny said.

The icepick behind his back. From the refrigerator bar. The door to the room closing. The detective turning toward him.

"It's very nice of you to . . ."

The icepick thrusting.

"Because an icepick is a phallic weapon," Dr. Hirsch said.

"I thought a knife was supposed to be phallic," someone said.

"Also," Dr. Hirsch said, with a curt nod. She had a faint German accent. The word came out "Ahlzo."

A man whom Carolyn introduced as Buddy Johnson of CBS News told Dr. Hirsch—and the several other people who were now gathered to hear the inside story —that his people had come up with some particularly grisly footage that the police wouldn't allow them to show because . . .

There *had* been a lot of blood, Sonny recalled.

. . . only the killer would know all the details of the crime.

Wrapping him in the quilted bedspread, checking the hallway to make sure it was empty, hearing the chambermaids chattering in Spanish down at the far end. Dragging the body down the hall and dumping it into a wheeled laundry cart standing alongside a service elevator. Scoop-

ing up a handful of dirty towels and sheets lying on the
service alcove floor, tossing them in over the body. Making
sure the body would not be linked to room 2312. And
buying time as well. The longer it took them to discover the
corpse, the further away he'd be.

"How about those *other* two?" a woman said. She was
wearing purple slacks and a white silk blouse unbuttoned very low on her tanned chest.

"Got to be some kind of satanic cult," the man with
her said. He was wearing a boldly striped Tommy
Hilfiger sports shirt.

"The newspapers didn't say what *kind* of tattoos,
though, did you notice?" someone else said.

Sonny was instantly alert.

"Or *where* on the body they were located."

"Probably you-*know*-where," a woman said, and gig-
gled.

"Tell us where, Sally," a man suggested.

"Two women with tattoos, I think that's odd," another
woman said. "You don't find too many women with tattoos these days."

"Oh, there must be *thousands* of them, Jean."

"Two women with tattoos? Both of them shot with the
same gun?"

"Very odd."

"Very *very* odd."

"I think this new one is even odder. A man in a laundry bin? Jesus!"

"Wasn't a musician killed on the roof of the Hilton a
little while back?" a woman asked.

"That was Carnegie Hall," the man with her said. "The roof of Carnegie Hall. She was some kind of musician."

"Lincoln Center," someone said.

"A cellist," someone said.

"I thought a flautist," someone said.

"Watch your language," someone said, and everyone laughed.

"Will you be covering the President's speech on the Fourth?" Sonny asked the man from CBS.

Geoffrey was telling her that once, when he was thirteen years old, he pretended he'd had a fist fight—and faked a resultant black eye—just to impress a girl with hair as blond as Elita's.

They were sipping their cocktails and munching on the complimentary *bruschetta* their waiter had brought to the table. The place was an Italian restaurant on Fifty-third and Third. Geoffrey had earlier told her that he often came here for lunch, but that it sometimes got hectic at dinnertime.

"Unless you enjoy looking at Woody Allen," he'd said.

Woody Allen wasn't here tonight. Nor was the place particularly crowded at a little past seven o'clock.

"Although hers was curly," he said.

"Mine used to be curly," Elita said. "It got absolutely straight when I turned twelve."

"A miracle," he said.

211

"No, I think it had something to do with . . . well, never mind. But how can anyone fake a black eye?"

"With water-soluble pencils," he said.

"With what?"

"They're these colored pencils you can draw with dry, or else dip them in water and use them like water colors."

"I still don't . . ."

"I used them wet. Under my left eye. To draw a bruise. I must tell you it was an absolutely perfect shiner, all blues and greens and yellows, magnificent, a bruise of monstrous proportions. Judith never once doubted its authenticity. That was her name. Judith. I was madly in love with her. Well, with her hair, actually."

"But why'd you pretend you'd had a fist fight?"

"To show her how much I *adored* her. I told her a great bully of a boy had said something derogatory about her honor, and I'd punched him halfway round the crescent before he landed a solid blow to my eye. I allowed the bruise to fade a bit each day, using the wet pencils, changing the color. It was quite the most brilliant bit of art I'd ever done."

"Do you still draw?"

"Not under my eye anymore. And only every now and again."

"Are you good at it?"

"Not very."

"I can't draw a straight line."

"I do it because I find it relaxing."

"No one's ever faked a black eye for me," she said.

"I'll paint one on the next time I see you," he said. "I still have the pencils."

She imagined him at thirteen, probably long and lanky, with the same eyelashes he had now, lashes a girl would kill for, standing before a mirror and decorating his eye with blues, yellows, and greens . . .

The scimitar.

Under Sonny's left pectoral.

The brightest green imaginable.

The green of a lizard's eye.

She visualized him standing before her naked . . .

"Something?" Geoffrey said.

She blinked at him as though coming out of a trance.

"You seemed very far away for a moment," he said.

"Sorry, I was . . . just thinking how hungry I am."

"Shall we get some menus then?" he asked.

"Do you live in New York?" a woman was asking Sonny. Except for Carolyn, she was quite the most attractive woman here. Sonny expected she was somewhere in her fifties, with a face-lift engineered by an expert. She was standing very close to him. Dark hair cut close to her face. Brown eyes looking up at him.

"No, I'm from San Diego," he said.

"Where in San Diego?" Carolyn asked. She had not moved an inch from his side the moment the brunette appeared.

"Well, El Cajon, actually," he said. "Are you familiar with it?"

"No," Carolyn said, "not really."

"I live on Garwood Avenue," he said, making up a name on the spot.

"I love San Diego," the brunette interrupted.

Careful, he thought.

"But I haven't been there in years," she said.

"It's changed a lot," he said.

"I'm sure. What do you do out there?"

"I run a small cable company," he said.

"You do? How exciting!"

Careful, he thought again.

"We do informational programs," he said. "Mostly medical."

Back to safer ground.

"Like what?" Carolyn asked.

"Oh, a wide variety of topics intended to keep the layman informed. As for example, how to detect the early signs of various diseases. Or when to consider surgery. Or how to . . ."

"Are you married, Mr. Hamilton?" the brunette asked.

"No, I'm not. And call me Scott," he said. "Please."

"Then it's Sally," she said, and smiled.

"Sally," he repeated, and returned the smile.

"Sally," Carolyn asked sweetly, "when does your husband get back from Boston?"

"The food's really quite good, don't you think?" Geoffrey said.

"It's delicious."

"But do you see what I mean about it getting sort of crowded and noisy?"

"That's okay, I like noisy places," she said.

"You do?"

"Yes. This pasta is fabulous."

She was eating penne with broccoli. He was eating the red snapper.

"I'm glad you like it," he said. "Shall I order another bottle of wine?"

"No, no. Whoo, no," she said, covering her glass with the palm of her hand. "So is New York the first assignment you've ever had?" she said.

"No, my first one was in Dublin."

"Is Ireland nice?"

"Oh, terrific. Well, not where they're shooting and killing people. But, yes, Dublin is . . ."

"How about that murder right here at the *Hilton*?" she said, and rolled her eyes.

"The city's getting absolutely *frightening,* isn't it?"

"Getting?"

"Well, it is *already,* isn't it? You're quite right."

"I didn't catch all of it, I turned it on when I came out of the shower. Was he a guest there, or what?"

"No, a detective. The victim, do you mean?"

"Yes."

"A detective. Actually, it's the oddest thing. I *know* him."

"You *do?*" she said, and opened her blue eyes wide, causing him to want nothing more in that instant than to lean over the table and kiss her.

"Well, he's not a *personal* friend or anything near," he said, "but we did have some business of a sort. Do you remember the two women I told you about? With the tattoos and the false passports?"

"Yes?"

"He was the detective who . . . you don't suppose they're *related*, do you?"

"The women?"

"No, the murders. His murder and theirs. He was investigating them, you see. The other murders. Do you think they know that?"

"Who?"

"The police. His superiors."

"I would guess so."

"Perhaps I should give them a call. Mention the possibility."

"Might not be a bad idea. But I'm sure they know what he was working on. That's something they'd check immediately."

"Yes, I'm sure you're right. Do you really enjoy noisy places?"

"Yes. Truly."

"Do you like to dance?"

"Yes."

"Would you like to meet Margaret Thatcher?"

"Sure," she said breezily. "Frank Sinatra, too."

"You're really quite lovely, do you know?" he said.

"Thank you," she said.

"Would you like to walk up to Fifth?" he asked.

216

"When we're finished here? I love Fifth Avenue in the summertime, don't you?"

"I love it *all* the time," she said.

"Well, shall we then?" he asked. "We can walk up to Fifth and then up Central Park South to Rumpelmayer's. Do you like ice cream sundaes?"

"I love them," she said.

"In England, we're sadly lacking places that specialize in them, more's the pity. There's one called Marine Ices, on the way to Hampstead, in Chalk Farm, but it's not widely known and not very central. There's always Fortnum's, I suppose, but really there's nothing in London quite like Rumpelmayer's. Do you think you might care for some ice cream?"

"Yes, I think I would."

"Well, splendid," he said, beaming. "Super!"

"Sunsets out here always remind me of a Syd Solomon painting," Carolyn said.

Sonny didn't know who Syd Solomon was.

"A marvelous abstract expressionist," she explained. "He lives out here part of the year. Sagaponock. I met him at a party once. He's a delightful man, and a wonderful artist."

The crowd was beginning to thin, one or two guests disappearing each time the sun dropped a bit lower on the horizon, the brilliant colors of the sunset dissipating, the sky becoming streaky and blurred.

"Looks like we should be leaving," she said. "Before

they put the chairs up on the tables. Let's say good night to our hosts, shall we?"

She took his arm, and led him off the deck, back into the house. Out on the ocean, the sun was all but gone, the sky stained a violent purple immediately above the water, the color graduating to a deep blue, and then the blackest black high above, where only a single star shone.

"Good night, Phil," Carolyn said to their host, and offered her cheek to him. "Marge," she said, and kissed her hostess as well.

"Thank you for including me," Sonny said.

"It was a pleasure having you," Marge said by rote, and turned to another departing guest.

"Want to walk back on the beach?" Carolyn asked.

"Sure," he said.

They climbed the wooden steps over the dune. The night was still except for the sound of the waves rushing the shore. She took off her sandals, holding his hand for support. Still holding his hand, the sandals dangling by their straps in her other hand, she began walking with him up the beach.

"If we're going into town," she said, "we'll need a car. That is . . . well . . . would you *like* to have dinner together?" she asked.

"Sure," he said.

"I should have asked first," she said. "I just thought . . ."

"I'd really like to," he said.

"Good," she said. "Though to tell the truth, I'm not all that hungry."

"Neither am I," he said.

They walked in silence for several moments. He could hear the murmur of the ocean against the shore. He could hear her breathing beside him in the darkness.

"Why don't I take some hamburgers out of the freezer?" she said.

"Okay," he said.

They walked a bit farther in silence.

"Start a little fire on the grill," she said.

"Okay," he said.

She stopped suddenly. Turned to him. She was still holding his hand. Standing quite close to him now. Sandals hanging from the other hand. She looked up into his face. Raised the hand holding the sandals, and draped it over his shoulder, the sandals dangling. Moved in closer to him, released his hand, and brought her liberated hand up behind his neck, the fingers widespread. He heard her catch her breath.

"Start a little fire," she whispered, and kissed him.

10

Tuesday morning, the last day of June, dawned bright and hot and harsh. In the four-poster bed in the master bedroom of Martin Hackett's beach house, Carolyn blinked her eyes open as sunlight struck her full in the face, a single slash of light knifing its way through the narrow opening where the drapes failed to meet. Disoriented for a moment, the blink of annoyance turned to one of confusion. Where . . . ?

And then she remembered.

And rolled over to see if he was still there, her delicious swordsman with the green tattoo on his chest.

There were only rumpled sheets beside her.

"Scott?" she called.

There was no answer.

"Scott?"

"Yes?"

Thank God, she thought.

"Good morning," she called.

"Good morning."

His voice was coming from the bottom of the stairs. She got out of bed, went to the chair where she'd tossed her slip the night before, and slipped it on over her head. Not quite as form-fitting as the one Kathleen Turner had worn in *Cat*, but that one had been hand-tailored, and this one was snug enough. Carolyn was thirty-nine years old and knew that whereas total nudity might be wonderful at the Metropolitan, it wasn't too terrific when it came to seduction.

Nobody had eaten any hamburgers last night.

They'd come directly back here, which she'd preferred, anyway, just in case the gentleman turned out to be a dud, a premise she'd sincerely doubted after their first kiss, when she was standing close enough to him to make some fairly accurate predictions and entertain some reasonably great expectations. Better nonetheless to be in *his* bedroom, or at least Martin Hackett's bedroom, where she could leave whenever she chose, rather than in her own bedroom, where she might have difficulty evicting a poor lover at best or a violent maniac at worst.

Barefoot now, and wearing only the white slip, she stepped into the doorframe at the top of the stairwell. He was standing below, looking up at her.

"Hi," she said.

"Hi."

"You're up early."

"I got hungry."

"Is there coffee?"

"Eggs, too, if you'd like me to make some."

"I'll be right down," she said.

She went into the bathroom at the end of the hall, squelched a desire to peek into Martin Hackett's medicine cabinet, washed her face instead, squeezed toothpaste from a tube on the sink, used her forefinger to brush her teeth, and then performed what The Late Colonel used to call her "morning *toilette*"—didn't his redheaded driver ever *pee*?

She went back into the bedroom, and debated putting on the high-heeled sandals again; the first time he'd fucked her last night, she was wearing only the sandals. She decided they might look a little trashy so early in the morning, opted instead for the Barefoot Contessa look, and went downstairs to where he was sitting at the kitchen table reading *The New York Times*. He was wearing a black silk robe sashed at the waist, a red monogram over the breast pocket, the letters MH. For Martin Hackett, she thought. Wears a black silk robe, how about *that* for a lobster fisherman?

He put down the newspaper at once.

"How would you like your eggs?" he asked.

"No good-morning kiss?" she said, and went immediately into his arms.

"Good morning," he said.

"Good morning," she said, and kissed him fiercely.

"Listen, if you want those eggs . . ." he said.

"You know what I want," she said, and kissed him again.

She could feel him growing immediately hard in the opening of the black silk robe, pressing his naked hardness against the thin nylon of the slip. Let him suffer a bit, she thought, and pulled away from him, and said, "Know how to make an omelette?"

"How many eggs?" he asked, and grinned. Knowing the game. Enjoying it. The grin telling her he was going to fuck her brains out the minute she finished breakfast. Good, she thought. Do it.

"Two," she said, and sat at the kitchen table, and crossed her legs.

"Want some orange juice?" he asked.

"Please," she said.

Watching him. The way he moved. So sinuously.

He poured a small glass of juice for her, carried it to the table. She picked up the glass, drank.

"Coffee now or later?" he asked.

"Some now, some later," she said.

"Mmm," he said, and slid his hand up her leg and under the slip.

She let his hand stay on her for a moment, working her for a moment, then gently took it away.

"My coffee," she said.

He went to the stove, poured her a cup, carried it back to the table. She poured a little milk into it, and then sipped at it. It was strong and it was hot. At the stove, he was cracking eggs into a bowl.

"What's in the paper?" she asked, and picked up the *Times*.

"I didn't get past the front page. Bush is coming to town."

"So I see, the bastard."

223

"You don't like him?"

"Do I like scorpions? I wish someone would shoot him."

"That would leave us with Quayle."

"Shoot him, too," she said, and turned to where he was beating the eggs. There was an odd look on his face. Smile on his mouth, eyebrows raised in surprise. "Don't tell me," she said. "You're a staunch Republican, right?"

"No. But . . ."

"Then surely you can see through this, can't you?"

"How do you mean?"

"This speech at the Statue of Liberty. It's a *campaign* speech, that's all. New York's going down the tubes, but *he's* going to make a speech about freedom and opportunity. Why can't he . . . ?"

"Where does it say that?"

"Say what?"

"That he's going to talk about freedom and opportunity?"

"It doesn't. But why do you think he's chosen the Statue of Liberty? I can write his speech from memory," she said, and shook her head sourly and opened the paper to page twelve where the story was continued.

"How do you want this omelette?"

"Not too runny," she said. "Says he'll be speaking at twelve noon. Catch the West Coast while it's waking up, right? CNN and the three networks'll be covering it. What'd you think of Buddy Johnson, by the way?"

"Nice man. Would you like some toast?"

"Please," she said.

He popped two slices of bread into the toaster, and came to the table to pour fresh coffee for her.

"Oh, lookee," she said, "the Marine Corps Band'll be there, too. Play a few choruses of all the old wartime favorites, and end with a rousing rendition of 'God Bless America.'"

"Here we go," he said, and brought her omelette and toast to the table. He poured himself a cup of coffee and sat beside her. Last night, they had enjoyed the passion only strangers could bring to the act of making love. Now, this morning, sitting here at the kitchen table, sipping coffee with him, eating the omelette he'd made . . .

"This is very good," she said.

. . . she felt more comfortable than she had on far too many mornings-after. A friend of hers once confided that some men weren't worth the shower afterward. She had often felt that way herself. But sitting here with Scott Hamilton, she felt entirely at ease—and this time, she did not want the morning to end.

"How long will you be staying out here?" she asked.

"Until after the Fourth, at least."

"Will you be going to the fireworks?"

"I didn't know there'd be any."

"The Hamptons without fireworks?"

"I'll have to see what Martin's plans are," he said.

"Where do you go from here?"

"Back to San Diego."

Careful, he thought.

"Back to your cable TV station."

"Yes."

"What'd you and Buddy talk about, by the way?"

"Oh, mutual interests."

"He's great at getting seats to the U.S. Open, you know."

"Yes, he mentioned that."

He put down his cup and leaned gently into her. She lifted her face to his. Their lips met. Their kiss tasted of coffee. He picked her up, cradling her in his arms, and they kissed again. She could not remember the last time a man had carried her into a bedroom. Smiling, one arm around his neck, the other resting on his chest, her hand just above the green scimitar tattoo, she closed her eyes as he negotiated the narrow stairway to the second story of the house, and did not open them again until he lowered her gently to the canopied bed. He stood beside the bed for a moment, staring at her the way he had from the deck yesterday, his grey-green eyes consuming her. Then he untied the sash at his waist, and let the black silk robe fall to the floor.

Selly Colbert was very proud of the security precautions his intelligence people had coordinated for the Canada Day gala.

"If you'll look at this floor plan of the Baroque Room," he said, and spread the drawing on the conference table:

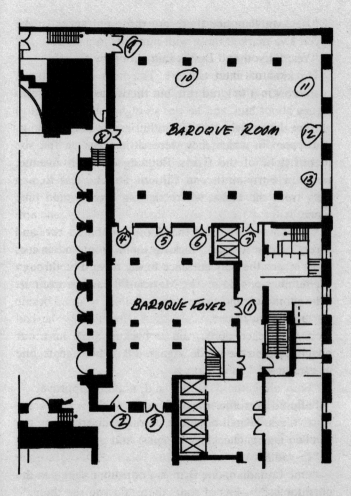

". . . you'll notice there are three entrances to the foyer. I've marked those with numbers in a circle . . ."

"Yes, I see that," Dobbs said.

He kind of liked Colbert. The man looked like a scarecrow in a tailored suit, but there was an air of efficiency about him, and he was so obviously dedicated to getting things right that his enthusiasm was contagious. The room in which they were sitting was on the sixteenth floor of the Exxon Building on Sixth Avenue, between Forty-ninth and Fiftieth Streets, less than a mile from the Plaza, where the big event would take place.

"We'll be closing off the doors numbered two and three," Colbert said, "locking them from the inside. That means the only entrance to the foyer'll be through the number-one door. The Mexicans'll have people outside doors two and three . . ."

"How many?"

"One at each door. And as backup, we'll have our own people on the inside. Again, it'll be two agents, one at each door."

"Four altogether," Dobbs said, nodding approval.

"Should be sufficient, don't you think?"

"Oh, yes. Who'll be at the entrance door?"

"Two agents checking the guest and press lists . . ."

"Canadian?"

"One Canadian, one British. Four other agents in the corridor itself—lots of stairs there, do you see them?"

"Yes."

"We'll have two agents at each of the stairwell entrances—British, Canadian and Mexican—and another two agents here at the elevator banks . . . do you see the X's? They indicate elevators."

"Um-huh."

"There'll be agents at each of the doors marked four, five, six and seven, leading into the Baroque Room itself. We'll be locking the doors marked eight, with agents standing inside and out, just in case an emergency requires them to be unlocked in a hurry. Fire, what have you."

"Um-huh."

"The number-nine doors lead to the service pantry, so we've got to leave them unlocked. Again, there'll be two agents on either side of them."

"How about the room itself?"

"The dais'll be set here at the far end, where you see the four pillars—those little black squares, do you see them? I've marked the spot with the number ten."

"Um-huh."

"It'll be a U-shaped dais . . . you already have the seating plan . . ."

"I do."

". . . agents behind it, and to the left and right."

"How about the windows?"

"Agent at each window. That's eleven, twelve and thirteen. Have you seen the room?"

"Yes."

"Big tall windows looking out on the park. A beautiful room."

"Beautiful," Dobbs agreed.

229

"How many people will you be using?" Colbert asked.

"I'm planning on a man at the foot of the steps here," Dobbs said. "Just outside the number-nine doors."

"Okay."

"Another man at the top of the steps . . ."

"Okay."

"And two in the corridor up there. There's elevator access, you know . . ."

"Yes, and another staircase as well. Fire stairs. But our intelligence people figured the men at the number-nine doors could handle anything originating . . ."

"Well, I'd just like to be sure."

"Okay, that's four."

"Have you got any people in the pantry itself?" Dobbs asked.

"No, but . . ."

"Then I'd like to put a man in there. Robert Kennedy was shot in a hotel kitchen, you know . . ."

"Yeah, that's right."

"Anyway, where there's food, you've always got the danger of . . ."

"Right, our people should have thought of that. Will you need backup there?"

"I don't think so. One man should be able to keep an eye on whatever's happening."

"Plus we've got those number-nine doors covered."

"Right. And I'll be in the Baroque Room itself."

"So how many will you be altogether?"

"Six, not counting whoever he brings with him. He's

got his own detail, sticks with him day and night. They'll be with him every minute."

Both men looked at the floor plan again, studying it, trying to locate any loopholes in the security arrangement. They nodded at almost the same moment, but it was Dobbs who said, "Looks air-tight to me."

Carolyn had already explained that the idea of the game was for each of them to drive each other to the very brink of total insanity by teasing but not satisfying, manipulating but not gratifying, withholding pleasure until it became unimaginably excruci . . .

A knock sounded at the door downstairs.

"Damn it," she said, "who's *that*?"

He got out of bed, pulled on the black robe, and shouted, "Just a second!"

"It's called Brink," she said. "The game."

"I'll be back," he said, and disappeared down the stairwell.

She had taken off her watch and placed it on the night table beside the bed. She looked at it now. A little past eleven. She put the watch back on the night table, stretched languidly, and smiled in anticipation. She could hear muffled voices below. Scott talking to someone she supposed was a delivery man. The man telling him he had to sign for all three cartons. Scott thanking him. The man telling him to have a nice day. Yes, come on up here, she thought, the nice day is just about to begin. She heard the door closing. The lock clicking. And then silence.

"Scott?" she called.

"Be right up," he said.

She stretched again.

Hurry up, doll, she thought. I'm going to teach you the ecstasy of denial.

"Scott?"

"Yes, just a second," he called.

She waited another three or four minutes, and then got out of bed, and tiptoed naked down the stairs. He was standing at the dining room table, his back to her. Three white FedEx cartons were on the table. He'd already opened one of them. Styrofoam pellets had fallen to the table and the floor. He hadn't heard her yet. She moved up behind him, stealthily, quietly, intending to surprise him, cover his eyes with her hands from behind him, press herself against the back of the black silk robe, guess who, baby? But a board creaked under her weight, snapping into the silence of the room like a rifle shot. He whirled from the table.

"What the hell's wrong with you?" he shouted.

There was a brown bottle in his hand.

It seemed for a moment that he would hurl it at her.

"I'm sorry," she said, "I didn't mean to . . ."

"No, no, *I'm* sorry," he said, regaining his composure at once. He put the brown bottle back into the carton, came to her where she stood midway across the room, naked and still frightened by his outburst. He took her in his arms. He whispered, "You startled me." He hugged her close. Over his shoulder, she could see the side of one of the unopened cartons. A big red label was affixed to it. Bold white lettering on it. Red and white striking sparks in the morning sunlight.

"Come teach me your game," he whispered.

She wondered what was in that carton.

Even at this distance, she was sure the bold white letters on the big red label spelled out the words HAZ-ARDOUS MATERIAL.

Elita was still asleep when the telephone rang that morning. Her first thought was *Sonny*. She picked up the receiver at once.

"Hello?" she said.

"Elita, it's Geoff."

"Oh, hello," she said.

"Is this a bad time?" he asked.

"I don't know, what time *is* it?"

"Twenty past eleven."

"No, that's okay," she said.

She listened to him telling her that he'd burrowed through his cupboards and had located his precious watercolor pencils and was hoping that sometime this evening he might . . .

"Well, no, I . . ."

". . . demonstrate the faking of a perfectly decent shiner."

"I . . ."

"I'd do it for you tomorrow night, but I don't think Mrs. Thatcher would enjoy it."

Mrs. Thatcher again. What was all this about Mrs. Thatcher?

"You *will* be joining me tomorrow night, won't you?" he asked.

"Joining you? Where?"

"At the dinner-dance."

"What dinner-dance?"

"I thought we'd discussed it."

"Well, no, you asked me if I liked to dance . . ."

"Yes, and you said you did . . ."

"Yes, but you didn't mention . . ."

"It's the big Canada Day celebration at the Plaza . . . do you remember the room we went to?"

"Yes?"

"That's where it'll be. Drinks, dinner, and dancing, black tie—do you have a long dress?"

"Yes, but . . ."

"Good, I'll come by for you at six. Drinks are at seven, but the consular people are supposed to be there a bit earlier, greet Mrs. Thatcher, and so on. Will six be all right?"

She hesitated, thinking why am I sitting here waiting for that son of a bitch to call when here's a perfectly decent person who was a lot of fun to be with last night, and now he's inviting me to a black-tie dinner-dance, what the hell's the matter with me? Maybe Mom's right, maybe I *don't* have the tiniest bit of pride and self-respect.

"When can you show me how to paint the black eye?" she asked.

* * *

Carolyn had gone back to her own house, and he was alone now for the first time since six-thirty last night. He went to the phone and immediately dialed Arthur's private number at SeaCoast. There was no answer. He dialed the general office number and got the Balinese girl.

"SeaCoast Limited, good morning."

Virtually singing the name.

"This is Scott Hamilton," he said. "May I speak to Mr. Hackett, please?"

"I'm sorry, he's gone for the day."

"Tell him I called," Sonny said, and hung up.

He'd wanted to ask Arthur about this second murder. He'd found nothing about either of the women in this morning's newspaper. But if someone was consistently eliminating their people, Sonny needed to know; perhaps the more *immediate* mission was to find the assassin.

The three cartons Arthur had expressed to him were still sitting on the dining room table. He picked them up and carried them into the kitchen, where he set them down on the counter alongside the sink. Arthur had simply used the original packaging, attaching a fresh FedEx label to each unopened carton. Sonny had already read the label on the bottle of isopropyl alcohol, and knew it was exactly what he'd ordered. He took a knife from the rack on the counter now, and slit open the tape on the second carton. Feeling around among the Styrofoam chips, he took out another brown bottle, this one labeled ISOPROPYLAMINE. Satisfied, he placed the bottle back onto the chips again, and slit open the last carton.

Burrowing under more Styrofoam pellets, he found a small paint can near the bottom of the box. He lifted the can out gingerly, opened a kitchen drawer to remove from it a butter knife, and pried off the lid. The paint can was filled with vermiculite. He felt around under the fine brownish packing flakes, found what he was looking for, and lifted out a sealed plastic envelope some three inches wide by six inches long. Inside the envelope was a glass ampoule with an amber-colored fluid in it. He read the label on the ampoule, and then put the plastic packet back into the paint can. Making sure there was a second ampoule in there, he resealed the lid, and put the can back into its packing carton. He would be running his reaction here at the kitchen sink, under a window open wide for ventilation. For now, he pushed all three cartons to the left of the counter, in the corner under the hanging wall cabinet, where they would be safe until he did the actual mixing.

The chemical name of the nerve agent he planned to produce was isopropyl dimethyl sulfonofluoridate. Its common name was sarin, an imperfect acronym derived from the names of its German creators: Schrader, Ambrose, Rüdriger and van der LINde. Sarin. A so-called G-agent, sarin was a deadly substance that short-circuited the nervous system, interfering with the enzyme necessary to muscle relaxation. Within seconds after ingestion or absorption, muscles all over the body would go into spasm, causing nausea, choking, vomiting, diarrhea, convulsion, coma, and death.

A drop of water weighed fifty milligrams.

For a man of the President's weight, the lethal ingested dose of sarin was .65 milligrams. This meant that an amount only 1.3 percent the weight of a water drop would kill him if he swallowed it.

If Sonny's reaction went to completion, he would have made a bit more than twenty *thousand* milligrams of the nerve agent. More than thirty thousand times the lethal ingested dose. He did not expect the President to swallow any of the stuff. But the liquid was immediately absorbed through the skin and the membranes of the eye.

He now needed only one other ingredient—to give a little body to the mix, he thought, and smiled. He would look for that today. And try to find his delivery system at the same time. Something that might allow him to walk away safely—although in his heart of hearts he did not believe escape afterward was possible. He had carefully planned tomorrow night's escape route. Push open the doors that led to the pantry on the left and—dead ahead—were the steps leading upstairs to the business offices. Past the offices, down the narrow corridor, turn right at the elevator, then down the fire stairs leading to the lobby. But he knew security would be thick, and he knew that only a miracle would take him safely from that dais to those doors on the left.

He accepted his possible death as the risk of service to his leader and to God, knowing full well that his reward was not here on this earth but in Paradise. It was written in the Koran, "Think not of those who are slain in Allah's cause as dead. Nay, they live, finding their sustenance in the presence of their Lord." If Sonny died tomorrow night, it would be with the certain knowledge that he had killed the man responsible for the murder of young Hana.

He wondered now if the two women he'd known as Priscilla Jennings and Annette Fleischer had met their deaths in the same cause.

Today he would look for whatever else he needed.

The rest was up to God.

Carolyn was in the shower when Sonny's car pulled out of the driveway. She did not know he was heading into town, and probably would have asked to go along with him had she known. She had never felt this way about anyone in her life. That he had fallen into her lap out of the blue was ample proof of the rewards of leading a clean life. Smiling as she lathered herself, she planned what she'd wear when she went over there later today.

She called Sassoon as soon as she was dressed, making an appointment for a haircut next Tuesday, when she planned to be in the city again. The next call she made was to her daughter.

"Have you heard from your Sonny Boy yet?" she asked.

"Not since Saturday," Elita said.

"Then he *did* call."

238

"Yes, he called."

"Did you see him?"

"Yes, I saw him."

"Where?"

"We went to the Statue of Liberty."

"Did you take him back to the apartment?"

"We came back here, yes."

"I hope you had a lovely time," Carolyn said.

"Yes," Elita said. "We had a lovely time."

"But you haven't heard from him since."

"No."

"Mm," Carolyn said.

Elita hated when she did that. Intimated through a murmur or a grunt or even the faint lifting of an eyebrow that Elita had somehow been . . . *duped* again, *gulled* again, led down the goddamn garden path again by yet another unscrupulous male bent on humiliating her. In retaliation, she said, "I'm going to meet Margaret Thatcher tomorrow night."

"Oh, *are* you?" Carolyn said.

The tone of her voice indicated that she thought Elita was the victim of a severe delusional system and needed immediate observation. Elita hated when she did *that*, too, used that condescending tone.

"I've been invited to a formal at the Plaza," she said curtly. Stiffly, actually. Coldly, in fact. Hoping her mother got the message that she wasn't particularly enjoying her little thrusts this afternoon.

"What will you wear?"

"I thought the blue gown. The one . . ."

"Yes, I know the one," Carolyn said. "Who invited you?"

"A man from the British Consulate."

"My," Carolyn said. "Thatcher, hm?"

"Yes. It's a big Canada Day celebration. She'll be there, and so will a lot of other important people."

"My," Carolyn said again, but her tone sounded somehow different.

"I may get to meet her," Elita said.

"Maybe you can ask her out to Westhampton."

"Maybe I will."

"What's this man's name? From the consulate."

"Geoffrey Turner."

"Where'd you meet *him*?"

"It's a long story."

Which Carolyn knew meant mind your own business, Mom.

"Will you be coming out to the beach this weekend?" she asked.

"I'm not sure yet."

"When will you know?"

"I'll call you Friday."

"Because I was hoping you'd bring out some clothes for me."

"What do you need?"

"Some of the things in my lingerie drawer. The bikini panties from Bendel . . . there're six of them in different shades . . ."

"Uh-huh."

"And you should find some garter belts in that same drawer . . . a black one, a red one . . ."

Her mother had met an interesting man, she guessed.

"And a white one," Carolyn said. "They're all in that same drawer."

There was a silence on the line.

"Elita?" she said.

"Yes, Mom."

"Did you hear me?"

"Yes, Mom."

"Do you know the white garter belt I mean?"

"I'll look for it."

She didn't have to look for it. It was hanging over the shower rod in her bathroom, drying with the . . .

"And the sheer white hose to match it," Carolyn said.

How do mothers *know*? Elita wondered.

"Elita?"

"Yes, Mom."

"Can you do that for me, darling?"

"Yes, Mom. *If* I come out."

"I wish you would. And, oh, yes . . ."

The red shoes, Elita thought.

"There's a pair of high-heeled red shoes in my closet . . ."

"Uh-huh."

"If you can bring those out, too, I'd appreciate it."

"Okay, Mom."

"You can put all of it in that little Louis Vuitton bag on the top shelf in my closet."

"Okay. If I come."

"Well, I hope you will. Have a nice time tomorrow night."

"Okay."

"And give my regards to Maggie," Carolyn said, and hung up.

"My wife is allergic to plastic," he explained to each of the pharmacists. "Don't you have an old *glass* eyedropper someplace back there?"

No, they did not have any old glass eyedroppers back there. Everything was plastic nowadays. Which was fine unless someone was planning to measure a corrosive chemical.

But Sonny had been taught to believe that a man's fate was written on his forehead and that a destiny appointed by God was impossible to avoid.

He went into the hobby shop looking only for a beginner's chemistry set, and he found several such, all of them containing glass test tubes and glass stirring rods and what appeared to be glass droppers—but he couldn't be certain. He asked the salesperson—a young woman whose name, ANNETTE, was lettered on a plastic tag pinned to her meager chest—to open one of the sets for him so he could take a good look inside, something she was reluctant to do until he flashed a plaintive smile at her. He would have settled for a dropper made of linear high-density polyethylene, but the dropper in the kit for adult-supervised ten-year-olds was made of glass. Genuine glass. As valuable to him as any diamond. A glass dropper plus a lot of other stuff he couldn't use and didn't need, including a dozen or more chemicals like calcium oxide, and sodium silicate, and silver nitrate, and cupric chloride.

Pleased by his discovery but annoyed by its price tag —twenty-nine dollars and ninety-nine cents, plus tax— he paid for it at the cash register and was about to leave the shop when it occurred to him that a place like this just might carry the delivery system he needed.

"I'll just look around," he said, and began wandering the shop.

He knew just what he was looking for.

In this most materialistic of nations, there had to be a *toy*, a *game*, an *entertainment* designed for children—as were the chemistry sets—which would prove useful to his needs. Each and every one of the water pistols was made of plastic. One of them was made to resemble an Uzi; the things Americans taught their children. He felt certain that any of the plastics used in their manufacture would melt when brought into contact with the reagents he planned to use. Besides, if he drew a fake gun and leveled it at the President, it would provoke the same response as a real one.

He kept searching.

In one section of the shop, he found shelves and shelves of little jars of paint and—stacked alongside them—boxes containing what the manufacturer called an "Airbrush and Propellant System." The back of the box explained that this was a complete airbrush system including ozone-safe propellant, and that it could be used for "painting plastic models and other arts and crafts projects." The side panel listed what the set included: the aforementioned ozone-safe airbrush propellant; a six-foot-long flexible hose; a color-mixing pipette; the propellant control assembly; three half-ounce jars; an organizing tray; a single-action, external-mix airbrush; and a complete instruction manual. The photographs on the box made it apparent that the set was made of plastic. But since it was designed to accommodate paint, he felt certain the plastic would be inert.

He looked for Annette. She was busy with another customer, but she kept tossing him a look that said, "I'll be with you in a second, darling, please don't go away." She was possibly the ugliest young woman he'd ever seen in his life; he flashed a smile that said, "Take your time, my adorable one, I have all day."

When finally and breathlessly she joined him, he asked if he could see the instruction manual inside the box.

She said, "Oh."

"Is there a problem?" he asked.

"Well, the box is sealed."

"Yes, I see that," he said. "But there aren't any chemicals in it . . ."

"Well, no, but . . ."

". . . and you *did* open the other one for me," he added, subtly reminding her that they'd already been illicitly involved, in a sense. She considered this now. His steady smile and penetrating gaze were quite unsettling her.

"I guess I can let you have a look," she said.

"I would appreciate it," he said softly.

She slit open the single strip of transparent tape sealing the box. Her eyes met his. She slid out the contents for him. As delicately as if he were raising the hem of her nightgown, he picked up the instruction manual. She got so flustered he thought she might faint. Another customer came in. She debated devotion versus honor and duty and went reluctantly to the front of the shop, tossing a love-lorn look over her shoulder. He quite pitied her.

The instructions told him what he didn't want to learn.

The kit was designed for spraying.

There was no way a steady stream could be propelled from the airbrush.

He carried the kit to the counter at the front of the store. A woman wearing green slacks and a peach-colored blouse was standing at the counter with a doll in her hands.

"I'm sorry," he told Annette. "I don't think I can use this."

Not unless he hoped to attack from a foot away—in which case *hurling* the sarin into the President's face would be enormously more effective.

"I'm *so* sorry," Annette said.

"But thank you, anyway," he said.

"Come back again," she said.

"I will," he said.

"Soon," she said.

"Miss?" the woman in the green slacks said. "I *asked* you a question."

Annette rolled her eyes hopefully toward the door.

But Sonny was already gone.

She was wearing tight, very short black shorts, a white T-shirt without a bra, and white sneakers to match. When she got no answer at the front door, she tried the knob. The door was locked. She went around to the back of the house, tried the knob on the kitchen door, which Martin often left unlocked, and found that to be the case now. She opened the door a foot or so, called "Scott?" and got no answer. Coming into the kitchen, she called "Scott!" again, louder this time, and was about to leave when she saw the Styrofoam pellets on the kitchen counter. She scooped them up, using the flat of her hand to sweep them into the open palm of the other hand, and opened the door to the cabinet under the sink. The garbage pail was full. She tossed in the pellets anyway, lifted the plastic garbage bag out of its container, pulled the ties, and was about to carry the bag outside to where Martin stored his garbage for pickup, when she saw the three cartons sitting on the counter. All of them were open now. There was no doubt now about the red-and-white label on one of them. It read HAZARDOUS MATERIAL.

She put down the garbage bag.

Went to the carton.

Opened it.

And reached into a flurry of white Styrofoam pellets.

* * *

In the Westhampton supermarket, Sonny dropped a pair of medium-sized Playtex HandSaver gloves into his shopping basket. They were marked a dollar ninety-nine. He went down the aisles looking for baking soda, and found a four-pound box of Arm & Hammer that cost only ninety-nine cents. In a section devoted to cooking aids, he found a plastic measuring cup with markings in both ounces and milliliters for only a dollar fifty-nine, three dollars less than the glass one. He also found something he could not have named and whose use he could only imagine.

The item was a plastic tube about a foot long and an inch or so in diameter, narrow at its open end, thicker at its other end, where a yellow rubber bulb was attached. He guessed housewives used it to baste roasts or decorate cakes or whatever. He didn't know and didn't care. He knew to what use *he* would put it. It only cost a dollar seventy-nine; he tossed it into his basket.

Pleased with all his little economies, he carried his items to the checkout counter.

The paint can was labeled with the same words as those on the carton.

HAZARDOUS MATERIAL.

Her heart was suddenly pounding.

She looked in the counter drawers for something she could use to pry off the lid, and found a screwdriver in a tray alongside a handful of serving spoons. There were brown flakes inside the can. Were *they* the hazardous

247

material? She did not think so. Cautiously, tentatively, she poked one finger into the can and began feeling around under the flakes. She felt something in there. Reached in with several fingers. Pulled it out. It was a plastic bag inside of which was some kind of slender glass vial with a brownish fluid in it. There was a label on the vial. It read:

GEM INORGANICS

37469   Dimethylsulfoxide difluoride
10g   LOT #08172

Danger: Corrosive Irritates Eyes Lungs

For research and development use only. All properties and hazards may not be known.

Consult MSDS

He was looking for carbon tetrachloride.

This had been the solvent of choice when he was learning at Kufra. Inert. Not very volatile. Nonflammable. You used a solvent to promote mixing when you were running a reaction, adding it to your starting materials so that there'd be enough to stir. A solvent also absorbed heat, reducing the risk of the reaction being carried away. Carbon tetrachloride did all these things. He did not know that its sale had been prohibited in New York State for the past ten years.

He drove up and down the Hamptons, stopping at hardware stores and art supply shops. He could find no

carbon tetrachloride. He began looking for a substitute.
All of the hardware stores carried paint removers or
thinners containing what the labels called "petroleum
distillates," a general term for products distilled from
petroleum. But without more specific information, he
was unwilling to risk any unforeseen reaction.

He found a paint stripper that contained methylene
chloride, another solvent that would have been ideal for
his purposes, but among the product's ingredients, the
label also listed . . .

Well, ammonia was okay, because it was a base . . .

And petroleum wax was inert, so that was okay, too.

But he was worried about the methanol and anhydrous alcohol. One of his reagents was isopropyl alcohol. Adding two *additional* alcohols to the mix might
make the ratio of alcohol to DF too high.

DF.

The toxic chemical which when mixed with alcohol
would provide sarin, a compound a thousand times
more deadly.

In his mind, he went over the reaction yet another
time:

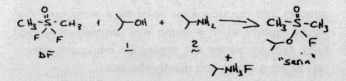

He now had everything he needed but a solvent inert
to the reaction.

He kept searching.

He was about to give up when he found among the cleaning solutions in one of the hardware stores a product called Carbo-Trichlor. Its label listed its main ingredient as 1,1,1-Trichloroethane. Perfect. The quart can cost only $5.99. Even better; he loved a bargain. He picked up a glass cutter from the tool section, and began prowling the shop again, still searching for his delivery system. When he passed a shelf full of rat traps, he paused for a moment, seriously considering whether it might work.

At Kufra, they had taught him how easy it was to obtain the ingredients essential to the manufacture of sarin—especially in a democracy, where few questions were asked and most questions were easily parried. Dimethylsulfoxide difluoride—or DF, as it was commonly called—was an admittedly dangerous insecticide, but when mixed with alcohol it became lethal. The beauty of sarin, in fact, was that its reagents could be stored separately, reducing the risks of corrosion or weeping, until it was time to unite them. This meant that it was possible to place the separate chemical components into canisters kept apart by a membrane that would rupture when a bomb was dropped or a shell fired, thereby mixing the separately innocuous chemicals to form a new and deadly chemical.

Sonny had been taught to do this on a smaller scale. No bombs, no shells.

Just a rat trap and a pair of test tubes.

Isopropyl alcohol and isopropylamine in one of the tubes.

DF in the other.

Tape both test tubes to the wooden base of the trap, side by side.

Set the trap, pulling back the bow and fastening it in place with the locking bar.

Toss the trap at your target.

The locking bar would be jarred loose, and the powerful spring would release the bow, shattering the test tubes, combining their contents, and splashing the created sarin into the air.

Simple, inexpensive, and effective.

The only risk was breaking your own finger while you were setting the trap.

Or getting caught in the lethal splashout.

But this delivery system had been designed for use in a crowd. Drop the trap from above, let it fall where it might, spattering the sarin onto random victims. His target tomorrow night would not be a random one. Accuracy was imperative; this was a No-Fail mission. So whereas the thought of using a rat trap on a rodent like Bush seemed appropriate, he decided against it.

In the gardening section of the store, he found a pump-top spray container that looked like a fat flying saucer. The little advertising placard on the wall behind it advised him that the grip was shaped to fit the hand, and the spring-loaded thumb plunger allowed for tireless operation. The nozzle was adjustable from a fine-spray mist to a 25-foot jet stream. His gaze zoomed in on the last two lines of copy:

Made of shock-proof, non-corrosive, injection molded plastic.

The shape of the container was awkward, making it enormously difficult to conceal. But the plastic was what he wanted, and if he could find nothing else, it would have to do.

He kept searching.

She stood at the kitchen counter looking down at whatever the hell it was inside that glass tube that didn't have any kind of stopper on it, just a tube sealed all around, wondering why Scott Hamilton was having a hazardous, corrosive material dangerous to the eyes and lungs delivered here to Martin Hackett's beach house. She wondered, too, if Martin Hackett knew Scott Hamilton was here in his house, knew in fact that *anyone* was staying here. She hastily put the little plastic packet with its glass vial back into the paint can, and replaced the lid, and put the can back into the carton. The other carton contained a bottle of alcohol and a bottle of something called isopropylamine, which she couldn't even pronounce.

She wondered if she should call Martin Hackett at his office, ask him if he knew anyone named Scott Hamilton.

She wondered where Scott was now.

Wondered when he'd be coming back.

And decided to look around the house a bit, see if there was anything that would connect Scott to Martin, a personal note of some kind, telling him where to leave the key or how to start the generator, anything that might spare her the embarrassment of a possibly foolish phone call.

As she started for the upstairs bedroom, Sonny was looking down into a basket brimming with dusty plastic bottles.

The basket was on the floor in a far corner of the hardware store, and it contained what had to be at least fifty plastic spray bottles of varying shapes and sizes, some with pump-top plungers, others with triggers, all of them less awkward than the one he'd earlier considered—but all of them most certainly vulnerable to the materials he'd be mixing.

Disappointed, he began looking for some of the other items he wanted. A penlight. Two batteries in it. A roll of monofilament fishing line, forty-pound test. A glass cutter. Should he buy the injection-molded bottle, after all? Find some way to conceal it? It cost only six dollars, which wasn't very much to spend for insurance. He was starting back toward where he'd seen it in the store, when suddenly he passed . . .

This had to be fate.

This had to be written on his forehead.

A shelf displaying insecticides.

And on that shelf a white plastic bottle with a green-yellow-and-black label, a green plastic screw cap, and a green nozzle. The label gave the name of the product as Raxon's Multi-Bug Killer, guaranteed that it would kill house pests and garden pests, and told him that the nozzle could be adjusted to either a spray position or a stream position that would squirt for a distance of fifteen to twenty feet. The label also mentioned that 99.6 percent of the active ingredients were inert. He turned the bottle to look at the label on the back. In tiny print at the bottom of the label, he read:

> ENVIRONMENTAL HAZARDS: This pesticide is toxic to fish. Keep out of lakes, ponds or streams. Do not contaminate water when disposing of equipment washwaters. For additional information write Roweena Walsh, Raxon Products, Inc. P.O. Box 732, Hattiesburg, Mississippi, or call toll free . . .

The twelve-ounce bottle cost five dollars and twenty-nine cents.

He had nothing to lose.

He studied the bottle carefully, examining its cap, examining the nozzle. If he did in fact use it later on, he would also need a roll of transparent tape and a fast-drying glue. He went looking for them.

What the hell was he?

Who the hell was he?

Different names on each of the laminated ID cards she'd found in the leather Mark Cross portfolio. Gerald Ramsey on the Plaza Hotel card with the word SECURITY printed across its bottom. A driver's license with the same name on it. Detective Second/Grade James Lombardo on a card for the NYPD's First Detective Squad. Same name and same photograph—Scott's—on another card for the Eighteenth Detective Squad. And lastly, a Federal Bureau of Investigation card with the name Frank Mercer on it.

Why all these different means of identification?

The Plaza.

Hadn't Elita told her . . . ?

She was suddenly frightened.

Hastily, she began putting the cards back into the leather folder.

That was when she heard the key turning in the door downstairs.

His trained eye immediately caught the black plastic garbage bag sitting on the floor in the kitchen. He had not left the kitchen that way.

He listened.

A trained listener could hear a flea breathing.

He heard nothing.

But someone was in the house, of that he was certain.

His gun was upstairs, in the night-table drawer on the right-hand side of the bed.

"Scott?"

Carolyn's voice. Calling from the bedroom. What . . . ?

He went up the steps. She was lying on the bed naked. Black shorts and bikini panties thrown onto a chair together with a white T-shirt. Sandals on the floor beside the chair. She was lying on her side, one elbow bent, head propped on her hand, long blond hair trailing.

"Hi," she said.

Smiling.

"Hi," he said.

Eyes flicking the room.

The closet door was ajar. He hadn't left it that way.

"I thought you'd never get back," she said.

"How long have you been here?"

"Oh, five minutes or so."

The brown leather Mark Cross portfolio was sitting on the small desk across the room, where he'd left it. But it had been moved to the center of the blotter. He shifted his eyes back to her. Her face was flushed.

"How'd you get in?" he asked.

"Back door was unlocked."

He walked to the closet, opened the door all the way. His eyes swept over the hanging clothes he'd brought from Los Angeles. Sports jacket and slacks, dark suit, raincoat.

"Why don't you come over here?" she whispered.

"In a minute," he said.

One of the pocket flaps on the sports jacket was twisted so that the lining showed. She had been inside that pocket. He'd carried only three ties from L.A. He took one of them from the tie rack now. A red tie. Red silk. She smiled as he came across the room to her.

256

"Gonna tie me to the bed?" she asked, and sat up against the pillows, watching him as he approached.

He did not answer her.

He came to the bed and sat on its edge, the tie in his right hand.

"What'd you find?" he asked.

"What?" she said.

"You were searching the house. What'd you find?"

"Searching the *house*? Don't be ridiculous."

Blue eyes wide. Frightened.

"Did you find the ID cards?" he said.

His voice was very low. He was holding the tie with both hands now, the tie dangling loose between his hands.

"What ID cards?" she said.

Her voice was quavering. She was lying.

"What else did you find?" he asked.

"Nothing," she said. "I didn't find anything."

But her voice was still quavering.

"You're lying," he said.

The tie whipped out, looping over her head, forming a sling behind her neck, yanking her off the pillows. He dropped one foot to the floor, the opposite knee still on the bed, and coiled the tie around her neck. She felt herself being pulled off the bed, sliding off the bed, put out a hand to stop her fall, and then felt herself being yanked up sharply by the tie. "No, please," she said, and grabbed for his hands looped into the tie, tried to loosen the hands tugging at the tie from either end. He stood with both feet solidly planted on the floor now, using the tie to lift her from her knees, raising her to her feet, the tie tightening relentlessly. She gasped for air, clutched at the tie with both hands, felt it cutting silkily into her flesh, tried to force words into her constricting throat, begging for her life, please, please, *no*, the words screaming silently, her fingers emptily clawing the air now, clawing for purchase, for life, for air to breathe, clawing, screaming silently, eyes bulging, please, no, please, please, please, the tie merciless, his hands pulling it tighter and tighter, narrowing the gap between life and . . .

She collapsed against him.

He kept the tie taut between his hands until he was certain she was dead.

Then he allowed her to drop to the floor at his feet.

11

There were people in Washington, D.C., who believed there was no such thing as the CIA. These people reasonably surmised that any intelligence agency so blatantly blundering had to be a cover for America's *real* spy network. Alex Nichols didn't work in Washington, but he was one of those people. Moreover, he worked for the CIA.

His recruitment had taken place on a bright fall day at the University of Michigan in Ann Arbor, the clock tower bonging the hour, playhouse posters announcing the arrival of a PTP play starring James Whitmore and Audra Lindley. Something called *The Magician*. Or *The Conjuror*. Or *The Illusionist*. Something like that. Young Alex—he was only twenty-one at the time—noticed the posters only peripherally. His head was full of visions of derring-do, a spy! He could hardly wait to tell his mother.

That was twenty-three years ago. Alex was now forty-four, and more convinced than ever that he was merely part of a gigantic cover operation that concealed a spy mechanism too awesome to behold. The two men with him today in the New York field office were also part of the cover. They could not possibly have been as stupid as they seemed. This was all a masquerade. Outside the office, the first day of July had announced its arrival in a determinedly sizzling fashion. The men were in their shirtsleeves. It was nine o'clock in the morning. They were here to discuss the letter on Alex's desk.

"It's obviously a fake," Peggot said.

Moss Peggot, unfortunately named in that his features were somewhat porcine and spooks everywhere around him called him "Miss Piggy," albeit behind his back. A measure of his quality as a spy was that he still didn't know about the nickname. Short and squat, the armpits of his shirt stained with sweat, his face florid and damp, he looked to Alex for approval. Alex was his boss.

"I'll bet Moss is right," Templeton said.

Conrad Templeton, a spy who dressed like a college professor in the vain hope that anyone on his trail would accept him as a professor of English literature at Columbia University, where in fact he did teach a course on Milton. Were it not for the heat, he would be in tweeds and a ratty wool cardigan sweater. Then again, the school term would not begin till September. Not to be denied, he was puffing on a pipe. Professor Conrad Templeton. You could've fooled me, Alex thought.

The letter on his desk looked genuine enough:

OFFICE OF THE VICE PRESIDENT

WASHINGTON

April 10, 1986

Dear Mr. President:

I have now carefully studied the intelligence reports supplied by
Mr. Casey and have met with Colonel North and heard his views on the
meetings of the Crisis Pre-Planning Group. There is now no doubt in
my mind that:

1) Libya provided the passports, money and terrorist training for the
two airport attacks in December of last year, one in Rome, the other
in Vienna. Five American civilians were killed in those attacks, one
of them an eleven-year-old girl.

2) Intercepted telephone calls to Tripoli from the People's Bureau in
East Berlin, prior to and immediately following the bombing of the
La Belle Discotheque in West Berlin on April 4 this year, constitute
irrefutable "smoking-gun" evidence that the bombing was planned and
executed by Libyans working for the People's Bureau in East Berlin,

under direct orders from Colonel Muammar Quaddafi. One American was
killed and twenty-three other Americans injured in the attack.

3) There is now hard and convincing evidence that Quaddafi divulged to
President Megistu of Ethiopia his plan to have the President of the
United States killed while traveling in a presidential convoy. CIA
reports confirm that Libyan hit teams operating on a "stray dog" basis
have targeted the President of the United States for assassination.

Given the failure of the economic sanctions imposed upon Libya in
January of this year, having carefully studied the reports cited above
as well as those of my own Task Force on Combating Terrorism, it is now
my duty and obligation to ask that you disregard the CIA's advice
against seeking the removal of Colonel Quaddafi through a surgical
bombing attack on Libya, and proceed with the recommendations proposed
by the Crisis Pre-Planning Group.

Mr. President, the time has never been more propitious for Quaddafi's
removal. The American people perceive Quaddafi as an eccentric
troublemaker spoiling to bring open conflict to the Middle East. There
is a built-in animosity toward the man, supported by recent reports of
his bizarre personal behavior. The public is ready to accept whatever
action we may take to curb the mad dog of the Middle East.

I urge you, therefore, to confer at your soonest convenience with
Messrs Regan and Weinberger, Vice Admiral Poindexter, Colonel North,
and the Joint Chiefs of Staff to implement at once a plan for immediate
military action.

My kindest regards,

George Bush

"Has the signature been checked?" Alex asked.

"It's a good forgery, but not good enough. Here's the President's *real* signature—from letters he wrote back in 1986," Peggot said, and put the sample on Alex's desk:

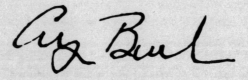

"But the signature on the letter more closely resembles *this*," Peggot said, and produced another document:

"This is the President's *current* signature. Signatures change over the years, you know . . ."

"Yes, I know," Alex said drily.

"What I'm saying," Peggot said, "is that the signature on this letter was obviously premised on the President's *current* signature. The letter could not possibly have been written in April of 1986, as it purports to have been."

Purports, Alex thought. A typical Peggot word.

"How about the stationery?" he asked.

"Well, this is a *copy* of the letter, of course," Templeton said, puffing on his pipe and stinking up Alex's entire office. "But vice-presidential stationery would be relatively easy to come by."

"Anyone worth his salt," Peggot said, nodding in agreement.

"We've tracked the typewriter type," Templeton said. "The letter was typed on an IBM Selectric. A fair number of them are still shipped to the Middle East, by the way. The typeface is Prestige Pica 72."

"Are you saying the letter originated somewhere in the Middle East?"

"Possibly."

"*Very* possibly," Peggot said, and nodded again.

"Where'd it turn up?"

"The letter? You understand we haven't located the actual typewri . . ."

"Yes," Alex said, and refrained from rolling his eyes heavenward. "The letter. Where did it surface?"

"A digger in Tripoli passed it to one of our people."

"Reliable."

"Our man?"

"No, the digger."

"Oh. Yes, so far."

"Where'd *he* get it?"

"She. Someone at GID copied it for her."

"Who?"

"Confidential source. She won't reveal it."

"Mm," Alex said.

The General Investigation Directorate, familiarly called the GID by American and British agents, was once headed jointly by Police Colonel Mohammed Al-

Ghazali and a man from Benghazi named Sáed Bin Umran, who'd been recently muzzled and put on the shelf. Al-Ghazali reported directly to the Secretariat for External Security, which was formed in 1984 by order of the General People's Congress, and whose responsibilities included the supervision and coordination of all Libyan intelligence and counterintelligence operations, including those of the GID. There was only one intelligence group controlled directly by Quaddafi, with no intermediaries. The only thing the CIA knew about this elite organization was its name: Scimitar.

"My suggestion is to forget all about the letter," Peggot said.

"Why?" Alex asked.

"It's obviously false," Templeton said, and looked into the bowl of his pipe to see if it was still lit.

"What's it doing in Libya?" Alex asked.

"What difference does it make?" Peggot said.

"How'd it get there?" Alex said.

"Who cares?" Templeton said. "It's a forgery."

Which is exactly the point, Alex thought.

Sonny set the nozzle on the plastic bottle to the STREAM position.

Standing on the beach, he pulled the trigger.

A stream of insecticide shot out some fifteen to twenty feet, exactly as promised on the bottle's label. To make certain the first shot wasn't just a freak, he tried it a dozen times. Not once did the stream fall short of the advertised distance. Moreover, he was able to trigger off fifteen shots every five seconds.

He first practiced on the flat because that was what the terrain would be tonight. But if he had to wait till the Fourth, he had to be certain he could hit the President with a deadly stream of poison from *above*.

In the sand below the upstairs deck of the beach house, he positioned a metal pail some eight feet out from the house. He estimated that the deck was eighteen feet or so above ground level. He climbed the staircase, and took position behind the railing, the bottle of insecticide in his hand. He felt as if he were standing at the counter of a carnival shooting gallery, aiming a water gun at a bull's-eye that would move a mechanical rabbit uphill. Each time a stream of water hit the bull's-eye, the rabbit would move up a notch. Whenever one of the rabbits went over the top, a bell would ring, signaling a winner.

No bells went off in the sand today.

But after a handful of test shots, he found he could accurately direct a stream that fell in a shower of smaller droplets into or onto the pail. Nor was it even necessary to hit the exact center of the pail each time; the radius of the falling drops was wide enough to encompass at least some part of it, and that was quite enough.

But he kept practicing.

A little girl walking toward the steps leading over the dune stopped to watch him.

"What're you doing?" she asked. Five or six years old, he guessed, and fascinated.

"Trying to get this stuff in the pail," Sonny said, and went right on with his work.

The little girl kept watching.

Different agendas, he thought.

"Why?" she asked at last.

"Oh, just for fun," Sonny said.

"Can I try?" she asked.

"Nope," Sonny said.

"Why not?"

"Too dangerous," he said.

The little girl watched awhile longer and then, bored, climbed the steps and disappeared from sight. Sonny kept practicing, triggering off three shots every second, swinging the bottle in an arc now to cover an even wider radius each time.

If the tiniest bit of sarin fell on the President's head, it would be absorbed immediately into his scalp. If he brushed at whatever fell onto his hair, it would touch his hand, magnifying his exposure and his vulnerability. Either way, he was a dead man.

There was just one other thing to check.

He dialed the 800 number on the plastic bottle, and got a recorded voice.

"Thank you for calling the Raxon Consumer Research Center. All lines are busy just now. Please hold and our next available representative will help you."

He waited.

A live voice came on the line. A woman.

"Research Center," she said, "may I help you?"

"I hope so," he said. "I have a bottle of your Raxon Multi-Bug Killer . . ."

"Yes, sir?"

"And I was wondering what the plastic is made of."

"In the bottle, do you mean?"

"Yes, please."

"Well . . . I'm not sure, let me check."

He waited.

When she came back on the line, she said, "We don't have a number on that. I can tell you that the EPA doesn't recommend recycling of the bottle. What'd you want to use it for?"

"It's such a good spray bottle," Sonny said, "it would seem to have a lot of uses. I'm just wondering if the plastic would be inert to organic solvents."

"Well . . . let me take another look," she said, and was gone for another five minutes.

He waited.

"Hello?" she said.

"Yes, I'm here."

"Sorry to keep you waiting. I would *guess* the plastic is polyethylene, but we don't have that information. In any case, we don't recommend recycling, because traces of the chemical might remain in the bottle and . . ."

"Yes, I can understand that. But you don't know for sure whether it's polyethylene, is that right?"

"No. Some of the others are, so I'm guessing this one is, too. What'd you plan to use it for?"

"Some of the others, did you say?"

"Pardon?"

"Are made of polyethylene? The bottles?"

"Oh. Yes."

"Which ones, can you tell me?"

"Well, there's Raxon's Flying Insect Killer, for one. It comes in a number-two bottle made of hi-density polyethylene. But I can't say for sure that the Multi-Bug . . ."

"Well, thank you very much," he said, "you've been very kind."

"Thank you, sir," she said, and hung up.

He dialed the 800 number again.

Got the same recorded voice telling him that all lines were busy and asking him to wait for the next available representative. If he got the same woman again, he would ask her to repeat the name of the product. But he got a man this time.

"Research Center, may I help you?"

"Yes," Sonny said. "I have a bottle of your Flying Insect Killer. Can you tell me what the plastic is made of?"

"I know the code doesn't permit recycling of that bottle, sir."

"Yes, but can you tell me what the plastic . . ."

"That's the white plastic bottle, isn't it?"

"Yes."

"Just a moment, please."

Sonny waited. All the time in the world. Canada Day was only tomorrow.

"Hello, sir?" the man said.

"Yes?"

"That's a code-two bottle, hi-density polyethylene."

"Thank you very much," Sonny said, grinning.

He had his delivery system.

All he had to do was run to the hardware store again.

Then he could begin mixing his formula.

At ten o'clock that morning, Elita tried the number at the beach house and got no answer. Thinking she might have misdialed it, she immediately tried it again, slowly and carefully punching out the numbers this time because sometimes the phone's computer system or whatever it was didn't work as fast as you could hit the buttons. The phone rang and rang on the other end.

She tried her mother again at ten-thirty, wanting to ask if she could borrow her blue Judith Leiber bag with the big mabe pearl set into its clasp; Elita didn't have anything dressy enough for the formal tonight, and the bag would be perfect with her blue gown.

She let the phone ring a dozen times.

Come on, Mom, she thought.

It was another scorching hot day, she was probably on the beach.

She tried the number again at eleven.

Let the phone ring off the hook.

Still no answer.

She had once met the man who owned the house next door. Someone named Martin Hackett, who was in the fish business or something. She wondered if she should call him, apologize for breaking in on him, tell him this was something of an emergency and ask if he'd yell down to the beach, if that's where her mother was, tell her to call her daughter in New York. Sounded like a good idea.

She looked for her mother's personal directory, but of course she'd taken that out to the beach with her. She called directory information and asked for a Martin Hackett on Dune Road in Westhampton Beach, and lo and behold, the operator came up with a phone number, would wonders never?

Elita dialed the number.

The phone on the kitchen counter in the Hackett house rang and rang.

The extension in the bedroom upstairs rang and rang.

In the basement, her mother lay unhearing in a shallow grave covered with sand.

In the kitchen, Sonny did not answer the phone because he was mixing his formula.

He worked with the kitchen windows open. Sarin evaporated swiftly, and its vapors were deadly. Even though the only truly dangerous chemical he'd purchased—his DF, the dimethylsulfoxide difluoride—was still cooling in the refrigerator, he was nonetheless wearing the yellow rubber gloves he'd bought in the supermarket. The chemistry set had come complete with a pair of eye goggles. He was wearing those now. He had also opened the box of Arm & Hammer baking soda, poured it into a bucket of water, and stirred it until it dissolved. The bucket now stood in preparation on the counter top; in solution, baking soda and water would decompose any sarin accidentally spilled or splashed.

In preparation for running his reaction, he had emptied the twelve-ounce bottle of Raxon's Flying Insect Killer into the toilet, flushing the contents out to sea or wherever, he didn't know and didn't care. He had then washed out the plastic bottle with some of the isopropyl alcohol he'd ordered from the J.D. Bowles lab in St. Paul, shaking the bottle out and setting it on the sink rack upside down, so that the alcohol vapors would flow out, allowing quicker drying. The empty plastic bottle, uncapped, now sat upright in a bowl of ice cubes and water, cooling. When he began running the actual reaction, he did not want the mixture to heat too rapidly. Heating would cause evaporation. Breathing in the escaping fumes could kill him.

Into the graduated measuring cup he'd bought on his trip to the supermarket, he poured ten ounces of trichloroethane, the inert cleaning solution that was his solvent. Holding the pouring lip of the cup against the glass stirring rod from the chemistry set, he allowed the liquid to run down into the white plastic bottle.

The clock on the kitchen wall read 11:22.

He could not use the measuring cup for his reagents; the lowest graduated marker on it was fifty milliliters. Sticking a strip of transparent tape to one of the glass test tubes from the chemistry set he'd bought, he'd earlier calibrated a one-milliliter setting—twenty-five drops equaled a milliliter—and also a five-milliliter setting. He

271

had twenty grams of DF, which was the equivalent of twenty-five milliliters. To this, he needed to add 16.6 grams each of alcohol and amine. The conversion came to twenty-one milliliters of alcohol and twenty-four milliliters of amine.

He picked up the jar of anhydrous alcohol. Anhydrous simply meant water-free, unlike the common rubbing alcohol you could buy in a pharmacy, which was only ninety percent alcohol and ten percent water—the deadly enemy of sarin. He measured his units and transferred them to the plastic bottle sitting in its bowl of icy water. He measured out his amine and transferred that as well, to bind the formula. It gave off a pungent smell, rather like ammonia. The white plastic bottle sat in its icy bath, the mixture inside it still harmless.

All that was missing was the DF.

All that was missing was the ingredient which, when combined with the others, could kill Sonny if he wasn't careful.

The clock on the kitchen wall read 11:30.

In eight and a half hours, the guests at the Canada Day celebration would be called in to dinner from the Baroque Foyer.

World enough and time.

He allowed his mixture to cool.

Lower the vapor pressure. Keep the reaction going at a safe pace.

He looked up at the clock again.

He would not hurry.

At a quarter to twelve, he went to the refrigerator and

272

removed from it one of the sealed ten-gram ampoules of dimethylsulfoxide difluoride. Wrapping a dish towel around the thicker end of the ampoule, holding it so that his fingers were around it and his thumb was erect and facing him, he ran the blade of the glass cutter behind the nipple end of the sealed glass container, and began working it, scoring it, finally putting down the tool and—with a sharp snap—breaking off the end of the ampoule. Despite the hours of cooling, a puff of fume escaped into the air, startling him. He turned his head away instinctively, realized at once that this was merely a reaction with the moisture in the air over the ampoule, and allowed himself a few seconds to collect his wits before he picked up the glass dropper.

From this moment on, his life was in imminent danger.

What he was running was technically called the nucleophilic displacement of fluoride by alkoxide, a reaction in which a molecule of alcohol combined with a molecule of DF to produce equal amounts of hydrogen fluoride and the deadly nerve agent known as sarin.

Drop by careful drop, he dribbled the DF into the white plastic bottle containing his other reagents and his solvent.

He could not allow any of the product he was making to touch his skin.

He could not breathe in any of it.

Ten grams of DF in that ampoule, less than a half-ounce. Drop by drop into the plastic bottle to create his deadly brew. The solution darkening as the reaction occurred. Darkening. Darkening.

The clock kept ticking behind him.

In just eight hours, the President of the United States would take his seat on the Baroque Room dais.

And Sonny would kill him.

The ampoule was empty now. He dropped it into a plastic bag, and went to the refrigerator for the second ampoule. Patiently, he repeated the procedure until he'd emptied this one as well.

The plastic bottle now contained sarin.

Making certain the nozzle tip was turned to the OFF position, he screwed the green cap tightly onto the bottle, and set it down on the counter. Opening the bottle of quick-setting glue, he applied it to the seam where cap met bottle, creating a tight seal. He then cut a strip off the roll of transparent tape and wrapped it around the nozzle, securing it firmly in the OFF position. He set the bottle down in the corner of the counter where the walls joined. He did not think it could now accidentally spill its contents. He hoped not. Because if it did, the released sarin would kill on the spot whoever or whatever it touched—human, animal, or insect.

He put the second empty ampoule into the plastic bag, together with the stirring rod and the dropper. With his gloved right hand, he peeled the glove off his left hand so that only the fingertips were still covered. Using those fingertips, he peeled off the other glove entirely, dropped it into the plastic bag, and then shook his left hand until that glove fell into the bag as well. He dropped the goggles into the bag, sealed it, and carried it outside to Martin Hackett's garbage bin.

When he came back into the kitchen, the clock on the wall read twelve thirty-two P.M.

He was ready to leave for New York City, where he would welcome whatever destiny God had planned for him.

At two-thirty that afternoon—while Alex Nichols was reading through a mass of intelligence information about a phony British naval officer the allies had deliberately washed ashore during World War II—Sonny Hemkar was checking into a room at the Plaza Hotel.

The name he signed to the register was Anthony Logan. The American Express credit card he handed to the clerk was made out to that name. He gave two dollars to the bellhop who carried his bag to his room on the eighth floor, and exchanged only a few words of conversation with him. The bag contained a navy blue tropical-weight suit, a white shirt, a tie almost as dark as the suit, black shoes, blue socks, a white handkerchief, and a clean pair of striped boxer shorts. It also contained a 9-mm Walther P-38 pistol, half a dozen loaded magazines for the gun, and all the fake identity cards McDermott had made for him. The sealed plastic bottle of sarin was nestled in one of his shoes, in a snug corner of the suitcase. Sonny figured he had three hours before he should begin getting ready for tonight's festivities.

And *a little name plate,* the loquacious Miss Lubenthal had told him. *White lettering on black plastic. Totally discreet.* In this city, in the midtown area alone, there were dozens of shops specializing in the instant manufacture of such things. He would find one of them and have a tag made with the name G. RAMSEY on it—for Gerald Ramsey, the name on his Plaza Hotel security card. Then he would buy a walkie-talkie from the first Radio Shack he passed, and a Walkman radio wherever he could find one.

Then . . .

Ah, yes, then.

While he was still in medical school and students everywhere around him were studying for finals round the clock, popping pills and drinking coffee in desperate attempts to stay awake, Sonny would go to a movie. He'd walk over to Westwood, spend a few hours in a movie theater, sometimes went to two movies in the same afternoon. Then he'd go back to the dorm and study intensely for five or six hours before taking another break. Went for a hot fudge sundae with strawberry ice cream, his favorite. Almonds on it, too. Then went back to studying again. Paced himself and never panicked. World enough and time.

Later this afternoon, Sonny just might go to a movie.

The Secret Service men Dobbs had brought with him from Washington followed him up the fire stairs to the first floor.

"What we're doing here is blocking off rear access to the room," Dobbs told them. "No one in or out without proper ID. Dave, you take the top of the steps here . . ."

"See you later," Dawson said, and hung back from the group already walking toward the elevator at the end of the corridor.

"You here, Hank," Dobbs said, "outside the elevator. Rest of you follow me."

Dobbs planted another of his men at the top of the steps leading down to the Baroque Room, and a fourth one at the bottom. Two British agents were already there, flanking the doors leading into the room. The men introduced themselves all around. One of the Brits told Dobbs there were two Mexican agents on the other side of the doors, and then wondered aloud if it'd be all right to have himself a smoke before the guests started arriving. Dobbs told the Brit he thought it would be okay, and then led his remaining agent into the pantry, where he planted him at the doors leading to the Baroque Room.

He felt he had the place pretty well covered.

Nodding curtly, he told the man in the pantry to keep a sharp eye out, and then went to check the Baroque Room itself, see who else was on the job.

A limousine was waiting at the curb.

She was thoroughly impressed. A limo, my, my. The last time she'd been in a limo was when her mother's sister, Aunt Hildy, got married in Teaneck, New Jersey.

The chauffeur came around to open the rear door for them as they came out of the building. Geoffrey glanced at her sidelong, gauging her reaction. She turned to him and smiled. A casual, accepting smile, this was a mature young woman who was used to stepping in and out of limousines wearing an ice blue gown cut dangerously low over the swelling tops of her breasts. Long blond hair piled on top of her head. Pearls her grandmother Constance had given her on her eighteenth birthday. Her mother's blue Judith Leiber bag with the larger pearl to match, which she'd taken from its flannel pouch on the top shelf of her mother's closet, even though she'd never been able to reach her to ask permission. There were some things you just *did*.

"Thank you," she said to the chauffeur, using the voice Princess Di might have used to a menial, not even glancing at him as she pulled back the skirt of the gown and stepped into the car. Geoffrey came in behind her, looking quite handsome in a dinner jacket, although the tie was knotted somewhat crookedly.

"I have to call my mother," she said.

"What?" he said.

The chauffeur had come around to the driver's side now, and was getting into the car. The door eased shut with the solid simple click of luxury. "Excuse me," Geoffrey said to her, and then leaned forward and said to the chauffeur, "We'll be going directly to the Plaza now."

"Thank you, sir," the chauffeur said, and eased the sleek long limo away from the curb. Elita felt as if she were inside a tinted glass spaceship gliding soundlessly through the stratosphere, the city far below, obliter . . .

278

"I'm sorry," Geoffrey said, "you were saying?"

"I was? Oh, yes, my mother. If you don't mind, I'd like to try her again when we get to the hotel."

"Something wrong?"

"Well . . . I just can't believe she's *still* on the beach. Would you like me to fix that for you?"

"Fix what?" he said, looking alarmed.

"The tie. It's a little crooked."

"Oh. Yes. Please do."

They turned to face each other on the leather seat. She smelled of something wonderful, it reminded him of journeys to the Cotswolds when he was a boy, the hillsides covered with wild flowers, the sky a piercing, aching blue. Her hands were adjusting the tie now. Blue eyes lowered. Intent. He looked at her face and longed suddenly to kiss her.

"There," she said, and looked up, satisfied.

"Thank you," he said softly.

"This is nice, isn't it?" she said, and smiled and sank back into the yielding leather seat, and unexpectedly took his hand.

He'd gone into the shower at ten minutes to six.

Soaped himself leisurely and calmly, shampooing his thick hair into a luxuriant froth of foam, thinking of the movie he'd seen this afternoon, wondering if Julia Roberts was as pretty in person as she was on the screen. Only saving grace. Otherwise, a totally dumb movie. He wondered who she was sleeping with now that she'd dumped the Sutherland kid.

He came out of the shower at nine minutes past six.
Watch on the counter, ticking off time digitally.
6:09.

He was through shaving at 6:24 . . . no, 6:25, the
watch informed him, the numeral changing even as he
looked at it.

He combed his hair.

Sprayed deodorant under his arms.

Looked at himself in the mirror.

Winked.

And went into the bedroom to dress.

Geoffrey looked at his watch.

It was already six-thirty, and he was eager to get upstairs to the Baroque Foyer, where the reception line
would be forming. This would not be *the* P.M. arriving—
Major being too major for such a minor event, oh dear,
Geoffrey thought—but it was most certainly *a* P.M., and
Geoffrey wanted to be on hand to greet her. Shake her
hand and let her know he was a loyal servant of Her
Majesty the Queen, not to be forgotten if ever Maggie
shared tea and opinions along with the scones and clot-
ted cream at Buckingham Palace.

He was standing discreetly beyond hearing distance of
Elita, who was at one of the wall phones downstairs at
Trader Vic's, where the Plaza people routed anyone desperate to ring up anyone else. If he wasn't mistaken, she
was now dialing the same number yet again, or perhaps
a different number this time. She had slipped out of one
high-heeled blue satin pump and was standing with the

stockinged foot resting on the toe of the other shod foot, looking entirely girlish and adorable, but he did wish she would hurry up.

He looked at his watch again.

6:32.

Please, Elita, he thought, get off the phone or we'll entirely miss her arriv . . .

Ah. At last.

He began moving toward her as she replaced the receiver on its hook, hoping she didn't plan to dial yet another number, catching her elbow as she turned away from the phone, a concerned look on her face.

"Is everything all right?" he asked.

"I still can't reach her," Elita said, and fell silent, obviously troubled as he hurried her upstairs and through the main lobby now, toward the elevator banks.

"Are you sure you dialed the right number?" he asked.

"I know it by heart. I even called the man next door . . ."

"This way," he said, and led her into the closest elevator.

". . . but I didn't get an answer there, either."

She was nibbling at her lower lip now. He took her hand in his, gave it a little reassuring squeeze.

"Perhaps she's at a party," he said.

"I hope so. It's just . . . so odd. Her not being in all day."

He refrained from suggesting that her mother was, after all, a grown woman who did not need to inform

281

her daughter of her exact whereabouts at any hour of the day. The elevator had whisked them up to the first floor, and he allowed her to precede him into the corridor, which he immediately saw was afloat with security people bobbing like blue-suited buoys on a sea of tuxedos and dinner gowns. He took her elbow again and led her to the entrance doors to the foyer, flanked by two agents, one of whom held a clipboard.

"Geoffrey Turner," he said. "And Miss Elita Randall."

The agent with the clipboard flipped to the second page of sheets attached to it. The other agent kept checking the corridor, making occasional eye contact with the floating agents scanning the arriving guests, most of them consular personnel eager to be on hand when the heads of state rolled in with the tide.

"Turner, yes, I have that right here, sir," the agent at the door said, British from the sound of him. "And the other was Crandall, sir?"

"Randall," Elita said.

"Yes, of course, pardon me, Miss," the agent said, and ran his finger up the page to the R's. "Yes, here we are, step right in, won't you please? Have a nice time."

"Thank you," Geoffrey said.

Elita was thinking how very polite the British were.

Ozzie Carruthers stood at the top of the carpeted steps on the Fifth Avenue side of the hotel, watching the uniformed doormen opening the doors of limousines and ushering elegantly dressed men and women onto the sidewalk. A black plastic tag with white letter-ing on it was pinned just over the breast pocket of his jacket, O. CARRUTHERS. A laminated Plaza Hotel identity card was clipped to the lapel above that pocket. A walkie-talkie was in his right hand. In his dark suit, white shirt, and maroon silk tie, he looked discreetly official. He was waiting to say hello to the President, a man he'd loved—*still* loved—a man he'd voted for each and every time.

A limousine with miniature British union jacks flying from both front fenders pulled to the curb. One of the hotel doormen approached the rear door and was po-litely but pertinently shouldered aside by a man in a dark suit who took up a position at the curb while three other men covered the car front, rear, and driver side. The chauffeur came around and opened the rear door. The Right Honorable Margaret Thatcher accepted his gloved hand as he assisted her out of the limousine. The hotel doorman smiled graciously and bowed her toward the steps. Surrounded by the four British agents, she swept past Carruthers, who inhaled the faint scent of her delicate perfume.

The Canadian Prime Minister and his wife were at the head of the greeting line—this was, after all, *their* day. Margaret Thatcher, simply but elegantly gowned, her hair splendidly coiffed, wearing no jewelry but a pair of diamond earrings and a gold necklace with a dia-mond drop pendant, spent at least five minutes chatting with them before moving along the line. Her smile gracious and warm, she exchanged handshakes and a few words with each of the people from the Canadian, British and Mexican consulates. Elita could hardly wait till she reached them.

"How do you do?" she said, and offered her hand to Geoffrey.

"Mrs. Thatcher," he said, taking her hand, "I'm Geoffrey Turner, Her Majesty's Foreign Service."

"Delighted," she said.

"And this is Miss Elita Randall . . ."

"How do you do?" Mrs. Thatcher said.

"I'm a great admirer of yours," Elita said.

"Why, thank you," Mrs. Thatcher said.

"I admire you greatly," Elita said, and thought Oh *God*!

"That's very kind of you," Mrs. Thatcher said, and moved on down the line, offering her hand and a "How-do-you-do?" to Lucy Strident from Passports and Visas, and managing not to wince when Lucy blared out her name, rank and serial number.

His obligation fulfilled, Geoffrey led Elita from the reception line the moment the Prime Minister's security people escorted her to the bar, where one of them obtained for her a glass of white wine. Elita told Geoffrey she would love a scotch and soda, and immediately wondered if anyone here would card her. Waiting while Geoffrey went for the drink, she looked around dazzle-eyed at all the handsome men and beautiful women in the room, the buzz of conversation everywhere around her, the clink of ice in glasses, the floating sound of laughter on a summer's night, and wondered who else famous would be here tonight.

Sonny came out of his room at ten minutes to eight. The walkie-talkie he'd bought at Radio Shack was in his right hand. The plastic name tag he'd had made at a place called Jefferson Office Supplies on Third Avenue was pinned above the breast pocket of his jacket. G. RAMSEY. White lettering on black plastic, three inches long by three quarters of an inch wide, at a cost of eighteen dollars plus tax, which he thought was highway robbery. The Plaza ID card McDermott had fashioned for him was clipped to the right-hand lapel pocket of his suit jacket. GERALD RAMSEY. SECURITY. He was wearing the blue suit, the white shirt, and the quiet silk tie. He looked very much the way Carruthers did, except for one thing. Carruthers wasn't armed. Tucked into the waistband of Sonny's trousers was the 9-mm Walther. Single cartridge in the chamber, loaded magazine containing eight additional cartridges in the butt of the pistol. And in the inside pocket of the jacket, just under the handkerchief pocket on the left, Sonny was carrying the twelve-ounce bottle of sarin, the transparent tape removed from its nozzle now. He had practiced reaching inside the jacket to draw it; it was only a bit more difficult than yanking a pistol from a shoulder holster. He had practiced turning the nozzle from OFF to STREAM. It took no more than a micro-second.

He was ready.

He stepped out of the room, looked up and down the

empty corridor, and started walking toward the elevator bank. A chambermaid dressed in nighttime black came out of one of the rooms, carrying soiled towels.

"Security," he said. "Everything all right?"

"Oh, *yes,* sir," she said, and virtually curtsied him by.

The corridor outside the Baroque Foyer was crawling with spooks. Sonny could virtually smell them. He walked past them confidently—never explain, never apologize—and went directly to where several men and women in formal attire were having their names checked at the entrance door. Two more agents stood there, one of them consulting a clipboard to which was attached several sheets of paper, the other scanning the corridor this way and that, the way agents did when they wanted to look terribly eagle-eyed and alert. Sonny went directly to the head of the line.

"Excuse me," he said to a white-haired woman in a bouffant pink gown. "Plaza Security," he said to the agent with the clipboard, and showed him a page he had torn from the message pad alongside the telephone in his room. The Plaza Hotel logo was at the top of the page. Under it, he had scrawled *Dr. and Mrs. Harry Rosenberg.* He showed this to the agent now. "Young girl called the office five minutes ago," he said. "Told me she was their baby sitter, needed to talk to them. Said they're at the party here."

The agent with the eagle eyes had zeroed his laser beam in on the ID tag and the name plate. Sonny simply ignored him. The one with the clipboard seemed impatient to get on with his job. There were a lot of important people standing on line here, waiting to be admitted to the foyer.

"Are they on your list?" Sonny asked.

The agent flipped to the second page on his clipboard.

"How do you spell that?" he asked.

British, Sonny thought. Meaning dull and plodding and stupid.

"R-O-S-E," he said.

"That all of it?"

"Here, have another look," Sonny said impatiently, and extended the piece of paper again.

The agent scanned the R's. "No one of that name," he said. "Sorry."

"I'd better check inside," Sonny said, and nodded to the eagle-eyed one, and walked right past both agents into the foyer.

He did not arrive until almost eight o'clock.

His limousine was immediately surrounded by Secret Service men in dark blue suits. He stepped out, offered his hand inside the car, and helped his wife out onto the carpeted sidewalk. Escorted by Secret Service men fore and aft, he and his wife came up the carpeted steps toward where Carruthers was standing near the entrance doors.

"Welcome to the Plaza, Mr. President," he said, grinning.

* * *

The Baroque Room was crowded and noisy, the guests milling in from the foyer and searching the tables for place cards, people recognizing friends or associates, men shaking hands, women kissing air. The dais was set up precisely where the good Miss Lubenthal had said it would be, in front of the columns at the far end of the room, opposite the three entrance doors. There were two agents standing on this side of the doors in the corner of the room closest to the dais.

"Big crowd," Sonny said to one of them.

"Very beeg, yes," the agent answered.

Spanish accent. Part of the Mexican team, Sonny guessed. The other agent was checking out Sonny's ID card and name plate. Slow-moving Mexican eyes roving over them in seeming casualness. Checking out, too, the bulge under Sonny's jacket where the bottle of sarin nested in the inside pocket. Figuring it for a pistol, finding it permissible on security personnel; the agent himself was packing what looked like a howitzer. Through the oval portholes in the doors, Sonny could see other suited men in the corridor outside. His escape route.

"A que hora servirán la cena?" he asked, switching to fluent Spanish.

"A las ocho," one of the agents said.

"Pero no para nosotros," the other one said sourly.

Margaret Thatcher was moving toward the dais now, being escorted by her personal heavy mob, four of them in all, each and every one of them as wide as the Thames. Sitting to the left of Mulroney, the Canadian Prime Minister, exchanging pleasantries with him. She would be the second to go, the whore. The chair on her left was still empty.

The chair to the right of Mrs. Mulroney was similarly empty. Sonny assumed that this was where Bush would be seated. President of the most powerful nation on earth would naturally take precedence over the Mexican leader for the place of honor on his hostess's right. This would make things more difficult. If Sonny took out Bush first, he would then have to sweep to the right for his second target and that would take him further away from the exit doors.

He was beginning to think it no longer mattered.

The moment he squeezed off the sarin, first at Bush, next at Thatcher if there was time . . .

He could no longer see an escape.

Everywhere he looked, there were agents. Agents to the left and right of the dais, agents behind the dais, agents at each of the windows overlooking the park, agents outside and inside all the doors. Thatcher's heavy mob behind her, trying to look as cuddly as teddy bears, but coming off as grizzlies. Bush would have his own army of Secret Service men. There was no way Sonny could get out of here alive.

He closed his eyes.

The Mexican agents looked at him in surprise.

They did not know he was praying.

One of the men from the British Consulate was telling a joke about Red Adair, the man who had worked to put out all the oil fires in Kuwait.

"Adair's sitting in the lobby of a hotel there, y'know, when this American tourist begins chatting him up. 'I hear Red Adair's in Kuwait,' he says. 'So he is,' Adair says. 'I hear he's staying right here at this hotel,' the tourist says. 'So he is,' Adair says. The tourist says, 'I'd love to meet him, I'm a great admirer of his . . .' "

Just what I said to Mrs. Thatcher, Elita thought, still embarrassed.

". . . and Adair says, 'Well, you've met him—*I'm* Red Adair.' The tourist jumps to his feet, takes Adair's hand, begins pumping it madly, and says, 'Am I glad to meet you! I've been an admirer of yours forever! Are you still screwing Ginger Rogers?' "

Everyone at the table began laughing, except for a woman Geoffrey had earlier introduced as Lucy Phipps, who now blushed scarlet and sank lower into her chair. And all at once, the laughter trailed, and all conversation seemed to stop as well, not only at the table where Elita sat with the Brits but everywhere around the room. In the hush that followed, Elita turned to look toward the entrance doors.

Sonny opened his eyes when the room went silent.

The Mexican agents were looking toward the entrance doors.

"Aquí viene," one of them said.

Sonny looked.

And saw not President *Bush* coming through those doors with Barbara on his arm but President *Reagan* with Nancy on his arm. The wrong goddamn President!

Waving his familiar wave to the hushed and reverent crowd, grinning his familiar grin. And suddenly there was applause for this popular idiot, this fool who'd succumbed to his vice-president's advice: Send the bombers. Had the letter not fallen into their possession, they'd have believed forever that the blood was on Reagan's hands. But through the merciful goodness of God, they now knew that the man responsible for young Hana's death was the man who'd written that persuasive document: Send the bombers. Destroy the Beloved Leader. Murder the infant daughter where she sleeps in her bed.

Bush.

The murderer Bush.

Not Reagan, the easily led fool, here to take his place beside the great whore of Britain, his one-time infamous partner.

Sonny would have killed them both in the next instant, but his instructions were clear.

Bush was the target.

You must not do anything to jeopardize your main objective.

It would have to wait till the Fourth, after all.

"Buenas noches," he said to the Mexicans, and began striding across the floor, passing the orchestra where it was tuning up discreetly on his right, the applause for Reagan tapering as he took his seat beside the bitch of England, Sonny's eyes searing with almost blinding hatred for both of them, the doors not twelve feet away now, the two agents who'd earlier been checking names

now standing inside the doors, side by side, legs apart, hands behind their backs, six feet away, and . . .

"Sonny!"

The name stopped him as effectively as a rifle shot.

He turned, but only for a second.

And caught a glimpse of Elita rising from her chair at a table near one of the big arched windows.

He turned back to the doors again. Nodding to the agents, he said, "See you later," and they parted to let him through.

Behind him, he heard Elita calling yet another time. "Sonny!"

He did not look back.

12

Why had he run?

Hadn't he *seen* her last night? Heard her?

She'd screamed at the top of her lungs. Startled the Brits—especially Miss Lucy Phipps—out of their collective wits. Well, the *shock* of it. Seeing him there. In a business suit and wearing some kind of identification tag, was he the doctor in residence or something? I mean . . . what was he *doing* there? And why had he ignored her, dashed through those doors and out into the corridor as if there was an emergency someplace, calling Dr. Hemkar, emergency in the operating room, Dr. Hemkar, report to the operating room at once.

"Sonny!" she'd yelled, and "Sonny!" again, and then, embarrassed to death—first her gushing to Mrs. Thatcher and then bouncing out of her chair like a teenager—she almost whispered his name the third time, a question mark at the end of it this time, "Sonny?" and since she was standing anyway, she muttered, "Excuse me, please," and went after him. By the time she reached the corridor, he was gone. Penn Station all over again. And now, ladies and germs, it gives me great pleasure to present The Amazing Disappearing Dr. Krishnan Hem . . . oops, where'd he go? Amazing.

He probably hadn't seen her or heard her. There'd been a lot of noise in the place, after all, people talking and laughing and table-hopping, waiters bustling about, it was entirely possible that her voice had been drowned in the babble and boil. Because surely, after what they'd done together, after the intimacies they'd shared, he wouldn't just *ignore* her . . . would he? I mean, if he'd heard her or seen her, would he have just run *off* that way? Unless there was some kind of dire emergency that required a doctor. Which may have been the case, after all. His beeper had gone off and he'd . . .

Wasn't that a walkie-talkie she'd seen in his hand?

Well, a doctor.

She supposed doctors sometimes carried walkie-talkies. She guessed. Especially at a large important function like that one, where he was most likely the doctor in attendance, *that* was the word she'd been looking for. There to be on hand in case anyone had a fainting spell or a fit, I'm a doctor, ma'am, please let me through. Open the woman's blouse, put his stethoscope to her chest, lucky lady. Just thinking of him, she . . .

Damn it, she had to *stop* this.

He had heard her.

He had seen her.

He had ignored her.

Period.

She picked up the phone and dialed her mother's number at the beach.

She let the phone ring a dozen times, and then she hung up and punched out the numbers again, and let it ring another dozen times. On the offchance that Mr. Hackett next door might have gone out there by now—this was Thursday already and a lot of people were starting the Fourth of July weekend early—she dialed his number, too, and let it ring and ring before finally giving up.

In the basement of the Hackett house, Sonny was dissecting Carolyn Fremont's body.

He worked expertly, wishing he had a scalpel or a surgical saw, but settling for a cleaver he'd taken from the kitchen, and a hacksaw he'd found hanging on the basement wall. He planned to pack the separate body parts into plastic garbage bags, disposing of them tonight, after yet another glorious Hamptons sunset. Tie the bags loosely so that the air inside would eventually escape and cause them to sink. Toss them into the ocean on separate strands of isolated beach, miles apart, watch them floating away to Europe. The head, the torso, the severed legs and arms.

Even though he hadn't dissected a cadaver since medical school, the task was virtually automatic, requiring little thought. He found what he was doing somewhat relaxing, in fact, the way roller skating or riding a bicycle might have been, his hands reverting to a skill he had learned years ago, freeing his mind for other thoughts.

The idiot last night.

Calling out his name in a room thronged with strollers and spooks.

What the hell was she doing there?

She hadn't *followed* him there, had she? Well, no, she couldn't have. It was just one of those damn ridiculous coincidences that sometimes toppled empires. It all got back to the train again. The mistake he'd made on the train. Automatically giving her the Sonny Hemkar cover name instead of the Scott Hamilton double cover. Dumb. But excusable. No. Unforgivable. Because now she was here to haunt him, popping up like a nemesis where he'd least expected her, shrieking "Sonny!" at him across the room, when his name plate and his ID card read something entirely different.

Come *on,* he thought, and hacked again at the cartilage separating femur from tibia.

Perhaps he should call her.

Ask her to please stop bothering him.

No.

Better to let sleeping dogs lie.

He picked up the portion of leg he had severed, dropped it into a black plastic garbage bag, and set the bag on the floor beside the work bench.

Carolyn Fremont's lifeless blue eyes stared up at him as he began severing her head from her torso.

The two people staring up at the Statue of Liberty were not the slightest bit impressed by her awesome majesty. They were looking for good camera angles.

These were the President's advance men, and they were here to make certain that everything went well, campaignwise, on the Fourth of July. You could maybe fool some of the people most of the time and most of the people some of the time, but you couldn't fool anybody *any*time when it came to a good television show. Heather Broward—who was female but nonetheless one of the President's men—sometimes thought that America itself was one big gaudy television show.

"How about we line the band up behind him?" she suggested.

She was dressed for work—linen slacks, loafers, a sand-colored long-sleeved cotton blouse, a peach-colored ribbon holding her short brown hair, a Polaroid camera slung on a strap over her shoulder. Ralph Dickens, the man with her, was sixty-three years old and had been setting up Republican campaign stops from when Nixon was making his first bid for the presidency, but thirty-one-year-old Heather was his boss. He figured placing the band up behind The Man would steal his thunder, but he said nothing about it. He was thinking it was nice and cool out here on the island with the river breezes playing. He was wondering how hot it would be on the Fourth.

"Think they'd all *fit* up there?" Heather asked. "The band?"

She was indicating the area above ground level, some fifteen, twenty feet higher than where they were standing and looking up. White wall, looked like limestone or something, good backdrop for the podium behind which the President would stand, battery of network microphones on it. Blue suit, white shirt, red tie—the Republican uniform. White wall behind him. Above him the Marine Band in dress uniforms, all red-white-and-blue, and then the grey stone of the pedestal and above that the Lady herself all coppery green. Not bad, Ralph had to admit.

"How many people are in the band, anyway?"

"We can trim it to fit," Ralph said.

He'd been through this shit a thousand times before. The President of the United States wanted a four-hundred-piece orchestra, he got a four-hundred-piece orchestra. He wanted just one guy with a piccolo up his ass, he got that, too. When you were President of the United States, you got whatever you wanted, period.

"We'd better go up there, check out the width, see how many musicians we can fit up there," Heather said.

"Good idea," Ralph said.

"How the hell do you *get* up there?" she asked.

The more CIA Agent Alex Nichols studied the letter purportedly written by Bush when he was Vice President in 1986, the more he wondered *why* it had been written and how it had ended up at the General Investigation Directorate in Tripoli.

During World War II, MI5—in collaboration with Naval Intelligence and the Twenty-Two Committee—sent a British submarine to the coast of Spain. Its mission was to drop off the corpse of a so-called Major Martin of the Royal Marines, who incidentally happened to be carrying in his dispatch case plans describing a forthcoming totally fabricated Allied invasion of Greece. The Germans fell for the ruse, and were caught with their pants down when the Allies invaded Sicily instead.

When you got hold of something like this letter, you had to begin wondering why somebody had gone through all this trouble. Well, maybe not so much trouble, after all. Any intelligence agent worth his salt—as Miss Piggy Peggot had put it—could work up a piece of vice-presidential stationery and type on it any damn thing he felt like. The stupid part, the amateur part—and this was what separated the men from the boys—was that he'd used Bush's present-day signature on it, instead of . . .

He suddenly wondered if Mossad had cooked up the letter; he wouldn't put anything past the Israelis, they were the sneakiest fuckin' spies in the entire universe.

But why?

Work up a phony piece of goods, hide it like it was the family jewels till some sucker took the bait and nabbed it. Then sit back and wait for it to work its way into the hands of the GID. Which, if their information was correct, was exactly where it had finally surfaced, only to be pilfered yet again by a conscientious digger.

If the Israelis were behind all this, what were they hoping to gain?

Nothing that he could see.

In fact, what could *anyone* gain by faking a letter and making certain it got into Libyan hands?

And then, all at once, Alex remembered something

he'd been taught at The Farm, when he was just beginning to learn his craft. The instructor was a man who'd spent twenty-two years in the Middle East before coming back home to teach new CIA recruits like Alex. He'd been talking about Iraq's *Al Mukhabarat,* when suddenly he'd cocked his head to one side and said—somewhat wistfully as Alex now recalled—"There's an old Arab proverb that's saved my life more times than I can count. 'He who forgets is lost. He who forgives is doomed.' "

The fake letter had ended up in the hands of Libyan intelligence.

It placed directly at Bush's doorstep full responsibility for the air raid that had killed Quaddafi's fifteen-month-old daughter.

Alex figured he now had something to go on.

The telephones were secure. The one here at the beach, the one at SeaCoast. They could freely discuss whatever they wished, with no need for codes or veiled meanings.

"A man's fate is written on his forehead," Arthur said.

"I know that," Sonny said.

"If it had been fated for Bush to die last night, God would have willed it," Arthur said. "This means only that the Fourth will be a more propitious date."

"I'm sure," Sonny said.

He wasn't at all sure.

"I've been trying to reach you," he said.

"Yes, I have your messages. But I've been busy working for *you*, Sonny."

"Oh?"

"I don't know if you've heard or read anything about this second murder . . ."

"I have, yes."

"I've been trying to find out who or why."

"What do you think?"

"Well . . . I hope you haven't been targeted."

Sonny hoped so, too.

"What have you got so far?" he asked.

"Not much. But I have my very best people on it."

"Good," Sonny said.

He was thinking two of Arthur's very best people were already dead.

"In any case, I don't want you to be concerned about it."

No, huh?

"If it turns out you're in danger, you'll get all the protection you need."

Like the protection the two women got?

"But getting back to last night," Arthur said, "at least it gave you an opportunity to study the security setup."

"It won't apply," Sonny said.

"No?" Arthur said, sounding surprised.

"It wasn't representative," Sonny said. "There were agents from *four* countries there. It won't be that way on the Fourth."

"Lighter, do you think?"

"Almost certainly. The island will be closed to the

301

public till noon. If there're half a dozen people around him, I'll be surprised."

"That should make your job easier."

"God willing," Sonny said.

"But be prepared for . . ."

"I will be."

". . . the worst," Arthur said, the tone of impatience creeping into his voice again. "There's a saying you may not be familiar with. My mother taught it to me. It goes like this. 'When you hear of no robbers, lock the door twice.' It means . . ."

"I understand," Sonny said.

"They may *double* the security only because they feel *too* secure."

"Yes, I understand."

"So expect an army . . ."

"I will."

"And be happy with a platoon."

"I'll be prepared for either," Sonny said.

"I'll see you tomorrow morning," Arthur said.

"At ten," Sonny said.

"Is there anything I can do for you meanwhile?"

"Yes," Sonny said.

Elita caught the jitney to Westhampton Beach on Seventieth Street and Lexington Avenue at eleven-fifteen that Thursday morning. She had packed into her mother's Louis Vuitton bag the lingerie and shoes she'd requested, and she had packed for herself a small duffle containing a pair of blue jeans, four T-shirts, a half-dozen panties, a pair of sandals, and—just in case—a pair of French-heeled shoes and a black cotton shift. She planned to stay at the beach only through the Fourth, returning to the city sometime Sunday.

Her concern for her mother had given way to anger.

A person should know better than to go gallivanting around—an expression her mother was fond of using—without first informing any other person who might be worried about her. When Elita went off to UCLA a year ago, she and her mother made a deal of sorts. If ever one of them planned to be away for a while, even if it was just for a couple of days, she would inform the other, and leave a number where she could be reached. A simple bargain which Elita had, in truth, begun finding too restrictive in recent months, but which had served them both extremely well until then. Until *now,* actually, when her mother apparently felt it was perfectly okay to break a solemn contract and disappear from the face of the earth without so much as a lah-dee-dah. Just a phone call would have been sufficient. Hi, Elita, I'm off to Phoenix, Arizona, for a few days, here's where I'll be. But, no. Silence instead. And anxiety. Or anger. Which was how anxiety usually translated itself, thank you, Professor Jaeger, Psychology 101.

The jitney dropped her off in front of the Quogue Emporium Mall at a bit past one-thirty. She got into a waiting taxi and gave the driver the address on Dune Road. He didn't want to go into the sand driveway because his tires were either too low, or too inflated, or whatever the hell they were, she couldn't make any sense at all of what he was saying. Either way, he dropped her off at the top of it, for which discourtesy she tipped him only half a buck. Carrying the bags down the drive, she noticed a car parked at the Hackett house next door, and wondered why Mr. Hackett hadn't answered the phone all those times she'd called.

Shrugging, she went around the side of the house to the service entrance where her mother always hid the key in a little magnetized box fastened to the rear side of the fill spout for the oil tank. The key was where it usually was. Elita unlocked the kitchen door, put down the bags, blinked into the sunshine streaming through the window over the sink, and yelled, "Mom?"

There was no answer.

"Mom?" she yelled again, and stood stock still, listening.

Where the hell *are* you? she thought, and then, aloud, she shouted, "Mom? Where the hell are you?"

There was only silence.

In the driveway next door, she heard the car starting.

She went to the window and saw it backing out.

The sun glancing off its windshield made it impossible to see the driver's face.

Detective-Lieutenant Peter Hogan welcomed the opportunity to get out of the office. He had always thought of himself as an active street cop until he'd been promoted three years ago, and all of a sudden found himself pushing papers around a desk. The murder of one of his best detectives—and incidentally one of his closest friends—gave him the excuse he needed to get out into the field again.

He started the investigation into Al Santorini's death the way he'd have started any other homicide case. He tried to work it backward from the time Santorini's body was discovered in the laundry cart, hoping to learn what had brought him to the Hilton in the first place. The assistant manager who'd talked to Santorini informed Hogan that he'd clocked the call in at one o'clock sharp, and that all the detective had wanted to know was the name of whoever was in room 2312. He'd told him they had a man named Albert Gomez registered in that room, and that he'd checked into the hotel on Thursday, the twenty-fifth of June. That was it. The manager remembered that the call had come at one, because he'd just got back from lunch.

Hogan was trying to piece together a 24–24.

The twenty-four hours preceding a homicide were important because anything the victim had done, anyone the victim had talked to during that time, might provide information leading to his killer. The twenty-four hours following a homicide were important in that everything was still fresh during that time. The killer, unless he was more professional than most murderers Hogan had known, would not yet have covered his tracks. The trail would not yet have been obscured. The longer a murder case dragged on, the narrower became the hope of solving it. Al Santorini had been killed on Monday. This was now Thursday. As far as Hogan was concerned, the killer already had a three-day edge.

He went through the Detective Division reports Santorini had filed in triplicate. He'd been investigating two separate murders, the victims both women with British passports, both of them tattooed with some kind of green sword. One of them had lived on the Upper West Side, the other on the Upper East Side. East side, west side, all around the town, some fuckin' city. Santorini had been in contact with someone named Geoffrey Turner at the British Consulate and also with an FBI agent named Michael Grant, downtown at Federal Plaza. Nothing in the files told Hogan where Santorini had been on Monday before he ended up dead at the Hilton.

But the desk sergeant at the Two-Five, where Homicide North had its offices, told Hogan that the last time he'd seen Santorini was around ten-thirty that morning when he'd passed the desk on his way out. He'd said only, "Heading downtown, George," which was the desk sergeant's name. He did not say *where* downtown. Both of the dead ladies lived more or less downtown. Since the Two-Five was located at 120 *East* 119th Street, Hogan decided to check out the more convenient East Side location first.

He was in the upstairs bedroom—lying on the bed, looking through the newspapers he'd bought in town, hoping to garner more information about the President's Fourth of July speech—when the doorbell rang, startling him. He swung his legs over the side of the bed, called, "Just a moment, please," and then went downstairs. Standing just inside the front door, he asked, "Who is it?"

"Mr. Hackett?"

"No, I'm sorry, he's not here," Sonny said.

"I'm sorry to bother you," a woman's voice said, "but could you please open the door?"

Annoyed, he unlocked the door and opened it.

Elita Randall was standing there.

There was, for each of them standing on either side of that doorjamb, an identical shocking instant of recognition. It was as if they had run into each other again at the base of Victoria Falls or the summit of Kilimanjaro, or for that matter any other unlikely, unforeseen, and totally unexpected location. Here across the open doorway of a house at Westhampton Beach, they stared at each other uncomprehendingly, and wide-eyed, and literally open-mouthed, neither of them able even to breathe a name, each separately stunned into mutual speechlessness.

And then—just as there'd been separate agendas for each of them on the day they visited the Statue of Liberty—there were now separate recoveries and separate wonderings and separate fears and separate hopes and separate plans for the future.

She was the first to blink her way out of the silence.

"Jesus," she said, "what are *you* doing here?"

"I . . . Martin is a friend of mine."

He was shaking his head in wonder now. How the hell had she *found* him?

"Mr. Hackett?" she asked, still astonished.

"Yes. But . . . what . . . how . . . ?"

"My mother has the house next door," she said, and nodded in the direction of the house where first he'd seen Carolyn Fre . . .

Her *mother*?

His heart was suddenly beating very fast.

She was thinking how gorgeous he looked barefooted, in blue jeans and a T-shirt.

He was thinking her mother was in black plastic bags in the basement.

"This is . . . I just can't . . . I just came over to ask Mr. Hackett if he'd seen her. And here I find . . . God, this is . . ."

"It is amazing," he said, and smiled.

He was thinking she was trouble.

She was thinking she'd never let him out of her sight again. Now that she'd found him again, she'd . . .

"Was that you at the Plaza?" she asked.

He had still not moved out of the doorframe.

He was thinking he could not let her into this house.

"The Plaza?" he said.

Trouble, he thought. She's trouble.

"Wasn't that you? In a blue suit? With a walkie-talkie in your hand?"

"No."

"I was *sure* it was you."

"No."

"Aren't you going to ask me in?"

"Well, I . . ."

"God, I'm so glad to *see* you again," she said, and

threw herself into his arms, virtually knocking him out of the doorframe and back into the living room. "Listen," she said, her arms around his neck, "you'd better not run out on me ever again, you hear?" She kissed him on the mouth, a light little peck. "Have you got that?" she said.

"I've got it," he said.

"Gee, I've never been inside this house," she said, taking his hand and leading him deeper into the living room. "It's really very nice, isn't it?"

"Yes, it's lovely," he said.

Sunlight was streaming in through the French doors. Sunlight glowed like molten gold on the water beyond.

"How do you happen to know Mr. Hackett?"

"A friend of my parents," he said.

Careful, he thought.

"I called you in Los Angeles, you know," she said.

"Called me? Where?"

"At your apartment . . ."

"How'd . . . ?"

"And also at the hospital. I spoke to a doctor named BJ something, he said you'd better have a good story for Hokie. What's in here? The kitchen?" she said, and was about to push open the swinging door when he shouted, "Don't!"

The plastic bottle of sarin was in the refrigerator. He didn't want anyone going anywhere *near* that bottle.

"It's a mess in there," he said.

"Okay," she said, "let's try the bedroom instead," and looked at him, head cocked, one eyebrow raised in faint inquiry. "Must be a bedroom, no?" she said, and smiled in invitation, her eyes narrowing smokily. "No?" she said again.

He shook his head.

"I have work to do," he said.

"Okay, later," she said airily, but her heart was pounding. "I've got to make some calls, anyway, find out if any of her friends . . . hey, *you* didn't see her, did you?"

"No," he said.

"Blond, blue-eyed? People say we look alike?"

"No, I didn't see anyone like that."

She came to where he was standing. Stood very close to him.

"I'll be back," she said. "Don't go away."

"I won't," he said.

The place smelled as if a tiger had been let loose in it. Hogan folded his handkerchief into a triangular-shaped mask, and tied it over his nose and mouth. He knew that the Nineteenth had already been through the apartment and had probably bagged and tagged anything there'd been to find. He was guessing, too, that Santorini had been through *both* apartments with a fine comb, this one here on the east side and the one further uptown on the west side. What he didn't know was whether or not he'd found anything that had led him to Albert Gomez, who- ever the hell *he* turned out to be; with race relations bubbling close to the boiling point in this city, all the police needed was some crazy Latino fuck running around sticking icepicks in cops' eyes.

My *God*, the lady must've let her pet tiger piss all over everything in the place.

Hogan wondered if Santorini had gone through the garbage.

He did not want to go through the garbage.

He went into the lady's bedroom instead. Same stink in here, how could anyone have *lived* in this joint? He checked out the closet and the dresser drawers. Didn't find anything but a lot of frumpy clothes. He sure as hell didn't want to go through that garbage. There was a small desk in one corner of the room, gooseneck lamp on it, some envelopes sitting on the desktop, right where the lady had left them. The detectives from the One-Nine had probably gone through them, figured they weren't going to be of any help to anybody, left them sitting there. A bill from Con Ed, another bill from a dry cleaning establishment named Madame Claudette's, a third one from Citibank, that was it. He reached into the Citibank envelope, removed from it what turned out to be a MasterCard bill. Scanned the bill, nothing of any importance he could see on it, restaurants, shops, the usual . . . well, wait a minute . . .

No.

Saw the word United, thought it might be United Airlines, which would've meant the lady had taken a trip someplace. But it was only a charge to something called United Neighbors, which he guessed was some kind of Upper East Side Do-Gooder association to which she'd contributed twenty-five bucks which she should've spent on a cleaning lady instead, get rid of the tiger piss. He gave the bill another run-through, and then put it back into its envelope.

There was a drawer over the kneehole.

He opened it.

One of those Month At A Glance calendars. He guessed the One-Nine had gone through that, too, and found nothing significant in it, otherwise it wouldn't be sitting here like a lox. He looked through it, anyway, comparing the month of June to the month of May to see if the lady had done anything special or unusual that might have led to her murder on the twenty-sixth. He found nothing extraordinary. Well, two calendar entries for appointments at a place called SeaCoast, which he guessed was a restaurant, one for twelve-thirty on the twenty-third of June and the other for the same time the following day. Eating in the same restaurant on two successive days seemed a bit odd to him, especially since the lady didn't seem to dine out all that often. He found a Yellow Pages directory in the bottom drawer to the right of the kneehole, and looked up SeaCoast under restaurants. There was no restaurant named SeaCoast in the city of New York.

He looked in the lady's personal telephone directory, which the One-Nine again had left behind, or perhaps brought back after they were done with it, such courtesies were not unknown in the NYPD, although exceedingly rare in cases where the owner of the property was no longer alive to complain. Either way, the directory was here to be studied, but there was no SeaCoast listed in it, so Hogan figured the hell with it. His eyes were beginning to smart from the stink of tiger piss in here.

In the middle drawer on the right-hand side of the desk, he found three little books with green covers.

He lifted the topmost book from the drawer, and opened it.

There was some kind of funny squiggly writing in it.

"Federal Bureau of Investigation," a woman's voice said.

"Agent Grant, please," Hogan said.

"Special Agent Michael Grant, yes, sir," the woman said, subtly correcting his error; in the FBI, all agents were *special* agents.

Grant came on the line thirty seconds later. Hogan introduced himself, told him what he was working, told him he'd found some kind of little green books with foreign writing in them, and wondered if Santorini had discussed these when he called.

"If this is the Green Book," Grant said, "then we . . ."

"Three of them. *Three* green books," Hogan said.

"Collectively, I mean," Grant said.

"Uh-huh."

"If this is what I think it is, then yes, we discussed it. In connection with the scimitar tattoos. Apparently he had some victims with scimitar tattoos . . ."

"Yeah, the green swords."

"Yes. And he wanted to know if I knew anything

313

about an Iranian terrorist group that called itself Scimitar."

"Uh-huh."

"I told him our current thinking was that they'd been inactive since the JFK bombing . . ."

"Uh-huh."

". . . back in 1989. So we sort of eliminated them as . . ."

"He was considering them as possibles, huh?"

"Well, I think he was looking for a place to hang his hat."

"Uh-huh. So where'd you go from there?"

"We talked about Libya a little. Because the tattoos were green, you know . . ."

"Uh-huh."

". . . kicking around the idea that this might be something Libyan, *those* crazy bastards. He wears women's dresses and makeup, you know . . ."

"Who?"

"Quaddafi. And goes to sleep with a teddy bear."

"I didn't know that."

"Yeah. Totally weird. Sends his people out to buy new bedsheets whenever he checks into a hotel room. Nuts."

"Uh-huh. So what'd you tell him?"

"Your guy? I said I didn't have anything new on Libyan intelligence, the whole thing sort of died down after the big scare six years ago, when everybody thought Reagan was on a hit list."

"Uh-huh."

"I told him he'd do better contacting the CIA. They'd

be the ones with any current stuff. He said he might do that."

"I don't see any indication he did," Hogan said.

"Well," Grant said.

They were both thinking he'd been murdered before he'd got around to it.

"Have you got a number for them?" Hogan asked.

"Sure, hold a sec."

Hogan waited.

When Grant came back on the line, he gave him the number of the New York Field Office of the CIA, and told him the man he usually dealt with there was a man named Conrad Templeton. Hogan thanked him for his time, hung up, and checked through Santorini's files again, to see if he'd missed anything about a call to the CIA. There was nothing. He dialed 755-0027, got a woman's voice saying, "Central Intelligence," and asked for Agent Templeton.

"One moment, please," the woman said.

Hogan waited, wondering how a nice Irish kid from Staten Island had grown up to be a man phoning secret agents all over the fuckin' city. He was hoping this really *was* some kind of crazy green spy shit from Libya; you could always unite New Yorkers by telling them some lunatic foreigner was running around hurting innocent people. Though, tell you the truth, most people in this city thought cops *deserved* to get stabbed in the eye. He kept waiting. He was just about to light a cigar, when a man came on the line.

"Alex Nichols," the man said.

"This is Detective-Lieutenant Peter Hogan," Hogan said. "Homicide North."

"Yes, sir."

"I was trying to reach Agent Templeton . . ."

"In the field just now. I'm his superior, maybe I can help you."

"I hope so," Hogan said. "One of my people was killed during a double-homicide investigation. The victims were tattooed with green scimitars, and I just now found three little green books that the Feds tell me . . ."

"Where are you?" Nichols asked at once.

She sat at the desk just to the left of the windows facing the beach, thumbing through her mother's telephone directory, sorting out city people from beach people. The next beach name she recognized was Mc-Nulty, James and Amanda. She dialed the number and waited.

"Hello?" a woman's voice said.

"Mrs. McNulty?"

"No, this is Helga," the woman said. "Who's calling, please?"

"Elita Randall."

"Hold on, please."

"Tell her it's Caro . . ."

But she was gone.

Another woman came onto the line.

"Hello?"

"Mrs. McNulty?"

316

"Yes?"

"This is Elita Randall, Carolyn Fremont's daughter?"

"Hello, Elita, how are you?"

"Fine, thanks, Mrs. McNulty. I'm sorry to bother you . . ."

"No bother at all."

"But I'm trying to locate my moth . . ."

"Helga! What is that dog *doing*? Excuse me, darling. Helga!"

Elita waited. In the background, she could hear voices and barking. At last Mrs. McNulty came back onto the line.

"I'm sorry, darling," she said, "we're getting ready for a Fourth of July party, and the caterers are here, and the dog decides at this very moment . . . well, never mind, it's been taken care of. You were saying?"

"I'm trying to get in touch with my mother, would you happen to know where I can reach her?"

"Well, I'm sure she's out here, have you called the house?"

"I'm *at* the house now, Mrs. McNulty. I came out when . . ."

"Well, I wouldn't worry, darling, I'm sure she's all right."

"It's just . . ."

"Helga! Will you please get that damn dog . . . ? Excuse me, darling," she said. "Helga! How many times do . . . ?"

Her voice faded. There was more barking. More yelling. Elita waited a moment longer, and then hung up and began leafing through her mother's directory again.

Except for the bag containing her head, all of the black plastic bags were bulky and awkward to handle. He loaded all five of them in the trunk of the car, and then went back into the house for his suitcase.

The suitcase was packed much as it had been yesterday, when he'd checked into the Plaza. In addition to some casual clothes he planned to wear tomorrow, there was the same blue suit and muted tie, a fresh white button-down shirt, clean underwear and socks, the same polished black shoes. The sealed plastic bottle of sarin was inside a shoe again, a fresh strip of transparent tape holding its nozzle in the OFF position. He got nervous each time he handled it. He was nervous now as he placed the suitcase on the floor behind the passenger seat. He went back into the house for a last-minute check, making sure all the lights were out and the faucets turned off, and then he locked the front door, and got into the car.

In the house next door, Elita didn't hear the car starting because she was on the phone with a woman named Sally Hemmings who'd just told her she'd seen her mother at a cocktail party this past Monday night.

"Actually," Elita said, "I spoke to her after that. On Tuesday. But I haven't been able to reach her since, and I'm beginning . . ."

"Well, I'm not surprised," Sally said.

"What do you mean?"

"She's probably in San Diego."

"San Diego? Why would she . . . ?"

"That's where the young man lives," Sally said.

"What young man?"

"The one she was with Monday night."

"Do you know his name?" Elita asked.

"Scott Hamilton."

"And you say he lives in San Diego?"

"Owns a cable television station out there."

"Then . . . what's he doing in Westhampton?"

"I assumed he was visiting your mother."

"Visiting my . . ."

"*Staying* with her. That's the impression I got."

"Well, no, he's not here. Neither of them are here. I'm *at* the beach house, and it's empty."

"Like I said," Sally said knowingly. "San Diego."

The hotel Sonny had chosen was the Marriott Financial Center on West Street, just a short walking distance from Battery Park. He felt the room rate was exorbitant for this part of the city—two hundred and twenty-five dollars for a single—but the location was perfect, and there were five hundred and four rooms in the hotel, a number that virtually guaranteed anonymity.

He allowed a doorman to take his suitcase out of the backseat of the car . . .

"Anything in the trunk, sir?"

"Nothing."

. . . and left the car with a valet who gave him a

claim ticket for it. He checked in as Lucas Holding, Jr., showing a valid Visa card made out to that name. The bellhop carried his bag up to room 1804. He tipped him two dollars. The moment he left the room, he dialed Arthur's direct line at SeaCoast. The phone here at the hotel wasn't secure. He would have to go through the ritual.

"SeaCoast Limited," Arthur said.

"Arthur Scopes, please," he said.

"Who's calling?"

"Scott Hamilton."

"This is Martin, go ahead, Scott."

"I'm here. Room 1804."

"Fine. I have that item you wanted."

"I'll see you tomorrow then."

"And will you still be here at ten?"

"You can be sure," he said, and hung up.

From his room on the eighteenth floor of the hotel, Sonny could see the Hudson River and the Statue of Liberty.

He looked at his watch.

5:27.

Still time to do what had to be done.

He would go out for dinner at seven-thirty, eight o'clock, and then come back to the hotel for the car.

It was hard to believe that the two men from the Westhampton Beach Police Department were detectives. They looked as if they should be selling haberdashery in Oxnard, California. Then again, Elita's concept of what detectives should look like had been derived entirely from motion pictures and television. These two didn't seem like cops, but they seemed to be asking all the right questions, so she guessed they were okay.

One of them was named Gregors and the other was named Mellon.

They wanted to know what she and her mother had talked about on the phone this past Tuesday.

"Did she say where she might be going that night?" Gregors asked.

"Or the next day?" Mellon asked.

"No," she said. "Nothing like that."

"And you say some of these people you spoke to on the phone saw her on Monday night, is that what you said?"

"Yes. With a man named Scott Hamilton."

"Do you know anyone by that name?"

"No, I don't."

"Mother ever mention anyone by that name?"

"No."

"Better call these people she spoke to," Mellon said to Gregors.

"See if they can describe him for us," Gregors said.

"Can you give us their names?" Mellon asked. "These people you talked to?"

"I'll get my mother's book," Elita said.

She went over to the Hackett house the moment the detectives left.

Sonny's car wasn't in the driveway.

She rang the doorbell. No answer. And then knocked. No answer. She tried the doorknob. The door was locked. She went around to the kitchen door and tried that one, too. Locked. There were no lights on anywhere in the house.

She guessed he was gone again.

After the huge grey buildings of finance and justice closed their doors for the day; after all the work was done, and all the people were gone; after darkness fell, and the streets emptied, and the only sound was that of a patrolman's footsteps, or the hiss of a passing automobile, or the click of a traffic light; then here in this lower part of the city, there were only eyeless buildings and long shadows and emptiness.

Sonny was looking for garbage dumpsters.

Whenever he spotted one, he checked the street ahead and behind and if there were no pedestrians and automobile traffic, he stopped the car alongside the hulking metal container, popped the trunk from the button on the door to the left of the driver's seat, got out of the car at once, went around to the back, raised the trunk lid all the way, hoisted out one of the black plastic bags, and hurled it up into the dumpster.

Took maybe forty seconds.

By eleven o'clock that night, he had disposed of all five bags.

He wondered if he could still catch a late movie.

13

He was awake with the sun.

He felt alert and alive and anticipatory—but today was only the third, and tomorrow seemed an eon away. He ordered a hearty breakfast of orange juice, eggs over easy with country sausages, buttered biscuits, and coffee. He switched from morning show to morning show, hoping to catch a glimpse of where the networks planned to film the President's speech to the nation, but there was nothing. At a quarter to eight, he dressed casually and went downstairs.

At the camp in Kufra, they used to run the trainees ten miles every day in the desert heat. In Los Angeles, he used to do three miles around the UCLA track, morning or evening, depending on which shifts he pulled at the hospital. This morning, dressed as he was, he had to settle for a fast, brisk walk. This part of New York was strange to him, even stranger in that a holiday pall already seemed to have settled upon the city. Early Friday getaways were common enough during the summer months, but this was a long holiday weekend, and with the Fourth falling on a Saturday, most people didn't have to work next Monday. As he walked through the sparsely populated streets of the financial district, he had the sense of a city already abandoned, its inhabitants having fled to the mountains, the seashores, or the lakes.

He was alone in an alien land.

A country he had slept in for more years than he cared to count.

Awake at last.

Walking uptown along the East River Drive, he looked out over the water to where a red tugboat was churning through a mild chop, raised his gaze farther out to where a tanker plodded heavily along, and wondered what kind of river traffic he could expect tomorrow. He had already concocted what he believed to be a feasible means of escape by water—if ever he managed to get three feet from the scene without being gunned down. Getting killed was a distinct possibility. But losing his life was something to be desired, not feared. Only failure was to be scorned.

Tomorrow, he would get to the President by whatever means possible. If it meant unscrewing the cap of that plastic bottle and hurling the sarin at him from a foot away—he would do it. If it required running through a storm of bullets to reach him, tossing the poison into his face, into his eyes, onto his lips, killing the murderer before he himself was slain—he would do it. And he would seek no greater glory than the knowledge that he had served his God and his leader and his people. But if there was the slightest chance that he might live to serve again, then he would seize it.

He felt certain that his plan of attack would work.

The President would die.

He felt less confident about his means of escape, but here too he might succeed . . . if only because they were so very stupid.

Running along the river on the way back to the hotel, he grinned broadly, and felt as if his heart might burst through his chest, so joyous were his thoughts.

She had heard nothing from the police.

She called that morning at ten minutes to nine, and spoke to Gregors, who told her they had some very good descriptions of this Scott Hamilton person, which a police artist was putting together right that minute into a composite drawing they could circulate.

"From what we've been told," Gregors said, "from people who were at that cocktail party—men and women alike, by the way—this was a very handsome person, that's one thing they all agree on. You sometimes . . ."

She was wondering how her mother could've been so goddamn *stupid*.

". . . get descriptions that vary, you know, depending on who's doing the talking. You get brown eyes, you get blue eyes, you get green eyes, hazel eyes, whatever, this is the same person all these people are describing. What we've come up with, though, what the artist is working on now, is a male Hispanic—but a very educated one, no accent, nothing like that—in his late twenties, early thirties. Dark hair, light eyes, very handsome. Runs a cable television station in San Diego, by the way, we're checking out there right this minute, see if there's any paper on him. See if he's got a record, that is."

"When will you know?" Elita asked.

"Well, it isn't morning there yet, but they should be getting back to us soon. Meanwhile, we'll get these people back in to look at the drawing, fine tune it, you know, fix an eyebrow here, a nostril there, get it to look as much like the person as we can. We're working on this, Miss Randall, don't worry. You realize, of course . . ."

He hesitated.

She waited.

There was a crackling on the telephone wire. She wondered if a storm was on its way.

"There's no indication yet that any foul play is involved here," Gregors said at last. "Your mother was seen with this man at a party, but that doesn't mean anything has happened to her, or if something *did* happen to her, it doesn't mean this man is responsible for it. We'll have cases where a person will go off and not tell anyone where she's going and she'll turn up safe and sound right around the corner. All I'm saying is that we're working up the composite as a precautionary measure, in case we should need it in the future, but you mustn't think we're automatically assuming something has happened to your mother. Do you understand what I'm saying?"

"Yes, I do. Thank you very much."

"We'll keep in touch," Gregors said.

"Thank you," she said again, and hung up.

The house seemed utterly still.

She looked at her watch.

A little past nine. She wondered if Geoffrey was at work yet. She hadn't spoken to him since Wednesday night, hadn't even called to thank him for what had been a truly wonderful time. By now, he had to be thinking she was the most ungrateful jerk imaginable. She looked for his number in her handbag, dialed it, got a woman telling her this was the British Consulate, asked for Mr. Turner, and was sure that the next woman who came on the line was the absurdly strident Lucy Phipps, to whom she did not identify herself. She asked for Mr. Turner again and was put straight through.

"Elita!" he said. "I've been worried sick about you! Where on earth *are* you?"

She told him where she was and told him why she'd come out here, and all at once she found herself bawling into the mouthpiece, sobbing out the whole story of not having been able to get her mother by phone . . .

"Do you remember my calling her from the Plaza?"

. . . and no one having seen her since Monday night, and the police interviewing people and getting a composite drawing made . . .

"Oh, Jesus," she sobbed, "I don't know what to do!"

"I'm sure she's perfectly all right," Geoffrey said.

327

"Now listen to me, Elita. You can't help the situation an iota by sitting out there all alone and waiting for the phone to ring. Did you drive out there?"

"No."

"How did you get there?"

"By jitney."

"Can you take one back to the city?"

"Yes, but I don't think I should."

"Why not?"

"Suppose they learn something?"

"I'm sure they'll learn she's fine. Just give them your number in New York, and they'll . . ."

"Suppose she isn't," Elita said.

There was a silence on the line.

"Elita," he said, "whatever the case, I think you need to be with someone who cares about you. What time is the next jitney?"

"I don't know. I'll have to look at the schedule."

"Look at it," he said.

"All right," she said.

"*Now*, Elita. Look at it *now*, please."

She blew her nose, found the schedule, and went back to the phone. Still sniffling, she told him that the next bus left at twelve twenty-five and arrived in Manhattan at two-fifteen.

"Where in Manhattan?" he asked.

"Thirty-ninth and Third. And then it makes stops . . ."

"I'll be there to meet you at two-fifteen."

"Geoffrey . . . I really think I should stay here."

"Why?" he asked.

She could not think of a single reason why.

"Call the police and give them your number in New York," he said.

"All right."

"I'll see you in a little while."

"All right."

"Elita?"

"Yes, Geoffrey."

"I'm sure she's fine."

"All right, Geoffrey."

"Elita, please stop crying. You're breaking my heart."

Which words, for some odd reason she couldn't quite understand, almost broke hers. Or perhaps she'd just remembered what he'd said earlier. About her needing to be with someone who cared about her. That.

Arthur opened one of his desk drawers and removed from it a large manila clasp envelope. He unfastened the wing tips of the clasp, reached inside the envelope, and pulled out a thin rectangle of cardboard, somewhat longer than it was wide.

"According to your specifications," he said.

There was thick block lettering on the sign, black on white.

"Okay?"

"Yes, perfect," Sonny said, and then carefully put the sign back into the envelope. Arthur was still watching him.

"So," he said.

"So," Sonny said.

"All ready for tomorrow?"

"Almost."

"Would it were day, hmm?" Arthur said, and smiled. Sonny looked at him.

" 'Will it never be morning?' " Arthur said.

Sonny kept looking at him.

Henry the Fifth, " Arthur said. " 'Would it were day!' " he said, quoting again. "The French camp, near Agincourt."

"Oh," Sonny said.

"I still don't know your plan," Arthur said.

"I'll be laying in," Sonny said.

"I assumed. And when you surface?"

"I'll blend in. Till it's time."

"Do you know when he'll be speaking?"

"Twelve noon."

"High noon, hmm?"

"High noon, yes."

"Catch the West Coast, too."

"Yes."

"How will you do it?"

"From above. The level above him."

"Using?"

"Sarin."

Arthur raised his eyebrows appreciatively.

"Careful with that stuff," he said.

"I will be."

"Don't want to get any on you."

"No."

"Or even *breathe* any of it."

"I know how dangerous it is," Sonny said.

"Should do the job nicely, though."

"Yes."

"Then what?"

"Get away. If I can."

"How?"

"A boomerang," Sonny said.

"Ah. Yes. Good," Arthur said. "Very good. And where will you go afterward? Back to Westhampton?"

"I don't think so."

"Where then?"

"The hotel, I think."

"I'd like to know for certain."

"I'll call you," Sonny said. "*If* I get off the island."

"Oh, I'm sure you will," Arthur said. "Which is why I'd like to know where you'll be, hmm? So we can help you with your future plans."

"I'll call you," Sonny said.

"Please," Arthur said, and smiled.

The three men met in the CIA office in lower Manhattan, its exact location known only to the people who had legitimate business there, and incidentally to any foreign spy who happened to be tracking them. None of the men was *quite* sure an actual threat to the President existed, but they damn well wanted to make certain it would be properly addressed if it *did* exist.

Well, actually, one of the men frankly didn't give a damn whether the President got murdered or not. This

331

was Secret Service Agent Samuel Harris Dobbs, who saw this latest brouhaha as just another plot to keep him here in New York when all he wanted to do was go back to Washington where his wife was. Nobody had killed Reagan at the goddamn Canada Day thing the other day, and nobody was about to kill Bush tomorrow, either. But Hogan and Nichols, the two men with him, kept worrying the thing like a dog gnawing on a bone. Nichols was the one who seemed most convinced that a conspiracy was afoot; but he was CIA, so what could anyone expect? Hogan seemed desperately trying to understand the arcane terminology Nichols kept tossing around. He understood murders, though, and three people had been killed so far, and it looked possible that someone just might also have his sights on the President; crazier things had happened in this city.

"They call themselves *Sayf Quasīr*," Nichols said. "That means scimitar in Arabic. It looks like this," he said, and carefully lettered the word on a pad, and then showed it to the other men. Dobbs figured he was showing off.

يَطَقَان

"Pretty writing," he said.
"Pretty little tattoo, too," Hogan said.
Ta-2-2, Dobbs thought. Sounded like a robot in a sci-

ence-fiction movie. Tell the truth, this whole damn *thing* sounded like science fiction. A conspiracy to kill the President? The way he figured it, if no one had killed the son of a bitch yet, no one was *ever* going to kill him.

"It isn't so farfetched," Nichols said, as if reading his mind. "He'll be here tomorrow, you know. Coming in by jet to La Guardia, then by helicopter to the island."

"These two British ladies had tattoos," Hogan explained belatedly.

"What British ladies?" Dobbs asked.

"These two murder victims. Green scimitars."

"What?" Dobbs said.

"Just under their . . . ah . . . breasts," Hogan said delicately.

"What?" Dobbs said again.

"We think it's a means of positive identification," Nichols said. "A way of exposing impostors."

"What do they do?" Dobbs asked. "Open their blouses, flash their boobs?"

"In interrogation," Nichols said. "If they catch a double."

Hogan wondered what baseball had to do with this.

"Check him out," Nichols said, "they'll know right off."

"Flash their boobs," Dobbs said, refusing to let go of it. "Don't shoot, I'm a spy."

"Well, I don't know what they do, actually," Nichols said, looking offended. "We don't know very much about them, actually. But we feel certain the green scimitar tattoo identifies them."

"What time will the President be in?" Hogan asked, changing the subject. Schedules, he knew. Police investigation always entailed schedules. Time tables. Who was where when? He could deal with schedules.

"He'll be speaking at twelve o'clock. Probably get to the island minutes before. He's an old pro at this sort of thing."

A campaign speech, Dobbs thought. Pure and simple. Worst damn thing was he'd probably get re-elected. The thought of another four years of a Republican president —*any* Republican president—made Dobbs shudder.

"What if it rains?" he asked. "It looked like rain when I came in."

There were no windows in the office. For all they knew, it could already be raining.

"I don't know where he'll do the speech if it rains," Nichols said.

"Maybe stay in Washington," Dobbs said. Which is where *I* should be, he thought. "Do it from the Oval Office."

"Maybe. Statue of Liberty'd be better, though."

A Republican, Dobbs thought. Always looking for the angles, camera or otherwise.

"I keep wondering why those two broads were killed," Hogan said.

Murder, he could deal with. There were reasons for murder. Crazy reasons sometimes, but always reasons. If you were a homicide cop, you always asked why.

"Conflicting interests?" Nichols asked, and raised his eyebrows.

"Like?" Dobbs said.

"An agency that wants to keep the President alive."

"Like?" Dobbs said.

"Mossad?" Nichols suggested.

"What's that?" Hogan asked.

"Israeli intelligence. Better the devil they know, huh?"

Dobbs was thinking, This is a dumb waste of time.

"So what do you want from my team?" he asked.

"How many are you?"

"Six."

"Let's bring 'em out there tomorrow," Nichols said.

"How about us?" Hogan asked. Meaning the NYPD.

"More the merrier," Nichols said.

"I'll call the First, see if I can get some detectives out there."

"Better safe than sorry," Nichols said, and looked to Dobbs for approval.

Dobbs grimaced sourly, clearly in disagreement.

"Did anybody ask the Brits about those two women?" he asked.

"According to Santorini's reports . . ."

"Who's Santorini?"

"One of my people," Hogan said. "He was investigating the murders."

"He was later killed himself," Nichols explained.

"Conflicting interests?" Dobbs asked sarcastically.

"The Brits told him the passports were forgeries," Hogan said.

"Scimitar would have any number of good cobblers," Nichols said.

Hogan wondered what the hell shoes had to do with passports. He didn't ask. Dobbs didn't know what the expression meant, either, these fuckin' CIA jerks.

"Who told him that?" Dobbs asked. "About the passports?"

"A guy at the British Consulate," Hogan said.

Which was how Geoffrey Turner got dragged into it again.

When Elita got off the bus at a quarter past two that afternoon, Geoffrey was waiting in the pouring rain with a big black umbrella over his head. He looked very British with the umbrella and all, a big grin cracking his face as he hurried to her and took her bag, covering her with the umbrella and asking solicitously if she'd had any lunch. She told him No, she hadn't, but she wasn't very hungry . . .

"In which case," he said, "I'll make an early dinner reservation."

She was actually very glad to see him.

In the taxi on the way to the Park Avenue apartment, she filled him in more completely about her mother, and took enormous comfort from his genuine concern and little murmurs of reassurance. By the time they reached the apartment, in fact, she was beginning to believe that her mother *was* truly all right, and that her failure to communicate was merely inconsiderate.

She did not know that on Beaver Street at that very

moment, a policeman in a black rain slicker was opening the black plastic garbage bag containing her mother's head.

The story was news only because of the downpour.

Sonny caught it by accident, flipping through the dial, never expecting to find a news broadcast at two-thirty in the afternoon, surprised when the Statue of Liberty popped onto the screen. Standing in the rain. Hand with the torch held high over her head, rain pelting her. The camera panned down over her face, down, down past the tablet cradled in the crook of her left elbow, down over the folds of her robe, and then zipped on down to ground zero, where a roving reporter in a yellow raincoat, the hood pulled up over her head, her glasses spattered with raindrops, stood with a microphone in her hand, interviewing a pretty young woman whose blond hair was blowing in the wind.

"I'm here with Heather Broward," the reporter said, "who is organizing the President's appearance here tomorrow. How does it look, Heather?"

"Well, I'd have preferred sunny skies along about now," Heather said. *"But . . ."*

Both women smiled.

". . . hopefully we'll have good weather today."

Can't even speak their own language properly, Sonny thought. Wouldn't mind being in bed with both of them, though, rainy day like today.

"When do you think you'll be hanging the bunting?" the reporter asked.

"Well, Mary . . ."

Mary and Heather, he thought.

". . . I was hoping we'd have it up by now, but this rain . . ."

She shrugged prettily. Bad case of the cutes, Sonny thought.

"But the minute it stops, we'll begin draping the wall just behind the President," she said, and indicated the white wall behind the women. "The podium'll be here," she said, "just about where we're standing . . ."

Good, Sonny thought. Just where I figured.

". . . and we'll be decorating that, too, around the Presidential Seal, of course, and in keeping with the theme of freedom and prosperity . . ."

In this wonderful country of ours, he thought.

". . . in this great nation we're so lucky to live in," Heather said.

Close but no cigar, Sonny thought.

"Thank you, Heather Broward . . ." Mary said.

Thank you indeed, Sonny thought.

"This is Mary Mastrantonio at the Statue of . . ."

He clicked off the set. The manila envelope Arthur had given him this morning was sitting on the desk. He took the sign from it, studied it again, and then sat down behind the desk. Using a black Magic Marker, he added a handwritten message to the sign, and put it back in the envelope.

Then he began packing his camera bag.

* * *

338

The three men were waiting for Geoffrey when he got back to the consulate office. They introduced themselves and then began asking him all sorts of questions about the two women with the false British passports. He had frankly thought that both women were well behind him by now, and he was tired of explaining to everyone—*including* Joseph Worthy of Her Majesty's own infernal spy machine—that neither was in actuality British, and that therefore the British Government felt no obligation to pursue the matter further.

"Joseph *who*?" the one named Nichols said.

"Worthy," Geoffrey said. "He was called in when London learned the passports were false. Although, actually, I suppose it was the tattoos that alerted them."

"He knew about the tattoos then?" the one named Dobbs asked.

"Yes, of course."

"What'd *he* think about them?"

"He thought a Libyan intelligence group might be hatching a plot against the former Prime Minister."

"Mrs. Thatcher?"

"Yes."

"What sort of plot?"

"Assassination. Which turned out not to be the case at all. She's come and gone quite safely."

"Pretty good guess, though," Nichols said.

"Bush instead," Hogan said, and both other men cut sharp glances at him.

"Well, thanks for your time," Dobbs said. "We appreciate it."

"Not at all," Geoffrey said, and led them out, wondering what in blazes *that* had been all about.

After he'd left Arthur's office this morning, he'd made two stops. The first thing he'd bought was a black fedora. The next thing he'd bought was a camera bag. The bag was made of a sturdy black fabric, its flaps fastened with Velcro. There were removable panels inside it, to accommodate lenses and cameras of different sizes and shapes. There were pockets outside the bag, to hold film or lens paper or whatever. It was an entirely convenient bag, some seventeen inches long by at least fifteen inches wide and ten inches deep. The man at the camera shop told him it would hold a video camera, at least two still camera bodies, several lenses, and whatever Sonny chose to stuff in the pockets. He pointed out that there were two Velcro-fastened straps on the rear side of the bag, designed for carrying a folding tripod. It was an entirely convenient bag. Sonny packed into it:

The bottle of sarin, wrapped in a towel and sitting upright in one of the compartments.

The loaded 9-mm Parabellum pistol.

Two extra magazines for the gun.

The basting tool.

The walkie-talkie.

The muted silk tie.

The various identity cards McDermott had cobbled for him.

The sign Arthur had given him this morning.

The roll of transparent tape.

340

A four-foot length of the monofilament fishing line.
His Walkman radio.
And a box of toothpicks.

"How'd you happen to find this?" the cop asked.

The man he was talking to was from Pakistan. He had given the cop his name three times, and the cop still hadn't caught it. Something like Pashee. Or something. And the cop didn't know whether this was his first name or his last name or both names put together. The cop, whose name was Mangiacavallo, wished names were still simple in this city.

"I was throwing garbage in the dumpster," Pashee said. He had a terrible accent, but Mangiacavallo had been listening to him for ten minutes now and was beginning to believe he understood Urdu. Except for the guy's name. "I tossed up a bag, and it hit this other bag on top of the pile . . ."

"This one?"

"This one, yes. And it came toppling down."

"So how come you opened it?"

"It looked like something might be in it."

What was in it was a fuckin' human *head,* is what was in it. What the fuck did he *think* was in it?

"What'd you think might be in it, sir?" Mangiacavallo asked politely.

"It felt like something heavy. I thought it might be something good."

"So you opened the bag."

"Yes. And closed it again right away."

341

I'll bet, Mangiacavallo thought.

"What'd you do then?"

"Called nine-eleven."

So here we are, Mangiacavallo thought.

It was still raining, but only lightly, when the man walked out of the Marriott at three o'clock that afternoon. The man was wearing a dark blue suit, black shoes, and black socks. His white shirt was buttoned to the very top button, and he was wearing no tie. A black fedora rested atop his head, and he was carrying what appeared to be a black duffle bag. He looked somewhat like an Orthodox Jew.

The homicide cop who caught the squeal on the severed head was a detective/first grade named Max Golub, who worked out of Homicide South in the Thirteenth Precinct downtown on Twenty-first and Third. He dutifully typed up his report in triplicate and at three-twenty that afternoon, he gave one copy of the report to his lieutenant, whose name was Albert Ryan.

Ryan was eager to get home—he would be relieved at a quarter to four and didn't want to get involved in any long telephone conversations. But he knew that in cases where you found one part of a body, you could suddenly start finding *other* parts all over town. So he called Detective-Lieutenant Peter Hogan, his counterpart in Homicide North, and asked if any arms or legs had turned up in his bailiwick today? Hogan told him he hadn't seen any yet, thank God, but he'd keep his eyes open.

"Why?" he asked.

" 'Cause we got a head belongs to a white female down here, blond lady tossed in a dumpster on Beaver Street."

Which is how Hogan found out that Carolyn Fremont was dead.

Although nobody yet knew the dead woman's name.

He caught the almost empty three-thirty ferry to the island. The rain had tapered off to a drizzle. No one asked to look into his camera bag. He had not expected that anyone would. He wandered around the deck with the rest of the tourists—though there were not very many of them on this wet afternoon—eyes wide in wonder, looking like someone who might next visit Ellis Island to trace the history of an ancestor who had come here from Russia or Poland.

At Kufra, disguise was nonsense entertained only in fiction. In real life, it was better to teach annihilation and survival. He knew that to appear absolutely authentic, he should be wearing unshorn earlocks and a beard. But he'd have felt ridiculous applying crepe hair, and he'd reasoned—correctly, it now seemed—that the familiar costume alone would confirm his identity. People rarely saw beyond the uniform. Moreover, he carried himself with an air of solemn religiosity premised on an inner belief that he was, in fact, an Orthodox Jew on a rainy day's outing. Smiling thinly in his beard—the beard he *believed* he was wearing, although it did not in actuality adorn his face—he thought, To *me* I'm an Orthodox Jew, and to *you* I'm an Orthodox Jew—but to an Orthodox Jew am I an Orthodox Jew? There were no Orthodox Jews on the ferry today.

He stepped off the boat at five minutes to four. Again, none of the rangers on the dock asked him to open his bag. His good old friend Alvin Rhodes was not among them. Like a rabbi davening in prayer, he muttered his way past them. At five o'clock, he went into the restaurant and bought three hamburgers, a can of Diet Coke, a container of orange juice, and a hard roll. He sat at a table to eat the hamburgers and drink the Coke. He put the orange juice and the hard roll into the camera bag, in the compartment alongside the pistol.

At a quarter past five, the announcements started, telling visitors to the island that the last boat back would leave in half an hour.

He went into the base of the statue, and up to the men's room on the second level.

Two men were at the urinals.

He could see shoes and bunched trouser legs under one of the stall doors.

He went into a free stall, locked the door, and waited. At five-twenty, the man in the stall on the right flushed the toilet, stood up, pulled up his trousers, and left. Sonny heard water running in one of the sinks.

A man's voice—calling from the doorway, it seemed —yelled, "Last ferry leaving in fifteen minutes!"

A urinal flushed.

Silence.

Sonny took the box of toothpicks out of the camera bag. He grabbed a handful of them and stuffed them into the right-hand pocket of his jacket.

He took the loop of fishing line out of the bag and put it into his left-hand pocket.

He could hear a loudspeaker announcing that the last ferry from the island would leave in ten minutes.

He pulled his feet up onto the toilet seat.

The same man who'd called from the doorway earlier —an attendant, a ranger, whoever the hell—now came into the room and shouted, "Last ferry's about to go. Anybody in here?"

Sonny did not dare breathe.

"Last call for the ferry," the man said.

There was a long silence.

He heard the man grunt, and visualized him crouching to look under the stalls. Another grunt as he rose. Then his voice coming from the corridor outside, "Last call for the ferry," retreating down the hallway, "last call for the ferry, last call . . ."

And then silence.

Sonny came out of the stall at once.

He went to the wooden outer door, painted to look like bronze, and pulled it closed. If he had to, he was prepared to pick the lock on the utility closet door in the alcove—but the door was standing open, just as it had been last Saturday. He took a toothpick from the handful in his pocket, inserted it into the keyway, and snapped it off flush with the face of the lock. There was still room in the keyway's slit for another one. He slid one in, snapped it off flush, pressed both stubs in solidly with the flat side of a quarter, and then reached into the camera bag at his feet, removing from it the manila envelope bearing the sign Arthur had given him this morning. He took the roll of transparent tape from the bag and began fastening the sign to the door, a sliver of tape at each corner. The sign read:

OUT OF
ORDER
USE LADIES ROOM CLOSET

His hands were trembling.

He was putting the tape back into the bag when he heard footsteps in the corridor. Distant. But approaching. The attendant, the ranger, whoever, was coming this way again. He rushed into the closet and took the loop of fishing line from his pocket. Hooking it over and behind the thumb bolt, the only grip on the inside of the door, he was pulling the door toward him when he heard the man's voice again. Just outside the closed entrance door now.

"Who the fuck?"

Wondering who had closed that outside door.

Sonny tugged on the fishing line.

He heard the outer door opening.

The bag!

He'd left his bag outside the . . .

He shoved the door open again, reached down for the bag, and was stepping back into the closet when the man suddenly appeared in the alcove.

Tall and burly and wearing a ranger uniform.

Blue eyes and a reddish-brown mustache.

His mouth opening in surprise.

"What . . . ?"

But Sonny was already moving forward. As Rhodes reached for the revolver in the holster at his waist, Sonny brought his right arm back, the elbow bent, the hand coming up close to his left cheek. As the gun came free, Sonny released his cocked arm, chopping the hard edge of his hand across the bridge of Rhodes's nose. He heard the bone shatter, heard Rhodes yelp in startled pain, stepped around him at once, caught the back of his head in a double-handed lock, snapped it sharply forward—and broke his neck.

Rhodes went limp against him.

He dragged him into the closet and eased the door shut again. Tugging on the fishing line as hard as he could, he heard at last the heart-stopping click of the spring bolt snapping into the engaging strike plate. He was sealed inside now. No one could unlock that door from the outside, not with the lock effectively jammed.

He hunkered down beside Rhodes's body.

Settling his back against the wall, he stretched out his legs and sat back to wait.

It would be a long night.

Geoffrey had brought two flat tins with him, one filled with forty water-soluble crayons, the other with thirty water-soluble pencils, for finer work. He'd confessed at dinner that he no longer had the pencils he'd used to paint on the shiner all those years ago, and had gone to an art supply house the moment he'd left her this afternoon. Now, in her mother's Park Avenue apartment, he displayed his wares and asked her which eye she wanted done.

"Will it wash off later?" Elita asked.

"Of course," he said. "They're water soluble. In four languages."

Indeed, the printed matter on both tins read water soluble, *wasserlöslich, solubles à l'eau,* and *solubili in acqua.*

"Pick an eye," he said.

"Which do you think?" she asked.

"It's hard to decide, they're both so lovely," he said. "But let's try the left one. I'm right-handed, so it'll be easier to work on that side of the face."

"Are you sure it'll wash off?"

"Positive."

"You won't get any on my blouse, will you?"

"No, no."

"I hope not."

She was wearing a white long-sleeved silk blouse

she'd bought at Bendel's. The last thing she wanted . . .

"I'll need a glass of water," he said.

"What for?"

"To dip them in," he said, and started for the kitchen. "Actually, this isn't the proper way to use them, one should also have a brush. But it'll work this way as well." He found a glass on the counter drainboard, called, "Okay to use this?" and filled it with water. When he came back into the living room, Elita was studying the array of crayons in the larger tin.

"What gorgeous colors," she said.

Each of the crayons was wrapped with a band the color of the crayon itself. The range covered the entire spectrum, modulating subtly from shade to shade of yellow, red, orange, blue, violet, purple, grey, brown—and green.

She thought suddenly of Sonny.

And just as quickly put him out of her mind.

Geoffrey put the glass of water on the end table beside the easy chair in which she was sitting. Perching himself on the ottoman in front of it, he said, "I think an undercoating of yellow, don't you?" and chose from the tin the lightest of the three yellow shades. Dipping the crayon into the glass of water, he applied the tip gingerly to the flesh under her eye. She was still afraid he was going to drip this stuff all over her blouse.

"Listen," she said, "would it be all right if we got a dish towel or something?"

"Of course," he said, and went back out to the kitchen again.

"Inside the door under the sink," she called.

"I've got it," he called back, and returned to the living room. Like a beautician fussing over a client, he draped the towel over her shoulders, stepped back to look at the yellow undercoating he'd already applied, and went to work again.

It was clear from the start that this was to be an artistic creation. No mere application of makeup was this, oh no. Carefully choosing his shades—a bit of red, a bit of blue, a bit of violet—he painstakingly colored the skin, working slowly and carefully, putting down one crayon to pick up another, chatting all the while. He was telling her now about the visit he'd had today from a police lieutenant and two men he suspected were spooks . . .

". . . though, Lord knows, neither of the two identified himself except to offer a name, which was probably false anyway. These cloak and dagger people give me a severe pain in the arse, forgive me, don't they you?"

But she had stopped listening. The moment he'd mentioned a police lieutenant, her mind leaped back to Westhampton Beach and her last conversation with Detective Gregors. She hadn't heard a word from him since. She wondered now if she should call him again. She didn't want to make a pest of herself, but goddamn it, this was her *mother*!

". . . impression they're worried about President Bush."

350

"I'm sorry," she said, "what . . . ?"

"These men who came to see me. Do you remember my telling you about the two murdered women? The first time we had lunch togeth . . . ?"

Mention of murder caused her mind to leap to her mother again, and the awful possibility that something terrible had happened to her. She felt an uncontrollable urge to go to the telephone this very instant, and almost leaped out of the chair. But he was working so closely, concentrating so intently . . .

". . . the green tattoos," he said, and picked up a green crayon.

A green the color of a jungle glade in brilliant sunlight.

"Which they seem to think identifies some sort of Libyan intelligence group," Geoffrey said, and dipped the green crayon into the glass of water. "The green scimitar," he said.

"What?" she said.

"The tattoo on each of the women. A green scimitar."

His face was not six inches from hers. The green crayon was in his hand. A green the color of the scimitar tattoo on Sonny Hemkar's chest. Her eyes opened wide.

"A green *what*?" she said, and the telephone rang.

She leaped out of the chair at once, almost knocking over the glass of water on the end table, rushing to the phone at the other end of the room, yanking the receiver from its cradle.

"Hello?" she said.

"Miss Randall, please."

"This is she."

"Detective Gregors, Westhampton Beach Police."

But she had recognized his voice from his very first words.

"Yes, Mr. Gregors," she said.

"We've got a pretty good composite on this guy your mother was with the other night, and I was wondering how we could get it to you. I could have it messengered, I suppose . . . you don't have access to a fax machine, do you?"

"No, I . . . oh. Just a minute. Geoff!" she called. "Is there a fax machine at the consulate?"

"Yes, of course," he said.

"Can you let me have the number, please?"

Ten minutes later, Geoffrey unlocked the door to the consulate office, punched the security code into the panel to the right of the door, and ushered her in. The fax machine was at the far end of the room, near Lucy Phipps's desk. The fax from Detective Gregors was already sitting in the grey plastic receiving tray. Elita picked it up.

She was looking at a very crude drawing of Sonny Hemkar.

14

During the night, the body made sounds.

Rigor mortis setting in, tissues stiffening, the sounds of the dead. He shivered each time the body made another sound. He tried to catch some sleep, but the small insistent noises the body made kept waking him up from fitful slumber. He was afraid the body would rise up alive again, to slay him. He was afraid some of the sarin would somehow spill out of the sealed bottle and kill him. He was afraid they would find him here in the closet, force open the door, murder him like a trapped animal.

He must have dozed at last.

A new sound jerked him into startled wakefulness.

The lock. Someone trying to force a key into the jammed keyway. The key clicking, clicking, an effective burglar alarm.

A voice in Spanish.

"Mierda!"

Silence.

Reading the OUT OF ORDER sign.

Or trying to read it.

A heavy sigh outside the door.

Footsteps retreating.

He tapped the light button on his digital watch.

6:30 A.M.

He released the button. Beside him, the ranger's body kept stiffening, whispering of death.

He tried to sleep again.

Hogan kept wondering who had hung the shiner on the girl.

The Turner kid from the British Consulate was telling him about yet another green scimitar tattoo, but all Hogan could think of was what a beautiful shiner the girl was wearing. Had the Turner kid been knocking her around? You could never tell with the quiet ones.

"On his chest," the girl said now.

Elita Randall. Healthy-looking blond girl. Big blue eyes.

"On the left pectoral," she said.

He wondered how she knew this, but he made no comment. He was suddenly reminded of the two women who'd contradictorily described a word tattooed on a man's penis as SWAN and SASKATCHEWAN. Hogan was up to his ass in tattoos, and was beginning to wish he'd joined the Fire Department all those years ago. Besides, the two kids had been waiting for him when he'd got to work at a quarter to eight this morning, and he hadn't even had his coffee yet.

"You want some coffee?" he asked. "I'll send out for some coffee."

"This is the man her mother was last seen with," the Turner kid said.

"On Monday night," the girl said.

"What's his name?" Hogan said, and picked up the phone. "Harry," he said into the receiver, "order me three cups of coffee, willya? And some cheese Danish. How do you like your coffee?" he asked.

"Regular," the girl said.

"Black," the Turner kid said.

"Sonny Hemkar," the girl said. "His name."

"Two regulars, one black," Hogan said into the phone, and hung up. "How do you spell that last name?"

"H-E-M-K-A-R," the girl said. "And his first name is Krishnan, the Sonny is just a nickname. K-R-I-S-H-N-A-N."

Hogan was writing.

"What is he?" he asked. "Pakistani? Afghan? Something like that?" The guy probably drove a taxi; the city was full of camel jockeys these days.

"Indian," the girl said. "Well, his father's Indian. His mother's British."

"British, huh?" Hogan said, and looked shrewdly at the Turner kid, reminding him that the two dead ladies had been carrying British passports, no matter what *anybody* said.

"He's a doctor," the girl said.

"Here in New York?"

"No," she said. "L.A."

She gave him the name of the hospital where Sonny was in residence, and also the phone numbers Geoffrey had provided, and then she told him the Westhampton Beach police were looking into her mother's disappearance and suggested that he might want to get in touch with them. Hogan said he would.

The coffee came some five minutes later, by which time Hogan had asked a police clerk to photocopy the faxed drawing of Sonny Hemkar and to check with the BCI for any criminal record on the guy. Like a family sitting down to breakfast together, the three of them drank their coffee and ate their cheese Danish at Hogan's desk. The clerk came in just as Hogan was draining the last few drops from his cardboard container. He reported that Hemkar had no criminal record, was there anything else, sir? Hogan told him to call the hospital out there in L.A., see if they could fax them a *photograph* of this character, back up the drawing with something concrete.

"Could you call them now, please?" Elita said. "The police in Westhampton?"

"Sure," he said, though that wasn't what he really wanted to do right this minute. "Who was the person you spoke to out there?"

She gave him both detectives' names, and Hogan placed the call, asking for either Gregors or Mellon, and was told they were both out in the field just now. Hogan left a number and asked that they call back. The sergeant who'd taken the call said he'd make sure they did.

"So," Hogan said, and shrugged. "I'll get to you as soon as I can."

Actually, he didn't much care about where the girl's mother might be.

What he was eager to do now was talk to Nichols and Dobbs, tell them a fuckin' Indian with a green scimitar tattoo had surfaced in New York.

By a quarter past nine that morning, the haze had burned off, and the day was clear and bright. The weather forecasters on all the morning talk shows had promised wonderful weather for the Fourth of July weekend, and it seemed that for a change they were going to be right.

In the harbor at the approach to the Hudson River, the Statue of Liberty held her torch aloft and seemed to bask in the rays of a beneficent sun.

In the men's room supply closet on the second floor of the monument, Sonny sat in the dark with a dead body still making noises. An earphone button was in Sonny's right ear, its connecting cable plugged into his Walkman radio. The radio was tuned to CBS, 880 on the dial, traffic and weather every ten minutes. Eating the hard roll he had bought yesterday, drinking from the container of orange juice, he listened to the weather report. He had been fearing more rain. He now heard that the day would be sunny and fair, albeit hot.

He did not mind heat.

Nothing could be hotter than the desert sands of Kufra.

In the darkness, he smiled a secret smile.

Then he bit into the roll again.

The return call from Detective Gregors out in Westhampton Beach came at ten minutes to ten. To Hogan, the guy sounded like a hayseed. You'd think Suffolk County'd have somebody spoke English like the cops in New York did. Instead, there was this kind of molasses-dripping drawl. A fuckin' hick.

"We don't have any paper on this Hemkar character," Hogan said, "but . . ."

"Neither do we," Gregors said.

"But we're working some other murders that may be related."

He went on to tell Gregors all about the two British ladies with the tattooed tits . . .

"No kidding?" Gregors said, obviously impressed and probably wide-eyed, the jackass.

. . . and the murdered cop from right here at Homicide North . . .

"Boy," Gregors said.

Probably never saw a murder victim in his life, Hogan thought.

"Yeah," he said, "and since Hemkar has the same tattoo . . ."

"Didn't know that," Gregors said.

Well, you know it now, jackass, Hogan thought.

"Yeah," he said, "he does. So we're thinking there might be some connection. Can you tell me a little more about the missing woman? I had the daughter in here a while ago, but she was a bit distraught, if you know what I mean, and I didn't want to ask her too many questions about her mother. I think somebody's been batting her around a little, she was wearing a shiner the size of Staten Island."

"Didn't have one when I saw her," Gregors said, sounding surprised.

"Well, she's got one now. Anyway, can you fill me in a little on the missing woman?"

"I'll fax you what the daughter gave us, if you want," Gregors said.

"Well, just give it to me on the phone, if that's okay," Hogan said.

"Sure. Just thought I'd save time. Let me get it for you."

He was away from the phone for about three minutes, coming back with what Hogan guessed was a complaint form, and began to read from it like a kid reciting in class.

"White female," he said, "thirty-nine years old, five feet seven inches tall, a hundred twenty-five pounds. Blond hair, blue eyes, no identifying scars, marks or . . ."

"Blond, did you say?"

"Blond," Gregors said.

Hogan had suddenly remembered yesterday's call from Homicide South.

He hoped to God he was wrong.

* * *

The two plainclothes cops standing on the Battery Park dock were from the First Detective Squad, here to check the identification of anyone going out to Liberty Island on the special ferry. This was now ten in the morning, a glorious day, and the cops were grateful for a cushy assignment like this one, which certainly beat looking down into the face of a stiff on a city pavement.

An earlier ferry had carried to the island forty-two Marine Corps Band musicians in their dress blues, three members of the President's advance team, and four Secret Service men from the New York field office. Most of the people boarding the ferry now were from the three television networks and CNN, all of them wearing lucite-encased press cards, the rainbow peacock on the NBC tag, the black-and-white CBS eye on the Channel 2 tag, the big 7 on the ABC tag. Some of them were carrying cameras, others were carrying sound equipment, others seemed to be carrying only clipboards. All of them seemed happy to be outdoors on a nice day like today. Chatting amiably among themselves, here on a cooperative assignment where there was no sense of rivalry, the men and women boarded the ferry together with nine men wearing dark blue suits, white shirts, and muted ties.

The television people were savvy enough to know that these nine guys weren't a baseball team. Whispers ran around that this was Secret Service, but the surmise was only two-thirds correct. Six of the nine were, in fact, Secret Service: Dobbs and the men he'd brought with him from Washington, D.C. The other three were CIA: Alex Nichols, Moss Peggot, and Conrad Templeton.

None of them knew that Sonny Hemkar was already on the island.

Hogan hated this part of police work more than anything in the world.

They stood together in the stainless steel silence of the morgue. There were stainless steel tables with stainless steel cups brimming with blood. There was a burn victim on one of the tables, his fists clenched, his hands raised in the characteristic pugilist position. There was the stench of putrefying bodies. The clock on the wall read twenty-eight minutes past ten. It had taken him ten minutes to get to the Park Avenue apartment and another twenty minutes to drive them down to the hospital. Hogan was here to show Elita Randall the head Homicide South had recovered.

She looked at it and gasped.

Covered her face with her hands.

Nodded into her hands.

And turned away and ran out.

"Thanks," Hogan said to the attendant, and followed her out to the corridor, where she stood sobbing in Geoffrey's arms. "I'm sorry about this," Hogan said. She nodded, kept sobbing. "I'd have given anything not to have . . ."

"I know," she said, sobbing.

She was thinking that she'd been to bed with the man

who'd killed her mother. She was thinking she would never go to bed with another man as long as she lived.

"Miss Randall," Hogan said, "if you feel up to answering a few questions, I'd like to . . ."

"Yes," she said. "I'm all right."

"'Cause I'd like to get started on this right away," he said. "I tried to reach Nichols and Dobbs," he said, turning to Geoffrey, who'd met them yesterday, "but they'd already left for the island. Liberty Island," he explained. "So what I want to know . . . is that drawing a good one? The composite? 'Cause if it is . . ."

"Not particularly, no," Elita said.

"What I'm asking, if I had copies of that drawing messengered out to the island, would it help our people out there? Would they recognize this character from the drawing alone? When he pops up? If he pops up."

"I don't think so," Elita said. "Not from the drawing alone. I *know* him, but I'm not sure anyone who *didn't* know him . . ."

"Because what it is, we're having trouble getting that hospital out there to cooperate. All we want is a *photograph* of the guy, but you'd think we were asking them to fax us his *kidney* or something. Which brings me to my next question. Would you recognize this character if you saw him again?"

"Yes."

"Miss Randall, do you want to help us catch him?"

"Yes."

"Would you be willing to come out to Liberty Island?"

362

"Why do you want her out there?" Geoffrey asked.

Hogan hesitated. He knew he'd be placing the girl in harm's way, and ethics demanded that he tell her what she might be getting into. At the same time . . .

"It's my guess he'll be heading out there," he said. "One way or another, he'll get on that island, is my guess."

"Why would he want to do that?" Geoffrey asked.

Hogan hesitated again. This kid was from the British Consulate. How much of this did he want going out over the international wire? He decided to level with them both.

"We think he'll be trying for the President," he said.

Elita looked puzzled. Geoffrey was already nodding.

"To kill him," Hogan said. "He'll be trying to kill President Bush."

"I thought so," Geoffrey said.

They all fell silent. A doctor in a white coat, a stethoscope hanging out of his pocket, came down the corridor, pulled open the heavy door to the morgue, and went inside. There was the sudden whiff of decomposing bodies as the door whispered shut.

"If the picture's no good to us . . ." Hogan said.

"I know what you want," Elita said.

"Just stay with us," he said. "Point him out if he shows his face."

She nodded.

"That way, we'll maybe have a slight edge."

She was still nodding.

"Will you do it?" he asked.

"Yes," she said. "Of course."

"Good," he said.

Heather Broward was positioning the Marine Corps Band on the level above the podium. Three musicians deep, fourteen musicians wide, a human wall of red, white and blue above the red-white-and-blue bunting draped on the wall behind the podium. The podium itself had been hung with similar bunting on its sides and above the Presidential Seal on its face, but nothing could disguise its primary function. A Coast Guard cutter was moving in a circumscribed circle out on the water, waving off any boats approaching the island, but its presence was hardly necessary; every precautionary measure had been taken to circumvent any water-borne snipers.

"Which one of you is the leader?" Heather called up through a bullhorn.

The leader, who happened to be a brigadier general, didn't much enjoy being yelled at by a snip of a girl, but he raised his hand like a schoolboy asking permission to go pee.

"Could you stand just a bit forward of the others, sir?" Heather called, the *sir* mollifying him a bit, but not entirely.

Behind the podium, Ralph Dickens and his assistant were helping the television people set up their microphones. A technician from ABC accidentally banged into the CNN mike. Ralph caught it before it fell over completely, but he hit his elbow on the goddamn shield in the process. Muttering under his breath, he righted the microphone and scowled at the clumsy technician. Not three feet away, Heather was bawling into the bullhorn again. On such a nice day, too.

Ralph yawned and looked at his watch.

Ten forty-seven.

In about an hour and a half, it'd all be over and done with.

Sun dazzled the water, glinting like diamonds in the spray kicked back by the police launch. Against his better judgment, Hogan had allowed the Turner kid to accompany them. He would probably get all kinds of flak about this from the Chief of Detectives, but better to get the damn girl out to the island than to argue about it all morning with someone who could hardly speak the English language right.

"He took me out there, you know," Elita said, shouting over the roar of the twin engines.

"Who did? What do you mean?" Hogan shouted back.

"Sonny. We went out there last Saturday."

"What'd you do?"

"Walked around, took pictures."

She was thinking of what they'd done afterward. In her mother's apartment. In her mother's white lingerie and red shoes. How could she have been so utterly stupid? A wave of guilt and shame washed over her, almost overwhelming her grief, followed instantly by a rage so fierce it virtually blinded her. In that moment, the spray hitting her face as she stood on the open sunwashed deck with Geoffrey and the police lieutenant, she wanted nothing more than to strike back at Sonny Hemkar, cut out his heart, eat his heart, hurt him, kill him, *kill* him.

Geoffrey saw the look on her face.

And shuddered.

In the darkness of the supply closet, the Walkman clipped to his belt, the earpiece in his ear, Sonny listened to the news while he knotted his tie, slipping the silk under the collar of the white shirt, looping it under and over, smoothing it on his chest. The black fedora was sitting on top of the camera bag. He moved it to the floor and flicked on the small penlight, but only for an instant, time enough to locate the FBI tag McDermott had fashioned for him.

He clipped the tag to his lapel, took the walkie-talkie from the bag, and slipped it into the right-hand pocket of the suit jacket. He had earlier removed the bulb from the basting tool; he now slipped the plastic tube into the left-hand pocket of the jacket, together with the two extra magazines for the pistol. Picking up the gun with its attached silencer, he tucked it into his waistband on the left-hand side of his body, easily accessible for a cross-body draw.

He had not touched the bottle of sarin since he'd placed it in the camera bag yesterday afternoon.

He turned on the penlight again.

He knew this was a risk; light might spill into the

entrance alcove from the crack under the closet door. But the greater danger was to work with the bottle in the dark, risking a spill that would certainly kill him. Cautiously, his hand shaking, he peeled off the transparent tape around the nozzle, relieved when he saw that the nozzle was still turned to the OFF position. He would not turn it to the STREAM position until he was in place on the level above the President.

On the radio, a news commentator was saying that the Presidential jet had just landed at La Guardia airport.

Dobbs listened while the girl told her story.

Good-looking kid, he was wondering how she'd managed to get mixed up with an assassin. No question now about what Sonny Boy was or what he planned to do. Green scimitar tattoo on his chest, he was one of Quaddafi's chosen. Took her here to the island last Saturday, innocent boy and girl on a day trip, while meanwhile he's shooting pictures of everything in sight, planning his attack. He'd be here again today, no question about that, either. *If* he could get past them. Dobbs couldn't see how. He looked at the pencil drawing again.

"What color are his eyes?" he asked.

"A sort of greyish-green," Elita said.

Not a bad-looking man, Dobbs thought, but who said a killer had to be? The guy who'd chopped up all those people in Milwaukee was handsome as hell.

"How tall is he?" Nichols asked.

Didn't like feeling left out, Dobbs thought. If they

nailed this guy, the CIA would take all the credit, no question about *that,* either.

"Around six feet?" the girl said. "More or less."

Dobbs hoped he wouldn't get physical.

"Ever take you to his apartment?" Nichols asked.

"No," she said.

"Then you wouldn't have seen a weapon . . ."

"No."

"Anything he might use as . . ."

"No."

Nichols looked out over the water. Wondering if Sonny Boy planned to come in that way, Dobbs guessed. The Coast Guard boat was still maneuvering out there. Nichols nodded, still wondering. His walkie-talkie went off. He took it from his belt and put it to his ear.

"Nichols," he said, and listened. "Yeah," he said. "Uh-huh. Uh-huh. Got it, thank you." He tossed back his jacket, hooked the walkie-talkie to his belt again.

"The chopper just left La Guardia," he said.

Dobbs looked at his watch.

Twenty-five to twelve.

The girl seemed nervous.

He didn't know what to say to her, so he just let it go.

Sonny waited.

The radio was telling him nothing new. Local news, information about tonight's fireworks displays, traffic and weather conditions, but nothing further about Bush. His speech was scheduled to begin at twelve noon. Was there some problem?

Alvin Rhodes was beginning to smell.

Effluvial odors emanated from his distending organs.

Sonny tried not to breathe too deeply.

His digital watch read eleven thirty-seven.

The chopper came in over the water at a quarter to twelve, zooming out of the sun like an attack machine, the Presidential Seal painted on each of its sides, its big blades whirring furiously. From where Dobbs stood with the others, he could see it circling in toward the flagpole on the other end of the island. Hovering on the air now, virtually motionless, and then sinking lower and lower, below the treeline and out of sight.

He could not see the President when he disembarked.

He knew he would be surrounded by his own Secret Service people from Washington, who would rush him here to the base of the statue.

Sonny flipped through the dial.

One of the news announcers was saying that the president's speech would begin as scheduled in ten minutes.

He took this to mean that Bush was already on the island.

He was handsomer in person than he appeared on television, a tall, rangy man with the look of an outdoorsman, sporting the suntan he had acquired on his recent vacation to Kennebunkport, smiling affably as he approached Heather, his hand outstretched.

"'Morning, Mr. President," she said.

369

"'Morning, Heather," he said.

Knack of his. Called everyone by his or her first name, never forgot a face or the name that went with it.

"Beautiful morning, isn't it?"

"Gorgeous, Mr. President."

"They look terrific up there," Bush said, indicating with a wave of his hand the Marine Corps Band lined up on the level above. "Everything looks terrific."

"Thank you, sir," Heather said, beaming.

"I won't need makeup, will I?"

"No, sir, you look fine," she said.

"Because you know what Hitchcock used to say, don't you? Alfred Hitchcock, the film director?"

"No, sir, I'm sorry, I don't."

"He used to say, 'How can anyone respect a man who makes his living wearing makeup?' "

"Yes, sir."

"He was referring to actors. He hated actors."

"Yes, sir," Heather said.

Some of her best friends were actors.

"Hello, John!" Bush shouted, changing the subject, and raising his arm in greeting to the brigadier general who would be leading the band. "Got some nice tunes for us today?"

"Yes, Mr. President."

"Did a good job with the podium, too," he said, turning back to Heather, his Secret Service contingent turning with him as if they were all joined at the hip. Four men from the personal White House security platoon, two on each side of him, eyeballing the reporters and the other security people, checking the landscape for anything that looked even remotely alien. Dobbs walked over, introduced himself to the Secret Service man in charge. The two had a whispered conversation, Dobbs nodding in Elita's direction, the White House man looking her over and nodding in puzzled understanding. As he understood it, the blonde was here to finger some Libyan hit man out to get the President. Which seemed about as likely as a Bengal tiger leaping out of the East River. The White House man nodded uh-huh, uh-huh, uh-huh, clearly unconvinced.

From behind the podium, Bush said, "Do we really need this thing?"

"Open water out there, Mr. President," Heather said.

"I *hate* these darn things."

A network woman wearing earphones and cradling a clipboard said, "Four minutes, Heather."

"Can't we get rid of it?" Bush said.

"Not without messing up all the bunting, sir," Heather said.

"Mr. President, could we get a voice level, please?" one of the technicians said.

"Hello, Gabe," Bush said, calling to a reporter he recognized.

"If you'll just give me a ten-count, sir . . ."

"One, two, three, four . . ."

"Can we move that number-two camera a bit to the left?"

"Watch those cables, Harry."

"Bit more, Mr. President."

"Seven, eight . . ."

"Two minutes, Heather."

"That's good, sir, thank you."

"Didn't think I *could* count to ten, did you?" Bush quipped, and grinned.

A network person wearing earphones held up his hand, said, "Quiet, people," and then turned toward the podium and said, "Ready, Mr. President?" Standing behind the battery of microphones, Bush cleared his throat and nodded. There were four television cameras between him and the water beyond. The security people were spaced in a semi-circle behind the cameras, facing not the President but the possible approaches to him from any given compass point. Only Dobbs stood apart with Elita, farther back from the others, where they commanded a wider view of the President and the statue behind him.

"Stand by, please," the man with the earphones said.

"Thirty seconds," the woman with the clipboard said.

Everyone fell silent.

There was not a breeze stirring.

Out on the water, even the Coast Guard boat had cut its engine and was drifting idly, soundlessly.

"Ten," the woman said, "Nine . . . eight . . . seven . . . six . . ."

The man with the earphones held up his right hand for the President to see. Ticking them off on his fingers, he began counting the seconds to airtime . . .

". . . five, four, three, two, one . . ."

"Good afternoon, my fellow Americans . . ."

372

* * *

He turned off the Walkman the moment he heard Bush's salutation, yanked the earpiece from his ear, and dropped radio and cable on the floor beside Rhodes's body. Picking up the camera bag and the black hat, he came out of the supply closet, and pushed at the door, closing it firmly behind him, satisfied when he heard the latch clicking into the strike plate. He did not want anyone opening that door, not with Rhodes's body in there, not until he had done what he was here to do.

He went into one of the stalls, lifted the lid on the toilet tank, dropped the black hat into it, and replaced the lid. He dropped the camera bag into the restroom trash basket.

Boldly, he stepped into the corridor.

The FBI tag clipped to his lapel identified him as Frank Mercer.

But he knew who he was.

He was Sonny Hemkar, and he was stepping forward to meet his destiny.

". . . on this Fourth of July, a day we call glorious—not only because it *is* a glorious day here in New York—but because this day marks a day of glory for us and for the world, the day upon which freedom was born. Freedom," Bush said, and paused. "Well now," he said folksily, "that's a word we sometimes take for granted nowadays, especially since dramatic changes all over the world have brought freedom to peoples everywhere. But I can tell you, it's a word which wasn't so darned famil-

373

iar back then when the founding fathers thought of it. Back then, it was a new concept for these brave men to declare themselves free and independent and forge for themselves, and for all mankind to follow, a constitution that has survived the centuries, a document that has served as a model of inspiration for democratic nations everywhere. It was a good idea then, and it's *still* a good idea. And I'm here on this glorious—yes, *glorious*—day of celebration to tell you that America will continue to be the brightest star in a firmament of emerging democracies."

He paused for merely an instant.

Soberly, dramatically, he gazed into the whirring cameras.

Here it comes, Dobbs thought.

"Four years ago, I promised the people of America a thousand points of light. Well, four years later, we're living in a nation where none need go hungry and none need go poor, a nation of healthy, educated, employed, hard-working, proud and patriotic people who can achieve whatever their minds can conceive, who can aspire to whatever their souls . . ."

God, what bullshit, Dobbs thought, and turned his attention to Elita.

She wasn't watching Bush.

Her eyes were darting everywhere.

The President was already three minutes into his speech.

* * *

He took the steps up swiftly, the walkie-talkie in his right hand, quite official-looking in the event anyone stopped him, ten steps to each of the two flights, past the non-functioning telephone exhibit, and up the two shorter flights of steps leading to the star-shaped Fort Hood level.

No one in sight yet.

The three bronze-framed plate glass doors just ahead of him.

Deadbolts on all of—

He hadn't once thought—

God, don't let them be locked!

He shoved out at the middle door. It yielded to his hand. He caught his breath, came out into daylight. Stopped dead. Looked left and right. No one. His right hand went into his inside pocket, over his heart. His fingers closed on the bottle of sarin. Breathing hard, he lifted the bottle from his pocket, and turned the nozzle to the STREAM position. He hesitated a second longer, then walked swiftly to the steps leading to the level above. When he got up there, he would crouch down below the chest-high wall that enclosed it, and then work his way to a position directly above the President. The Statue of Liberty would be facing both of them; she would witness it all. He had practiced it a hundred times. Before anyone below knew what was happening, the President would be doused with a shower of poison that would kill him within minutes.

He started up the steps.

Came out onto the level above.

Ducked below the wall.

Half-crouching, half-running, he moved toward the corner where a right-angle turn would take him to the front of the monument. Above him, the lady clutched the tablet in her left hand. In the distance, he thought he could hear the President's droning drawl. He turned the corner. Still crouching, he lifted his head to get his bearings.

No, he thought.

No.

He was looking at a squad, a platoon, a company, a battalion, a goddamn *regiment* of marines in dress-blue uniforms!

One of them, a man holding what appeared to be a trombone, turned to look at him, puzzled. Sonny came to his feet immediately, as if recovering from a stumble, put the walkie-talkie to his ear, turned without glancing again at the man, and hurried back toward the corner of the monument.

But he had already been seen from below.

Dobbs had caught movement from the corner of his eye.

He'd glanced upward, seen what looked like one of their own people up there—blue suit, white shirt and dark tie, walkie-talkie in his hand—moving swiftly toward the corner of the monument, where suddenly he disappeared from view.

". . . in a nation where education and health are the birthrights of not only a privileged few but of everyone, where shining cities stand as beacons of achiev . . ." the President was saying.

Dobbs wondered what one of their own was doing up there with all those marines. And then he wondered if the tall man he'd seen *was* in fact one of their own. He decided to investigate. He was heading for the stairs leading up, when Sonny broke into the open at a dead run, a pistol in one hand, the bottle of sarin in the other.

In the instant that Dobbs yanked his revolver from his shoulder holster and rushed to intercept the man who was most certainly the one Elita had described, he knew that his worst nightmare was about to be realized: he was going to lose his life defending someone he despised.

The words propelling him were *No-Fail*.

The motives that drove him toward that podium were hatred and revenge, coupled with the realization that what he was about to do would earn him a place in Paradise. Like one of Khomeini's ten-year-old boys— the *Basseej* who'd rushed across Iraqi minefields, their forearms roped together, the black cloths of martyrdom tied across their foreheads, metal tags around their necks—like one of those young martyrs whose tag was a key to Paradise, Sonny now rushed forward to accept his fate.

It was not Dobbs who stopped him.

He dispatched Dobbs with two neat whispered shots, puffing on the still summer air, felling him in his tracks.

Nor was it Elita's shouted words that stopped him.

"There he is!"

Her finger pointing like an arrow at his heart.

He recognized her in that instant, but dismissed her as inconsequential, and continued his headlong rush toward the podium, where now he saw the President and heard his words and saw as well . . .

And this was what caused him to stop for just an instant . . .

And then turn from his course . . .

Swerve away from the podium . . .

And race for the nearest point on the star-shaped level.

He leaped over the wall to the level below, ran across a parched stretch of grass . . . Elita's voice shouting again behind him . . .

"Stop him! That's the man!"

. . . hit the pavement that ran straight to the water's edge . . .

"Stop him! Stop him!"

. . . shots behind him . . . stepped off the pavement in a zig-zagging maneuver . . . more shots . . . stop him . . . get him . . . reached the metal railing . . . climbed onto it . . . and dove into the water.

There was immediate darkness.

Cold wet darkness.

He swam some distance underwater, and then surfaced, gasping for air.

Shots puckered the water everywhere around him.

"Help me!" he shouted.

And went under again.

The cold wet dark of the river.

Surfaced again not a moment later.

"Help!" he shouted.

There were men at the railing now. They opened fire at once.

"Help! Help!" he shouted.

And went under again in a hail of bullets.

"He's failing!" someone shouted.

They spread out along the railing, guns ready, waiting for him to surface again.

"I think we hit him," one of them whispered.

There was no blood on the water.

They kept waiting.

He did not surface again.

Elita wondered if drowning was a painful death. She hoped he had died in agony.

379

15

At ten twenty-seven on Sunday morning, the fifth day of July, in the corridor outside the intensive care unit of Beekman Hospital, Detective-Lieutenant Peter Hogan of the NYPD and Agent Alex Nichols of the CIA's New York Office waited for word on the colleague with whom they'd briefly worked.

He'd been shot twice in the head.

Their conversation kept coming back to the events of the day before. Invariably, they kept wondering what the hell had been in Hemkar's right hand. It had looked like some sort of bottle. But what had he planned to do with it? And why had he changed his mind?

"Couldn't have been nitro," Nichols said, "the way he was handling it."

"That's why burglars stopped using it," Hogan said. "Your box men. Too unpredictable."

"Box men?" Nichols asked.

"Safe-crackers," Hogan said, flashing his expertise.

"Oh," Nichols said, and both men fell silent.

On the hospital wall, the clock kept ticking.

"Did you happen to see him when he dove in?" Hogan asked.

"We *all* saw him," Nichols said.

"So what'd he do with it? The bottle."

"Tossed it in the water before he jumped. The bottle and the gun both. Deep-sixed them. A person can't swim with his hands full, you know."

"You think he even *knew* how to swim?"

"He chose the river, didn't he?"

"Sure, but where else could he go?"

"Well, that's true, but . . ."

"He probably didn't know how strong those currents can get. Out there in the Narrows. Even a good swimmer could have trouble with them."

"Assuming he *was* a good swimmer."

"Did you see him go under three times?"

"What?"

"Before he drowned? They're supposed to go under three times."

"I wasn't counting," Nichols said.

He had begun wondering about that letter again. The fake Bush letter. Wondering how it had got into Quaddafi's hands. And then suddenly he realized who was behind it all. Who was responsible for forging that letter and making certain it surfaced in Libya. Forgetting that Hogan knew nothing at all about the document, he said aloud, "Who *really* wants him dead, huh?"

"Huh?" Hogan said.

"Bush. Who wants him dead more than anybody on earth?"

"I don't know," Hogan said. "Who?"

"Whose country did he destroy?"

"I don't know," Hogan said. "Whose?"

"Bombed it right back into the eighteenth century," Nichols said, nodding.

"I don't know who you mean."

"Can you think of a dictator who wears a mustache and a uniform?"

"Sure," Hogan said. "Hitler."

A doctor in a green surgical gown was coming down the corridor toward them.

"Are you the people with Mr. Dobbs?" he asked.

"Yes?" Nichols said.

The doctor hesitated. Nichols already knew from the look on his face that one of them would have to call Dobbs's wife.

He only hoped Hogan would volunteer for the job.

Less than a mile away, in Battery Park, a Hassidic Jew wearing a rumpled dark suit, an equally rumpled black fedora, and a tieless white shirt, got off the first ferry to arrive from Liberty Island that morning.

No one paid him the slightest bit of attention.

They arrived at the Thirteenth Precinct downtown at a little past eleven o'clock that Sunday morning. They had gone there to talk to Detective-Lieutenant Albert

Ryan, who'd invited Elita to his Homicide South office to ask whether or not he should clear her mother's case.

"What does that mean, clear?" Elita asked him.

"Well, clear it. Stop the investigation."

"Why do you need her permission to do that?" Geoffrey asked at once.

"I don't, actually," Ryan said. "This is a police matter, actually."

"Then why are you asking her advice?" Geoffrey said, and Elita realized all at once that she had a champion.

"Well, the Westhampton Beach Police are already working the case, so if we clear it here, we'll be saving a lot of duplication."

"I see," Elita said.

Never mind duplication. He was merely trying to save the city time and expense by stopping the investigation.

"I don't know what to tell you," she said, and turned away because she was on the verge of tears again. In her heart, she felt Sonny *was* the one who'd killed her mother. But suppose it had been someone else entirely? Suppose by giving her tacit approval to . . . *clear* the case, had he said? Suppose she did that, and the *real* killer escaped? Wouldn't it be better to have the NYPD investigating in tandem with the Suffolk County cops? Weren't the New York cops superior to a small-town police force?

"What are you *truly* concerned about, sir?" Geoffrey asked.

Her champion again. Directly to the point. Riding in on a white charger, her favor tucked into his gauntlet.

"I'm not concerned about anything," Ryan said, far too casually. "Now that the likely perpetrator is dead, we're just thinking of leaving the case to the department that had original juris . . ."

"That's the key word, isn't it?" Geoffrey said. "Likely."

"Well, yes. We have no positive proof that Hemkar . . ."

"Exactly. But if you clear the case here . . . by the way, that doesn't mean *solving* it, does it?"

"Well, no. Clearing is clearing, solving is solving. They're two different things. Related, but different."

"Related how?"

"In that the case would be closed."

"I see. And if five years from now, someone turns up . . ."

"That would be Suffolk County's . . ."

". . . and confesses to having killed Elita's mother and ten *other* women . . ."

"Suffolk would handle that eventuality."

"But that wouldn't look so good for New York, would it? That *eventuality*?"

"The case originated in Suffolk. If somebody kills somebody in Indiana, and the body washes up in the East River . . ."

"But how would it look if New York *cleared* a case and then the killer turned up later?"

"Young man . . ."

"Merely asking," Geoffrey said, and shrugged innocently.

Elita suddenly wanted to kiss him.

"If you'd like my advice," she said. "I think . . ."

"Well, that's why I asked you to . . ."

"I think New York should continue the investigation."

"Certainly. We appreciate . . ."

"We don't even know he's dead," she said.

"No, actually we don't."

"*If* he's the one who did it."

"That's right."

"And if he *isn't* the one, then you should *find* the one. You should find whoever's responsible for my mother's death."

"I can assure you . . ."

"Because she lived in New York, you see."

"Yes, I rea . . ."

"And she loved this city."

The room went silent.

"And we owe her at least that much," Elita said.

And her eyes filled with tears.

Arthur came to see him at the hotel at four o'clock that Sunday afternoon. It was a quiet day down here in the financial district. The two men shook hands, and then sat at the table near the windows overlooking the Hudson. They were not here to celebrate. Sonny was hoping that Arthur had come to discuss their next move. He had, after all, aborted the plan only so that he could serve another day. To sacrifice himself without having accomplished his mission would have been absurd. Arthur agreed with him.

"I was watching it all on television," he said. "I was puzzled at first, couldn't understand why you'd turned away, hmm?"

"Well, the moment I saw . . ."

"The shield, yes. I realized that later."

"Trimmed with bunting, but unmistakable."

"A bulletproof shield, yes."

"I wasn't expecting it."

"They sometimes use it."

"It just never occurred to me."

"You did the right thing. If there was no way to get to him . . ."

"I'd have given my *life* to've done it. My very *life* if only . . ."

"Yes, I know. But don't let it trouble you, truly. There'll be another time. He'll be repaid, don't worry," Arthur said, and smiled suddenly. "At least the boomerang worked, hmm?"

Sonny smiled, too.

This was not a joyous occasion they were sharing, but the thought of how easily he'd outwitted them was cause for at least some merriment. With great animation and obvious pleasure, he told Arthur how he'd swum *back* to the island instead of swimming *away* from it—the very principle of the boomerang escape he'd been taught at Kufra. Swimming underwater until his out-stretched hands made contact with the island's retaining wall, his lungs ready to burst, he'd taken the basting tube from his pocket, and pushed it toward the surface until only the thick end of it showed above the water. Capturing the narrow end in his mouth, he'd gently blown the tube free of water, and at last had been able to breathe again.

"That air tasted so sweet," he told Arthur now.

"I can imagine," Arthur said.

The makeshift snorkel in place, he'd worked his way underwater around the wall, until he reached the ferry dock. He'd lain hidden just below the surface then, clinging to one of the pilings, breathing gently through the tube, and did not climb ashore again until it was dark.

"And then what?" Arthur asked. "Did you go back to your lay-in position?"

"I couldn't. I'd left the door locked."

"Why on earth did you . . . ?"

"Has there been any news of a dead park ranger?"

"No. Should there have been?"

"I imagine there will be," Sonny said, and smiled again. "The island's almost deserted at night. I went back to the restroom, fished out my hat . . ."

"Your hat?"

"Too long a story."

"*Fished* it out?"

"Yes. And then spent the rest of the night outdoors, drying off. I caught the first ferry back at ten o'clock. I'm glad you're here, Arthur."

"I am, too," Arthur said.

"When do we try again?"

"Well, we'll have to wait for instructions, hmm?"

"Of course. But . . ."

"And in any case, you're known now, aren't you?"

"Yes, but disguises can . . ."

"Well, disguises. You know how we feel about disguises."

"Yes, but . . ."

"Mind you," Arthur said gently, "we know it wasn't your fault. Things simply didn't work out the way we'd hoped they would, hmm?"

"That's why I . . ."

"You mustn't think your efforts weren't . . ."

"But I really would like the opportunity to . . ."

"Yes, well . . ."

". . . serve again, to do the job properly this time."

"Well, that's quite impossible," Arthur said.

And suddenly there was a pistol in his hand.

Sonny blinked.

Arthur shrugged somewhat sorrowfully.

There was a silencer on the gun's muzzle; this would be swift and soundless.

"Why?" Sonny asked. "Because I failed?"

"No, no," Arthur said. "It would have been the same either way."

"Either . . . ?"

Sonny's eyes narrowed in total understanding.

He sprang at once.

It was one thing to die in the service of God and country, but it was quite another to die the way he now realized the two women had died. Total anonymity, Arthur had told him. Claim no credit, expect no retaliation. If there were no surviving links to Scimitar . . .

He was not two feet from the muzzle of the pistol, his

arm swinging in the backhanded deflecting swipe he'd been taught at Kufra—when Arthur fired. The first muffled shot took Sonny just below his nose, shattering the gum ridge and exploding from the back of his head. The second shot took him just above his Adam's apple as he fell over backward, his head tilting upward, his throat exposed. Arthur fired two more bullets into his lifeless body where it lay on the floor before the windows streaming late afternoon sunlight.

He tucked the pistol into his waistband, and looked down at Sonny one last time.

"It is written on our foreheads," he whispered.

And left.

AUTHOR'S NOTE

Sarin is real. Very real. And quite deadly. Its three essential reagents can be ordered from any major chemical supply house in the United States. I ordered them, and charged them, and they were delivered to my home by Federal Express.

But.

There is no such chemical as dimethylsulfoxide difluoride. It is wholly invented and it serves in this novel as a substitute for the real insecticide used in the production of sarin.

ABOUT THE AUTHOR

John Abbott was born in London in 1956. His father was a consul in Her Majesty's Foreign Service, and as a boy Mr. Abbott attended schools in India, Burma, Afghanistan and Paris before returning to London in the fall of 1967. His mother is Phyllis Rowland Abbott, the well-known American watercolorist, and his brother Peter—his elder by seven years—is an illustrator of children's books. Mr. Abbott now makes his home in Bucks County, Pennsylvania, where he breeds golden retrievers when he is not writing.